LONG-AGO LOVERS

Emboldened by his teasing and by the very rightness she felt clear down to her heels, Jenny threaded her fingers through the dark hair on his chest. "And what am I thinking?"

Brett's head dipped closer to hers. "I think you're thinking what I'm thinking."

Jenny's own pulse raced. "What is it you're thinking?"

"This." His lips brushed hers softly, then settled in place as gently as a fallen rose petal drifts to the dewy grass.

Jenny met him halfway.

There was no rush, no hurry. They took their time testing and tasting, taking each other up the slow, easy climb toward something neither questioned. There was no need to question, no need to hurry. This was—*they* were—meant to be. Each knew it somewhere deep inside.

Jenny knew that some part of her had known him forever. She prayed silently as he nibbled his way down her neck to her shoulder that somehow, in some way, his heart remembered hers, because she knew without a doubt that they had been together like this before. In some other place, some other time, she had loved and been loved by this man . . .

JANIS REAMS HUDSON

REMEMBER MY HEART

Janis Reams Hudson

P

PINNACLE BOOKS
KENSINGTON PUBLISHING CORP.

PINNACLE BOOKS are published by

Kensington Publishing Corp.
850 Third Avenue
New York, NY 10022

Pinnacle and the P logo Reg. U.S. Pat. & TM Off.

First Printing: October, 1995

Printed in the United States of America

*To the little girl who woke crying in the night, and to
her mother, for holding her and chasing away the fear.
Thanks, Mother.*

*And to the maker of the quilt that made me cry . . .
whoever you were, whoever you are. Whoever
you will be the next time around.*

Every soul . . . comes into this world strengthened by the victories or weakened by the defeats of its previous life.   *Origen (185–254 A.D.)*

It is absolutely necessary that the soul should be healed and purified, and if this does not take place during its life on earth, it must be accomplished in future lives.   *St. Gregory (257–332 A.D.)*

On nearly every subject under the sun, most men will believe almost any lie—provided it is big enough, absurd enough and is repeated often enough—and never dream of demanding proof. Likewise he will believe what he reads in the papers, and what he sees on the newscasts, as implicitly as if Moses had brought them down Mount Sinai engraved on stone. He will totally accept the election promises of a demagogue. He is blindly convinced that his lawyer, his doctor and his dentist are infallible and incorruptible. . . .

Apparently only reincarnation fills him with the superstitious dread, and only when he is plagued by dread as vague as that does he insist on proof so irrefutable that not even the Mother of All Living could supply it to his satisfaction.

Noel Langley in Edgar Cayce on Reincarnation

Chapter One

The Dream

A bolt of lightning flashed outside, illuminating the interior of the warehouse on the bayou, highlighting the tall, lean man in his formal black evening attire and the young woman in her yellow silk ballgown. They were entwined in a lovers' embrace. The moaning wind, rustling leaves, and creaking walls of the warehouse drowned out all other sounds, save the tender, fierce love words the two whispered against each other's lips.

It was their habit on warm summer nights to meet in the gazebo for privacy, but tonight there were too many people strolling the brick paths in the garden around their usual hideaway. The warehouse along the bayou's edge was all that was left to them, and even then, their time together was short. They had to return to the ball soon, before anyone noticed their absence—which was quite likely, since the ball was in their honor. Not only was it Anna's nineteenth birthday, it was also the night her engagement to Seth was to be announced. It wouldn't do to miss the announcement of their own engagement. But just one more kiss. One more. Then another.

"Thank you for the bracelet," she murmured sweetly against his lips. "It's a lovely birthday present."

Seth's lips moved on hers. "You like it, then?"

"Mmm."

His chuckle was low and vibrated through his chest to hers. "Is that a yes?"

"Yes." She kissed him again.

"Good." He trailed heated kisses across her cheek. "You have to marry me to get the matching locket."

She threaded her fingers through his hair. "Seems like a lot of trouble for just an ol' locket."

"Come on. It's heart-shaped," he tempted.

"Welllll."

He kissed the underside of her jaw and made her shiver. "It's gold."

"I don't need gold."

"I had it engraved."

"Hmm. What does it say?"

He nipped lightly with his teeth along the tendon down the side of her neck and made her breath catch. "It's the secret recipe for my Aunt Camellia's peach brandy."

Anna giggled. "It is not."

"Guess you'll just have to marry me and find out." He moved to the other side of her neck.

She let out a deep sigh. "I suppose you're right. Where is it?"

"I hid it so you wouldn't find it until after we're married," he said with a chuckle. "You can wear it to bed on our wedding night."

Anna's laugh was low and sultry. "I hadn't really planned to wear anything."

"Enough." He brought his mouth back to hers. "You're making me think things I'm better off not thinking just now. We have to go back."

"In a minute." She met his kiss and deepened it.

"Yes. In a minute. Or two."

They were so absorbed in each other that they were oblivious to all else. Neither one smelled the kerosene until it was too late. Before they were aware of it, a wall of flame burst from the stacks of cotton bales piled high all around their secret meeting place—between them and the door.

Anna choked and coughed at the thick, strangling smoke. Her heartbeat thundered in her ears.

Seth's head snapped up. With a violent curse, he thrust Anna behind him and faced the flames, searching desperately for a way out. Old, dry, and stacked to the rafters with cotton, the warehouse would go up fast. Already flames engulfed the doorway. Seth turned, pushing Anna before him toward the back wall.

Fear licked at Anna's soul. Fear for the man she loved, and for herself. To burn alive! My God, it was too horrible even to contemplate!

At the back wall, Seth raised his knee to his chest and kicked out at the upright slats standing between them and freedom. Smoke rolled thickly across his shoulders. He coughed, then kicked again. Anna coughed. The fire raced up behind them. The smoke grew heavier.

"It's no use!" Anna cried.

Seth hunched and kicked again. "We'll make it!" Determination etched strong lines across his face. He kicked again. And again. And again.

Anna heard his grunts of effort and the loud whack

of his boot striking the wall, but she couldn't tear her horrified gaze from the fast-approaching fire. Her heart knocked against her ribs. She tried to draw air, but there was no air. Only smoke, and searing heat.

Then there was a loud crack, followed by another, barely heard over the blood rushing in her ears. Tongues of flame leaped toward them. Smoke gushed past her face and out through the space in the wall where two boards had been.

He'd done it!

Seth grabbed her arm and thrust her out ahead of him into the dark night and the fresh, blessed air. Nothing had ever felt or smelled or tasted so sweet as that air. They stumbled across the clearing to the line of trees. Gasping and coughing, they fell to their knees, arms entwined.

When they'd caught their breath, Seth helped her rise. Orange light danced across the clearing and reflected off the dark water of the bayou. Anna leaned heavily against Seth's chest. The heat from the fire chilled her curiously. She shivered.

"Are you all right?" Seth asked.

Anna pulled back and gave him a trembling smile. "I think so."

He brushed her cheek with his forefinger, then hugged her close, giving her a fierce, passionate kiss. Anna clung with all her strength, her heart still racing at their close brush with death.

From out of the moaning wind and crackling flames came a piercing shriek—the sound an animal might make if caught in the fire. Or a tormented soul, plagued by unnamed demons.

A dark, billowing figure raced toward them, the shriek issuing from its throat.

Chills raced down Anna's spine. She pressed herself against Seth, her eyes wide, disbelieving, her mind nothing more than a confused jumble. "Maudie?" she whispered. Seth stiffened in her arms. "Maudie," she cried, "is that you? What are you doing here?"

In the eerie glow from the fire, Maudie seemed to float toward them in a cloud of royal blue. A flash of lightning bleached all color from her face, leaving it pale as death. "You!" she screamed at Anna. "Get away from him!" One of Maudie's eyelids drooped half shut, then began to twitch. "He's mine! He belongs to me!"

Anna looked into her cousin's eyes and trembled. There was nothing there even closely resembling sanity, much less a lifetime of companionship and shared girlish secrets. All the warnings from friends over the years, warnings Anna had ignored as she'd stoutly defended her cousin and best friend, filtered through her mind.

She's mean, Anna. Real mean . . .

She's using you, can't you see that, girl?

Remember that time her daddy whipped her? Funny how he fell down that well and broke his neck the next day.

Why, she'd stab her own mother for a harsh word, if the poor woman had sense enough to use one on the girl now and then . . .

I still say that was her up there in Martin's loft with that drifter last spring, just before they found him with his throat cut—

Thunder boomed close overhead, drowning out the roar of the fire. Anna shuddered. Some of the talk about Maudie was just jealous gossip, Anna knew. After all, Maudie was the prettiest girl in the parish. Then, too, Maudie wasn't always nice to everyone, the way she was to Anna, so some people took it out on her with talk.

Anna eased herself from Seth's arms. "What are you saying, Maudie? You know Seth and I are getting married. Daddy's announcing our engagement tonight at midnight.''

''No!'' Maudie waved her fists in the air. ''No, you can't marry him. He's mine!'' One hand dipped down into a deep, hidden pocket of her dark blue silk ballgown and came back out with her daddy's old pistol. She aimed it straight at Anna. ''You can't have him!'' Maudie shrieked.

Anna stared down the black bore and froze. Lightning flashed again. Maudie's finger trembled on the trigger. Her thumb pulled back the hammer. Her finger squeezed.

The gun barked. Seth shouted and gave Anna a mighty shove. Maudie screamed into the night.

Anna landed hard on her side, stunned, not realizing, not understanding, what had happened. After a long moment, Maudie's maddening screams finally pierced her dazed mind. She pushed herself up onto her knees, then halted. After a second of immobility, she scrambled frantically toward Seth's side.

He lay sprawled on his back, arms and legs outflung, blood pouring from a gaping hole in his left temple and forming a black puddle on the ground.

''Seth!'' Anna was at his side in an instant, tears streaming unnoticed down her cheeks. ''Seth, no! Don't die, Seth. You can't die. I love you. Do you hear me, Seth? I love you!''

Anna pressed her ear frantically on his chest. Nothing. No sound but her own harsh breath and her pounding pulse. She raised her head and stared down in shock and denial at the pale, still face of the only man she'd ever loved. ''Seth, don't leave me!''

But even as she begged, she knew it was too late. Stunned, devastated, she lifted her face at her cousin. ''You've killed him, Maudie. Seth's dead!''

Maudie's wild eyes darted from side to side. ''No!

Not me. *You* did it. This is *your* fault! If not for you, he'd have married me last summer." The crazed girl raised the gun and pointed it at Anna's head.

Anna watched, frozen by the horror of Seth's abrupt, violent death. It wasn't real. It couldn't be.

Maudie's eye twitched. She pulled the trigger.

The hammer struck with a loud click, but nothing more. The gun was empty. Anna flinched, stared with disbelieving eyes. Was she still alive? Was she? Without Seth, what did it matter whether she lived or not?

Just then the roof of the warehouse collapsed with a thunderous crash and roar. Maudie screamed and dropped the gun. A giant tongue of flame shot up into the night, setting fire to two overhanging live oaks. Maudie stared, fascinated by the dancing, leaping flames.

It all came clear in Anna's mind in that instant, all the big and little "accidents" that had befallen her lately. The loose wheel on the carriage, the broken cinch strap. The cottonmouth in her bureau drawer—Anna's father claimed he'd never seen a cottonmouth near the house before.

Maudie had been nearby each time.

And now Seth was dead.

Before Anna even had time to identify the emotion that threatened to choke her, Maudie turned her back on the fire and faced her. The gun was gone, but Maudie reached into her pocket again. The long, sharp blade of a knife flashed orange and gold in the firelight. Anna recognized it at once. Terror tightened her stomach.

It was the knife Old Saul used when he butchered hogs for Anna's mama. With all the talk lately about slave uprisings, Mr. Leonard, her father's overseer, kept close track of anything resembling a weapon. When he'd discovered the knife missing two weeks ago, Old Saul had sworn he'd returned it to the shed for locking up.

But the knife wasn't to be found, so Mr. Leonard didn't believe him. Anna still remembered the horror of Old Saul's bloody back after the whipping And the horror of Maudie's strange smile at the grisly sight.

Now that same blade danced in the firelight before Anna's eyes, mesmerizing her, holding her frozen to the spot, while Maudie stalked closer.

With a snarl of demented rage, Maudie flung herself at Anna. In sheer reflex, Anna sprang to her feet and grabbed Maudie's wrist with both hands. The two struggled, strained, each seeking advantage. The harsh sounds of their labored breathing filled the air. Anna clenched her teeth. Tears stung her eyes. Muscles shrieked in pain. Her chest burned. And terror filled her soul.

Maudie stepped closer. Anna stumbled over Seth's legs and fell backward with a cry.

Maudie fell with her and wrenched her hand free of Anna's grasp. She pulled the knife closer to her chest, then thrust it forward with a snarl.

Anna felt a sharp, burning sensation deep in her chest. Her eyes widened in shock. A small gasp left her lips. Then, darkness.

Ten-year-old Jennifer Franklin woke with a scream and grabbed at her chest. It burned! It burned! She kicked back the sweat-soaked sheets and rolled to her side, clutching the burning pain along her ribs. Her small, thin body trembled as she lay there sobbing.

She barely heard the click of the door latch. With her eyes squeezed shut, she didn't notice when the overhead light flicked on.

A warm, comforting hand touched her shoulder. The bed sagged.

"Jenny?"

At the reassuring sound of her mother's voice, Jenny rolled over and buried her face against Mama's fuzzy bathrobe.

One hand stroked Jenny's back, while the other brushed tear-soaked strands of hair from her face. "It's all right, sweetie. It was just a bad dream. Don't cry. Dreams can't hurt you."

Jenny sobbed, and words came pouring out. She couldn't stop them. "She killed me, Mama. Cousin Maudie killed me! She shot Seth and stabbed me."

The hands on Jenny's back and face stilled a moment, then resumed their stroking. "What an imagination you have, honey. You don't have a Cousin Maudie. It was just a dream."

Jenny pulled away from her mother and sat up. "No! It wasn't a dream. I can feel it. It hurts! She stabbed me, right here!" She pulled her pajama top up and pointed to the burning place along her ribs.

At the sound of her mother's gasp, Jenny looked down to where she pointed. She screamed. There, beneath her very own finger, on her very own ten-year-old chest, was a long, bloody mark on her pale white skin.

"It's all right, Jenny, you probably just scratched yourself in your sleep." Mama hugged Jenny to her chest and held her while Jenny cried. "It's just a scratch, sweetie. It was just a dream."

But Jenny knew better. Fear raised goosebumps down her spine. That was no dream. It was real!

Chapter Two

Twenty years later

Somebody was slumming, or showing off. A brand-new silver Corvette with the cardboard dealer's tag still in the back window occupied Jenny's usual parking spot. Swearing at the fancy car, she pulled her five-year-old Monte Carlo into the next slot. She gathered her purse, briefcase, and two diskette file boxes and mentally prepared herself for the hot trek between her air-conditioned car and her air-conditioned apartment.

A Corvette, of all things. Jenny shook her head. The car must belong to a visitor, because it was a cinch that no one who lived in the River Haven Apartment complex could afford one. The residents here were strictly middle-class all the way. Pickup trucks, four-door sedans, economy cars. And an old rattle-trap Monte Carlo, she added, with a wry twist of her lips.

She stepped out of her car and felt the heavy New Orleans heat press down on her. Ninety, they'd said on the radio a few minutes ago. She wondered if that was the temperature or the humidity. Probably both.

On her way to her apartment, she stopped at the mailboxes at the base of the stairs and collected her mail. Bill. Bill. Bill. Software catalog. Discount coupon for an oil change at Wal-Mart. A long-awaited letter from her parents in Oklahoma. As she tucked the mail into her purse and turned toward the stairs, she noticed the door of the apartment directly below hers standing open. Furniture and boxes filled the middle of the previously empty living room.

New neighbors.

Did they belong to the Corvette?

She really should stick her head in the door and welcome them to the complex, but she didn't. She could welcome them later. And explain the concept of assigned parking. Right now, she had something more important on her mind.

While climbing the stairs—*God, it's hot*—she fumbled in her purse for her keys. The briefcase hanging on her arm banged against her hip. *Damn it, why didn't I keep the keys in my hand when I had them?*

At the landing halfway up, the stairs took a sharp one-eighty, and Jenny nearly took a fall. With her head bent toward her purse as she finally located her keys, she never saw the bare bronze chest until she bounced off it.

"Whoa, there."

"Rob!"

He grabbed her arms to keep her from tumbling back down the steel and concrete stairs. "Got your mind off in another world, as usual, I see."

"Just trying to make it to the air conditioning before I melt," she said.

"Come on down to the pool with me. That'll cool you off."

"Maybe later," she said with a grin. "Right now I've got something I have to finish inside."

The six-foot-tall man shook his gorgeous blond head and rolled his eyes. "Work, work, work. That's all you do."

"Ah, but this isn't work, Robert, it's pleasure."

"You? Doing something for fun? I don't believe it."

Jenny stuck her tongue out at him. "Just shows you, you don't know everything. See ya later."

"Need some help?" he asked, eyeing the load she carried.

"No, thanks, I've got it."

Rob shook his head again at the expected answer. "What are you going to do in your apartment, alone, that's more fun than me?"

She wiggled her eyebrows. "I'll never tell."

Rob rolled his eyes once more and released her arms. "If you survive all this *fun* of yours, come on down to the pool for a while."

"We'll see," she said with a smile.

Rob shook his head and groaned on his way down the stairs. He knew she wouldn't show up. Jenny paused to stare after him. He was her next-door neighbor and closest friend, one of the best-looking men she'd ever seen in her life—tall, with broad, musclebound shoulders, trim waist, narrow hips, and long, powerful legs. Sexy was the word for him. A hunk. Even his bare feet were sexy. Dressed in swim trunks that looked like they'd been sprayed on, he was enough to make any red-blooded girl drool.

She let her gaze roam once more over the rippling muscles of his bronze back, then she shook her head. Her family was at its wit's end knowing dear, sweet, cuddly Rob was the only man in her life. They'd been sorely disappointed to learn that Rob was, as Jenny's father had so indelicately put it, "queer as a three-dollar bill."

To each his own, Jenny thought.

Inside her apartment, the rush of air conditioning brought a sigh to her lips. After leaning against the door a moment, she straightened, locked it, then headed for the living room. She dropped her briefcase, her diskette cases, and her purse on the couch, kicked her shoes off near the coffee table, and pulled her shirttail out of her skirt while unplugging the telephone.

With another sigh, she flopped down onto the recliner, pulled the lever that lifted the footrest, and picked up the heavy hardback book from the table on her right.

Now. She could finish reading it.

It was Friday, and she had nothing planned for the weekend. She didn't want any interruptions while she finished *This Raging Madness.*

She didn't usually buy books on the bestseller list—they often weren't as good as the hype promised. But Brett McCormick's books were always good—she'd read everything of his she could find—and the jacket copy on this one had particularly intrigued her. It was turning out to be well worth the exorbitant hardcover price.

Every time she picked the book up to read, she had the oddest feeling she'd read it before. That was, of course, impossible. The book had just come out last month. It wasn't that she knew what was going to happen, it was just that every now and then, a passage or a scene struck her as being somehow familiar.

Sometimes, while reading about the young Southerner and his girl, a strange sadness came over her, even though the scene itself wasn't sad. Maybe what she was feeling was envy.

The deep love the two characters shared touched something inside Jenny and sparked a yearning that surprised her. She hadn't known she wanted that kind of love for herself until now. The author was lucky. Surely, to be able to write so sensitively about such an intimate relationship, to be able to so effectively portray such powerful emotions with mere words on paper, he must have loved like that himself.

Jenny found herself in the absurd position of envying fictional characters. She ached to be loved by a man the way the girl in the book was loved. The slow, old-fashioned courting was just her style. She wanted a man who would take his time with her feelings, slowly build the trust between them until she couldn't help but fall in love.

So far, no such man had appeared in her life. Maybe that's why she felt this strange sadness. Maybe it was only envy, after all.

Jenny shook off the feeling and opened the book. Whatever it was about this book that appealed to her, she intended to read the rest of it without stopping. She had only a couple hundred pages to go.

By the time Jenny reached the last chapter, the room was growing dark. She switched on the lamp beside the chair. Her stomach reminded her she hadn't eaten since lunch, but she ignored it. She wasn't about to put this book down now. Not when the innocent young lovers from neighboring plantations had no idea a madwoman was stalking them.

Jenny settled on a more comfortable spot in the chair and turned to the final chapter. Tension coiled tight in her muscles as she wondered how the lovers were going to save themselves.

A bolt of lightning flashed outside, illuminating the interior of the warehouse on the bayou . . .

Jenny's hands trembled.

They had to return to the ball soon, before anyone noticed their absence . . .

An odd feeling stirred in the pit of her stomach.

"It's no use!" Anna cried.

"We'll make it!"

By now Jenny was shaking so hard the page before her blurred. Her throat threatened to close as she struggled for air. She slammed the book shut and clenched her fists. It couldn't be! It couldn't!

Yet it was. She knew it as surely as she knew anything. It was her old dream, her nightmare. The one she'd been having on and off for the past twenty years.

But it couldn't be!

With grim determination, she forced herself to reopen the book and continue reading. Tears streamed down her cheeks, but she kept reading. Her breath came in painful gasps, but she kept reading. Her mind denied it all, but she kept reading.

"Seth, no! Don't die, Seth. You can't die. I love you. Do you hear me, Seth? I love you!"

Jenny leaned her head against the back of the chair and waited for her heart to slow. It *was* her dream. Someone else, some man, some stranger, had written her dream. He'd even gotten the names right.

Reincarnation. That was the only theory that had ever made any sense to Jenny, the only explanation she had been able to come up with for the dream that had plagued her most of her life. She had read quite a bit on the subject over the years, enough to satisfy herself that if she was crazy, she was in the company of millions of others who adamantly believed that everyone had lived before. Jenny didn't much care about all that, except as it pertained to her dream. To her the dream was real, it had happened, and it had happened to her. *She* was Anna. Or had been, at one time.

That red mark her mother had seen on her chest the first time Jenny had the dream had never gone away. It looked like a birthmark, something she'd been born with.

Jenny thought of it more as a memory mark, put there the night her best friend and cousin murdered her, in some other place, some other time. It was as real to her as if it had happened yesterday. She'd accepted that years ago. She had stood there, as Anna, and watched that warehouse burn, watched Seth die, and then had been killed herself.

A clerk in a new-age book store had once urged Jenny to try hypnosis—past life regression. At the mere suggestion, Jenny had felt icy fingers of terror grip her spine. No, no past life regression for her. As far as she was concerned, there were some things people were simply better off not knowing. She didn't want to relive the death of the man she loved, didn't want to experience again her own murder at the hands of someone she trusted. God, who would want to go through that again?

Not her, that's for sure.

Yet here she sat, with a book in her hands, a book for which she had no logical explanation. Even knowing how it would end, she could not stop herself from reading on. With a churning stomach and icy hands, she focused on the page before her.

Maudie turned her back on the fire and faced Anna. Anna stared, mesmerized, while Maudie calmly, purposefully, reloaded the pistol.

Jenny frowned. Reloaded the pistol? That wasn't right.

With one eyelid still drooping and twitching, Maudie aimed and grinned. "Now die, bitch," she hissed.

That's not how it happened! The book was wrong!

Anna saw the finger squeeze the trigger. Something hot and hard struck her in the chest, knocking her to the ground. She looked down and gaped at the blood—her blood— gushing darkly over the front of her pale blue gown.

Blue? No . . . that's wrong. It was yellow.

She turned her head to gaze once more at her beloved Seth. A small gasp left her lips. Then . . . darkness.

The laughter of madness rang across the clearing, along the river, and echoed through the trees, drowning out the moan of the wind and the roar of the fire. Maudie rolled Anna's body aside and lifted the dead weight of Seth's lifeless head to her lap. "He's mine!" she cackled. "All mine! No one can take him from me! He's mine! This time, forever!"

The echo of laughter mingled with the smell of wood smoke and blood. Her skin prickling with ter- ror, Jenny gasped and raised her head with a snap, fulling expecting to see Maudie, a mad light in her glazed eyes, bearing down on her.

Shadows. Why were there so many shadows in her living room? Anyone could hide . . .

Get a grip, Jenny.

She tried, but couldn't. Her heart whacked against her ribs, her hands shook violently, and she couldn't breathe. Her throat was closed. *Oh, God, oh God!* She was choking, suffocating. There was *no air!*

She ordered herself to calm down, but some vital part of her wasn't listening. Trying to swallow, trying to breathe, she kept staring into the shadowy corners of the room, waiting . . . waiting for someone, some- thing. The crackle of flames, the rustle of a ballgown, the gleam of a knife. The sound of hysterical laughter.

There was no one there, of course. Jenny was alone in her own living room. Comfortable, modern furniture, bold colors. A dead begonia on the breakfast bar, a stack of newspapers ready for the recycling bin. No laughter, no smoke, no blood, except that which pounded in her ears.

Concentrate! Breathe! It wasn't easy. Air came hard, and with it, even though she knew it couldn't be, came the faint stench of burning cotton. With jerking motions, Jenny shoved the book from her lap and covered her mouth with shaking hands to hold back a threatening scream.

Her churning stomach gave a sudden heave. She crawled out of the chair and stumbled across the floor, barely making it to the bathroom in time.

Jenny tossed restlessly all night, unable to sleep for thoughts of the book and her dream. In truth, as much as it pained her to admit it, she was afraid to close her eyes. No amount of self-lecturing helped. It didn't matter that it was only a dream, only a book, that there was no real danger to her here and now.

She'd read somewhere once that the subconscious mind did not know the difference between something vividly imagined and something actually happening. Right then she believed it. No one had been near her. No fire, no knife or gun, no madwoman. Jenny *knew* that. But her subconscious apparently didn't, because it was sending out messages of fear strong enough to chill her to the bone. Fear and foreboding. As if the whole terrifying episode were going to happen again, to *her*—Jenny Franklin—rather than Anna. In the present, rather than the past. Someone was going to watch her, stalk her, kill her.

Dammit!

Jenny kicked the twisted sheet aside and crawled out of bed. She was being an idiot. She refused to cower before her own imagination. Reincarnation or not, it was in the past. It was only a dream. Only a book. It was *not* going to happen again.

In the kitchen she hit the light switch. In the freezer, she hit the ice cream. If she was going to be awake half the damn night, she might as well enjoy some part of it.

A few moments later she carried a heaping bowl of butter pecan to the living room, where, as a concession to the fear that refused to be banished, she turned on all the lights.

The first thing she saw was the book. It lay in the middle of the floor, where it had landed when she'd made her dash to the bathroom.

She circled it now, staying a respectful five feet away, as if it were a snake coiled to strike. She felt stupid. It was only a damn book. Yet she couldn't bring herself to get near it.

How had McCormick managed to get everything so accurate, including the characters' names, and then get the ending wrong? For that matter, how had he known any of it at all?

Wondering was useless, but she couldn't help it. It was just too much to be coincidence. Reading that final chapter had made her feel like . . . what was the old saying? Like someone had just walked over her grave. She'd never understood that saying. Until now.

Jenny eventually went back to bed, but she left all the lights on. "If I'm going to be a sissy, I'm going to do it right."

By morning she was exhausted. Her mirror revealed dark circles beneath dull gray eyes, and shoulder-length, honey-blond hair sticking out in tangled clumps, both the results of her sleepless night.

She groaned and turned away from the reflection. Coffee. She needed coffee.

Refusing to give in to the remnants of last night's terror, she stumbled to the kitchen and put filter, coffee, and water in their appropriate places in the coffee maker, switched it on, then sat down at the table to wait.

She couldn't stop thinking about that damned book. It was spooky, like someone had been crawling around inside her brain while she wasn't looking. How could a total stranger write something that she'd been dreaming, word for word, action for action, since she was ten years old?

Except for the ending.

She forced the thoughts away and poured herself a cup of coffee. Distraction, that's what she needed. In the living room she left the book where it still lay in the middle of the floor and flipped on the television, then flipped it off. She couldn't handle Saturday morning cartoons and had no burning desire to learn how to re-plumb her bathroom.

She read the letter from her parents, but for once, the news from home failed to distract her.

With inspiration, she found yesterday's *Times-Picayune*. Picking a spot as far away from the book as possible, she spread the paper out on the living room floor to read. She deliberately turned her back on the book. The headline accused another state politician of taking a bribe.

"Hell's bells. I thought they were supposed to report *news*." Since moving to New Orleans a few years ago, Jenny had learned that here, like everywhere else in the country, crooked politicians were a dime a dozen. Except for the fact that Louisiana seemed to have more than its fair share, there was nothing special about them. Certainly nothing extraordinary enough to be called "news."

She scanned the rest of the front page and found more "non-news." An oil company was being fined for polluting a swamp, and garlic really *could* inhibit the growth of some tumors.

"Yeah, but does it repel vampires? *That's* what the world wants to know."

The inside pages of the paper weren't much more informative. Crime was up, and expected to rise. With the new school term under way, women were being warned about date rape.

Well, there was one problem Jenny wouldn't have to worry about. She figured a girl had to have a date before she needed to worry about date rape. She hadn't had a date in months, and nothing resembling one was looming on her personal horizon. As for a steady boyfriend, it'd been so long, she wasn't sure she remembered what one was. She didn't have time for men. Her work took all her time.

With three older brothers and an older sister, there hadn't been enough money to send Jenny to college, and she hadn't really been interested anyway. Not in full-time college. She'd already spent twelve years of her life in school. By the time she'd graduated from high school, she'd been ready to get out into the real world.

During summers in high school she had worked at various office jobs in Chandler, the town nearest her family's central Oklahoma wheat farm. She'd saved all her earnings, and after graduation, she moved to Oklahoma City and got an apartment, and a job as an inventory clerk for an electrical supply company.

Three months later she'd quit and taken another

job, then another. She never stayed long at one place because she found she had absolutely no patience with antiquated office procedures. Any time she tried to change an established practice, she'd been told a flat no. "That's the way we've always done it."

After a particularly frustrating experience on one job, Jenny decided it was time for a drastic change. For as far back as she could remember, she'd been fascinated with the city of New Orleans. To her, the city spoke of a lazy, gracious style of living reminiscent of the old South. Considering the dream that had haunted her for years, she would have thought anything concerning the South would repel and frighten her, but it didn't. She couldn't swear to an eagerness to visit old plantations, but New Orleans seemed to call to her. She had the vague feeling that in that other life, before things had gone so drastically wrong, Anna had been happy in New Orleans. Jenny thought she could be happy there, too. Over the objections of family and friends, she had packed her belongings and moved to the Crescent City.

The job situation, however, did not improve—or rather, she herself did not change her attitude. One job followed another, followed another. Inefficiency abounded in the offices where she worked.

On the farm, her father had taught her to make every effort, every single motion, count for something. But none of her bosses, much less her co-workers, appreciated her efforts at improving efficiency. She supposed it had something to do with her age—she was usually younger than most of her co-workers—and that she was always the newest employee. An upstart, one woman had called her.

During all this job-hopping, Jenny became fascinated with computers and software. She took night courses in computer programming, and courses on specific commercial software applications, and discovered what she wanted to do for a living.

Her first real break came, of all places, at the grocery store. She overheard the manager complaining about having to set up a computer system for his office, as ordered by the owners of the store. He didn't know the first thing about computers, much less how to go about converting his current methods of operation.

Jenny had taken a deep breath, stepped up to the man, and said, with a thousand times more confidence than she felt, "I'll convert your office procedures to computer for you."

At noon the next day, Jenny had uncrated the new computer at the grocery store and started to work. The manager had received approval to hire her on a contract basis to set up the system, convert their present methods to computer, and teach him and his employees how to run "the damn thing."

Thanks to word of mouth, Jenny spent the next year setting up computer systems in one grocery store after another. Then she went on to other businesses as word of her skills spread. Now, five years later, she was a well-established, highly respected computer consultant with a list of recommendations a mile long.

Her business was flourishing, and she could pick and choose her clients, as her talents were always in demand. But life was expensive, and if she ever hoped to live in the heart of town amid the flavor, history, and atmosphere that was the real New Orleans, rather than her semimodern, moderately priced complex that looked like every other apartment complex in the country, she had to carry a full load of clients and save every penny she could.

When she wasn't with a client, she was home studying new computer software and hardware (Rob called it playing) and keeping abreast of the latest developments. That took all her spare time. No sooner did she learn the ins and outs of a particular program than the manufacturer issued a new, updated version. Then she'd have to start over.

No, she didn't have time in her life for men. Not that there hadn't been a few in her past. But lately, for the last couple of years, she hadn't met a man who'd even tempted her to shut off her computer for an evening.

Of all the crimes perpetrated against women, Jenny felt pretty damn sure that date rape was one she didn't have to worry about.

She tossed the entire front section of the paper aside and went for the funnies. Gradually her mind began to concentrate on what she read, and date rape, oily politicians, aromatic cancer cures, the book, and her dream were forgotten.

But not for long.

After the funnies, she worked her way back through the weekend entertainment section. A small ad caught her eye. There, in the lower right corner of the page, was a picture of the cover of *This Raging Madness,* followed by an announcement that the author, Brett McCormick, would be autographing copies of the bestseller at the Riverwalk Waldenbooks that afternoon at two.

Jenny hesitated only a moment before heading for the shower. She had to see this famous author who'd written her dream. If her knees turned to jelly at the thought, she ignored it. She wanted to look in his eyes, talk to him, find out how he'd known . . . She'd never told a living soul about that dream, except her mother, that first time. How had Brett McCormick known the story?

Coincidence. That's all it was. Just like the coincidence of the author living in New Orleans.

But how could nearly every detail of his book be identical to her twenty-year-old dream?

It made about as much sense as turning on the television and hearing Peter Jennings discuss her dream as though it were a current news item, or Barbara Walters wanting to interview her about all the gory details.

"Just between us girls, Jen—or should I call you Anna?—what was it like to be murdered?"

"Well, Barbara, believe me, it was a killer. A real killer."

Jenny forced a laugh at her own expense and tugged on her favorite New Orleans Saints T-shirt. When she stepped out into the muggy overcast day a few moments later, the silver Corvette was still parked in her space. Barely sparing it a glance, she got in her car. As heavy as the humid Louisiana air, that strong sense of foreboding pressed down on her again. With grim determination, she shook it off and drove toward the Mississippi River and the bookstore. For answers.

The Riverwalk Mall was located, as the name implied, on the New Orleans Riverwalk along the Mississippi. If Jenny had ventured clear across town on any other Saturday, she would have spent the day strolling the walk, losing herself in the crowds of tourists, ambling through the aquarium, or maybe even taking the ferry across the river and back, just to say she'd done it.

But this wasn't any other Saturday. It was the day she was going to meet the man who had written her dream.

The mall was packed with its usual Saturday afternoon crowd of teenagers turned loose for the day with Daddy's credit card, senior citizens taking their brisk daily walk in air-conditioned comfort, tourists from all over the world, and shoppers, shoppers, and more shoppers.

When Jenny neared Waldenbooks, she was astounded at the crowd of a hundred or more people jamming the wide doorway, each one shoving and jockeying for a position somewhere in the middle of the throng. Two cardboard displays filled with books threatened to topple.

Jenny eyed the crowd and groaned. Oh, to be six feet tall instead of five-two. Somewhere in the middle of that huge mass of bodies was the man she was after—the man who knew things he shouldn't know. How was she going to talk to him with all those people around?

She wasn't, she figured out a few minutes later. Just as she worked her way through the outer edges of the crowd, the store manager and a security guard made everyone line up single-file. Jenny ended up more than halfway back as the line snaked down the center of the mall.

Some of the people in front of her held copies of *This Raging Madness*. That made sense; they were here to get the author's autograph. After about fifteen minutes, Jenny had advanced only three feet closer to her goal. She used the time to try to think of what she would say to Brett McCormick. What could she say to him in front of dozens of people? "Excuse me, but why did you write my dream?"

Yeah, sure. Brilliant, Jenny.

A moment later the store manager came down the line announcing they were out of copies of *This Raging*

Madness. Anyone who didn't already have a copy in hand should come inside and have one ordered.

"But then we can't get them autographed," a woman in front of Jenny complained.

The bookstore manager smiled calmly. "Mr. McCormick has agreed to come back when your books come in and sign for those of you who didn't get to buy one today. When we call to tell you your book has arrived, we'll let you know when he's agreed to be here."

Jenny ignored the grumbling around her as she finally laid eyes on the man she'd come to see. At that precise moment, Brett McCormick raised his head and their eyes met. And locked. Jenny sucked in her breath sharply. Shock riveted her in place. She couldn't have described the feeling that swept through her as she stared into those deep blue eyes if the salvation of the free world had depended on it. It was too . . . overwhelming. Too powerful. And even though she knew she'd never met him before, it was, somehow, familiar.

Not the familiarity of having seen his picture dozens of times. No, this was different. This was more . . . personal. Intimate. It made her blood roar in her ears.

His face was darkly tanned, with high cheekbones and a nose proportioned by some world-class sculptor to fit perfectly in the center of his face. A square jaw and stubborn-looking chin enhanced the most sensual, most perfect set of male lips Jenny had ever seen. His striking face was surrounded by thick, black hair that hung down over his collar in back and looked as soft as silk. But it was his eyes that held her. Eyes a deeper shade of blue than any she'd ever seen.

Good grief, she thought. All those romance novels

she'd read were right. A woman *could* drown in a man's eyes. She'd never been so deeply affected by anything in her life. It was exhilarating. It was frightening. It felt like the most important thing that had ever happened to her.

For one brief flash, she read surprise in his eyes. Relief. Welcome. And something much, much deeper that she couldn't begin to interpret.

In shock, maybe in fear, Jenny broke the powerful connection and looked away. Beads of sweat dotted her forehead and upper lip. Her mouth felt as dry as sawdust and her chest ached. She hadn't realized until then that she'd been holding her breath.

Steeling herself, she craned her neck to catch another glimpse of the man who'd affected her more with a single glance than any man ever had. She couldn't see him. Too many people had shifted in front of her.

She could, however, see the woman who stood next to McCormick. A tall, graceful blonde who looked like she'd just stepped off the cover of *Vogue*. The woman leaned down and picked up her purse, and when she straightened, her gaze collided with Jenny's.

Grace Warren, Brett McCormick's publicist and friend, picked up her purse in preparation for leaving—Brett was in the process of signing the last copy of his current bestseller. When she straightened, her eyes caught those of the young woman Brett had stared at a moment ago. Stared at, hell. He'd practically eaten the girl alive.

Grace frowned. She'd never known Brett to give the women he met at book signings a second glance before, which suited her perfectly.

Not that Brett didn't like women. She knew he had

his share of affairs. But as far as she could tell, they'd been mere flings. Temporary, discreet liaisons with mature women, women who didn't interfere with his work. One-nighters, usually. That was fine with Grace. She wanted all his concentration focused on his writing. He didn't have time to get involved with some starry-eyed *child* who had "marriage" and "family" and "mortgage" written all over her face. Grace shrugged and smiled. Brett was too smart for that.

Beside her, Brett rose. Good. They could get the hell out of here and reach the airport in plenty of time for his flight to New York.

But Grace was obviously the only one pleased that she and Brett were leaving. The remainder of those in line, the ones without books in hand, surged forward, trying to shake Brett's hand or talk to him. The girl with the big gray eyes looked frantic. Grace watched, curious, as the girl elbowed her way forcefully through the crowd. The girl dug around in her purse and came up with a scrap of paper and a pen. She reached the table where Brett had been sitting just as he waved goodbye and turned toward Grace.

Grace glanced back over her shoulder, amused. The girl was writing a note. Grace had seen it before, women chasing after Brett, but she wasn't worried. He had more sense than to let himself get distracted by a woman. By anything, for that matter.

At the last minute Grace remembered the announcement she'd planned to make. She tugged on Brett's arm to stop him, then turned back to the group still surrounding the table. "Ladies and gentlemen," she called. "Brett will be back as soon as the books you're about to order come in. In the meantime, catch him on the *Today Show* Monday morning. Tuesday he'll be on *Good Morning America,* and Wednesday, the *CBS Morning News.*"

She and Brett both smiled and waved to the crowd, then she took his arm and they turned to leave. They hadn't gone three feet when she felt Brett stop. She turned to see that same damned girl staring wide-eyed at Brett, handing him a folded note. When Brett slipped the note into his pants pocket without reading it, Grace laughed silently.

Brett smiled at the girl, then turned back toward Grace. Grace glanced at the girl one last time and thought, *Give it up, honey. Better women than you have tried. You don't stand a chance.*

Chapter Three

They were almost at the airport before Brett realized he hadn't heard a word Grace had said since they'd left the mall. Disgusted, he silently acknowledged that he'd been thinking about big gray eyes and honey-blond hair, about that sharp zap of electricity that had struck him when their gazes had met. And wondering what was written on the note in his pocket.

As if he couldn't guess. Hell, this wasn't the first time a woman had slipped him a note. He might not know exactly what she was after, but if she was like damn near every other woman he'd ever met, given half a chance, she would start with sex. After a few tumbles between the ol' sheets, she'd finally get around to letting him know what she really wanted. Because it damn sure wasn't *him*. It was never him. Not in the long run.

Women always wanted something *from* him. Brett, the man, was only a means to an end. How long had he been a status symbol to females? A notch in a garter belt?

It had started in high school, he thought with a bitter grin. Hell, in high school he hadn't considered it a curse, but a blessing.

Fort Wayne, Indiana, hadn't been the most exciting place for a teenager to grow up. When he'd gone out for football his sophomore year, the team hadn't won more than three games in the preceding four years. By the time his senior year had rolled around, the starting quarterback spot belonged exclusively to him, and the state trophy plus two undefeated seasons were in the bag. The girls were all over him, and he'd damned well enjoyed it.

But the benefits of being looked at as an object, a trophy, a ticket to some girl's goal, had grown old quickly enough. One girl in high school had actually told him—after they'd fogged up the windows of her daddy's Buick out on a dark country road—that she'd come on to him because she wanted to know if star athletes "did it" any better than other boys. The hell of it was that afterward, she'd never told him one way or the other.

College had been more of the same, except he'd had precious little time for girls, what with working to pay his tuition and room and board.

When he'd started teaching, girls, young women, had come on to him in hopes of getting good grades. When his first novel had hit the *New York Times* best-seller list, the reasons had diversified. Some wanted him for his so-called fame, others thought he was rich. He'd even had a few come at him with the tenacity of bulldogs, thinking he could get their manuscripts published.

All in all, with a few exceptions, of course, Brett wasn't overly fond of women. So why was he having trouble putting this one from today's autographing out of his mind?

He knew why. Like it or not, something had happened when he'd met the woman's gaze.

As Grace pulled up beneath the American Airlines departure sign, Brett gave up trying to define what he'd felt in the mall when he'd looked up and fallen head-first into deep gray eyes. He, whose stock and trade was words, could not find the right words with which to describe what he'd felt, what he was still feeling even now, forty minutes later. And it pissed him off. Not the lack of words, but the feelings themselves. He didn't have the time or energy to spare on a woman.

" . . . Can change my plans if you want. Brett?"

"Hmmm?"

"Are you listening?"

"Sure."

"Well? Do you want me to come with you, or not? I know you said not to bother, but you seem distracted. If you've changed your mind, I can follow you to New York later today."

Brett didn't for a minute think that Grace was offering to go to New York for anything personal. Grace was one of the exceptions. All business, she was, and that's the way he liked her. Not once had she ever come on to him, nor he to her. She was the best damned publicist an author ever had. Neither one of them wanted to chance ruining the business relationship, nor the friendship, they had developed over the years.

"Hell, Grace," he said with exaggerated disgust as he opened the door. "Even I can handle three little interviews."

"Little?" she arched a brow. "I beg your pardon?

Three major network morning news programs? Little?''

He opened the back door and picked up his suitcase. ''I'll call you when I get home.''

''You'll call me every morning immediately after each interview and tell me how it went.''

''Yes, Mother.''

The bellman left the suite and closed the door quietly behind him. All Brett wanted to do was stretch out on the bed and sleep. He spent hours every day sitting in front of his computer while he wrote, yet being forced to sit for hours in a plane was different, and it always left him irritable and exhausted. He wanted a nap.

First, though, he had to call Kay. He smiled slightly as he dialed her number. Another exception. He could be himself around Kay because all she wanted from him was courtesy, respect, and a regular paycheck. He and Grace and Kay were business associates, even friends, but that was all. That was the way he liked it.

Even though she'd insisted from the beginning on being called his secretary, Kay Olsen was much more than that. She was his assistant, his right arm, his sounding board, and his first line editor. She helped with the research for his books, corrected his grammar, spelling, and punctuation, and kept his appointments and public appearances in order. He'd be a mess without her.

''Madam Secretary,'' he said when she answered. ''Did you find the floppies I dropped off before I left town?''

''Sure thing,'' came the soft, friendly drawl. ''How's New York? Are you all checked in?''

They traded small talk for a few moments, then Kay said, "I'll have these latest chapters cleaned up and printed out by the time you get back."

"No need to hurry," he answered. "I won't be ready to go over them until I finish the last half of the book."

They spoke for a few more minutes, then said goodbye and hung up.

Kay Olsen let her hand linger on the receiver long after she hung up the phone, as if by maintaining contact with the instrument, she could somehow stay closer to the man whose deep voice still resonated in her heart . . . Would always resonate in her heart.

With a sigh, she finally pulled her hand away. Brett didn't think of her in the same way; she knew that. He was a lonely, solitary man who would never admit how much he needed a woman in his life, one special woman who would love him.

Kay took a deep breath and turned back to her computer. One more hour of work, then she would climb back onto the skiing machine in her spare bedroom. Twenty more pounds. Twenty more pounds, and she would fit back into a size twelve. Then Brett would begin to see. He would notice her as a woman. And he would start to return her feelings.

Her fingers flew faster over the keyboard, entering corrections to his manuscript. She wouldn't short-change him on the work he paid her for. She wanted this manuscript to shine like non other.

And she was going to shine with it. By the time he finished writing this book . . .

This book was different, somehow. The emotion between the two protagonists was deeper than anything he'd ever written. The deep, desperate yearning they felt for each other was almost tangible.

That meant something inside Brett was changing. The call from New York was another indication. He liked her, genuinely liked her, and his feelings were growing. She could feel it.

Twenty more pounds, and he would no longer be embarrassed to be seen with her. Not that he'd ever acted embarrassed. Not that they'd ever been anywhere together that wasn't strictly business. But he was holding back, she could tell.

Not much longer, though. By the end of this book . . .

When Brett undressed for bed that evening, he emptied his pockets and found the note. "Ah, hell."

He'd meant to throw it away. He *wanted* to throw it away. Instead, he unfolded the scrap of paper and glanced at it, expecting to find a phone number. He found more than he'd bargained for.

> *Mr. McCormick:*
> *Loved your book, but would like to point out a couple of technical errors in the last chapter. First, Maudie's gown wasn't green, it was blue. Anna's was yellow. Second, Maudie didn't shoot Anna. She stabbed her instead, with a knife she'd stolen weeks earlier. Call me for details. 555–4671.*

Brett read the note again while he slowly lowered himself to sit on the edge of the bed. A flash of . . . something . . . he wasn't sure what, whipped through him. *Déjà-vu?* Foreboding? Disbelief, certainly.

How could she know? How could a total stranger know how he'd originally written the book?

It must be a joke. Someone was trying to pull one

over on him. It had to be Kay. Kay was the only one who saw the original version, except for Frank, his editor in New York. Frank was the one who'd talked him into changing it to the way it now read. It wasn't likely that the woman in the New Orleans Riverwalk Mall knew Frank. But she might know Kay.

Dammit, Kay knew how he felt about his work. He didn't like her talking about his writing with other people. He especially didn't care for the idea that she'd told someone details that didn't end up in the final book.

"Dammit, Kay."

He ground his back teeth and, swallowing the rest of the curses that rose to his tongue, picked up the phone and dialed Kay. The line was busy. He slammed the receive down and forced a deep breath, then another. It wasn't like him to lose his temper so easily. As far as he knew, Kay had never let him down, never talked about his work before. Was this one little slip-up worth destroying a perfectly good working relationship?

Of course it wasn't. It was no big deal. He was blowing things all out of proportion. He should just forget it. Hell, the woman at the mall had distracted him enough just by meeting his gaze. He wasn't going let her interfere in his professional life, and he damn sure wasn't going to waste any more time on her.

The next thing he knew, though, he was dialing her number. After four rings, she answered.

"Hello."

"This is Br—"

"This is Jenny Franklin."

"Yes, I—"

"I'm sorry I can't come to the phone right now—"

Brett felt like a jackass.

" . . . but if you'll leave your name and number and a brief message, I'll get back to you as soon as possible."

As the recorded beep sounded, Brett swore. "This is Brett McCormick. Cute note. I'd like to talk to you about it, but I'm in New York right now. I'll call you when I get home. By the way, how long have you known Kay?"

He swore again as he hung up the phone. What in Hades had possessed him to leave a message?

"Kay, I'm gonna murder you."

Jenny Franklin's voice was everything he hadn't wanted to hear. Soft and low and sexy, it oozed down his spine like cool honey. It left him anything but cool. He fought the feeling that night and throughout Sunday. By Sunday night he was irritated with himself for dwelling on her.

With a frown of irritation, he threw himself down on the bed, determined not to give her another thought. He had three important television interviews coming up, a meeting with his agent, meetings with his editor and the publisher's art and publicity departments, and a speech to give to a group of local librarians. He didn't need or want the distraction of a honeyed voice or big gray eyes.

When he got home, he'd be damned if he'd waste his time calling her.

He fell asleep thinking about Jenny Franklin.

Then he dreamed.

Seth drew up in front of the stables, dismounted, and tossed his reins to Joshua.

"Af'noon, Mastah Seth," the old black slave said with a wide white grin. "The big doin's is out front, and they's done started the barbecue without ya."

Seth smiled back. "Then I guess I'd better hurry, hadn't I?"

With a wave, he left the stables and strolled around the side of his neighbor's huge white mansion toward the front lawn. As he rounded the corner of the house, his steps slowed to a halt.

Was that Anna holding on to her father's arm? That lovely young lady? He blinked and stared again.

The last time he'd visited his best friend, Randall, a few months ago, Randall's younger sister, Anna, had been a cute little hoyden with a devilish sparkle in her eye who'd refused to move at any pace slower than an all-out gallop. Now, seemingly overnight, she'd turned into a breathtakingly beautiful woman, her hand resting lightly on her father's arm, strolling gracefully beside him as they greeted their guests.

Seth couldn't take his eyes off her, and his heart started racing. With a certainty that shook him, he suddenly knew he was going to marry his best friend's sister. He smiled and started forward.

"There you are, Seth darling."

Seth ground his teeth and tried hard to keep his smile in place. He glanced down at the dainty hand grasping the sleeve of his coat, then at the woman who held him. "Hello, Maudie."

"I declare, Seth, I was beginning to think you'd *never* get here. I've been waiting simply *hours* for you to show up."

Seth forced a deep breath between his stiff lips. Anna's and Randall's cousin, Maudie, was known far and wide as the most conniving, most vicious bitch in the parish, and she was the last person Seth wanted to deal with just then. He didn't want his name connected in any way with hers, especially since he was now determined to win Anna.

He'd known both girls for years, and the only way

to deal with Maudie was to ignore her. It didn't usually help much in getting rid of her, but encouraging her with conversation only made things worse.

He wished he could tell Anna all the nasty things Maudie said about her behind her back, but he knew better. Anna was the only person in the parish who befriended Maudie. Seth feared that one day Anna's fierce though misguided affection for and undying loyalty to her cousin would cause her untold heartache.

But Seth intended to be by Anna's side and protect her from Maudie's viciousness.

He looked back at Anna and drank in her cool loveliness. Without taking his gaze from her, he reached down and peeled Maudie's hand from his arm and stepped away.

As he rudely left her standing there, Maudie muttered loudly enough for him to hear, "She'll never have you. You're mine, Seth. Mine!"

He shoved away her words and the premonition of impending disaster they carried. He kept his gaze centered on Anna and walked toward his destiny.

Brett woke with a groan and fumbled for the alarm clock on the bedside table. Three-thirty. God, he hated these early-morning talk shows. Why couldn't the networks air their entertainment segments at a decent hour? He groaned again and pushed himself to a sitting position.

Something other than *The Today Show* nagged at the back of his mind. Something . . . foreboding. A strange sense of sadness and unease hung over him like a dark cloud. He felt like something was about to change in his life. Something important.

He had a sense of wanting something strongly,

yearning for it, yet at the same time, fearing it would never be his.

What was the matter with him? he wondered irritably.

Fragmented images drifted through his mind, then he remembered: the dream. He'd had the damn dream again.

With a self-deprecating laugh, he got out of bed and headed for the shower. There was nothing to fear in a dream. Especially not this particular one. It had brought him untold good fortune, since it was what had prompted him to write *This Raging Madness*.

Premonitions of doom, hell. It was just a dream.

As he showered, it occurred to him that something about the dream had been different this time. Some small, fleeting detail . . .

When he remembered what it was, he swore, then he laughed out loud. For a split second, he had a flash of the beautiful Anna strolling gracefully toward him across the lawn . . . wearing a New Orleans Saints T-shirt.

To hell with it, he thought as he dressed for his interview. Maybe he *would* call Jenny Franklin when he got home. Maybe when he met her, spoke with her, whatever it was about her that wouldn't leave him alone would . . . leave him alone.

Chapter Four

The Café du Monde on the edge of the Vieux Carré always reminded Jenny of the midway at the Oklahoma State Fair. Not the activity, although the café was almost as crowded, and not the decor, certainly—no wrought iron at the Oklahoma State Fair. No, it was the smell. If she closed her eyes and inhaled, she could picture herself at age six, standing impatiently, hopping from one foot to the other, waiting for her funnel cake to cook, a grubby dollar bill in her hand, knowing she would get the first one because she'd already threatened her older brothers with tears if she didn't.

It wasn't funnel cake she was smelling now, not Indian fry bread or doughnuts. It was beignets, and she had an unreasonable weakness for the fried sourdough treats sprinkled with powdered sugar. She could, of course, save on dental bills if she simply applied the little leaden doughnuts directly to her hips, because that's where they would end up anyway. But then she'd miss the taste, and what fun would that be?

Sitting at a small outdoor table at the Café du Monde, Jenny wondered precisely when it was that she'd lost her mind. Beignets aside, honesty had her admitting that this most recent insanity had started with the note she'd handed Brett McCormick last weekend at the mall. What a stupid, imbecilic, moronic, *stupid* thing to do. The man probably thought she was an escapee from the local loony bin.

Actually, she thought with chagrin, he probably thought she was a groupie. He was good-looking enough to make any red-blooded female's pulse pound. He was world-famous, and he was, by all accounts, stinking rich. If he ever dispensed with his "swinging single" image, the tabloids might very possibly go bankrupt. Women chased him from one end of the continent to the other. She'd bet her new CD ROM that she wasn't the first female to hand him her phone number.

God, she felt like an idiot. If she'd had any brains at all, she would have told him when he finally called back yesterday after he'd returned from New York that her note had been a joke—a rather lame one—and that she had no intention of meeting him in the French Quarter tonight.

Yet it was Sunday night, eight o'clock, and was she home checking out the latest Windows software upgrades or optimizing her hard drives? Nooooo. Not her. She was sitting at a small table in the Café du Monde in the French Quarter, watching tourists and locals alike stroll past Jackson Square, listening to the heartbeat of New Orleans, known to the rest of the world as jazz, ooze from a saxophone out on the sidewalk, inhaling the aroma of beignets and freshly ground coffee, and waiting for Brett McCormick.

"I'm an idiot."

"You say somethin', *cher*?"

Jenny forced a slight smile for the waiter. "Just talking to myself."

"Shure 'nuff. Your gen'lman, he be comin' soon?"

"Her gentleman is here."

Jenny whipped her head around to find the nation's hottest author taking the seat across from her. She'd come here tonight with equal measures of anticipation and trepidation. As Brett McCormick scooted his chair up to the table, she realized that anticipation had long since faded to some far-distant memory. Trepidation reigned supreme.

"Hello."

His deep, mellow voice made her mouth go dry. She managed a nod in response, impatient with herself. Hell, she was acting like she'd never seen a man before.

Maybe she hadn't, she thought as she finally met his gaze. It happened again, that instant, powerful . . . connection. And something more. Something elemental. Something . . . sexual. The heated stirring deep down inside, the humming in her veins, the sharp, sudden awareness that she was a woman and he was a man, startled her. The blue of his eyes turned deeper, darker. He seemed—she hoped—as shaken as she was.

She looked away, her cheeks stinging, certain he could see in her eyes what he was doing to her.

The waiter, wearing a smug smile, still stood beside their table. "Chicory, plain, or half and half?"

With a nod, Brett indicated that she should go first.

"Half and half," she requested, shuddering at the thought of attempting New Orleans coffee without filling the cup half full of cream.

Brett asked for the same, plus an order of beignets. When the waiter left, Brett McCormick changed.

It was as if an invisible wall went up around him. His expression hardened.

No, she thought, the change wasn't that drastic. Cooled. That was the word. He looked cool and reserved, where a moment ago, the heat in his eyes had nearly singed her.

Ah, she thought, folding her hands in her lap to keep from showing her nervousness by playing with her fingers. He'd remembered she was just some nutcase who had passed him a note.

If she was assuming correctly, then she had to ask herself why he'd invited her for coffee. Why does a good-looking, famous, stinking-rich man ask out a woman he thinks is a groupie?

Why else, you idiot?

"So." He folded his arms across his chest and leaned back in his chair. "How long have you known Kay?"

She'd expected a come-on. Maybe something trite like, "Your place or mine, babe?" She had not anticipated being quizzed about another woman. "Who's Kay?"

"The woman who put you up to writing that note."

"Put me up to?" Jenny frowned. "I don't know what you're talking about. No one put me up to anything. I don't know a woman named Kay."

Brett waited until the waiter deposited two thick white ceramic mugs filled with steaming coffee on the table along with a serving of beignets before he answered. While he waited, he studied the woman across from him. He didn't like realizing that just by looking him in the eye she had the power to make his blood heat. Didn't like it at all, but there it was, the unvarnished truth.

"You don't know Kay?"

She looked genuinely puzzled. "I don't know Kay."

Could she be that good an actress, or was she telling the truth?

He gave a mental shrug. He could always ask Kay. As a matter of fact, he would, tomorrow, when he went by her house to trade diskettes with her. He would even let her get away with claiming innocence. His mere asking of the question would serve to remind her that she wasn't supposed to talk about his work with anyone.

But if Jenny Franklin really didn't know Kay, what the hell had that note been about? "Explain your note."

With her index finger slung through the mug handle, she turned the mug back and forth on the table several times before meeting his gaze. "I thought it was pretty self-explanatory. Maudie shot Seth with the only bullet she had. She couldn't have reloaded and shot Anna. She stabbed her."

"With what?"

Jenny moistened her lips and studied the steam rising from her coffee. "With that old butcher knife— the big one that Old Saul used."

Brett's chest tightened. "You have to know Kay."

"I don't know any Kay." Jenny was getting irritated. "Who is this Kay person, anyway?"

"My secretary."

"Why do you insist that I have to know her?"

"I didn't describe the gun Maudie used," he said, ignoring her question. "Or the ammunition. Why would you think Maudie couldn't have reloaded, that she stabbed Anna?"

"Because that's the way it really happened."

At the words that flew from her mouth, Jenny froze. She wanted, desperately, to call them back. Brett McCormick was eyeing her like she'd sprouted a second nose right before his eyes. Who could blame him?

"Forget I said that," she said quickly. "I . . . oh, hell. Forget I said it. That's just the way I thought the book would end, that's all. Look, I'm not crazy or anything, at least not any more so than the next person. I guess your book just got to me, that's all."

She was lying, Brett realized. But about what, he couldn't imagine.

"Where did you get the idea for the story?" she asked quickly.

Could she be a reporter? A freelance journalist trying to get a story? "I made it up."

She blinked. "Oh."

No. Not a reporter. At least, not a good one. Not even a bad one. She couldn't seem to come up with anything else to ask.

And he couldn't figure out why he didn't care. Something about her intrigued him. He could find no logical reason for it, but then, he wasn't always a logical man.

Sure, she was nice looking. Better than nice, actually, with her honey-blond hair hanging in loose curls to her shoulders. Her chin was a little on the stubborn side, but it added character to a face that was almost too perfect.

Still, he knew a number of beautiful women, but he'd never felt the pull he was feeling now. Not like this. There was heat, yes, but there was something else he couldn't name.

Damn, but this was frustrating.

The eyes had something to do with it. Those clear gray eyes, looking like winter mist over Lake Pontchartrain, could suck a man in and take him under before he knew what had him.

"Have dinner with me," he found himself saying.

After a brief flash of pleasure, wariness clouded the gray. "Dinner?"

"Tomorrow night." He couldn't believe he was inviting her to dinner. He didn't have time to socialize. His manuscript was due at the end of the month and he was nowhere near finishing it. Besides which, he didn't trust women in general and had no use for ones who slipped him their phone numbers at autographings. "Seven o'clock."

Jenny was tempted, more than she wanted to be. Unnamed emotions were pulling her toward this man, but at the same time, her brain screamed caution. Something dark and fearful bloomed in the back of her mind, something to do with the stranger across the table. "I . . . thank you, but no."

"You went to a lot of trouble to get my attention last weekend. Have dinner with me and tell me why."

Why? He wanted to know why? Hysterical laughter threatened. "Look." She pushed her coffee mug away, grabbed her purse, and stood. "This was a mistake. I'm sorry I bothered you. Good night."

Bemused, confused, and more than a little irritated, Brett watched her flee as though her skirt was on fire. In seconds she had dashed across the street, barely avoiding being run over by a horse-drawn carriage. When the carriage moved on, she was gone.

Absently Brett picked up a beignet and took a bite, then swore as powdered sugar drifted down the front of his shirt.

Why had she run out like that? She had made the first move with her note. If she hadn't wanted something from him, why the hell had she written it?

*   *   *

Brett had thought putting Jenny Franklin out of his mind would be easy. By Friday night, he was forced to admit otherwise. She was there at every turn, lurking at the edges of his thoughts. Jenny, with her honey-blond hair. Jenny, with her beautiful, perfect face. Jenny, with her mesmerizing gray eyes. Jenny, with her damn note.

She'd really seemed to be telling the truth about not knowing Kay, and yesterday Kay had denied ever telling anyone anything about his work, had in fact seemed hurt that he would ask. But if Jenny didn't know Kay, what was the deal with the note?

He rubbed his eyes again and stared at the blinking cursor on his screen. How the hell was he supposed to finish this manuscript if he couldn't concentrate? Reviewers were calling *This Raging Madness* his best book yet. As an author, the thought intimidated the hell out of him—how was he going to top it? The reviewers' comments also irked him. *Madness* might be his best to date, but as far as he was concerned, it could have been better. Should have been better. To him, there was something lacking in the love story subplot. It wasn't . . . emotional enough.

He wanted more feeling in his books. More depth of emotion from the characters. Where was it supposed to come from? Him? Ha! What did he know about the heart-wrenching anguish, the overwhelming joy of being in love? And why, God help him, when he thought of love, did Jenny Franklin's face appear in his mind?

That was absurd. She had nothing to do with anything.

He knew nothing of falling in love, of being in love. *Nada.* Zero. Zilch. If regret tugged at him at the thought, he ignored it. If Jenny Franklin's face swam through his mind, he ignored that, too. He didn't know a damn thing about love, and even less about women.

Not that he wanted to know. Not firsthand, anyway. He liked his life just fine the way it was. He felt no burning desire to plunge himself into all that emotional upheaval that came with what people called love.

But dammit, he ought to be able to write about it anyway. He'd never murdered anyone, but he could write about that with spine-tingling clarity—or so he was told.

But love? All he knew on that subject was what he'd read or what he'd heard from others. The same with murder. So why was he having so much trouble writing about one, while the other came more or less easily?

Maybe it said something about his psyche that he didn't want to know. Maybe it meant that he had it in him to murder someone, but not to love. Terrific.

Maybe he was losing his ever-lovin' mind. He didn't want to fall in love—or murder anyone. He only wanted to write about those things.

Fresh air. Maybe that and another beer would help.

Shirtless, he pushed his chair back from the computer. His office, set up in the spare bedroom, wasn't any smaller than the last one he'd had. Maybe it was knowing the apartment itself was so much smaller than the old house that had him feeling closed in. That, and the fact that every available inch of wall space was filled with books, clear to the ceiling.

Yeah, fresh air couldn't hurt. Neither could a beer.

In the kitchen he grabbed his second Jax of the night and stepped out onto his postage-stamp-sized enclosed patio. The balcony of the apartment above covered half his patio. When he wanted shade, or shelter from the rain, that was fine. Tonight he wanted more than that.

He stepped beyond the overhanging balcony and threw his head back to look at the stars. Not too many were visible from here in the city. Not like there would be up the river, away from the bright lights, at some of the old plantation homes. Someday he'd buy a place in the country, up along some nice, quiet bayou. Until then, he'd have to satisfy himself with the view from New Orleans.

The night air was heavy and warm and carried the fragrance of honeysuckle and cut grass from somewhere beyond his six-foot-tall privacy fence. Late night traffic on Interstate 10 a few blocks away hummed and whined in disharmony with mosquitoes, frogs, crickets, cicadas. A movement of air, not strong enough to be called a breeze, quietly stirred the five-foot-long leaves of the banana tree in the corner of the yard.

The latter—the sounds of nature—he enjoyed. But when the renovations were finished on his house in the Garden District, he damn sure wouldn't miss the noise of interstate traffic.

Or the sound of neighbors so close, he thought irritably as the patio door of the apartment directly above his slid open. From the sounds, someone was staggering onto the balcony, gasping for breath. Something hit the wrought-iron railing. A woman sobbed.

Concerned, yet not wanting to intrude, Brett turned and glanced up. A woman wearing white panties and a white sleeveless tank top lay crumpled over the railing like a balloon losing air. She was clutching her ribs. Her crying, sounding as though it came straight from the depths of her soul, was the most gut-wrenching sound he'd ever heard. He'd never known a person could hurt like that and still live.

He took at step forward. "Are you all right?" It was a stupid question—she was obviously not all right—but it was too late to call it back.

The woman raised her head and peered down at him, her body wracked by violent shudders. Then she froze.

So did Brett. *She* was his upstairs neighbor? "Jenny?"

She peered down at him, looking confused and disoriented. "Seth?"

A chill raced up Brett's spine. "It's Brett. Brett McCormick. Are you all right?"

With a hoarse cry, she turned and stumbled back inside her apartment.

Brett debated with himself for maybe half a second, then dragged his wooden picnic table beneath the edge of her balcony and climbed up. It occurred to him a moment later, as he slipped through the sliding glass door she'd left open, to wonder if she was alone, but frankly, he didn't think he cared. Something was obviously wrong. He couldn't stand by and do nothing.

The balcony door led directly into her bedroom. Brett found her kneeling on the bed, doubled over, with her arms around her middle and her face pressed against the tangled sheets. She was moaning and crying and rocking back and forth, mumbling. "Seth, no! Don't die . . . don't leave me!"

Another chill raced up Brett's spine. Good God, she was reciting snatches of dialog from the end of *This Raging Madness*.

"Jenny." Was she dreaming? "Jenny, it's Brett McCormick."

He placed a hand tentatively on her shoulder. Her

skin felt like ice, but at his touch she seemed to relax. "Are you all right?"

She wilted beneath his hand, then, with a cry, rose to her knees and turned. "You're alive!"

Stunned by her response, he stood still while her cold hands raced over his bare chest and arms, his neck, his face.

"Thank God, thank God," she whispered tearfully. "I thought you were dead, but you're alive. You're . . ." She blinked rapidly, then jerked back. "Brett?"

"It's me. Are you awake now?" He cupped her arms gently in his hands. Her skin was cold. Ice cold. "You must have been having a nightmare."

She glanced fearfully around the room as though expecting to find the devil himself crouching in a corner, ready to attack. Her gaze came back to Brett and her eyes widened. She reached toward him. "You're all bloody."

"What? Where?"

She looked down at her hand. He followed her gaze to find her palm smeared with blood. Then she motioned toward him. "Your arm, your neck. Your face."

He saw the blood on her tank top. "It's not mine. Christ, you're the one who's bleeding. What happened?"

Jenny glanced down her chest and saw the blood. Slowly she sat back on her heels. "Oh." A hard shudder racked her. "It's . . . nothing."

She sounded dazed. "Nothing, hell, you're bleeding. Let me help you. Come on, lie down."

She hesitated for a minute, then lay back on the bed.

"I'll be right back," Brett said.

Jenny watched him round the corner into the hall,

her mind still fogged. The dream. She'd had the dream again, for the first time in more than a year. This time it had seemed even more real than ever, and she couldn't fight the overwhelming sense of loss. She couldn't stop the flow of tears.

When Brett had touched her a moment ago, she had thought, for one wild, thrilling moment, that Seth . . .

That's crazy, Jenny.

Yes, it was crazy. So was the blood. She had never bled from her dream before. Flinging an arm across her eyes, she wondered frantically what was happening to her.

She heard Brett return a moment later, but didn't uncover her eyes—she couldn't stop the damn tears.

The bed gave as he sat beside her. When she felt him tugging her tank top up over her ribs, she flinched and grabbed his hand.

"It's all right." His voice soothed something inside her. It shouldn't have, but it did. "I just want to clean you off and see how bad it is. What happened?"

The sound that burst from her throat was half sob, half hysterical laughter. *Oh, nothing much. I've just been stabbed. Murdered. But it was only a dream, you see, so the blood can't be real.*

Her next sound was a gasp as a cold wet washcloth touched her skin.

"Sorry." The way her stomach muscles quivered beneath his touch did something to Brett inside, something hot and wild. "It, uh . . ." He stopped and cleared his throat. "It looks like you must have scratched yourself. It's odd, though."

"Odd?"

"Yeah. This little scratch doesn't look capable of letting that much blood."

Beneath his fingers as he wiped away the last smears, her muscles tensed.

"Oh, well," she said. "I guess it's no big deal, then."

Pressing the cloth against the three-inch mark along her ribs, Brett glanced up to see that tears still seeped from her eyes. "Bad dream, huh?"

She swallowed. "Yeah. I guess so."

When he realized his cleaning had turned into caressing, Brett deliberately lifted the cloth from her ribs. He wiped the blood from her hand, then placed a bandage over the scratch on her ribs and forced himself from the bed. "While I rinse this out, why don't you change out of that shirt?"

In the bathroom, the vanity was cluttered with bottles and jars, makeup, lotions, perfumes, mousse, gel, hair spray. Female stuff. To him, foreign, alien stuff. Yet . . . intriguing. Why, he wondered, when women as a whole did not normally intrigue him?

He rinsed out the washrag and hung it next to a pair of sheer pantyhose on the shower curtain rod. With his hands braced at his hips, he stretched his neck to relieve an ache and tried to forget the softness of her skin, the tears on her face. The way she'd looked at him and touched him when she'd first turned toward him—as if he was the answer to her most fervent prayer. As if he was the very center of her world. As if . . . as if she loved him more than life itself.

God, what would it be like to have a woman look at him like that? To look at him and see *him,* not some phantom from a dream? To know and understand *him,* Brett McCormick, and still love him that much?

He glanced at his reflection in the mirror and smirked. *In your dreams, McCormick. In your dreams.*

He made sure he gave Jenny plenty of time to change clothes, then he returned to the bedroom. Instead of another rib-hugging tank top, she now wore an oversized white short-sleeved T-shirt. Her cheeks were still wet, and her long, golden legs were covered with goosebumps. She was shivering, even though the room was warm.

"Come on," he said, concerned. "Get back in bed. You're freezing."

She frowned at him, her eyes still somewhat glazed. "Where did you come from? What are you doing here?"

Brett straightened the top sheet on the bed, then folded it back and reached for her. "I came from downstairs, by way of your balcony."

"Downstairs?" She stared at him with wide eyes.

When he held out his hand, she slowly took it and let him tuck her in.

Unwilling to let go of her just yet, Brett eased down beside her, on top of the sheet, and propped himself on one elbow. Her gaze never left his.

"Yeah," he finally answered, smoothing a strand of hair from her damp cheek. "I moved in the day before my autographing. Some coincidence, huh?"

When she didn't comment, but continued to stare into his eyes, Brett's concern deepened. "Are you sure you're all right?"

She closed her eyes and nodded.

"That must have been some dream."

"Yeah." She swallowed. "It was."

"Do you want to talk about it? I know I'm practically a stranger, but I'm told I'm a good listener. Sometimes talking about it helps."

She tried to smile but couldn't quite pull it off. "I'm okay. Really." Another hard shiver made a liar out of her.

"Come here. You're freezing." Slipping an arm beneath her neck, Brett lay down and pulled her close. After tensing for a moment, she relaxed against him, and gradually her shivers subsided.

He lay still for a long time, afraid to move, afraid she would remember he was there and he would have to let her go. He'd never felt such a compulsion to hold a woman, a particular woman, before. This one, Jenny Franklin, felt tailor-made to fit in his arms. The thought surprised him.

Then guilt ate at him as he recalled the words she'd been muttering when he'd found her doubled up on the bed. Words from his book. Words he'd written had caused her nightmare.

More guilt filled him when he admitted that in all likelihood, if not for her nightmare, he might never have had any contact with her again. Being neighbors, they might have run into each other occasionally, but after the way she'd run out of the Café du Monde the other night, he figured she wanted nothing more to do with him.

He'd tried to convince himself that he felt the same way, yet he hadn't been able to stop thinking about her.

Now he was holding her, and he couldn't work up the energy to be sorry.

Her breathing eased, and he realized she'd fallen asleep. Was she used to falling asleep with men she barely knew? Did she instinctively know that he meant her no harm, or was she just a naive, trusting fool?

No, he didn't think she was a fool.

Brett himself had never slept with another person sharing the bed. He'd never felt that comfortable, not even with women he'd made love to. He wouldn't sleep tonight, with her, either, but he couldn't bring himself to slip away. His computer and lights were on downstairs. The patio door was unlocked, but the front door was locked, so he wasn't particularly worried.

He didn't want Jenny to wake up in the middle of the night and find herself alone. What if she had another nightmare?

No, he wouldn't leave. He could always sleep tomorrow.

Chapter Five

Jenny woke to the most delicious warmth curled around her. She opened her eyes slowly and somehow wasn't surprised to find that the warmth came from the man holding her while he slept. Brett McCormick.

What had happened last night? She'd had the nightmare for the first time in ages. It had been stronger, she'd felt the pain deeper. Brett had been there. Why wasn't she surprised to remember that as Anna had held the dying Seth in her arms, Seth's face had become Brett's?

He had come to her straight out of her dream. He'd died in her arms, then reached out beyond death to comfort her and hold her and wipe her tears away. Yet this was no ghost who held her this morning as the sky beyond her balcony door lightened. He was flesh and blood, warm with life. His breath fluttered the hair at her temple. One arm reached beneath her and cradled her against him. The other draped over her, his hand resting familiarly on her hip.

And it felt . . . right. *He* felt right. *She* felt right in his arms.

A logical, practical person by nature, Jenny knew she should pinch him awake and toss him out on his ear. Just because he'd been there for her last night when she'd needed him did not give him the right to spend the night in her bed.

No, helping her didn't give him the right. But something did, something deep inside her that had let her fall asleep with this man who for all practical purposes was a stranger. Yet he was no stranger at all. Waking in his arms felt as familiar as seeing her own face in the mirror, and infinitely more comfortable. Infinitely more intriguing.

And she was infinitely more aware of him as a man than any other man she'd known.

Beneath her hand, his heart beat slow and steady. Tentatively, hoping not to wake him, she flexed her fingers against his smooth, tanned skin and felt hard muscle underneath. His heart rate increased. His hand flexed against her hip.

Jenny tore her gaze from his chest and found him looking at her. Blue eyes drew her in and held her effortlessly.

"I've never slept with a woman before."

Jenny fought against grinning and lost. "You're kidding, right?"

Brett's answering smile bordered on wicked. "I said *slept*. I believe I've done what you're thinking a time or two."

Emboldened by his teasing and by the very rightness she felt clear down to her heels, Jenny threaded her fingers through the dark hair on his chest. "And what am I thinking?"

His head dipped closer to hers. "I think you're thinking what I'm thinking."

Jenny's own pulse raced. "What is it you're thinking?"

"This." His lips brushed hers softly, then settled in place as gently as a fallen rose petal drifts to the dewy grass.

Jenny met him halfway.

There was no rush, no hurry. They took their time testing and tasting, taking each other up the slow, easy climb toward something neither questioned. There was no need to question, no need to hurry. This was—*they* were—meant to be. Each knew it somewhere deep inside.

Jenny knew that some part of her had known him forever. She prayed silently as he nibbled his way down her neck to her shoulder that somehow, some way, his heart remembered hers, because she knew without a doubt that they had been together like this before. In some other place, some other time, she had loved and been loved by this man.

Embers glowed low and hot. Jenny gave herself up to the pleasure of him, and Brett feasted, taking what she offered, giving of himself. There was no need to wonder why he'd done the unthinkable and fallen asleep holding this woman. She, he knew, although he didn't know why, was *the* woman. The one woman he'd never thought he'd find, had never known existed. But he knew now. He knew by the way she fit against him, by the way she melted at his touch while he hardened at hers. He knew by the way she filled up an empty, lonely spot inside him that he hadn't even realized existed.

Something important was happening here in her bed. Something life-altering. Brett didn't like the idea of his life being altered, but with Jenny, whatever was happening felt right. He returned to her mouth and kissed her deeply. She was his, part of him. The knowledge was buried deep inside his soul, and he refused, for now, to question it. Instead, he slowly undressed them both.

Flames danced along nerve endings. Hearts raced. Skin tingled. Breath to breath, body to body, they kissed and stroked and spoke only with sighs and looks and slow, heated touches.

For all its slowness, their loving held no lack of intensity. As the morning sky grew lighter, the intensity in the room grew sharper, and soon the slowness began to fade.

Brett settled between her thighs and teased her and himself by stopping just short of giving them both what they craved. The blood in his veins pounded heavier and harder with each breath.

Jenny, with her eyes locked on his, smiled and shifted beneath him, brushing against him once, twice. He kissed her and eased his hardness into her softness. Two deep sighs, one light and feminine, one heavy and all male, filled the room.

The teasing slowness gave way to a deep, primitive rhythm that drew them into its spell. Yet for all its heat, for all the throbbing need that surged between them, there was still no hurry. They had forever, or so it seemed.

Then the earth tilted and together Brett and Jenny slipped over the edge into the realm of completion.

"Believe it or not," Jenny said some minutes later, as she lay curled against Brett's side, "I don't normally do this sort of thing."

"What?" Brett drew lazy circles on her hip. "Lure men up to your room and have your way with them?"

"Funny, McCormick. Real funny."

"I thought so."

"As soon as I get the energy, I'll get you back."

With his eyes still closed, he grinned. "You're scaring me, Ms. Franklin."

She let out a long, satisfied sigh. "You should be scared."

"I know. Right now I couldn't defend myself against a gnat, much less a vengeful woman."

"Vengeful?" She was starting to get her energy back. "I'll show you vengeful." Jenny reached up and tickled him behind his left ear.

Brett hooted. He batted her hand away and scrunched his neck before she could reach him again.

"I thought that might get your attention."

Her tickling had broken his peaceful lassitude. His laughter ended abruptly as he stared at her. "Who *are* you?"

The change in him from lighthearted to serious confused and hurt her. Trying not to show it, she forced a laugh. "That's a heck of a thing to ask, considering the circumstances." She sat up and scooted toward the edge of the bed.

Brett grasped her forearm. "No. I mean it, Jenny. Who are you?" he demanded. "Why do you know things you shouldn't know?"

Feeling the tension in his grip, she frowned. "What are you talking about?"

His glare sharpened. "How did you know that's the one spot on my body that's ticklish?"

Jenny stared, astounded. "What's the matter with you? There's no way I could have known that. It was just a lucky guess."

"And my book?"

"What about your book?"

"How did you know about the original version?"

The temperature in the room seemed to drop twenty degrees. "The what?"

"Cut the games." Brett's hand tightened on her arm. "Tell me the truth, Jenny. Do you know Kay?"

"The only Kay I know is Kay Canfield, of Chandler, Oklahoma," Jenny bit back. He was making her both angry and uneasy. She had no idea what had set him off. Until a moment ago he'd been gentle and teasing and loving.

Then the truth hit her. *Good God, I've made love with a stranger!*

The full ramifications of her reckless abandon finally sank in. She'd let a man she barely knew spend the night in her bed. She'd been as intimate with him as a woman could be. She'd given him her body without question, without thought. What was the *matter* with her? The man could be the neighborhood ax murderer! "Let go of my arm."

Brett looked down, seeming surprised to find his hand squeezing her forearm. He loosened his hold but didn't let go. "Answer me. How did you know about the book?"

Sunday night at Café du Monde, Jenny had told him, "That's the way it really happened." She remembered the way he had casually dismissed her explanation. She wasn't about to mention her dream, even though he'd walked in on the tail end of it last night. As a matter of fact, she didn't think she was going to tell him anything. She was feeling too raw just then.

She slipped from his hold and pulled on the T-shirt she'd slept in. "If you're saying that what I put in my note is the way you originally wrote the book—" A cold shiver raced down her spine at the thought. "—Naturally I didn't know that. It just seems like having Maudie's gun be empty after the first shot would have made more sense, considering that you never specified the gun was a revolver."

"The gun *was* empty. I had her reload, if you'll remember."

"Yes, but you deliberately showed the reader when Maudie stole the gun, and again when she retrieved it the night of the ball. You went into considerable detail both times, yet you never mentioned extra ammunition, so it was jarring to see her reload."

Brett stared hard at her, but Jenny couldn't meet his eyes. A huge wave of humiliation towered over her head, threatening to break any moment and swamp her. Good God, she thought again. She'd made love with a stranger! It made her feel like the cheapest hooker on Bourbon Street. Her logical mind told her that in this day and age she should at least have demanded he use a condom.

She slid out of bed. "I'm going to take a shower. You don't need to be here when I come out."

"What the hell is that supposed to mean?" He bolted out of bed stark naked and followed her.

Jenny marched to the bathroom without stopping. "I believe the words were in English." She slammed the bathroom door in his face and pushed the lock.

It wasn't him she was angry with, but herself. Never in her life had she done anything so irresponsible. And maybe angry wasn't the right word, either. Sick seemed more appropriate as nausea rolled in her stomach. She'd let her dream interfere with reality, and somehow, in her mind, she had pulled Brett into it.

She wouldn't make that mistake again.

That's what last night—or rather, this morning—had been. A mistake. A big one. The biggest mistake of her life.

She stood in the middle of the bathroom cringing, unable to look at her own reflection in the mirror over the sink. Dear God, she couldn't believe she'd actually made love with a stranger. *A stranger!*

"Be downstairs in forty-five minutes," Brett called through the door, his voice gritty with anger. "I'll buy your breakfast."

Jenny leaned against the wall next to the towel bar and squeezed her eyes shut. She couldn't see him again, couldn't face him. She'd been serious when she'd told him she didn't normally do this sort of thing. Until this morning, she hadn't been with a man in more than two years.

But after this morning Brett McCormick would never believe that. He must think . . . Lord, what he must think.

"No, thank you," she called back to him.

"I *said* I'll buy your breakfast."

"*I* said, *No thank you.*"

Out in the hall, Brett gave the door a single heavy thump with the side of his fist. "Forty-five minutes, or I'll come up here after you."

He didn't know why he was insisting. Hell, she hadn't given him a straight answer since he met her. He had no business carrying things between them one step farther.

He turned from her bathroom door, pissed at himself and Jenny. What had she done to him? Why hadn't he been able to get her off his mind all week? Why had he fallen asleep in her bed? And why, heaven help him, hadn't he left as soon as he woke up?

Indiscriminate, gratuitous sex wasn't his style.

If he was going to be honest, though, what had taken place in Jenny's bed this morning had been neither indiscriminate nor gratuitous. There had been purpose. He wasn't sure what purpose, but it had been there. Every move each of them had made had been slow and deliberate, as if choreographed.

As if . . . ordained. Destined.

The more he thought about it, the more incredible it seemed.

But there were things she wasn't telling him. He'd known that, of course. He couldn't forget that business in her note. She was hiding something.

Brett cursed as he climbed down her balcony and let himself into his apartment through the patio door because he hadn't taken his keys with him last night when he'd played Tarzan and climbed to her rescue. He'd known better than to get involved with her. She wanted something from him. Women always wanted something from him.

With angry motions, Brett stripped and stepped into his shower. He didn't exactly trust women. He had no reason to trust his upstairs neighbor at all. She was hiding something. He intended to find out what.

Chapter Six

Forty-seven minutes after Brett's ultimatum, they were in his car and pulling out of the parking lot. Brett had been surprised to find Jenny stomping down the stairs when he'd stepped outside. Frankly, he'd been surprised that he himself hadn't just said to hell with it and crawled into his own bed.

The breakfast he'd promised was sure to give them both indigestion—they had yet to so much as look at each other.

"So." Jenny sat as close to the passenger door as her seatbelt would allow. She had her arms folded tightly across her chest and her lips puckered up like she'd been sucking on a green persimmon. "You're the one."

"The one what?"

"The one who doesn't understand the concept of assigned parking."

"I suppose you're going to explain that remark."

"It's simple." Her chin jutted out. "Nearly every day since you moved in, your car has been in my spot."

Brett pulled up at a red light and stopped. "That's because someone else has usually been in mine." He revved the engine, because he could—this was the first sports car he'd ever owned.

From the corner of his vision he saw Jenny's eyes narrow, but she said nothing. For spite, he revved the engine again.

Look at him, Jenny thought peevishly. *Gunning the engine like some macho high-school stud.* What the hell was she doing here? Why in the world had she given in and come with him?

She must be out of her mind. She'd slept with a stranger, made love with a stranger; now she was apparently going to eat breakfast with a stranger.

She was a fool. That was the only plausible answer. A total idiot. The minute they got back to the apartment complex, she would tell him so long and that would be the end of it. She would have nothing more to do with him.

If some little corner of her mind thought it knew better, she ignored it with an audible sniff of disdain.

Brett heard the sniff, but ground his teeth to keep from responding. A few minutes later he pulled into the parking lot of his favorite breakfast place. He left the car idling, flexed his hands around the steering wheel, and told himself that falling asleep in her bed last night was merely a fluke. He'd been staying up all hours working on his manuscript. He'd been tired, that was all.

He told himself that what he and Jenny Franklin had shared that morning had been nothing more than sex. Great sex, he allowed, but only that. He'd merely imagined that strange, elemental connection, that filling of some cold, empty hole inside himself, that feeling of destiny being met.

No, he hadn't felt any of those things. Not need,

not an end to a loneliness he didn't really feel, none of it. He'd only imagined it. Writers had great imaginations, or so he was told.

He should never have climbed that damn balcony. "Tell me you're on some kind of birth control," he said, keeping his eyes forward instead of looking at her.

He heard a small intake of breath. "I'm on some kind of birth control."

He looked at her quickly, then away. She, too, stared out the windshield. "Are you really?" he asked.

"Yes." A low snarl accompanied her terse answer.

Brett flexed his grip on the steering wheel again and silently counted the bricks across the side of the restaurant. "A couple of months ago the city held a big AIDS Awareness campaign. A bunch of local so-called celebrities volunteered to let news crews cover their blood tests. I'm HIV negative. I thought you'd like to know."

Some of the starch went out of Jenny's shoulders. After a long moment, she spoke. "Last Christmas I gave blood. They tested me first. I'm negative, too. I haven't . . . there's no way I could have contracted the HIV virus since then."

"Last Christmas? Nine months ago? What did you do, join a convent or something?"

"Don't I wish," she muttered.

Brett gave a single sharp nod and killed the engine. "Me too. Believe me."

With no other words between them, they got out of the car and entered the restaurant. Grimly, as if marching through the fires of hell, they followed the hostess to their table, picked up their menus, studied them as if perhaps they contained the answers to the puzzles of the universe.

Brett raised his gaze over the edge of his menu. "Why did you come with me?"

Using her menu the way a Southern Belle would a silk fan, Jenny fluttered it, gave him a fierce smile that looked more like a grimace, and batted her lashes. "I've always been a sucker for such a gracious invitation."

Brett snorted and tossed his menu aside. As the saying went, ask a stupid question . . .

A waitress who looked like a basset hound in drag stopped at their table. "Y'all ready to order?"

Jenny handed the woman her menu. "I'll have orange juice and wheat toast."

The farm boy in Brett, the one who'd had it hammered into him the first twenty years of his life that breakfast was the most important meal of the day, couldn't keep quiet. "That's it?"

Jenny folded her hands together on the table and looked disinterestedly past his shoulder. "It's plenty. I'm not hungry."

Brett frowned. Dark circles hung beneath her red-rimmed eyes, her face was ashen, and he'd bet his next royalty check that she had no idea he'd seen the way her hands had trembled before she'd clenched them together to still them. They were fine hands, he thought. Feminine and graceful. Even with short, unpolished nails, her fingers looked elegant. He remembered how they felt against his skin . . .

Hell.

The bones on her wrists stood out. She needed to eat.

To the waitress he said, "Bring me coffee, and we'll help ourselves to the breakfast buffet."

"Two buffets?"

"Two."

"One," Jenny corrected.

"Two." Brett countered.

The waitress smirked. "Give it up, honey," she told Jenny. "He looks like a man used to gettin' his own way. I'll have that juice and coffee out in a jiffy."

Brett watched Jenny while the waitress sauntered off. "She's right, you know. I am used to getting my own way."

Jenny met his gaze squarely. "In light of my recent firsthand knowledge, I'm certainly in no position to argue that."

"What's that supposed to mean?"

She tossed her head and looked away. "Not a thing."

"Are you trying to say I'm solely responsible for what happened between us this morning?"

Jenny's face flamed. Her eyes cut back to his. "Keep your voice down," she hissed. "I have no intention of discussing my private business in a public restaurant."

"You're right," he said with a nod. "It's better left until later, when we're alone."

The glare she shot him practically screamed that if she had her way, they would never be alone together again. Where the hell did she get off acting like this? He hadn't taken a damn thing she hadn't freely offered, yet she was acting like he had somehow wronged her.

Before he could say something he knew he would regret, he shoved himself from the booth. "I'm going to the buffet. You coming?"

She turned her head away again. "I told you, I'm not hungry."

He supposed he couldn't force her to eat. He shrugged. "Suit yourself."

At the buffet he grabbed a plate and piled it high with cholesterol—moist, fluffy scrambled eggs, sausage links, bacon strips, greasy hash brown potatoes instead of the grits he'd never learned to like, and three beignets, even though he knew they wouldn't be as good as the ones served in the Quarter. These national chain restaurants never quite got them right. And they never gave a man a big enough plate, either. He'd just have to come back for seconds in a few minutes.

By the time he returned to the table, his coffee was waiting, and Jenny was sipping orange juice. A small plate of anemic-looking toast sat before her. He put his plate on the table and slid into the booth.

One glance at her had him looking away. Dammit, what was it about this woman? A single look and he was hot all over. Again. "What do you want from me?"

She looked startled. "What are you talking about?"

"I'm talking about the same thing I talk about every time we see each other. And this time I want answers. Why did you write me that note?"

"I'm asking myself the same question," she said in irritation.

He didn't think she realized what she was doing when she snatched a strip of bacon from his plate and started munching on it.

"Why did you write that book?" she asked.

Brett sat back, his fork held loosely. "It's what I do. I write books."

"I know that." She waved the half-eaten bacon strip before her. "But why this particular story? Where did the idea come from?"

Brett rolled his eyes. "Ask any writer where he gets his ideas and if he's honest, he'll tell you that most of the time, he has no idea."

She polished off the slice of bacon and reached for another. "But don't some writers get ideas from news stories, from a snatch of overheard conversation,

things like that? Maybe even from, oh, I don't know
. . . dreams?"

Brett shrugged. "Sure. For a writer, anything can
spark an idea."

"So what sparked this one for you?"

He speared a sausage link with his fork. "Why do
you want to know?"

Jenny's heart thundered. "Just curious. Nosy, I
guess. No big deal." Except she felt as if her life
depended on his answer. She forced herself to look
away.

"I guess the original idea came from a dream," he
said casually.

A hot tingling started at the base of her skull and
worked its way down her spine. A dream. Oh, God,
oh, God. "What—" She had to clear her throat to
continue. "What kind of dream? You mean, like a
nightmare or something?"

"Like the one you had last night?" he asked.

Jenny blushed and held her breath.

"No, nothing like that," he said, answering his
own question. "Remember the scene when Seth first
realizes Anna is all grown up?"

"At the barbecue? Yeah."

"I built the rest of the story around that scene."

Jenny felt . . . stunned. In light of her reaction to
him, both last night and this morning, maybe she
shouldn't. He'd dreamed a scene—not the same
scene she had dreamed—and written the rest of the
book. "The, uh, the ending . . . did you dream that,
too?"

"No."

As the shock of his revelation faded, a calm acceptance settled easily over Jenny. A feeling of . . . inevita-
bility. The incidents might have been different, but
she and Brett had both dreamed of the same two

people, people who, as far as anyone knew, had never lived.

What did it mean? Was there some psychic link between her and Brett that made them both dream of Seth and Anna? Jenny frowned. From what little she knew of so-called shared dreams, the two parties involved shared the same dream, or extremely similar dreams, at the same time.

"Do you mind my asking when you had this dream?"

His lips quirked. "In my sleep."

"Cute. No, I mean, was it years ago, and you just never had a chance to do anything with it? Did you dream it often, just once, what?"

"Does it make a difference?"

"Of course not," she lied. "I'm just curious, that's all."

Curious, about a man who should have been a stranger but wasn't, a man whom some part of her, deep inside, knew and recognized. Before he'd touched her, she'd known the feel of his fingers. Before he'd kissed her, she'd known his taste. His smile, his clear direct eyes, his heat were all familiar to her. Somewhere, in some other time, she had known this man before.

Instead of shaking her, the thought comforted, and with the comfort came the memories of what they had shared in her bed this morning. Her blood stirred.

Brett watched the expression in her eyes change. Wondering what was going through her mind, he leaned back in the booth and folded his arms across his chest, hoping to give the impression that he was relaxed.

He was anything but. She was thinking about this morning, in her bed. He could read it in her eyes, the way her nostrils flared slightly, the way her lips parted.

His own body's reaction was swift, definite, and startling. Jesus, all it took was a look from those gray eyes and he was ready to launch himself across the table to get at her.

And she wanted him to tell her about his dream? Hell, just then the only dream he could think of was the dream he'd thought he'd had this morning, when he'd awakened to find her curled up next to him as though she belonged. He'd *felt* as if she belonged, felt as if they'd been originally carved as one unit, then sliced apart, only to finally fit themselves together after a hundred years apart. That's what she'd felt like in his arms.

It hadn't been a dream, dammit. He really had awakened in her bed this morning. They really had made love as if they'd been loving each other for years. And he wanted to do it again. Right here, right now.

He forced himself to look away from those hot gray eyes.

Dream. She'd asked him about his dream.

Brett didn't see the need to tell her any more than he already had. Hell, he'd already said more than he'd intended. If he told her more about his dream, what else would he tell her about? His house? He wasn't about to talk about the day he'd first seen the house on Chestnut. The sun had been going down, casting long shadows across the overgrown lawn. The property was run-down, boarded up, with absolutely nothing to recommend it. It had needed extensive renovations. He'd felt an instant . . . need. He had to have that house.

There was a slight obstacle in his way, though. It

wasn't for sale. Even if it had been, he wouldn't have been able to afford it, not back then.

But that hadn't stopped him. It had taken him months to track down the absentee owner, and literally years to convince the old lady to sell.

Now it was his. Every weed, every peeling wall, every warped board, every damn cobweb. He'd be living there right this minute, but both the roof and the floor were in danger of caving in.

He'd still be in his old house, the small ranch-style he'd bought in the suburbs when he couldn't get the house he'd wanted, except he'd made the mistake of listening to his Realtor.

"Get the contractors started on the new house, and list this one. Trust me, it'll take months, maybe longer, to sell. Nobody's buying right now. Don't put off listing it."

Normally she would have been right. The local economy sucked, and nobody was buying. Which, of course, had nothing to do with anything when he'd listed his house, because it had sold almost immediately.

So instead of his plain but comfortable previous house, or his new but unlivable 1857 relic in the Garden District, he'd had to get an apartment. Right downstairs from Jenny Franklin, no less. A woman he apparently hadn't yet had enough of. He shook his head. Fate was playing games with him.

"Well?" she asked, licking bacon grease from her thumb.

God, he wished she wouldn't flick her tongue out like that. "I had the dream three years ago, right after I moved here," he said tersely.

The dream had come that very night, less than a dozen hours after he'd first seen the house—or The House, as he mentally called it. As far as he was concerned, it deserved capital letters. He'd thought that writing the book would get the dream out of his system, but it hadn't.

He'd thought that making love with Jenny Franklin would get *her* out of his system. He'd been wrong about that, too.

He watched her reach for her third slice of bacon. "Okay, I've answered your questions. Now—"

"Why did you change the ending?"

"What is it with you and the ending?"

"You said this morning that the things in my note were the way you originally wrote it. Why did you change it?"

Frustrated—in more ways than one—and irritated, Brett tunneled his fingers through his hair. "Because my editor thought adding the knife to the scene just complicated things. He wanted a quick, explosive ending. Now, suppose you tell me how the hell you knew about the knife?"

"Why did you change the color of Maudie's dress?"

Kay. The knife and the dress had to have come from Kay. "What makes you think I changed it?"

"Why don't you want to answer my question?"

"Why are you asking it?"

Jenny's throat went dry. She couldn't tell him about her dream, she just couldn't. Oh, he knew she'd had the nightmare last night, but he didn't know the rest of it.

Think, think. Surely she could come up with a logical reason for wanting to know about Maudie's dress. Surely . . . "I just thought I remembered that in an earlier scene the dress was mentioned as being a different color. Blue. Dark blue silk, I think it said. I'm kind of a stickler for details. I just wondered at the discrepancy, that's all."

"Dammit, I hate it when they do that," Brett muttered, venting on his publisher his frustration over wanting Jenny again when he knew he shouldn't.

"When who does what?"

"The house—my publisher—changed the color of the dress because they wanted to use Maudie in that scene on the back cover, and they didn't like dark blue. It was a last-minute thing, so I didn't get to check over the final changes. Since you saw a different color mentioned somewhere, that means they must have missed something."

In irritation, Brett reached for a slice of bacon, only to realize Jenny had taken the last one. He'd yet to get a piece for himself. "Well, hell." He slid out of the booth, eager for an excuse to get out of range of those haunting gray eyes.

A shudder skipped down Jenny's spine as she watched him stomp off. His apparent rudeness, if that's what it was, didn't make a dent in her calm acceptance that she was somehow tied to Brett McCormick. Fundamentally, elementally tied, through time, to him.

But that acceptance was the only thing about her that was calm. Inside she was a riot of heat and hunger, want and need. The blood fairly sang in her veins.

She wanted him, and it stunned her. She had never reacted this way to a man.

He came back to the table a few moments later with another plate piled high with food.

"No wonder you wanted to come here," she said, looking at a two-inch stack of bacon. "You must have been starving."

Brett grunted as he slid back into the booth. "Damn right, I'm starving. Somebody ate all my bacon."

Puzzled, Jenny followed his gaze to her hands. Good grief. Her fingers were greasy. She sniffed them tentatively and frowned. Bacon. She definitely smelled bacon.

By the time they left the restaurant, Jenny had eaten more than her share of food and Brett felt like his insides were tied in knots. Every movement of her lips, every swipe of her tongue, built the heat inside him to an inferno.

Dammit, he wasn't some pimply-faced teenager in the grip of raging hormones. But he sure as hell felt like one. And unless he was reading her wrong, Jenny was feeling the same way.

At the parking lot of their apartment complex, Brett scowled. "See what I mean? Nobody pays any attention to the rules." He waved toward the parking space in front of his door—the space now occupied by a black pickup.

Grumbling, he drove around until he found an empty spot on the other side of the complex.

When they got out of his car, Jenny gave him a long look Brett couldn't interpret. Then she thanked him for breakfast and started for her apartment.

Brett caught her hand as she neared the stairs. Without a word, he tugged her to his apartment door, then inside.

"What are you doing?" she asked as he locked the door, sealing them in alone together.

"What were you doing? Walking away? Thanks for the fun and the food, but so long, sucker?"

"That was uncalled for."

"Maybe, maybe not. But you *were* walking away, and we're not finished, you and I."

She swallowed. Her gray eyes darkened to smoke. "We're not?"

"You know we're not. Something happens between us, something strong."

Jenny smirked. "Is this the old, 'Don't fight it, baby, it's bigger than both of us' line?"

"If the cliché fits." Still holding onto her hand, he pulled her close, closer, until their bodies were almost touching. "I don't know if it's bigger than both of us, but it's damn sure strong."

To prove it, he kissed her. Whatever magic had held them that morning, that slow, sweet madness that had them moving together like two streams of poured molasses, was gone. In its place raced something hot and desperate. It caught them both instantly and held them, demanding they surrender to its primitive force.

The power that gripped them got no quarrel from Brett McCormick or Jenny Franklin. Their loving was hot and hard and fast, and damn near took place on the living room floor, but somehow, Brett managed to carry her in his shaking arms all the way to his bed.

Clothes landed in untidy heaps across the room. Breath hitched, lips clung, flesh slid across flesh. Friction and fire. Greedy touches, hungry moans. Volatile. Intense. Explosive. It swept them up and hurled them beyond the edge of the world. Beyond the edge of time. Into bright, bursting lights and harsh cries of pleasure. Together. And it was . . . right.

Chapter Seven

Jenny and Brett spent the rest of the weekend together, most of it in bed. It was, Jenny thought, the strangest experience of her life. Never had she abandoned all good sense this way before. Her mind tried to argue with her heart, but her heart won. She stopped questioning the logic of her feelings for Brett, stopped trying to define them and analyze them. She simply let them come, and enjoyed.

He was the most attentive, most tireless of lovers. She had never imagined a man could make a woman feel so special. They loved hard and fast, slow and hot. Every way there was.

It was as if they were under some sort of spell. They loved, they laughed, and Jenny's heart was so full she thought it might burst from sheer joy. She'd never been in love before and wondered if this was what it felt like.

Saturday afternoon they ordered pizza delivered. Jenny learned that Brett hated anchovies. Brett learned how erotic it could be to taste cheese and

Jenny at the same time, and how amusing it was to watch Jenny let her piece of pizza grow cold while she reached over and stole pepperoni slices from his.

His publicist called to nail down some details about an ad layout. "Whatever you think, Grace," Brett told her. "You're the expert."

He was seated on the sofa with Jenny, and she rose to head for the kitchen to give him some privacy for the call, but Brett grabbed her wrist and whispered her name.

Then, to Grace, he said, "Sorry. Distracted? Well, I guess you could say that." With his eyes locked on Jenny's, he gently tugged her back to his side. "No, Grace, as a matter of fact, I'm not alone. Yeah, Monday." He said goodbye and hung up. His lips were on Jenny's in an instant.

Later they shared a bowl of microwaved popcorn and were forced to confess to each other that, to hell with cholesterol, they wanted butter, the real thing, melted and drenching and greasy. When Brett licked the mess from her fingers, Jenny's breath caught. The tingling heat that had yet to completely ease from her core sprang to life again.

After that, the melted butter ended up in the most unusual places, on both of them. They didn't bother with a shower until considerably later, after they had exhausted much more intimate methods of butter removal.

Sunday morning, Brett learned that Jenny liked Sugar Crisp cereal straight from the box. "How can you eat it like that? You sure you don't want a bowl and milk?"

"What? And ruin it? No, thank you. That's worse than putting catsup on prime rib. I'm a Sugar Crisp purist."

Sunday afternoon they fought over the funnies and

worked the crossword together. That evening they sat together on his patio and watched clouds build overhead.

Deep in the night, they lay curled up in Brett's bed and talked. Brett asked about her work, and she confessed to being a computer nerd.

"You are not," he protested.

" 'Fraid so. It earns me a living."

They talked about her job, his writing, Louisiana politics, and listened as autumn rain tapped gently at the window over the bed. There would be fog in the morning.

Someone had once told Jenny that being in love was scary, but if this was love, she wasn't scared. She was in heaven. She barely knew him, yet she'd known him forever. What she felt for him was undeniably powerful.

"What did you do before you started writing?" she asked.

"Taught history."

Jenny laughed. "Of course. What else would a historical novelist have done? How does your family feel about your success?"

Beneath her cheek his shoulder tensed. "My mother won't say it, but she'd just as soon I stay home and run the farm with my brother."

Jenny's first impulse was to ask about his father. Why was his brother running the farm? But she didn't, because Brett hadn't mentioned it. She let it go and gave him a laugh. "I knew we were kindred spirits. My family's farm is in Oklahoma. Where's yours?"

"Indiana. Near Fort Wayne."

By his tone, she guessed that his family farm left him with no pleasant memories. The tension that moved through his muscles, the way his hand tightened on her arm, warned her away from the topic. With mixed emotions, she took the hint. She wanted nothing to spoil the magic of their time together. The real world would intrude soon enough, when she had to go to work Monday. For now, she would not ask why mention of his family farm seemed to upset him.

But someday she would. She would have to, because she had a deep, burning need to know everything there was to know about Brett McCormick. If something upset him, it would upset her. If he hurt, she would hurt. But not now, not yet. Her feelings for him were too new and special to deliberately ask for pain. So she let it go and kissed him.

His arms came around her in a tight embrace that felt laced with urgency. Heat and need exploded deep in the center of her. Brett fed both emotions until she was mindless with them. Their joining was hard and urgent and fast. And when they reached the peak, they slid back down the other side wrapped in each other's arms and slept.

Monday morning they climbed out of bed and made their way to the living room to face reality. Jenny had to go to work.

"Are you sure?" Brett asked, nibbling the spot where her shoulder and neck met.

Jenny shivered as his mouth sent tendrils of heat spiraling to her core. God, she couldn't believe she could still respond to him after all the times, countless times, they'd made love over the weekend.

"You don't really have to go yet, do you? It's only eight-thirty."

There came that damn reality again. Jenny groaned. "I have to be at a client's across town in an hour." She smoothed her hands up from his denim-clad hips to his bare chest. Lord, how she loved touching his chest. "And you have a book to write," she reminded him.

"Ah," he murmured, pulling her closer. "You know what they say about all work and no play."

"Trust me." Jenny pressed a teasing kiss to his jaw. "Your name's not Jack, and there is absolutely nothing," she said, moving to his lips, "dull about you."

Brett grinned. Against her lips, he said, "I'm glad to hear it."

Their kiss was full and deep, but short lived—not through any intention of either Brett or Jenny, but because just when things were heating up, the front door burst open.

Startled, they jerked apart. Brett instinctively put himself between Jenny and the door. In shock, Jenny gripped his upper arm and stared at the woman who'd just used what appeared to be her own key to let herself in.

"Kay," Brett said, his tensed muscles instantly relaxing.

The woman at the door flinched and looked up from pulling the key from the lock. Her eyes widened as her face turned red. "Oh! Brett! I . . . that is . . . your car wasn't out front, so I thought . . . oh, I'm . . . so sorry!"

Jenny felt the skin of Brett's arm flush with heat. The blush spread to his face. Who could blame him, she thought with a sick feeling in her stomach. One woman—*who had a key to his apartment*—had just found him in the arms of another woman. If he hadn't exactly been caught with his pants down, it was a near thing—they weren't zipped.

Something warm and wonderful shriveled into a

cold, hard knot in the pit of Jenny's stomach. So, this was Kay. If Brett hadn't said her name, Jenny would have still known, by the four-inch oval key ring with K-A-Y spelled out in red glitter. A key ring that held a key to Brett's apartment.

Jenny couldn't say she blamed him. She had never seen a more strikingly beautiful woman than the one standing before them with shock on her face and pain in her eyes.

Kay was tall, probably five-ten. A comfortable height for a man of Brett's six-two. She could probably stand to lose a few pounds, but her generous curves were in all the right places. And with a face like hers, what possible difference could a few pounds make? The woman was intimidatingly gorgeous, with flawless olive skin, dark, deep-set eyes, and shoulder-length hair so smooth and glossy, such a shiny black that it looked almost blue.

In the face of such outstanding beauty, Jenny, with her mousy brown hair, ordinary looks, and skinny body, could have held her own head high, could have swallowed her insecurities, her envy. But the woman named Kay had one thing Jenny could not deal with, the one thing she realized she would give anything for—the right to have her own key to Brett McCormick's apartment.

Yet she had no such right, and this woman obviously did. Jenny had never thought to wonder if Brett was seeing someone else. The possibility didn't fit within her fantasies of past lives and lost loves reunited, of destiny and fate.

Fate? How about blind, stupid foolishness?

Once again the thought surfaced, the thought she had purposely ignored—she had been intimate with a man she knew virtually nothing about. More than intimate. She'd actually thought she'd fallen in love!

With a stranger! The knot in her stomach tightened as she prayed for the floor to open up and swallow her.

When her prayer went unanswered, she did the only sensible thing she could. "Excuse me." She slipped past Brett, grabbed her purse from the couch, and bolted out the door.

Brett called her name.

Jenny ignored him and hit the stairs at a dead run. They were damp and slippery from last night's rain and this morning's fog. Jenny's only thought was to barricade herself behind her closed door, where she would never have to face Brett McCormick again. Maybe there, the humiliation and self-disgust wouldn't taste so bitter. Maybe the pain wouldn't cut so sharp.

But it did. Closing her door behind her and bolting it held no magic remedy. The bitter taste still stung her tongue, the knife-edged pain still sliced deep. Her computer, the stacks of diskettes, piles of computer magazines, the dead begonia on the bar between the kitchen and living room . . . there was nothing here to soothe her. She could still feel Brett's skin against hers, could still feel the heat in her blood. Could still feel his presence in her apartment.

With an anguished cry, she turned and pounded her fist against the door. Why? Why had she been so damned *stupid?* She'd actually talked herself into believing he was her reincarnated lover. At least, that's the excuse she thought she'd settled on for her bizarre behavior.

Reincarnated lover, *ha.* He was a man on the prowl, and she'd welcomed him with open arms, practically begging to be taken advantage of. And boy, had he taken advantage. Advantage, and everything else she had to give.

Jenny wanted so badly to sink to her knees and give in to tears, but she refused herself the luxury. All of this, every bit of it, was her own damn fault. She'd always considered herself a logical person, analytical, someone who thought things through and weighed the odds. That was why she was so comfortable with computers.

But from the minute she'd seen Brett McCormick's blue eyes, she'd been operating on pure emotion.

"Mistake, Jenny girl," she told herself. "Just about the biggest damn mistake you've ever made."

Reincarnated lover.

Ha!

Grinding her teeth to keep from screaming at herself, she pushed away from the door and headed for the kitchen to make a pot of desperately needed coffee. She was halfway there when someone pounded on her door.

Brett made his excuses to Kay and left her standing in his doorway while he took the stairs outside two at a time. *Dammit, Jenny.* He reached the landing in time to find a half-naked man with the physique of a body builder pounding on her door.

"Open up, Jenny," the man called. "I know you're in there. I'm gonna stand out here and pound on your door all day until you answer me."

Brett's knees locked. In the instant that Jenny opened her door and the man stepped inside her apartment, he had a sudden insight as to what had sent her running from him moments ago. A sharp sense of betrayal stung him at the thought of her with another man.

Hellfire. What did he really know about Jenny Franklin, anyway? He knew that some inexplicable force drew him toward her. He knew he'd never felt anything so strong for a woman before. He knew he felt as though he'd been searching for her all his life. But he didn't know, had never thought to ask, if she was involved with another man.

The man's voice rang out through the open door. "Well, at least now I know you're still alive. Where the *hell* have you been all weekend? When you didn't show up Saturday afternoon and I couldn't roust you that night or Sunday, I damn near went nuts."

Brett couldn't hear Jenny's muffled reply, perhaps because his own blood was roaring in his ears. He couldn't have been that wrong about her. She couldn't be that good an actress. She'd shared herself with him all weekend the way no other woman ever had. She *couldn't* have been involved with this bronzed, musclebound beach boy and still have given herself to him the way she had.

A brief picture of the look on her face a few minutes ago when Kay had burst in on them made him frown. Was this what she'd been thinking? That he was involved with Kay? Was that what had sent her running?

If she could jump to such an erroneous conclusion, was he doing the same thing? Maybe he'd better find out, he thought, before the situation got any more screwed up.

The next thing he knew, he was striding through her open door.

"Brett!"

With his hands on his hips, Brett jerked his chin toward the other man. "Who the hell is he?"

Rob Evans narrowed his eyes at the intruder in Jenny's doorway. Whoever he was, he was sure riled. Gloriously riled. Rob took in the man's appearance with a slow, lingering glance. The tall, lean build, the bare feet and chest, thick, black, finger-combed hair, the rough shadow of a day-old beard. Tight jeans, mostly zipped, totally unsnapped. The man was, Rob thought, magnificent. And probably didn't have a thing on under those worn jeans.

A quick look at Jenny's face had Rob biting back a sigh. That was the trouble with having a heterosexual female for a best friend—all the men she introduced him to were straight. The guy was obviously hers. He was most likely the one who'd taken the color from her cheeks and put that pinched look around her mouth and that wary look in her eyes.

Jenny was Rob's friend, and he didn't like to see his friends hurt. "You want me to throw him out?" he offered.

Horrified at the sudden hostility in the air, Jenny could only stare as Brett looked Rob up and down and said, "You could try."

She took a deep breath for calm. "Stop it, both of you." She looked at Brett. "Rob lives next door." To Rob she said, "Brett lives downstairs. And no, I would appreciate it if you didn't throw him out. But since I have an appointment across town, I'd like you both to leave."

Rob eyed her closely. "Are you sure?"

She tried for a smile. "I'm sure. And Rob, I'm sorry about Saturday." She had promised to fill in for an absent team member on the volleyball court behind the complex, then, because of Brett, had forgotten. "I hope I didn't cause problems?"

Rob studied her a moment longer, then smiled. "No, everything worked out." Then he leaned down and kissed her. It wasn't the first time he'd kissed her. She and Rob had been close friends for a couple of years. But this was not his usual peck on the cheek.

This time, with a definite, devilish twinkle in his eye, he kissed her full on the mouth.

In shock, Jenny felt his lips cover hers, felt his hand on her shoulder to keep her from pulling away. And then, because her eyes were wide open, she met his gaze and he winked at her.

"Okay, babe," Rob said, releasing her lips with a grin. "If you need me, just bang on the wall and I'll come running."

Brett followed Rob's departure with a glare. When the door closed behind Rob, Brett turned on her. "How many more men do you have wrapped around your little finger?"

"How many more women have a key to your apartment?" she flung back.

"None," he answered sharply. "Kay Olsen is my *secretary*. She was returning the first four chapters of the book I'm working on. My car wasn't in sight, so she assumed I was gone. She was doing what I pay her to do. We're friends and business associates and not a damn thing more."

Jenny fought against believing him because she needed her anger to keep her upright while her knees threatened to buckle. But his eyes . . . his eyes said he spoke the truth.

"Anything else you want to know?" he demanded.

She remembered another set of eyes, dark and mysterious, beautiful. Those eyes had said something else entirely. "Yes. How long has she been in love with you?"

"Kay?" Brett cried. He shook his head and laughed. "Boy, have you got that wrong. I told you—"

"I saw the look on her face when she realized . . . what she'd interrupted."

"No, you're wrong." His voice softened. "Kay's a

friend, she's my secretary, but that's all, Jenny. No other woman has any hold on me." *Except you.*

Jenny's chest tightened. Had she heard those last words, or only imagined them because—But no, she didn't want to have a hold on him. This whole thing between her and Brett, whatever it was, was crazy.

"You don't believe me," he accused.

The flash of pain came and went so fast in his eyes, she thought maybe she'd only imagined it. She couldn't think straight while looking into those eyes. She turned away. "It doesn't matter."

"If musclebound beach boys are more your type, then I guess you're right."

"He's just a friend," Jenny said, echoing Brett's earlier defense. She could end any questions about Rob easily, but her friend's sexual preferences were his business. She didn't feel she had the right to reveal something so intimate about him.

"I guess I should consider myself lucky that he wasn't the one who climbed over your balcony," Brett snapped.

"Why did you?" Jenny turned slowly to face him. A curious numbness settled over her. She felt as though she were speaking from a great distance away. "Why did you come here that night?"

"Because I thought you were in trouble, dammit."

"Why did you stay?"

"Because you *were* in trouble."

"And in the morning? Why did you . . ."

"Why did you?" he asked in return, his voice now as quiet as hers.

Jenny turned away again. "I thought you were . . . I think maybe things have moved too fast for us."

"Why?" he demanded, all softness abruptly gone from his voice. "Because my secretary has a key to my apartment? That's crap and you know it. What's going on, Jenny?''

"I don't . . . know what you mean.''

"I *mean* that we've been all over each other, inside and out, all weekend. I know it happened fast, but it happened, and you loved every minute of it as much as I did. Two days ago you welcomed me like I was some long-lost lover. Now you're acting like I've got the plague.''

Long-lost lover. If he only knew. If he knew what she'd thought, what she'd felt, he'd have sent her straight to the nearest nuthouse. Maybe she should send herself, Jenny thought, for despite everything, she still couldn't deny the feeling that Brett McCormick had never been a stranger to her.

She shook her head. "I need some time, Brett. This, everything that's happened, it's all too fast for me.''

Brett clenched his fists at his sides to keep from grabbing her and shaking her. He'd finally let himself believe that a woman wanted him for himself, and now she didn't want him at all. She wanted *time.* Hell, less than an hour ago they'd been rolling across his bed in each other's arms. Despite that, he was more than ready to fall to the floor with her here and now. He wanted her, fiercely.

And she wanted *time.*

He'd been a fool.

"Suit yourself, Jenny. You know where to find me when you're ready for stud service again.''

Jenny gasped, his words slicing through her like so many knives. She whirled to deny the accusation in time to see the door close sharply behind him as he left.

*   *   *

Kay Olsen drove home from Brett's with her hands wrapped so tightly around the steering wheel, she knew her fingerprints were permanently impressed. It was a miracle she made it home at all, the way her vision kept fogging up. But she determinedly blinked the tears away and repeated to herself over and over, "I will not fall apart. I will not fall apart. I will not fall apart."

After all, Brett didn't know how she felt about him, so there was no reason for her to feel this sickening sense of humiliation, of betrayal. The pain, however, was unavoidable. She couldn't argue it away. Seeing him with another woman, knowing they had just come from his bed, was more than Kay could bear.

"It is not," she told herself firmly as she pulled into her driveway. "I'll bear it because I have to. I have no choice."

She entered her home and went straight to the ski machine. "I'll just have to lose a few more pounds. Then he'll notice me. He won't need that other woman. Won't need her at all. Won't even remember he ever knew her."

Chapter Eight

As she had done every day for a week, Jenny pulled into her parking spot—miraculously empty and waiting for her every evening—and sat for long moments before shutting off the engine. For the first few days she'd lied, telling herself that she sat there so long because she was tired. She was merely gathering her strength before getting her mail and climbing the stairs to her apartment.

Actually, she was tired. Drained was more accurate. She hadn't slept a full night all week. Her nightmare was back now on a nightly basis, filling her with the horror over and over. When she worked with her clients, her shoulders sagged and her feet felt weighted down. Walking, talking, even thinking had become strenuous tasks.

But she'd finally admitted to herself that exhaustion was not why she sat in her car every evening. She sat in hopes that Brett would appear and she would be able to catch a glimpse of him. Just a glimpse, that's all she wanted.

Or rather, all she would be able to stand. She missed him so much she ached deep inside. Missed his quick smile, his ocean-blue eyes, his deep voice. Missed his touch, his taste, the feel of his skin beneath her fingers.

How were these feelings possible? She barely knew the man.

But no, that wasn't true. She'd known him forever.

God, why had she pushed him away? Why had she listened to her head, when it was her heart that now suffered?

She forced herself from the car. He wasn't going to suddenly open his door and invite her in. His car was next to hers, as it was every day. He was home. All he had to do was look out the angled blinds of his living room window and see her car to know she was home. Yet he hadn't come to her, hadn't called. He'd left it to her.

As much as she wanted to see him, be with him, she could not take that first step. She couldn't quite ignore the voice in the back of her mind that kept telling her to be careful, to stay away from Brett McCormick, for his sake as well as hers.

They made no sense, these wild warnings, yet she could not silence them.

That's why she waited in her car every evening, hoping Brett would take the decision from her hands by opening his door.

"Why should he?" she muttered to herself. She'd acted like . . . she couldn't even come up with a word to describe her bizarre behavior. Sleeping with a man she barely knew, spending the entire weekend with him, then running from him and pushing him away.

She climbed the stairs to her apartment, dreading the coming of night, for she knew the dream would return.

* * *

Harry Pilanski had been the manager of the River Haven Apartments for four years. Before that, he'd operated a small motel in East Texas—until his then-wife had run off with the electrician and a month's receipts.

In his line of work, he saw all kinds of people. Kinda made a hobby out of making up stories about them in his head. When the bell over the office door jingled Saturday afternoon, he gladly tuned out *Geraldo* and grinned. Oh, yeah, this one was a doozie. He could stay up all night making up stories about her.

She was tall, maybe 5'9" or better. At 5'5" himself, Harry had a thing for tall women. This one was blond and good looking, with clear eyes and a pair of full, lush lips that looked like they could suck chrome off a bumper. Didn't look like she was on drugs, thank the Lord, but something about her appearance wasn't quite right. Maybe it was the tits. Couldn't rightly say he'd ever seen a set quite that big before. At least, not in person, so to speak. Looked like she was smuggling a pair of cantaloupes in there, but he sure as hell hoped not. He'd like to get his hands under that pretty red sweater and squeeze.

"Help ya, ma'am?" He'd like to help her, all right. He'd like to help her out of her clothes and onto her back.

"Yes. I'd like to rent an apartment. Furnished."

Harry smiled to himself, temporarily distracted from her finer attributes in favor of cash money. He liked renting furnished apartments. Being an enterprising sort of fellow, he always tacked on a little extra to the rent, even more than the already higher price for furnished, and pocketed the, ah, excess revenue.

It never amounted to much, but it would buy his beer.

"Yes, ma'am. I believe I've got just what you're looking for. If you'll just fill out this application, I'll take you right on around and show you the sweetest little one-bedroom furnished apartment this side of the Mississippi."

As she took the clipboard it finally occurred to him to wonder if she was really a *she.* This was New Orleans, after all, and sometimes a body just couldn't tell for sure.

The prospective tenant waited until he handed her a pen, then she sat in the chair before his fake wood-grain desk, making certain to lean just right to show off a chest that was meant to be shown off. "I do hope you have one that has a balcony facing north, overlooking the pool." A slow, suggestive smile accompanied the voice.

Harry rubbed his hands together in glee. "Uh, well, I'm sure we can find just what you need."

Pesky little man, the new tenant thought, the way he practically drooled, acting like he'd never seen a chest before. She ought to let him look, the creep. Wouldn't he be surprised?

She stared down at the form, pen in hand. The first blank to be filled in presented a problem. Name. Of course they would want a name. The idea shouldn't have come as a surprise, but it did.

Name. What name to use?

Under the guise of scratching her head, she gave a slight tug to the blond wig, hoping to relieve the nagging itch over her right ear.

Name. Name.

Mary. Millie. Marie.

No, they didn't suit.

She racked her brain, concentrating hard, and sud-

denly it came, soft and familiar and right: Maude.
Her name would be Maude.

By Friday afternoon, Brett had had all he could
take of Jenny's stubbornness. Every day he'd stood
just close enough to the miniblinds at his living room
window to avoid being seen and watched her pull up
in her car and sit there. She stared at his door as if
willing it to open. The look of yearning made his gut
clench.

And every day when she opened her car door and
got out, he held his breath, waiting. Would this be
the day she came to him?

But no, every day she squared her shoulders, collected her mail from the box unit in the breezeway
next to his apartment, and hurried upstairs.

Dammit, he'd had enough. She'd said she wanted
to slow things down. If things got any slower between
them they'd have to reintroduce themselves to each
other.

He checked his watch and frowned. Five-forty-five.
She was late. She'd been home by five-fifteen every
day this week.

After pacing the floor for what seemed an eternity,
he checked his watch again. Less than two minutes
had passed. He swore. If he didn't know better, he'd
swear he was becoming obsessed with Jenny Franklin.
Hell, maybe he didn't know better. What else but
obsession would make a man stand at his window
every day just to watch a woman *not* come to his door?

When he'd walked away from her last Monday
morning, he'd actually thought he could put her out
of his mind. He hadn't even made it to his own door
before he'd known he was wrong. Hell, if he hadn't
been able to forget her after they'd met for coffee

in the Quarter, what fool notion made him think he'd succeed after spending the weekend in bed with her?

And that was another clue to his obsession—he'd never brought a woman to his home before, never spent the weekend with a woman before. Right now all he could think was, he wanted to do it again.

Something happened when they were together, something elemental, primitive. Something powerful. He didn't know what it was, but he knew it was still there. He could feel it pulsing somewhere deep inside.

He shook his head, unable to explain it even to himself, and checked his watch again. Five-fifty-two.

The one who called herself Maude stood behind the sheer drapes at her balcony door and slipped the strap of her binoculars over her head. She couldn't have asked for a better view.

The apartment manager had been a little surprised when she'd selected this unit. There were others available with nicer furnishings and newer appliances, but this was the one she'd wanted. She'd signed the lease immediately. This was the one that let her look out across the parking lot, beyond the swimming pool, to the next building. To the door to apartment 103. And to *her* apartment, upstairs. The apartment of the woman Maude was determined to find a way to get rid of.

Maude lifted the binoculars to her eyes and studied the front window of 103. She would watch, and she would wait. She had to know what was going on. If the woman was only a passing fancy, there was nothing to worry about. But Maude had to be sure.

An aging Monte Carlo pulled in near Brett's car

and parked. Nothing happened for several moments. Finally, a woman got out. A small woman with honey-blond hair. It was her.

Maude's hands tightened around the binoculars as a vice of pain tightened around her head. "Bitch."

Jenny took a deep breath and squared her shoulders. She was going to do it. She was going to ignore the nerves quivering in her stomach, ignore the rapid shuddering of her pulse and the sweat on her palms. She was going to march up to Brett McCormick's door and knock. If he answered . . . she didn't know what she was going to do then, except maybe smack him in the face for that crack he'd made Monday morning about stud service.

All she really knew was that she wanted very badly to see him. She had to know once and for all if what she'd felt the first time they'd kissed was true. Was he some missing part of her soul, a love lost in another time and finally found again? How was she to know?

It was crazy, this obsession she had developed when she met him, but she couldn't seem to do anything about it. Staying away from him the past week hadn't put him out of her mind. It had only made her miserable.

She stopped at the foot of the stairs. She could turn left and take those stairs up to her apartment, and the logical side of her brain would congratulate her. Or she could walk straight ahead to apartment 103 and knock. Anxiety would eat holes in her stomach, her hands would shake, and he might not even answer the door. But something deep inside urged her forward.

She was two yards from his door when it opened. Her feet stuck themselves to the sidewalk as Brett stepped to his threshold. Jenny's parched emotions drank in the sight of him as though she'd been lost in the desert for months and he was a sparkling pool of water. He had his sleeves rolled up and the collar open on a white dress shirt, as though he'd been working. His jeans were old and faded and snug and did things to Jenny's heartbeat that were astounding.

But it was to his face that Jenny's gaze was drawn. Deep lines around his mouth and eyes spoke of exhaustion, but the eyes themselves, those vivid blue eyes she wanted to fall into, were shuttered, revealing nothing, making her ache.

"You said you wanted time." Brett folded his arms across his chest and leaned casually against the door-jamb. "You realize, of course, that if we take things any slower, we'll have to get somebody to introduce us to each other."

The tight fist of anxiety in Jenny's chest loosened its grip at Brett's words. Her tension eased even further when she noted a hint of wariness in his gaze. She stepped forward slowly, her heart pounding, her breath locked in her chest. "Hello," she offered quietly. She shifted her purse and her bulging briefcase to her left hand and held out her right. "My name's Jenny Franklin."

"To hell with that." Brett wrapped his hand around her wrist and pulled her to him. "I know exactly who you are. You're the woman who's been driving me crazy since the day we met."

He lowered his head to hers slowly, giving her every chance to back away. She wouldn't have backed away if she'd been able. As their lips met, she whispered his name.

Brett felt his heart stop. There was an ache in her voice that matched the one in chest. He'd missed her even more than he'd thought. To know that she'd missed him, too, sent relief sluicing through him. He covered her mouth with his and kissed her deeply, tasting her need, letting her taste his.

He wanted to step back and pull her into his apartment, then shut out the world. He wanted to feast on her and give her so much pleasure that she wouldn't dream of shutting him out again. But he didn't want her to be reminded of that instant when Kay had opened the door on them, didn't want Jenny thinking about it, remembering it, and being in his apartment might bring it all back to her. He eased his lips from hers and looked down into gray eyes gone soft and needy. The look sent heat and heaviness to his loins.

"Are you going to invite me upstairs, or am I going to have to invite myself?" he asked quietly.

For the length of two long breaths she didn't answer. Then she said, "Do you want to come upstairs with me?"

"More than anything," he said with feeling.

She smiled slowly. "Then why don't you try the front door this time instead of the balcony?"

"Ah, a kind and generous woman. Thank you. The front door sounds fine. Don't move. I'll be right back."

It took him less than a minute to grab his wallet and keys, lock up the apartment, and follow her upstairs.

Jenny's hands were so clammy that she nearly dropped her keys while unlocking her door. All week she'd been miserable with missing Brett. Now that he was beside her, so close she could feel his heat, she should be relieved, happy. She supposed she was, but she was also fast turning into a nervous wreck.

"You look tired," Brett told her as he followed her inside and closed the door. "Haven't you been sleeping well?"

Jenny set her purse and briefcase on the table by the door. "Not really," she answered with a shrug.

Brett pulled her into his arms and hugged her. "That's what comes from sleeping alone."

A nervous giggle burst from her. A giggle, she thought with chagrin. At her age. "As I recall, neither one of us got much sleep last weekend."

Brett grinned. "Good point."

Jenny stepped back from his embrace. "Let me go change clothes, then I'll see about fixing something to eat."

"You change. *I'll* see about supper. I didn't invite myself up here so you could stand on your feet and cook for me, when you look like you're ready to drop."

Jenny looked at him solemnly and took a slow, deep breath. "Why did you invite yourself up here?"

"Because I've missed you," he said candidly. His eyes darkened to midnight blue. "Because something happens when we're together, Jen. Something powerful. Something I don't understand, but that I can't walk away from."

Jenny's heart calmed. Certainty replaced nervousness as she accepted that Brett, too, felt the elemental pull between them. He might not feel the past history between them as she did, but he felt something. It was enough, for now.

"Go change clothes," he told her. "I'll ransack the kitchen."

Brett's "ransacking" resulted in the best Chinese fried rice Jenny had ever tasted. "You surprise me," she admitted.

"Why? Because I can cook?"

She shrugged. "I guess. You said you grew up on

a farm. So did my brothers, and believe me, they would starve to death if they had to feed themselves.''

"What's growing up on a farm got to do with it?'' Brett asked.

"Come on, you know there's always a woman on the farm to do the cooking.''

"Why, Ms. Franklin, what a chauvinistic comment.''

"I'll bet your mother fixed three meals a day seven days a week for the entire family. Big meals.''

"So?''

"So? So, I bet you and your brother and your dad never even so much as made your own sandwiches.''

At the mention of his father, Brett's throat closed. His heart sped up and his stomach churned.

"Am I right?'' Jenny asked, smiling.

He held his fork in a death grip, fighting the urge to run. He knew he couldn't run fast enough or far enough to outdistance the memories. He battled the tension inside with slow, deep breaths. Jenny was too sharp not to notice his reaction if he didn't get himself under control, and he had no intention of answering any questions that might result. He was better off answering the one she'd already asked.

"I guess so,'' he offered.

"And I further bet that you didn't learn to cook for yourself until after you left home.''

"You'd win that one, too,'' he said, feeling the tension ease. "There was no need to learn at home. But when I moved out, it was either cook or starve.''

"My brothers found another way.''

"What'd they do, eat out?''

"They got married. No single life for them. They each in turn had it all arranged before they left home. They went straight from having Mom take care of their every need to having a wife do the same thing.''

"You're laughing.''

"Yeah, I know. Because I was the youngest and the smallest, I always had to fight twice as hard to prove I wasn't helpless. It wasn't until right before I moved here that I realized all three of my brothers are as helpless as babies."

Because Brett had cooked, Jenny wouldn't hear of letting him help with the cleanup, but he declined her suggestion that he watch television while she loaded the dishwasher. Instead, he sat at the breakfast bar and tortured himself with the way her shorts stretched tight across her backside every time she leaned down to put something in the bottom rack of the dishwasher.

Nothing like a sexy woman to take his mind off things he didn't want to remember.

But no, that wasn't exactly true. He'd never met a woman before who could so totally occupy his thoughts.

He mentally shook his head. The woman was playing with his mind. Less than two hours ago, he'd been missing her so much he ached with it. Then he'd seen her, held her, kissed her, and all he'd been able to think about had been getting her out of that damn sexy business suit. He'd never considered a woman's business suit sexy before.

A few minutes later he'd turned himself into Harry Homemaker so she wouldn't have to cook when she was so tired. Then she'd mentioned his father and he'd been catapulted back in time and—

No. He wouldn't think about it. Not now, not here with Jenny. This time with her was special, and he didn't want to spoil it. Because now he'd come full circle in his emotions. He wanted her again. Damn, he *craved* her.

The woman was playing with his head, and he couldn't make himself care.

It wasn't just sex and hormones, he acknowledged to himself. It was everything. The way she smiled, her soft laugh, the way the light flashed through her hair striking gold here, paler sun streaks there. The way she moved, even in the simple act of rinsing plates and wiping the cabinet. She was so graceful. And those hands. Not a single wasted motion, yet she never seemed to hurry. Her hands were pure poetry, and that didn't take into account their softness or the way they made him feel when she touched him.

Yeah, there were a lot of things about this woman other than sex that drew him, but he'd be lying to himself if he said he was in no hurry to feel her stretched out naked and warm against every inch of him.

With a final movement, she closed and started the dishwasher. Then, with her back to him, she stilled for one breath, two, three. When she turned slowly toward him, her eyes widened at what she saw in his face.

Brett felt his pulse pound low and hard as his body responded to the answering warmth in her eyes. They didn't need words just then. He wanted her; she wanted him. Simple. Elemental. And it shook him.

She came to him without a word and took his hand. Silently, her revealing gaze locked on his, she led him down the short hall to her bedroom.

Brett paused in surprise. She had readied the room for him. The lamp was on and the bed covers turned down. What could have seemed like a calculating come-on was instead made sweet by the sudden uncertainty he saw in Jenny's eyes. He couldn't remember the last time anyone had done anything for him that was so utterly . . . touching. An aching tenderness blossomed inside him.

Jenny watched him from the corner of her eye as

he took in the preparations she'd made. Another case of nerves assailed her. Had she been too forward to lead him to her room this way? What was he thinking as he eyed the turned-down covers? Why didn't he say something?

"Thank you," he whispered.

"For what?"

"For this. For making me feel welcome."

"Did you think you wouldn't be?"

He took her hand and toyed with her fingers, sending electricity shooting from her hand to her heels. "For all I knew, you'd changed your mind." Slowly he pulled her against his chest and wrapped his arms around her. "It was a hell of a long week without you, Jen."

His admission dissolved her uncertainty and she melted against him. This was where she was meant to be. "It was awful," she admitted.

He nuzzled the sensitive spot behind her left ear. "What do you think we should do about it?"

Jenny felt her knees turn to jelly. "Oh," she breathed, "I can think of a couple of things that might start to make up for it."

With a low growl, Brett tumbled them both to the bed. "So can I." He threaded his fingers through hers and stretched her arms out to her sides, then settled his weight in the cradle of her thighs. "God, I never thought I could miss anyone the way I've missed you."

Her lips parted in reaction to his words and he took decisive advantage.

Jenny felt her senses reel as he kissed her. She was drifting, floating, soaring, and he was with her all the way. Her blood rushed and her heart pounded while her lungs labored for air. Just then she didn't care if she never breathed again, as long as he went on kissing her. His lips were firm and sleek and hot, his tongue textured to match hers, and his taste, dark and mysterious, drove her wild. The weight of him pressed between her legs started an urgent pulsing deep in her core.

Brett worked his way from her mouth to her jaw. At her neck he ran into the barrier of her T-shirt. Trailing his lips back up to her mouth, he slid one hand beneath the fabric and smoothed his palm up her ribs to cup one firm, resilient breast. She must have been made especially for him, he decided, because she fit his hand so perfectly.

Her heart beat hard and fast beneath his touch. His beat harder, faster. The first time they made love had been slow and easy. Then they'd argued and he'd thought . . . hell, he didn't know what he'd thought, but when he'd brought her home from breakfast later that morning, they'd been desperate for each other.

After that, the weekend blurred from one love scene to the next. They'd explored each other, enjoyed each other. They'd laughed and played like two teenagers in heat.

Tonight, what started slow would not stay that way, he knew. It couldn't. He felt the urgency rising in him like a flood tide. Because now he knew what it was like to exist for days without her. It was hell. A dark, cold, lonely place filled with nothing but silence and a sense of loss so deep and profound it was all out of proportion for a relationship as new as theirs. She was in his blood, a fire raging out of control, singeing him, burning him, engulfing him.

Jenny felt the change in him, felt the tension in his muscles increase. Without words, she thought she understood his sudden urgency. She, too, was desperate to wipe out the past lonely week. When he freed her hands and pulled off her T-shirt, she reached for the buttons on his shirt. In seconds they were naked. The exquisite sensation of hot flesh on hot flesh made her gasp with pleasure.

Then he stole her breath again, this time with his mouth on hers. She tasted his hunger, and suddenly she was greedy for more, for all of him.

All of him was exactly what he gave her. He sank into her, his hardness into her softness, in one powerful thrust that shook her to her soul, for she recognized that only when they were one, only when they were joined was she complete. She whispered his name.

Brett heard the sound with his heart as well as his ears. He felt it in every pore, along every nerve of his body. He watched, entranced, as her eyes grew darker and darker with every thrust he made.

Being inside her, feeling her surrounding him with her welcoming heat, felt more like coming home than anything he'd known in his life. Somehow, some way, he knew deep inside that he and Jenny were meant to be together. As the urgency built and his blood raced hotter and faster, he lost all thought but that one. They were meant to be. Meant to be. Meant to—

The thought was cut off in the middle, because thought was not possible when a man and woman were catapulted into oblivion together.

Brett's chest was still heaving when he felt himself surge to life inside her again.

Jenny looked at him in wonder and amazement.

He supposed he should laugh or make a joke, but he couldn't. "This has never happened to me before. Damn, Jenny, I hope you meant it when you said you wanted me, because tonight I think you're going to have more of me than you bargained for."

His—his what, threat? Promise? Whatever it was, it sent a searing weakness gushing through Jenny even as Brett seemed to grow stronger before her eyes.

And he was stronger. He felt the fire and strength surge through his blood, bones, muscles. He'd never felt so strong, so powerful, in his life.

"Whatever you've done to me," he whispered roughly, as he took her lips again, "it'll either kill me, or make me immortal."

At his words, the ice of foreboding shivered down Jenny's spine, but in seconds, the heat of his kiss burned it away.

Ordinarily Jenny would have spent Saturday morning lolling in bed. This particular Saturday morning, she didn't feel capable of doing anything but, nor did she have any desire to leave the strong arms that held her so securely.

For a moment she let herself remember the instant when fear had washed over her last night, when Brett had claimed she might be killing him. Thank God he hadn't seemed to notice anything was wrong. Her fear was irrational, she knew that. Whatever connection she and Brett had, whatever had happened in their past lives, couldn't touch them now. She was Jenny Franklin and he was Brett McCormick, and this was the twentieth century—what was left of it. This was their second chance. She felt that in her bones. Her heart remembered his, and this time . . . this time they would find the happiness that had been ripped from them in the past. This time they would make it. There was nothing to fear.

She might have stayed curled up against him all

day if her accountant hadn't called at nine, in a panic because his computer suddenly refused to boot up and he had a client coming over at three to pick up reports that weren't yet completed.

Jenny smothered a sigh. "Okay, Joe, I'll be there in about an hour."

Brett's arms tightened around her. "Trouble?" he asked, as she hung up the bedside phone.

"Work." Jenny turned over and met his questing lips. She should have told Joe two hours.

When Jenny finally grabbed her briefcase and left her apartment—twenty minutes late—Brett left with her. The day was sunny and warm, with no breeze to stir the air. A hint of magnolia teased her senses. Jenny took a deep breath, not minding the humidity, just glad to be alive. The day was beautiful, life was grand, and the man she was falling in love with was whistling a jaunty tune at her side.

At the foot of the stairs, Brett's whistle ended on an abrupt sharp note. Jenny followed the line of his stare and let out a cry of dismay. In shock, she gaped at her car. Slowly she walked around it counting. One. Two. Three. Four. Four flat tires.

"How?" she cried.

Brett squatted down first at one flat, then another, a stream of vicious curses following in his wake. "They've been slashed."

"What?"

He stood and turned toward her, grim faced, anger in his eyes. "Slashed. Somebody slashed all four of your tires."

Stunned, Jenny glanced around the parking lot. "The other cars look fine. Why mine, for Pete's sake? Who would do a thing like this?"

* * *

Across the way, the curtains at an upstairs balcony shifted. The one called Maude peered through binoculars and smiled. The sharp headache that had plagued her all night disappeared as she watched the woman inspect the flat tires.

"Take that, you bitch." Maude chuckled grimly. "Every time you go near him, you're going to pay. You'll keep paying until you get the message. Leave Brett McCormick alone."

Satisfaction in dealing Jenny Franklin a blow was fleeting. Sheer rage came next, when through the binoculars she saw Brett hand Jenny the keys to his new car. The little bitch kissed him, right there in front of God and everybody—and damn him, he kissed her back—then she got in his new car and drove off.

The pain behind Maude's eyes slammed back with a vengeance.

No more, she decided. No more "messages." She wouldn't bother with warnings. Jenny Franklin would have to die.

Chapter Nine

Brett and Jenny spent that night in Brett's apartment, and Jenny's restless sleep woke him just after midnight. He pressed her close and tried to soothe her with his touch without waking her. He'd had to practically force her to take his car so that she could make it to her appointment this morning. She'd been shocked and angry over her slashed tires and probably not in the proper frame of mind to deal with a client, but she'd finally agreed to go.

After she'd left, Brett had called the police. They'd told him exactly what he'd expected to hear—there wasn't a damn thing they could do. No witnesses, no clues, no other cars in the lot vandalized. One officer had asked if Jenny had anybody mad enough at her to pull a stunt like this. Brett hadn't had an answer.

When the police left, he found her insurance papers and called in the claim. By the time Jenny had returned from her appointment, the tire shop had come and gone. Her car sported four brand-new tires.

Brett grinned in the darkness. She had thanked

him profusely and . . . inventively for not having to deal with the mess herself. Afterward, he'd spent the better part of an hour showing her how welcome she was to any- and everything about him.

She stirred in her sleep again and whimpered. A bad dream, Brett figured, and it bothered him. He didn't like the idea of her having nightmares. She'd had one last week, the night she'd stumbled out onto her balcony and stared down at him. Hell, his own damn book had given her that particular nightmare. He hoped to God that wasn't what she was dreaming tonight.

He didn't know whether to wake her or not. He tried soothing her with soft words and touches as he'd done a few minutes earlier, but this time she merely grew more agitated.

"Jen?"

She cried out in her sleep. Fighting against the confining covers, she thrashed until her arms were free. Afraid she might get out of bed and hurt herself, Brett reached for her. "Jen. Wake up, Jen."

She placed her trembling hands on his face and her fingers were like ice.

"Jen?"

Again and again she ran her hands across his face. A wild, anguished moan rose from deep inside her.

The sound reached down and grabbed something vital inside Brett and made him shudder. "Jenny, wake up!"

"No!" she cried. "Oh, God, Seth, no—"

Seth? Brett's stomach clenched. Not again! "Jenny!"

"Don't die, Seth, please don't die."

"Jenny!"

She rose above him on her knees and clutched his

head tight. "You can't die. I love you. Do you hear me, Seth?"

Brett swallowed the bile that rose in his throat. Damn that book, and damn his own dream that hadn't left him alone until he'd written it. "Jenny—"

"I love you," she cried, tears streaming down her cheeks. "Seth, don't leave me!"

Her words—words he had written and that were now tormenting her—tormented him. "Ah, God, Jenny, wake up, baby, please."

"You've killed him, Maudie!"

"Jenny, you're having a dream. It's just—"

She scrambled away from him until she backed into the headboard, her arms out as if to ward off an attacker. In the dim glow of the security light outside, he could see that her eyes were open. The wild terror there sent icy fingers of dread down his spine. She wasn't seeing him at all, but some unknown demon in her dream.

No, not unknown. It was *his* demon she was seeing, the evil woman he'd invented in his mind and transferred to paper.

"What are you doing with that knife?" she shrieked.

Goddamn. He had no doubt that she was dreaming the end of *This Raging Madness*, but she wasn't dreaming it the way it had been published. She was dreaming it the way he'd originally written it, the way she insisted it should end. Either way, she was about be murdered in her dream. The mere idea chilled him to his soul. He had to wake her. "There's no knife, Jenny. Do you hear me? You're having a dream."

Suddenly Jenny's eyes widened. Her hands clutched at her ribs. A small gasp left her lips.

"Jenny!" Good God, he had to wake her! Brett

grasped her shoulders and shook her. "God damn it, wake up!"

A gurgled scream rose from her throat, then, with her chest heaving as though she'd run a marathon, she stiffened beneath his hands and stared wildly around her.

"Jenny?"

She jerked as though shot and looked at him. "B-Brett?" she whispered.

"It's me, Jen."

"Oh, Brett," she cried. She flung herself into his arms and trembled violently.

"You're all right now." He held her close, feeling her heart pound hard and fast against his.

"You're all right," he managed through his tight throat. "You're safe in my bed and everything's okay. It was just a dream. Just a bad dream, Jen."

Jesus God, he'd cared for so few people in his life, deeply cared, yet they seemed to be the very people he managed to hurt the most. He'd written his latest book for the same reason he'd written the others. For his readers' enjoyment. Sheer escapist fiction. But it was his book that now tormented Jenny. The book's success tasted bitter on his tongue. In that moment, he hated himself for writing it.

He held her gently and rocked her and tried his best to soothe her for what seemed like hours before she finally calmed in his arms. Her heart eased its pounding and her breathing slowed.

"Better now?" he asked softly.

Jenny sniffed and shifted to a more comfortable position against his chest. "I'm okay. Embarrassed as hell, but okay."

"You don't have a damn thing to be embarrassed about," he told her. "Nobody can control what they dream. I just wish to God I'd never written that damn book,'' he added fiercely, tightening his arms around her.

Jenny eased back until she could see his face. With a hand to his cheek, she asked, ''You know what I dreamed?''

He gave her a wry smile. ''You talked.''

She closed her eyes, and Brett kissed her soft lids. ''I'm so damn sorry, Jen.''

Her eyes flew open. ''It's not your fault.''

''Isn't it? My book is giving you nightmares. That makes it my fault. I wish I'd never written it.''

''Brett, no.''

The look she gave him then was one he couldn't interpret. Part sadness, part trepidation. Part resignation, and a dozen other indecipherable emotions.

She closed her eyes briefly, took a deep breath, then met his gaze again. ''If you hadn't written the book, we might never have met. The thought of spending my life without ever knowing you . . . it doesn't bear thinking about.''

Her words humbled him. ''I like to think we would have met anyway,'' he said candidly. ''It—this—you and me . . . feels like, I don't know, like destiny. I wish we'd met without the book. That's the second time I know of that you've had that dream. If it keeps up, one of these days you're going to decide I'm not worth the torment my book puts you through.''

''Never,'' she answered swiftly, tearfully. Her hands clutched at his bare back. ''Never.''

''Okay, it's okay. Shh. Shh,'' he soothed. ''Let's not talk about it. It doesn't matter anyway, because I already wrote the book, and it already gave you bad dreams.''

''No.'' She leaned away and met his gaze again. ''I . . .''

''What is it?''

Her chest expanded on a deep breath, pushing her bare, glorious breasts out, giving him ideas on how to take her mind off her nightmare. A slow, steady warmth started in his loins and radiated outward. As he watched, her nipples tightened. The slow warmth turned into a rush of heat.

Jenny made a sound of dismay. "No, don't look at me like that."

Startled, Brett jerked his gaze to her eyes. "What's wrong?"

"I . . ." She stopped and licked her lips—nervously, he thought. "There's something I need to tell you."

The seriousness in her tone sent apprehension snaking down his arms. "What?"

"I can't let you blame yourself or your book for my nightmares."

"Actually," he said with a quirk of his lips, "I don't think you need to let me. I think I'm managing to blame myself just fine all on my own."

"No." She shook her head. "You don't understand. Your book isn't the cause of my nightmares."

"Jenny, you were quoting my dialog word for word."

"I don't doubt it." She licked her lips again.

There was no mistake this time. She was definitely nervous. He felt a new tension running through her muscles. "What is it you're trying to tell me?"

She squeezed her eyes shut a moment, then, as if she'd come to some sort of decision, she gave a slight nod and looked at him. "Your book is not responsible for my nightmares, because I've been having that exact same nightmare for a lot longer than your book has been out."

Brett stilled. "Jenny, that's impossible."

"I know. But it's true."

"Maybe you heard the storyline in the advance publicity and—"

She was shaking her head before he finished. "No, Brett. The first time, I had the dream exactly, word for word, like the last chapter in your book—except, like I said, Anna was stabbed instead of shot, and Maudie's dress was a different color—"

"Jen—"

"The first time I had the dream, I was ten years old."

Shock glued his tongue to the roof of his mouth. For one unbelievable moment, he thought she'd said—With a silent, rueful laugh at his own foolishness, he shook his head and pulled her into his arms. "Damn, baby, I'm sorry. I knew it was bad, but I guess I didn't realize it was so bad it makes you feel like you've been having it all your life."

Jenny squirmed out of his hold. "I didn't say it felt like it. I know you're going to find this hard to believe, but I swear it's true. The first time I had this dream was when I was ten."

"Jenny—"

"It was the middle of the night, I think. I guess I must have screamed, because my mother came running into the room and turned on the light. By then I was crying so hard I could barely breathe. I was terrified. I kept looking around the room waiting for Maudie to jump out at me with that huge knife."

Jenny paused and shuddered, and for the life of him, Brett couldn't get a single syllable to cross his vocal chords.

"I remember Mother asking me what was wrong. I told her Cousin Maudie had stabbed me. I could still feel it, a deep, burning sensation straight through my ribs, clear down inside me. Mother had to pry my hand away from my ribs. She pulled up my pajama top, and there was this red mark on my chest that hadn't been there before."

Brett's breath lodged in his chest, locked there by an eerie premonition of what she was about to say. He'd seen that mark. The night he'd climbed onto her balcony, the mark had been bloody. When he'd cleaned it, the skin there had looked barely scratched. There had been no way that amount of blood could have come from something that hadn't really even broken the skin, but he'd shrugged it off that night to concentrate on calming her down.

The mark was still there. He could see it right now in the dim glow of the streetlight, a thin dark line across the pale skin over her ribs. It looked like a birthmark.

"She said I must have scratched myself in my sleep," Jenny continued. "But even then, as young as I was, I knew better. You've seen the mark, Brett. You know it's still there."

"There was blood on you," he whispered without thinking. He wanted to call the words back instantly. Dammit, something was really wrong here if she thought she'd actually dreamed his book before he'd even written it. He didn't want to encourage her, for Christ's sake.

"That was . . . strange," she said. Then she gave a wry chuckle. "Stranger than usual, anyway. It's never bled before, or since. Just that one time, the night I made it out to my balcony and looked down and saw you there."

"You—" He stopped and swallowed, knowing he was crazy to say anything but unable to help it. "You thought I was Seth."

"Yes."

When she didn't say anything else, Brett reached over and turned on the bedside lamp. After their eyes adjusted to the light he studied her closely. To her credit, she met his gaze head on. What he saw in her eyes chilled him. "My God, *you believe it.*"

"Believe what, that I've been having this same dream—"

"No, not just the dream. You think—good God, you think I'm him, don't you? You think I'm Seth."

Jenny trembled at the raw disbelief in his voice. What had she expected? Had she really been foolish enough to think he would believe the things she believed?

She shook her head. "No," she told him softly, sadly. "I know who you are. You're Brett McCormick."

"You didn't know that last week," he reminded her harshly. "You looked down at me from your balcony and you called me Seth. You did it again a few minutes later when I climbed into your room. You thought I was him."

Jenny closed her eyes against the flare of anger in his and let her head fall back against the headboard. "I was dreaming. You know that."

"Yeah, and you were dreaming again tonight, the same damn dream. You were dreaming my book, but with your ending. And you claim you've been dreaming it for years. What the hell is going on, Jen?" he demanded.

What the hell, she thought, resigned. "Do you believe in reincarnation?"

"*What?*"

"Do you be—"

"I heard you, dammit." He lunged from the bed and stood beside it, his naked skin glowing golden in the lamplight. His chest heaved; his fists clenched at his sides. "The answer is not only no, but hell no, I don't believe in that crap."

A laugh wouldn't have surprised her, nor skepticism, nor even outright scoffing. But the vehemence of his answer did. "Why?"

"Because it's nothing more than a sop," he cried, pacing back and forth beside the bed. "To make fools feel better about dying."

Curious, feeling as though she'd struck some personal chord with him, she cocked her head and asked, "Is that so bad, wanting to take away the fear of dying?"

"It's bad because it's a crock of shit. When you're dead, you're dead, and that's all there is to it."

"There's about a billion people in the world who'd disagree with you."

Suddenly he stopped pacing and turned toward her, hands braced low on his hips. "Why are we talking about this? Are you trying to tell me you think . . ." His eyes widened and his jaw fell slack. "Good God, that's it, isn't it? That's what this has been about from the beginning."

A chill raced through Brett. Was she . . . crazy? A psychopath? A certifiable loony-toon? Or was it even worse? She had come to his book signing specifically to meet him. Had she been stalking him? It happened to people in the public eye all the time. Someone—a fan, maybe—could become obsessed. She'd handed him a note guaranteed to get his attention, mentioning things no one could know. She'd met him in the French Quarter and left him sitting there, making her dramatic escape, making it impossible for him to forget her. Then she'd stumbled out onto her balcony and practically called for him to come up to her bed, where she'd . . .

Brett shook his head. Even looking for a reason to condemn her, he couldn't buy the scenario he was building in his head. *He* was the one who'd moved into her apartment complex. She couldn't have arranged that. She couldn't have known he would choose that night to step out onto his patio. And nothing short of believing that she and Kay were both liars could explain how Jenny had known the original ending to his book.

But none of it made sense, and the talk of reincarnation set his blood to boiling. Pictures flashed through his mind, sharp in their centers, fuzzy along the edges. A flower-draped casket. Tearstained cheeks. A permanent sickness settling into his gut. Guilt—God, the guilt. A deep, moaning wail in the dark corners of his mind, the wail of an animal in unimaginable pain. Quiet murmurs. Chanting. The rising of hope, the dying of faith. "Shit." He squeezed his eye shut.

"Does it matter to you what I believe?"

Brett opened his eyes and blinked, having for a moment forgotten she was there, forgotten he was there, in his apartment in New Orleans, rather than—

"How *can* you believe it, for crying out loud?"

"Because I don't know how else to explain sitting in my living room and reading a book written sometime in the last year or two by a man I've never met that ends almost word for word with a dream I've been having for the past *twenty years*. And when I saw you that first time, at the mall, when you looked up at me . . . how do you explain what happened then?"

Brett remembered the shock that had felt like some kind of soul-deep . . . recognition. Hell, he was as crazy as she was. "Nothing happened," he said with a low growl.

"It did for me," she admitted softly. "It happened for me again when I woke up last Saturday morning and found you beside me in my bed. You looked at me and everything seemed to fall into place."

"It's called chemistry," he nearly shouted. "Look, I won't deny there's something pretty damn powerful between us. Hell, I couldn't deny it if I wanted to, and I don't want to. Why can't we just take it at face value and see where it leads us? Why do you have to try to make something more out of it than what it is?"

"And just what is it, Brett? If what we feel for each other isn't from the past, if we haven't been cheated out of each other before and this life is all we have, then just what—" She squeezed her eyes shut and fell silent.

"Then just what?"

"Never mind." She shook her head. "I guess it doesn't really matter."

"It obviously does matter, to you."

"But not to you. I can't make you believe in reincarnation."

"Jen, the damn book is *fiction*. I made it up. The people in it *never lived*. Even if I did believe in reincarnation, I damn sure can't believe in the reincarnation of a fictional character."

"If you made it up, how did I know the ending?"

"That's the sixty-four-thousand-dollar question, isn't it? Hell, maybe it was nothing more than coincidence."

"And is it another coincidence that you dreamed about the same people I've been dreaming about since I was ten?"

For the life of him, he couldn't think of a damn thing to say.

"Forget it," Jenny said, sounding exhausted. "Just forget I ever said anything."

"Damn right I will," he muttered. "There's no such thing as past lives and rebirth and all that crap.

Dead is dead, and that's all there is to it. And dead people don't come back.''

Jenny watched him carefully, trying to ignore the ache in her heart and concentrate instead on the thread of something in his voice she couldn't quite identify. He sounded almost as though he were trying to convince himself ... no, that wasn't right. He believed every word he was saying. And then it dawned on her. "Who died?" she asked gently.

His head snapped and his shoulders jerked. "What?"

"Who died and left you and didn't come back?"

His blue eyes turned cold and hard. "I don't know what you're talking about."

She felt his pain from halfway across the room. Oh, God, she felt it to her bones. She breathed his name and watched his eyes turn dark. What right did she have to expose his pain?

"I'm sorry," she whispered. "I'll ... go." Trembling, she moved to the edge of the bed.

A sudden panic seized Brett. He knew he wasn't thinking straight. He never did when thoughts of his father's death intruded. But one thing he knew was that despite whatever weird things she believed, he wasn't ready to let go of this woman.

"Why?" he demanded. "Because I don't believe in reincarnation? For that, you're going to just walk out?"

She whipped her head around, her mouth and eyes wide in surprise. "Of course not. If it doesn't matter to you that I believe in it, why should it matter to me if you don't?"

"Then why are you leaving?"

Cool air-conditioned air washed over her skin and raised goosebumps. "You're angry. I ... I guess I thought you wanted me to go."

Brett leaned across the bed and dragged her slowly to his side. "Then you thought wrong. It's true that I don't believe in past lives and rebirth, but I believe in what happens between you and me when we're together. It's real and it's here and it's now. Can't that be enough?"

There was no answer but yes for Jenny, and she whispered it as she met his lips with hers. Yes, it would be enough, because she would take him any way she could get him. If he didn't believe, so be it. She knew the truth, though—knew it deep in her soul, deep down where her heart remembered him even though her mind didn't. They'd lost each other once, in another lifetime. She would let nothing come between them in this, their second chance. Nothing.

As she pulled him down onto the bed with her, she vowed to love him no matter what. Someday maybe she could find a way to ease the terrible pain she'd seen in his eyes, but for now, she would simply love him.

Chapter Ten

Brett didn't see any need to worry about Jenny's belief in reincarnation. If she wanted to buy into that line of crap, that was her business. By the time the pounding on his front door woke him the next morning, he'd put Jenny's weird theories completely out of his mind.

He rolled over with a groan, irritated by the intrusive racket. He and Jenny hadn't exactly gotten a hell of a lot of sleep last night, between her nightmare and the way he'd done his level best to make her forget it.

The pounding on the door came again.

Jenny mumbled and started to rise.

"Stay put and go back to sleep. I'll get rid of whoever it is." Brett crawled out of bed and stepped into his jeans. Remembering the morning Kay had walked in on them, he made sure his jeans were zipped and buttoned before he answered the door.

He was not in the least pleased to find Jenny's next-door neighbor, Rob Something-or-Other, standing on his doorstep. She'd said the guy was nothing more than a good friend, and Brett had no real choice but to believe her. That didn't mean he wanted to become pals with the guy.

"Yeah?" Brett greeted gruffly, his voice still scratchy from sleep.

"Sorry to bother you, but Jenny's not answering her door. Do you have a key to her apartment?"

Brett blinked. "You mean you don't?"

Rob laughed a little harder than Brett thought necessary. "No, I don't," he managed. "We're not that close."

"Then why do you want to get into her apartment?"

The man at the door sobered. "I'm worried about her. I heard her—"

"Rob?"

Brett turned to find Jenny staggering sleepily toward him wearing nothing but the shirt he'd worn yesterday.

"There you are," Rob said, sounding relieved.

Jenny glanced from Rob to Brett, wondering at the tightness around Brett's mouth and the wariness in his eyes. He couldn't still think there was something between her and Rob, surely. But just to make certain, she snuggled up to Brett's side and slipped her arm around his waist. "You've been looking for me?" she asked Rob.

"I've been pounding on your door for the past hour."

She smiled. "I didn't answer, did I?"

Rob's lips quirked. "I don't guess you heard me." His gaze flicked down Brett then back to Jenny. "Can't say I blame you, either."

"Why were you looking for me?" she asked.

"Because your shower's been running since around four this morning. I heard it come on right after I got home. I can hear it through my wall. I was worried maybe you'd fallen and hit your head or something." He cocked his head toward Brett. "He must be pretty damn distracting if you can walk out and forget to turn off your shower."

A cold tingling started at the base of Jenny's skull and whooshed down her backbone. "Brett is definitely distracting. But I haven't been upstairs since yesterday afternoon. And I know I didn't leave my shower running."

Waiting only long enough for Jenny to pull on some clothes and grab her keys, the three of them rushed upstairs to her apartment. The instant Jenny opened the door she knew someone had been there. She could feel it in the way the hair stood up along her arms. There was something in the air, something foreign, something . . . angry. She could sense it, taste it. And she could hear the shower. The shower she had not used.

With a shiver of apprehension, she started toward the bathroom.

Brett stopped her with a tug on her arm. "Let me go first, just in case."

Her eyes widened. "Just in case what? You don't think somebody's still here, do you?"

"That's what I want to find out."

She shook her head. "There's no one here," she said with certainty. Then, in a quiet voice, she added, "Not now."

Brett wouldn't give in, so she let him go first, but she followed right behind him. It was as she'd known. There was no one else in the apartment.

Jenny stood next to Brett at the door of her tiny bathroom with Rob behind them in the hall. Water hammered into her tub from the shower nozzle, sending damp, cool air wafting over her. "I know I didn't leave the shower running," she said, hugging her arms.

"I know you didn't, too," Brett confirmed as he stepped into the bathroom and turned off the water.

Nothing looked out of place. Jenny studied the bathroom carefully, then the bedroom, then the rest of the apartment. Everything looked exactly the way it should. But it didn't *feel* the way it should.

Rob shook his head. "I came home around three-forty-five and went straight to bed. I remember thinking how quiet it was when my air conditioner shut off. Then I heard the water come on in Jenny's apartment. Somebody was in here," he said grimly.

Jenny shivered.

"Are you sure," Rob said, "that you didn't come up here in the middle of the night and—"

Jenny was shaking her head before he finished. "Even if I had, you know I don't take showers."

Rob's lips quirked. "If you don't want to offend people, I suggest you give it a try."

"Very funny." She made a face at him. "You know I prefer a bath to a shower."

Brett knew that little fact about her, but he damn sure didn't like it that Rob knew. He started to say something, but swallowed the words. He would save it for later, when he and Jenny were alone. There were other matters to deal with now. "Do you want to call the police?" he asked Jen.

"And have them tell me I need new washers on my shower? No, thank you. There's nothing they can do. I doubt they'd even believe me. Maybe I *do* just need new washers."

"Dollface," Rob said, "if you needed new washers, the water would not have turned off." He looked at his watch. "Damn, I'll have to leave you two to figure this out. I promised Mom I'd be there for lunch. See you later, sugar." He leaned down and kissed Jenny on the cheek.

Brett lost it. With a low growl, he took a step toward Rob, his fists clenched.

"Ease off, big boy." Rob grinned at him. "I'll grant you, she's adorable, but frankly, you're more my type." Before he turned and sauntered out the door, he reached around and patted Brett on the ass. "I'm a sucker for a set of tight buns like yours."

Jenny took one look at Brett's outraged face and burst out laughing.

"Well, hell," Brett grumbled a moment later, "you could have told me the guy was gay."

By the time Brett and Jenny had showered and dressed at his apartment, Jenny was still upset, but unwilling to talk about it and still not willing to call the police. To take her mind off it, Brett suggested they get out and go somewhere.

"The Garden District," Jenny said emphatically, before Brett could make a suggestion of his own. "Let's ride the streetcar from one end of St. Charles to the other."

Because it was a ride he always enjoyed, and because it would take him near his house, Brett readily agreed. They grabbed a bag of beignets on the way, and in just over an hour they had boarded a St. Charles Avenue streetcar at Canal.

"God, I love doing this," Jenny said, taking in a deep breath and letting the tension slip away. They had traveled the length of the Central Business District, passed Lee Circle, crossed Jackson, and were now in the Garden District.

"What?" Brett asked, grinning. "Playing tourist?"

"A lot more than just tourists ride the streetcars and you know it," she countered. "I just love this part of town. When I can afford it, I'm going to live here."

It was more than just the beautiful old homes that drew Jenny to the Garden District when she could spare the time. It was the way the venerable old trees arched overhead and created a living canopy above the streets. It was the lush green lawns, the vivid rainbow hues of a dozen varieties of flowers that bordered sidewalks and foundations and sprung from planters and flowerpots at every house. It was the streetcars clanging down the center of St. Charles all day and all night. It was the cracked sidewalks, the feeling of closeness; yet an air of privacy, the surprise of a small neighborhood store tucked in among the houses.

Brett took her hand and smiled at her. "I know what you mean. There's no place else on earth like the Garden District."

"Wouldn't it be great to live in one of these enormous homes? Heck, I'd settle for a small apartment over a garage."

They held hands, traded smiles, and rode the streetcar almost to Audubon Park, which they decided to save for another day. By the time they hopped off and walked a few blocks toward the river to catch the Magazine streetcar back, powdered sugar from the beignets dusted their clothes. Neither of them cared.

It was a magical afternoon. The air was warm and damp and heavy, ripe with the perfume of magnolias. And Jenny fell just a little bit more in love with Brett McCormick every hour.

Brett, too, felt the magic and was glad they had gotten out of the apartment for the day. But the day's pleasure for him was tempered with feelings of guilt and confusion. As they crossed Washington on their way back downtown, he did the same thing he'd done earlier when the St. Charles streetcar had taken them across Washington in the other direction—he struggled to keep from leaning out the window to see if he could spot his house. He couldn't, of course, as the house was in the middle of the block between Washington and Sixth on a street that paralleled Magazine and St. Charles.

He was being a jerk. He should just tell Jenny about the house and take her to see it. She would see the possibilities in the half-renovated property. She would be able to envision the graceful elegance of the past and recognize his efforts to restore it. She would love the house, he was sure.

Yet he said nothing. Oddly, his reticence wasn't caused by his old feeling that all women wanted something from him and that Jenny would want him only for his house. He knew her better than that. She wanted him now and didn't know about the house.

No, he kept silent because for an instant, just one small fraction of a second, his initial reaction to the house when he'd first seen it years ago—that he had to have it, that it was meant to be his—somehow connected in his mind with Jenny's talk of reincarnation, and it shook him. Which was absurd, because he honestly did not believe in reincarnation. It was a fool's dream to think a person could live again after dying.

But if Jenny somehow learned how obsessed he'd been about acquiring the house, she might start in again with her wild theories. He didn't want to argue with her, nor did he want to hurt her by scoffing at her beliefs. Explaining his house in the Garden District was better left to a later time.

* * *

By late Monday afternoon Brett was still debating with himself over whether or not he should have shown Jenny his house. The silent argument was pointless, because he'd let the perfect opportunity pass yesterday. They had stayed on the Magazine Street Car until Canal Street, then strolled the French Quarter until they got hungry. Instead of dinner, they'd munched on salted raw oysters, then returned to Brett's apartment to prove that salt did nothing to harm the oyster's reputation.

Now Jenny was working and Brett was on his zil-lionth cup of coffee for the day, wishing he'd gone ahead and taken her by the house. When the knock came at his door, he was in no mood to answer it. Dammit, if he'd wanted the outside world to intrude he wouldn't have switched off his phone. And after the last time someone had knocked on his door—yesterday, when Rob had come to tell them about Jenny's shower—Brett wasn't any too anxious to see who was doing the knocking. He didn't need any more distractions or strange happenings. In between bouts of arguing with himself over his house and trying to work on his novel, he still hadn't stopped thinking about that business with Jenny's shower.

Jenny seemed to have put it behind her, though. She hadn't mentioned it again since they'd decided to ride through the Garden District, so neither had he. He didn't see any point in getting her upset by rehashing the subject. When she'd kissed him good-bye and headed across town to a client's an hour ago, there had been no lingering shadows in her eyes that would have hinted at troubled thoughts. He would just make damn sure she didn't spend the night alone in her apartment.

He wished he could say his mind was as clear as hers. His thoughts seemed to be troubled. The damn book was going nowhere because he couldn't concentrate on it for thinking of Jenny. When he thought of her, his thoughts went in spirals.

He was addicted to her, obsessed with her, yet he had no desire to do anything about it except indulge himself in her. Nothing like this had ever happened to him before. He didn't believe in her reincarnation theory, not for a minute. He didn't believe in past lives or rebirth or karma or any of that crap. But maybe he believed in fate, in destiny.

He shook his head and ignored the repeated knocking at his door. All he knew was that when he was with Jenny he felt whole in a way he'd never felt before. He didn't want to analyze it or theorize over it or question it. He just wanted to live it while it lasted.

The pounding on the door thundered through his apartment again. "Goddammit." Giving in, he pushed back from his computer and went to answer it.

"Well, it's about time," Grace said as she sailed past him and into the living room. "I was about to call the police to have them look for your body. Have you given up returning phone calls, or have you even bothered to listen to your messages all weekend?"

"Hello to you, too," he said, watching her strut past him. As he closed the door, she sat on one end of the couch and tossed her purse to the other. When she crossed her long legs and leaned back, the hem of her narrow skirt rose to just above her knees. With one arm along the back of the couch, the other braced on her hip, she could have looked sultry and seductive. She was, after all, a beautiful woman.

Not so pretty today, though, with that pinched look

around her mouth and eyes. Suddenly her head came up and her nostrils flared. Then one elegant eyebrow slowly arched. "Well, well," she drawled. "No wonder you haven't returned my calls."

"What's that supposed to mean?"

"Brett, dear, either you've had a woman here, and recently, or you and I need to have a little chat about your choice of cologne."

Brett was so used to Jenny's fragrance by now that he only really noticed it when it was gone. It was there on the air in his apartment, but only subtly. Grace must have a nose like a bloodhound to have detected it.

"My answering machine's broken," he lied. "What did you need to talk about?"

The second eyebrow rose to match the first. "Is this the same woman who was here last weekend? This isn't like you, Brett. Should I worry?"

"Prying into my personal life isn't like you," he countered softly. "Should I worry?"

For a moment, just a quick, sharp instant, Grace's beautiful face hardened. It happened so fast and was gone so quickly, Brett wondered if he'd imagined it. And if he hadn't, he wondered what the hell it meant.

Then she gave him a sheepish smile. "Touché. Sorry. None of my business, I know. I just don't like to see women use you. I happen to think your energies are better spent on your books than on some little fan or groupie."

It was on the tip of his tongue to ask her why she thought the woman whose perfume she smelled was nothing more than a fan or a groupie, but he kept his mouth shut. Grace had always been a little possessive of him, but with her it was all related to business. She'd spoken the truth when she'd said she would rather he work on his book. If she could figure out a way that he wouldn't need to eat or sleep or take a leak, he thought wryly, she'd do so at once so nothing would interfere with his writing. Unless it was one of her promotional tours. Then, to hell with whatever book he was working on; he was expected to drop everything and play at being a celebrity.

He sighed inwardly. Her tenacity was one of the reasons he'd hired her. He had no right to complain if at times her attitude grated on him. Besides, if he'd been involved with any woman other than Jenny, Grace would have been dead on with her remark about a fan or groupie. That seemed to be the only type of woman he attracted. Until now. Until Jenny.

Hell, if it were any woman other than Jenny, he admitted, he wouldn't *be* involved. He might have indulged in a night or two of hot sex at her place, but that would have been the end of it.

"What did you want?" he asked, taking the chair next to the sofa. "What's so important that you had to drive all the way over here?"

"*The Rampage.*"

Brett winced. God, he hated that title. His publisher had come up with it for the sequel to *This Raging Madness*. In truth, he hadn't been able to think of anything at all for a title, other than *This Raging Sequel*. He was no good at titles. But *The Rampage* definitely sucked just as bad as *This Raging Madness*. His publisher had come up with that one, too.

"What about it?" he asked.

"It's a December release with an in-store date of mid-November. I'm setting up a series of national television appearances in New York and Chicago for the second week of November."

Brett nodded. "Okay." Then he smiled, wondering if Jenny could get away and go with him.

"What's that look for? You never smile when I mention sending you out of town."

"Maybe I won't go alone this time."

"What does that me—. Oh, I get it. The one with the perfume. She's not the same one who was here last weekend, is she?"

"Why?"

"Because I've never known you to stay with one woman a whole week. In fact, I've never known you to have a woman spend the night at all."

He wanted to ask what made her think she knew him well enough even to be talking about this, but he didn't. She knew him that well because he'd allowed her to. Over the years they'd become friends. Obviously he'd told her more about himself than he should have.

"You're starting to sound like my mother again," he warned, trying to keep an easy tone in his voice.

Grace laughed. "Not hardly, dear. This is business, remember? You've built up an image as one of the country's most eligible bachelors. A swinging single, but one who doesn't go in for wild parties and drugs. It sells books, Brett. If you start showing up around the country with a woman in tow, it could cause problems. It was bad enough that you took Kay to the American Booksellers' convention last spring. In case you haven't been paying attention, your secretary is becoming a bit more fond of you than is wise."

When Jenny came home from work that evening, Brett was strolling out of his apartment with a tall, beautiful blonde. The two were laughing, and the woman's hand rested familiarly on Brett's upper arm. Jenny had no trouble recognizing her as the same woman who'd been with Brett the first time she'd seen him, at the autographing in the mall. He knew this woman well. They were more than casual acquaintances.

A sharp pain struck Jenny in the ribs. Uncertainty shattered her confidence. Just because she felt that destiny had decided to give her and Brett a second chance, that they had been reborn for the specific purpose of finding each other, that didn't mean he was obliged to fall blindly in with the plan. He'd already told her he didn't believe in reincarnation.

Jenny shook her head. She was being stupid. She didn't want Brett to want her simply because he had loved her in some other life, had died to protect her. She wanted the man he was now, Brett McCormick, to love Jenny Franklin. She *had* to stop comparing them to Seth and Anna. Even if that was who they had been in the past, that's not who they were now. *And I'd better start remembering it,* she warned herself. Brett was not hers by right, he was hers only as long as he chose to be.

Right now, he apparently chose to be on the arm of a beautiful blonde. And it hurt.

Then he looked up and saw her as she got out of her car, and the way his eyes changed, heated, darkened, shook her all over again. But this was a good shaking. That was not the look of a man enamored of another woman. Jenny's spirits soared.

Then his jaw squared, and she wondered at the look of firm resolve in his eyes as he urged the blonde down the sidewalk toward Jenny. He looked determined, as though he had something to prove.

"Jen, perfect timing." Brett stepped away from the blonde and slipped his arm around Jenny's waist. Her knees weakened in relief. "I want you to meet my publicist, Grace Warren. Grace, Jenny Franklin."

Jenny held out her hand in greeting. The other

woman's smile did not quite reach her eyes as she slipped on a pair of designer sunglasses before shaking hands.

"Nice to meet you," Jenny offered.

"The pleasure is mine. I won't keep you two."

Jenny had to admire the woman's poise. The casual observer would have thought Grace Warren didn't have a care in the world as she slid into her sleek foreign sports car and drove off. But Jenny had seen the anger way back in those eyes before the sunglasses had hidden it.

Jenny stared after the sports car as it pulled out of the parking lot onto the street. "She's very beautiful."

"She is that," Brett answered. "Does that bother you?"

Jenny turned to find him eyeing her curiously. "Should it?" she asked.

"She's my publicist, Jen. We've worked together a long time, and we're friends. That's all there's ever been between us, all there ever will be. Does that answer your question?" he added softly, with a hint of a smile.

It was hard for Jenny to imagine a man being nothing more than friends with a woman as glamorous as Grace Warren, but she knew if she didn't accept Brett's explanation she would drive herself crazy worrying. Besides, if there was anything between Brett and Grace, why would he have left the woman's side and put his arm around *her*?

The answer to that last realization let her return his smile easily. "Yeah, I guess it does."

Brett's smiled widened. He leaned down and brushed his lips across her cheek. "Good."

From just that simple contact, his lips against her cheek, his warm breath against her ear, Jenny felt the tingling rush of heat clear to her toes.

Brett pulled away with a laughing groan. "Don't look at me like that while we're on a public sidewalk."

Jenny forgot all about publicists and beautiful blond women and everything else. For right now, this minute, Brett McCormick wanted her, Jenny Franklin, and Jenny didn't intend to waste a minute of her time with him. "Look at you how?" she teased.

He grinned wickedly. "Like you're starving and I'm dinner."

Jenny laughed. "Speaking of dinner—" She moved toward her car.

Brett followed and saw the grocery bags in the backseat. "What's all this?"

"Dinner," she answered. "I'm cooking. You interested?"

He wiggled his eyebrows up and down. "I'm always interested in you."

Feeling suddenly free and lighthearted, Jenny gave him a wink and a grin. "That's desert, big boy. How about spaghetti for the main course?"

"Spaghetti?" He opened the car door and hefted two sacks. "Are you inviting the whole complex?"

"Just you. I also bought French bread, salad makings, and ice cream."

"You're making me hungry."

"Were you writing so feverishly that you forgot lunch?"

"Don't I wish. Actually, I was staring at the screen feverishly, trying to figure out what to write. I forgot to eat."

Jenny shook her head. "That's pathetic."

"Tell me about it."

Brett followed her upstairs to her apartment and unloaded the groceries onto the kitchen counter while Jenny changed clothes. He hadn't mentioned the potential trip to New York and Chicago. He'd wanted to, but something had held him back.

Something, hell. *A rose by any other name, McCormick* . . . Fear held him back. Asking her to go with him meant making plans beyond today. It indicated a commitment of sorts, the kind he'd never offered a woman. Inviting her to New York and Chicago in November would be an admission that he would still want her, would still be in her life more than two months from now. The thought terrified him—he'd never stayed with one woman more than a night or two, let alone a couple of months. But as much as the idea scared him, it didn't scare him nearly as much as the thought of *not* being in her life come November.

Jenny's spaghetti sauce was simmering, sending taste bud–awakening tendrils of aroma directly to Brett's nose, carrying messages that tried to convince his brain he hadn't eaten in a week. Damn, but that sauce smelled good.

When the phone rang, he urged Jenny to answer it. "I'll watch the sauce." So what if his grin was a little on the wolfish side? So what if there wasn't quite as much sauce in the pan when she got off the phone? She left him in charge, and it was his solemn duty to taste it.

A few minutes later, Jenny came back to the kitchen smiling.

"Good news?" he asked.

"A new client down in the Central Business District. A referral. That's always good news. But it means I'll be working late tomorrow night."

"In the CBD? How late?"

She shrugged and took the ladle from his hand to take a sip of sauce. "Mmmm, good."

"You do know that area isn't safe at night, especially for a lone woman."

Jenny rolled her eyes at him. "Yes, Daddy, I know that."

Brett refused to wince. Jenny was much too important to him for him to back off from cautioning her. "I just want you to be careful, that's all. I don't like the idea of your working late downtown."

"Neither do I," she said casually. "Which is why I'll be in my locked car, probably all the way home, long before the sun sets. Did you check the spaghetti? Is it done?"

"You promise you'll be careful?"

She batted her eyes. "I'm always careful with spaghetti."

"Okay, okay." He raised his hands in surrender. "I'll shut up, but if you aren't home before dark, I might just come looking for you. What the—"

He broke off, too astonished to finish, as he watched Jenny dip a fork into the spaghetti and pull out one long string from the pot. She brought her arm back as though to pitch the spaghetti across the room. He blinked, astounded, when she did just that. The spaghetti made a small *splut* sound as it hit the wall next to the refrigerator, then bounced off and fell to the floor.

"Nope," she said as she picked up the limp pasta from the floor. "Not done yet."

She turned, saw him gaping at her, and broke out laughing. "I guess your mother didn't teach you how to tell when spaghetti was done, huh?"

Brett pursed his lips. "No, she wasn't in the habit of flinging food at the walls."

Jenny chuckled. "Not that you know of, anyway."

She grabbed a sponge and wiped off the wall and the floor.

"Are you going to tell me what the point of that was?"

"The point is, if the spaghetti sticks to the wall, that means it's done."

"Aside from being messy," he said wryly, "don't you find it just a little on the unsanitary side?"

"Don't worry," she answered, stirring the pot again. "I won't make you eat anything off the wall or the floor."

"So," Jenny asked after dinner was over and the kitchen was clean, "are you ready for dessert?"

Brett grinned and stalked toward her, a definite heat in his eyes. "I thought you'd never ask. How about we go downstairs to my place?"

Jenny pursed her lips to keep from grinning back at him. "I meant ice cream, McCormick. Why should we go to your apartment for that, when the ice cream is here?"

"Funny, Franklin. Ice cream here, the real dessert at my place. How does that sound?"

"What's wrong with just staying here for the night?" she asked. "We could always take the ice cream to bed."

"Sounds too cold to me." Brett didn't want to stay in her apartment. Since the night someone had played the shower game, not to mention that business with her tires, he didn't want Jenny spending the night here, even with him at her side. "Besides, my bed's bigger. More room to roll around in, if you get my meaning."

"I get your meaning, I'm just not convinced. There's something to be said for closeness."

"I've got a brand new unopened box of Sugar Crisp cereal for your breakfast," he tempted.

"Oh." Jenny blinked and smiled. "Why didn't you say so?"

Twenty minutes later the one called Maude focused her binoculars on the man and woman coming from the upstairs apartment across the parking lot. They were easy to follow in the glow of the complex's security lights.

They touched, they laughed, they strolled down the stairs side by side and disappeared into Brett's apartment.

The throbbing behind Maude's eyes intensified.

"Enjoy tonight, bitch," she spat into the dark. "It'll be your last."

She lowered the binoculars and let them hang by the strap around her neck. This time tomorrow night, the Franklin bitch would be history. The thought was cheering.

Maude had always found it useful to do favors for people. It left her in the position of being able to ask for paybacks. She'd called in a couple of markers this evening.

She smiled softly to herself. Men could be so greedy. Some would do anything for money.

Her smile widened. The pain behind her eyes eased.

Chapter Eleven

Jenny ran her fingers through her hair in frustration. Her new downtown client, Terrance Reeves, had more serious problems with his office computer system than he'd led her to believe. Upgrading his word processing program to the latest version, as he'd requested, would have taken her no more than the hour she'd allotted herself to get home by dark. If only life, and computers, were that simple.

"Is it that bad?" the balding Mr. Reeves asked plaintively.

Jenny gave him a wan smile. "It's not good. The reason you started having so many problems with your old software had nothing to do with the program itself. I'm afraid you picked up a virus somewhere. It's already destroyed some of your files. That's just the teaser, though. It's got a timer set to wipe out your entire hard drive next Monday at noon."

"My entire hard drive?" he cried, his face paling. "Can you stop it?"

Jenny sighed. "Yes, but it's going to take a lot longer than the hour we agreed on to clean up the mess."

"I don't care," he said fervently. "I can't function without my computer. Whatever it takes, just do it. Please. I'll pay whatever you ask, just fix it."

Jenny gave a last lingering glance out the window toward the lowering sun. It wouldn't be dark for a couple of hours yet. "All right. I'll stay and do it now."

Brett checked his watch for the fourth time in as many minutes and swore beneath his breath as he offered Kay another cup of coffee.

"Thank you," she answered. "I would like another, unless I'm keeping you from something."

"Of course you're not."

"Oh." She glanced toward the watch he kept checking, then away as she smoothed her hand down her skirt. "I just wondered."

With a wry grin, Brett raised his wrist and jiggled it. "Sorry. It's just that I was expecting someone, and she's late enough that I'm starting to worry."

Kay's hand jerked once, then fell still. "Oh. I didn't realize you had a date."

"It's not really a date." Brett moved to the breakfast bar and refilled her cup. As he carried it back to her, he said, "You've met her, actually."

Kay blushed. "Oh."

They both remembered the morning Kay had used her key and let herself into his apartment. They both remembered his half-dressed state and the way he and Jenny had been wrapped around each other.

With a toss of her head, Kay flipped her hair back

from her face. She'd done something different to both, Brett realized. Her hair looked a little shorter, just brushing her shoulders, and more stylish than usual, although he couldn't put his finger on what, other than the length, was different.

The new look of her face, though, was due to makeup, something he'd never noticed her wearing before.

Those things, plus the sometimes shy, sometimes bold way she looked at him, along with this unexpected visit, reminded him of Grace's warning the night before, that Kay was becoming more fond of him than was wise, and Jenny's question the morning Kay had burst in on them. *How long has she been in love with you?*

Brett felt his heart sink to the pit of his stomach. Surely Grace and Jenny were wrong. Surely these changes in Kay had nothing to do with him.

"Do you mind if I stay until she shows up?" Kay asked quietly, yet with a hint of challenge in her voice.

"Of course not." Hell, what else could he say? He handed her the refilled cup of coffee, then took the chair opposite hers, the one that gave him a view out the open blinds to Jenny's empty, waiting parking space.

It was after ten when Jenny finally finished and left the gray stone office building housing Terrance Reeve and Associates. As near as she could tell, Reeve had no associates, and not many manners, either, she thought as he hustled down the sidewalk and left her alone on the deserted downtown street.

"Thank you for offering, Mr. Reeve," she whispered with sarcasm, "but you don't need to go to all that trouble. I'm sure I can get to my car just fine. Jerk.''

But the jerk had paid her well for her time and expertise, and his computer system was now up and running, sans virus, and hell's bells, she'd walked herself to her car hundreds of times. It was only a few blocks away. No big deal. She didn't need an escort, for crying out loud.

But he could have asked, the bum.

Brett's words of caution about the Central Business Distict being dangerous after dark played through her mind as she hiked her purse strap firmly on her shoulder with one hand and gripped her briefcase with the other. She was just glad he didn't know she had to traipse clear to the Superdome—the most unsafe area in town—to get to her car.

She'd known finding a parking place in the CBD on a weekday afternoon would be difficult if not impossible. Because the parking garages had been full, she'd been lucky to get a spot at all. But if she'd known she would have to traipse the deserted downtown streets at night she might have taken a cab.

No, she thought with a sigh, she wouldn't have taken a cab all the way from her apartment. She was too cheap. She would have done exactly what she had—parked as close as she could, then bitched to herself about the walk back to her car.

But there was nothing to worry about. The streets were fairly well lit and she saw no other pedestrians as she walked briskly toward the corner in the opposite direction taken by Mr. Terrance Reeve.

At the end of the street she turned right. Her car was up two streets and over three. Downtown seemed eerily quiet this time of night. The sound of a car a block away echoed between high-rise buildings, bounced off brick and stone and glass quietly, as if trying not to disturb the shadows. The rush of traffic on I-10 a few blocks away held no such reverence for the empty streets. It roared and whooshed and hummed, but not loudly enough to cover the sound of her own footsteps, which seemed unusually loud.

From somewhere behind her a scraping sound, like a hard-soled shoe on concrete, made the hair on the back of her neck stand up. Instinctively Jenny walked toward the edge of the sidewalk, as far from the shadowy recessed doorways as she could get without stepping into the street. With one hand she dug in her purse and located her car keys. She did not want to have to fumble for them when she reached her car.

By the time she reached the next street she'd decided she'd merely imagined the sound behind her, because she had heard nothing since. She stood on the curb beneath the street light and waited for a cab to pass, then crossed and headed up the next block.

Three doors down, she heard the sound again. Then again. And yet again. She was not mistaken. There was a rhythm to the scrapes. Those were footsteps behind her. With a sudden feeling of vulnerability she'd never experienced before, she gripped her purse and briefcase tighter and walked faster. At the next corner she couldn't resist the overpowering urge to glance behind her.

There! Was that a shadow darting into a darkened doorway?

Jenny, get a grip.

Shadows didn't dart into doorways, except on television. Whoever she'd heard walking behind her had obviously gone elsewhere by now. She was alone on the street.

She wasn't alone on the street. There were sidewalks and buildings and street lights and somewhere not far away, traffic and people. And behind her once again, footsteps.

Were they getting closer, gaining on her?

Without breaking her stride, she glanced back again. Another shadow dodged into a doorway.

Okay. Okay. So her palms had a reason to turn damp. She was being followed. If it were an ordinary pedestrian minding his own business, he wouldn't jump into hiding every time she turned around.

One more block, then across the street to her car. She was almost there. She would be fine if she just didn't panic. The man was still half a block behind her.

The street beside her was deserted, as were all the buildings. The faster she walked, the faster the footsteps came behind her. Her heart was racing now, and her mouth was as dry as a month-old corn husk. At the corner, the street she had to cross was as empty as the darkened Superdome a block away.

She stepped from the curb to cross the street. A rush of sound. A stirring of the heavy, damp air. A hand grabbed her shoulder from behind and dragged her to an abrupt halt.

Jenny screamed. Without thought, she swung her heavy briefcase in a wide arc and slammed it against her assailant's head. The man was just under six feet and as stocky as a wrestler. His broad, thick shoulders swallowed his neck.

He grunted and staggered back beneath her blow and grabbed the side of his head where she'd hit him, but he managed to hold on to her shoulder in a grip that she knew would leave a bruise.

The man recovered instantly. With a low growl he took a step forward.

With a half dozen keys clenched in her right fist, and one key jutting out between her knuckles like the blade on a Swiss army knife, Jenny let fly and jabbed him in the eye with her ignition key.

The man bellowed in pain. He released her shoulder and grabbed for his eye with both hands.

Jenny ran. She darted across the street and up the block to her car. She was shaking so hard she would have dropped her keys when she unlocked the door, but her fist wouldn't come unclenched from around them.

As she jumped into the car and locked the door, she looked up and saw the assailant still standing at the corner, still clutching his eye.

She was safe!

Her hand came unclenched in time to cause her to drop her keys when she tried to start the car. Using words that would have curled even her brothers' ears, she felt along the floorboard until she found them. Finally, *finally*, she managed to get the key into the ignition and turn it.

Nothing happened. Absolutely nothing. Not a crank, not a clink, not even so much as a whir!

Glancing frantically out the window, she spied the man moving toward her.

"Start," she begged the car. *"Start!"*

Not so much as a whisper of sound came from beneath the hood.

The man was getting closer.

On the verge of panic, Jenny tried to start the car again. She glanced away from the man coming after her for only a second. When the car still wouldn't start she looked back up. The man was gone.

Gone where? Oh, God, where was he?

Suddenly a large shadow loomed just outside her window.

Jenny flinched and bit back a scream.

Something heavy rapped sharply against the window.

Her scream broke loose.

Chapter Twelve

Brett had the blinds open and was sitting where he could watch for Jenny to pull into her vacant parking spot. Kay had gone home around nine, partly, no doubt, because Brett had been too distracted over how late Jenny was to hold up his end of the conversation. Then again, he'd yet to figure out why Kay hadn't turned around and left as soon as she'd delivered the diskette containing the chapters she'd cleaned up for him. She'd never stayed before.

Grace's warning and Jenny's question echoed through his mind again. Maybe they weren't so far off base after all, Brett thought with dismay.

He shoved his fingers through his hair in frustration. His whole life seemed to be slipping beyond his control. His secretary was acting strangely, Grace was getting possessive, and Brett was falling hard for Jenny Franklin, who should have been home hours ago, dammit.

Where was she? Why hadn't she called?

The knock on his door startled him. "What now?"

he grumbled. Jenny's parking space was still empty, so it wasn't her at the door, and he didn't feel like talking to anyone else. That it was after ten and he knew few people who would come this late sent unease slipping down his spine.

The pounding came again before he could reach the door.

"McCormick!" came a man's voice.

Brett opened the door to find Rob, Jenny's next-door neighbor, standing there in rumpled jeans and nothing else.

"What's happened?" Rob demanded, before Brett could speak.

Brett tensed. "What do you mean?"

"Where's Jenny?"

"I'm waiting for her to get home from work. What do you mean, what's happened?"

Rob braced his hands on his hips and glared at Brett, a defiant look in his eyes. "Okay, here it is, and don't give me any crap about it. I sometimes get . . . premonitions, or something. It's like this big thump in my chest, and it means something's wrong. I felt it a minute ago and immediately thought of Jenny. Something's happened."

Brett thought of Jenny working downtown late at night. Icy fingers of dread encircled his throat and squeezed.

Jenny felt her own icy fingers of dread.

"Ma'am?"

The deep rumble of the male voice paralyzed her with terror. Her heartbeat stopped for an eternity before she realized the man beside her car was a uniformed New Orleans police officer.

"Oh, God." With a giant thud, her heart resumed its racing beat. She slumped in relief.

"Is everything all right, ma'am?"

Jenny swallowed and cranked down her window. "No," she managed past her parched throat. "There's a man—" A quick glance up and down the street told her the man who'd grabbed her was gone.

"A man?" the officer prompted.

"I don't see him now," Jenny said. "He followed me for several blocks. When I got to that corner—" She pointed with a finger that shook. "—He grabbed me. I got away and ran to my car, but it wouldn't start."

The officer, a burly older man with a broad chest, bushy white eyebrows, and an accent straight out of the Bronx, glanced sharply up and down the street. "Seems he's gone now. Can you describe him?"

Jenny would have sworn that the face she'd seen looming over her as she'd struggled for freedom was indelibly etched in her mind, but when she opened her mouth to describe the man, nothing came out. The picture in her mind was blank. Frustrated and angry with herself, she shook her head. "I guess I wasn't paying enough attention. The only thing I remember is he was around five-ten and stocky, like a wrestler. If you find a man with a keyhole in his eye," she added grimly, "that'll be him."

"A keyhole?"

Jenny told him about jabbing the man with her key.

The officer nodded. "Good for you. Do you think you'd recognize him if you saw him again?"

Jenny pressed a trembling hand to her forehead, as if that simple act could bring her assailant's face to mind. Still frustrated, she shook her head. "I don't know."

The officer tried to talk her into accompanying him to the police station to file a report, but all Jenny wanted was to go home. To Brett. She was all for doing her civic duty, and she would love to see the creep who'd grabbed her get caught, but she knew that wasn't likely, particularly since she couldn't even describe him.

The policeman reluctantly agreed that her going to the station and filing a report would most likely be an exercise in futility.

"All right, then," he said. "But if you think of anything you forgot to tell me, you call, you hear?" He gave her a card with his name and the station's number. "Now let's see about your car. Won't start, you say? Give it another try."

She did, but as before, nothing happened.

The officer raised the hood and used his flashlight to check the engine. A chill trickled down Jenny's spine when he discovered that her battery cables had been disconnected.

"You realize," he said, "that this puts a new slant on things."

Jenny tried to swallow but her mouth was too dry. A new slant indeed.

"Of course," he went on, "it could just be a coincidence that your car was tampered with on the same night you were followed and assaulted."

"But you don't think so," Jenny said.

"No, ma'am, I don't think so. That's just a little bit too coincidental in my book. And if it wasn't a coincidence, then either the man saw you park your car, watched you walk away, then disconnected your battery cables and followed you, waited until you started back for your car, and tried to grab you . . ."

"Or?"

"Or he knew you, or at least knew where you would

be, about how long you'd be there, knew you'd come back to your car alone. In my professional opinion, ma'am, this does not look like a random act.''

Jenny shivered in the warm night air.

In the end, Jenny went to the police station to give a statement. While there she looked at mug books, to no avail. She debated with herself the entire time about calling Brett to tell him where she was, but decided against it. She'd lived her whole life beneath the overprotective shadow of her father and brothers. She was on her own now, independent. She had no business whining to the first man she became involved with just because she'd had a little scare.

Okay, so it was a big scare. So Brett McCormick was more than merely a man she was involved with. She had enough to deal with without adding a worried lover to the equation.

She could have saved her arguments, however, for when she finally got home near midnight and saw the look on Brett's face, and he saw her ashen pallor, there was no keeping the truth from him.

Across the parking lot, the woman called Maude cursed a blue streak as Jenny Franklin got out of her car.

"Goddammit, can't anybody do anything right anymore?"

She'd paid good money, and lots of it, to ensure that Jenny didn't make it home tonight, and there the bitch was, getting out of her car and falling into Brett's arms as though they'd been separated for months instead of hours.

Bile rose in Maude's throat. At the sight of Brett

holding the other woman in his arms, the sharp pain returned behind Maude's eyes.

"Damn them. Damn them both to hell and back. He's *mine*."

Her knuckles whitened as she gripped the binoculars tighter.

"Next time, I'll just have to take care of things myself."

"Next time you work downtown late in the day, by God, I'm coming with you."

Jenny snuggled against Brett's side and felt his arm tighten around her shoulders. Making love had a marvelous way of chasing away the remnants of her fear, and she bit back a smile. "Whatever you say."

"You're making fun of me, but dammit, Jen, what happened to you tonight—what could have happened—scares the hell out of me."

"Believe me," she said with feeling, "it scares the hell out of me, too. I guarantee I won't be caught downtown after dark again. You don't need to worry about that."

"I'm glad to hear it."

Brett's hand wandered from her shoulder down her arm beneath the covers until he traced circles on her bare hip.

Jenny smiled again as he deliberately stirred their banked heat to flames. There was something to be said after all for a possessive, protective man.

Later that night, Brett held Jenny close as she slept in his arms. He couldn't close his eyes, for when he did, he pictured how pale and shaken she'd been when she'd come home. He pictured some bastard grabbing her from behind and her having to defend herself. He pictured all the grisly things that could have happened to her alone on the dark, deserted streets of downtown New Orleans. The pictures scared the shit out of him. He could have lost her for good tonight.

The thought tightened his throat. His throat stayed tight into the next day and the day after that. It was the middle of the week before he was able to admit to himself that his fear for Jenny's safety was more than a humane desire that a woman not come to harm. His fear was rooted much deeper than simple humanity. He thought it might be possible that he was actually falling in love.

No, he couldn't be. He didn't have it in him to love a woman, or he would have fallen in love years ago, surely.

Whatever he was feeling would certainly pass, but before it did, he would use it. While Jenny worked during the day, Brett poured himself and all his emotions, the fear, the wanting, the sheer need to be around her, into his manuscript. And it was good. Damn good, if he did say so himself.

But putting his feelings on paper did not lessen their intensity in his gut. That had to mean something. In the past, he'd always been able to work through his anger or doubt by using those emotions in a scene in his book. By the time he'd finished writing them, the emotions had faded.

Not this time. Could it be the real thing? Could he be falling in love with Jenny Franklin?

He didn't want to. God knew he didn't. Things were just fine the way they were without complicating the situation. Hell, he couldn't be falling for a woman who believed in reincarnation. What if that crazy belief of hers was more important to her, had more of an influence on her, than she'd admitted?

Was it him she wanted, Brett McCormick, or was she so caught up in his book and the so-called past that she didn't even see the man he really was and thought of him as Seth?

Scary. It was all too damn scary for him. They were much better off without love, both of them.

Chapter Thirteen

Three hours of intense writing and fierce concentration Wednesday afternoon left Brett tense. While he was up stretching his muscles and debating on whether to have another beer, he made the mistake of answering the phone. As a result, Grace was on her way over to talk about the promotional tour again.

To give himself credit, he had to admit that if he hadn't answered the phone, Grace probably would have just shown up unannounced. She was a bulldog about promotional tours, and his publisher was paying for this one, so she took it even more seriously than usual. He'd had the feeling for months that she was angling for a job in New York.

The tour was seven weeks away and he'd yet to mention it to Jen. He didn't know why he was holding back, because he genuinely wanted her to go with him.

*   *   *

When Grace arrived, it didn't take her and Brett long to go over the details of the promotional tour. TV and radio talk shows, newspaper and magazine interviews, book signings, and meetings with whole-salers.

"You don't think we're hitting the networks again too soon?" Brett asked. "I was just in New York a few weeks ago."

Triumph laced Grace's smile. "*They* asked for *you* this time, my boy. They want you back. It was interest-ing to note that the producers for all three programs are young women. Just what did you do while you were up there the last time, you sly devil? They were practically begging me to send you back."

Brett felt a flush start at his neck and work its way up. He ignored it and waved away her words. He hadn't done any more than shake hands with any woman in New York. "Maybe they just liked my book."

"Yeah, right," Grace said smugly. "So says the nation's most eligible bachelor."

There it was. He hadn't said anything more about taking Jen with him on the tour since their last discus-sion on the matter, but he'd been waiting for her to bring it up. Now she was going to remind him again how much better off his career was if he kept up the *single* image. She sure had taken her sweet time getting to it, he thought as he realized she'd been there longer than he'd guessed. It was nearly four-thirty, and she'd arrived at three. He started to answer her comment, but she cut him off.

"I'd better be going." She rose and picked up her purse. "I have to find someone this afternoon to help me figure out what to do about the office computer system."

"What's the matter with it?" He asked the question

more because he felt it was expected of him than because he really wanted to know. His mind was already working on asking Jenny to go on the tour with him.

"I've outgrown the entire system," Grace said, as she headed toward the door. "It's time to upgrade my hardware and my software, but I really don't know where to start."

Brett paused and thought, why the hell not? Maybe if Grace could get to know Jenny, she'd ease up on her cracks about his bachelorhood. "Jenny could help you."

"Jenny?"

He grinned. "The one with the perfume."

Grace arched an eyebrow and smiled. "Oh, really?"

"Yes, really. She's a professional computer consultant. She has clients all over town. Why don't you call her this evening and talk to her?"

"And where," she said slowly, "should I call her? Here?"

"Here. Anytime after six."

Grace looked away suddenly to dig in her purse for her keys. When she found them and reached for the doorknob, she looked at him and smiled. "Thanks. I think I will call her. I appreciate the information. I really had no idea who to call."

Grace did call Jenny that evening, and they set up an appointment for two days later for Jenny to go to Grace's office and advise her on her hardware and software needs.

Later that night Brett bit the bullet, so to speak, and asked Jenny to go with him on the promotional tour in November.

"You mean it?" she asked, her eyes lighting with eagerness.

Brett's tension disappeared. "No, I was just fooling. Of course I mean it."

"I'd love to go. But wait—what about Thanksgiving?"

"What about it? We'll be back by then."

Jenny scooted next to him on the sofa and put her head on his shoulder. "Do you go home for Thanksgiving?"

"Yeah," he said quietly, only then realizing the holiday would mean being away from Jenny. She probably went to Oklahoma to see her family. "Do you?"

"Yeah. Every year. Thanksgiving, Christmas, Mother's Day, Father's Day, all the biggies."

Father's Day. Brett pushed the thought away.

"I'll miss you," Jenny told him softly. When she looked up at him her eyes were clouded with sadness.

What could he say? He would miss her like hell. He let a kiss be his answer.

The day before Jenny's appointment with Grace, three days into a late-season heat wave of daytime highs in the nineties, the air conditioner in Jenny's car quit.

"I am absolutely going to suffocate tomorrow if the temperature doesn't drop."

Acknowledging to himself that he'd poured about as much emotion as he could into his manuscript for the time being, and that a breather would be welcome, Brett offered to switch cars with her the next day and take hers to the shop.

"You're offering me your 'Vette?" Jenny asked, incredulous.

"Why not?"

"No reason," she said quickly. "I just wanted to make sure I heard you right. You griped for an hour the last time because I left the seat scooted up."

"But this time you'll push it back so I can actually get in, right?"

"Yes, sir!" She gave him a snappy salute.

"Don't sweet-talk me. I know you're just after my car."

"Let's put it this way. If I don't come back for a week or two—"

Brett grabbed a throw pillow from the sofa and tossed it at her head. "You can drive my car to call on your clients, and that's all, woman. And while you're at it, you can drop a diskette off at Kay's on your way to Grace's office."

Jenny grinned. "Sure. Let's see. The only Kay I remember knowing is the one back on Oklahoma, and that's a day and a half away. If I leave first thing in the morning—"

Another pillow hit her in the face.

In the middle of the night, the one called Maude stood beneath the dim light over the kitchen sink of her furnished apartment and scrubbed furiously at her fingers with a nail brush.

"Damn, if I ever get all this oil and grease off, I'm going to need a manicure for sure."

But it would all be worth it. Tomorrow little Miss Jennifer Franklin would get in her car to meet Grace at her office. Jenny would, of course, have to take I-10 to get there. What a pity she wouldn't be able to slow down at that sharp exit. That sharp, elevated exit. The one with the flimsy aluminum guardrail.

Maude laughed as she scrubbed harder at the grime beneath her fingernails. Oh, yes. This time it would

Wish You Were Here?

You can be, every month, with Zebra Historical Romance Novels.

AND TO GET YOU STARTED, ALLOW US TO SEND YOU

4 Historical Romances Free

A $19.96 VALUE!
With absolutely no obligation to buy anything.

YOU'RE GOING TO LOVE GETTING
4 FREE BOOKS

These books worth almost $20, are yours without cost or obligation
when you fill out and mail this certificate.
*(If the certificate is missing below, write to: Zebra Home Subscription Service, Inc.,
120 Brighton Road, P.O. Box 5214, Clifton, New Jersey 07015-5214*

4 FREE BOOKS!

Yes! Please send me 4 Zebra Historical Romances without cost or obligation. I understand that each month thereafter I will be able to preview 4 new Zebra Historical Romances FREE for 10 days. Then, if I should decide to keep them, I will pay the money-saving preferred publisher's price of just $4.00 each...a total of $16. That's almost $4 less than the publisher's price, and there is no additional charge for shipping and handling. I may return any shipment within 10 days and owe nothing, and I may cancel this subscription at any time. The 4 FREE books will be mine to keep in any case.

Name _____

Address _____ Apt. _____

City _____ State _____ Zip _____

Telephone ( ) _____

Signature _____
(If under 18, parent or guardian must sign.)

LF1095

Terms, offer and prices subject to change without notice. Subscription subject to acceptance by Zebra Books. Zebra Books reserves the right to reject any order or cancel any subscription.

ZEBRA HOME SUBSCRIPTION SERVICE, INC.

120 BRIGHTON ROAD

P.O. BOX 5214

CLIFTON, NEW JERSEY 07015-5214

work. This time Jenny Franklin would be out of Brett's life for good.

"And he'll be mine. All mine."

She laughed again, and if her laughter was tinged with a touch of madness, there was no one there to hear but her and the lone cockroach watching from the edge of the cabinet.

The sleek silver Corvette gave a throaty rumble as Jenny drove it out of the parking lot the next morning. The sheer power that she felt through her hands on the steering wheel sent a heady sense of strength and freedom rushing through her veins. Lord, but it was going to be hard to go back to the old Monte Carlo after driving this dream again.

She followed Brett's directions to Kay's house in a nice middle-class neighborhood, lamenting the fact that she hadn't had to get on I-10 to get there. A car like Brett's was not meant to be driven at speeds under forty, for crying out loud. She wanted to *drive*.

She would get her chance soon, though, because to get from Kay's to Grace's, the most logical route was via I-10.

With anticipation humming in her veins, she pulled into Kay's driveway, grabbed the diskette Brett had given her, and went to the front door.

Kay opened the door with a huge smile. It was instantly plain by the way her face froze that Jenny was not who she'd expected to find on her doorstep. It was also plain that Kay had no trouble recognizing her.

"Hi," Jenny offered, trying to forget the circumstances under which she'd first seen this woman. "I'm sorry to bother you, but Brett asked me to drop off this diskette. I'm Jenny Franklin."

Kay struggled and failed to keep her smile in place. She glanced past Jenny's shoulder toward the gleaming silver car in the driveway. "Is he coming in?"

"He's not with me," Jenny told her. "We traded cars for the day."

The look of shock on Kay's face was almost comical. "He let you . . . I mean, when I saw his car, I assumed he was with you."

"Yeah, pretty incredible, isn't it? If it was mine, I doubt I'd let my own mother near it."

Shock faded to longing on the woman's face— longing for Brett, Jenny assumed, uncomfortably, rather than his car.

"The air conditioning in my car went out," Jenny found herself explaining. "He took pity on me."

Kay swallowed and reached for the diskette Jenny still held toward her. "Oh. Well, uh, thank you for bringing this. Tell him . . . tell him I'll get it back to him right away."

In mere moments Jenny was back in the Corvette and zipping down I-10, trying to hold the car down to sixty on her way to Grace Warren's office. Some of the pleasure of driving the high-performance vehicle was dimmed by the memory of the pain in Kay Olsen's eyes as she'd watched Jenny drive away in Brett's car.

The rest of the pleasure Jenny expected from driving the 'Vette was completely gone as she drove home from Grace's office in the early afternoon. *Needed a computer consultant, my foot,* Jenny thought peevishly. Grace Warren had needed a computer consultant like New Orleans needed humidity. The woman knew almost as much about computers and software as Jenny did.

There'd been only one reason Grace had wanted Jenny to come to her office, and that was to warn her away from Brett. All those little comments about how valuable his reputation as an eligible bachelor was to his success. All those remarks about how women were naturally drawn to him, but that they never meant anything to him, how he used women, then tossed them aside in favor of his writing.

Grace's constant little jabs during the course of their visit would have sent a lesser woman running for cover, but not Jenny. Why should she believe Grace over Brett? Why should she place more credence in some other woman's words than in Brett's actions?

One thing was certain, though. Brett might think he and Grace were merely friends and business associates, but it was apparent to Jenny that Grace Warren had other ideas.

She shook her head as she pulled into the apartment parking lot. She wasn't about to say anything to Brett concerning her day. Kay, Jenny still felt, was in love with Brett. The idea left Jenny feeling uneasy.

But Grace . . . there was something different there, something strong and possessive, but it didn't seem like love or even affection. Not to Jenny. She couldn't put a name to it, but it was there, and it was disturbing.

No, she wouldn't mention any of it to Brett. She might feel semiconfident that he had strong feelings for her—at least, she *hoped* he did—feelings he wasn't ready to admit, but she wasn't quite sure enough of herself to go planting ideas in his head about how much these other women in his life probably wished her to hell and back.

Jenny's Monte Carlo and Brett were both gone. Jenny went to her apartment feeling at loose ends.

It was barely three o'clock, yet she had no more calls to make for the day, and Brett wasn't home.

Thirty minutes later, when someone knocked on her door, she ran to answer it, hoping it was Brett, expecting no one other than him.

It was Rob. Despite her disappointment that it wasn't Brett, she was still glad to see her friend.

"It must be love," he told her.

"What must be love?"

"I saw you pull up in McCormick's car. Any man who lets a woman drive his brand new Corvette must either be in love, or stupid. He doesn't strike me as stupid."

Jenny's heart thundered at the possibility that Rob might be right. Oh, not that nonsense about the Corvette, but maybe, just maybe, Brett was starting to love her.

"Don't look so anxious, dollface. Come on down to the pool and go for a swim. Take advantage of this damn hot weather. A little dip to cool you off, a little soak in the sun will do you good. Besides, it'll drive him crazy to come home and see you strutting your stuff in that nothing little bikini you wear."

Jenny laughed. "I don't know about driving Brett crazy, but a swim sounds like a heck of a lot more fun than watching my hard drive copy itself onto a backup tape."

"Fine. I'll meet you at the pool in ten minutes."

It didn't take Jenny even that long to change and get down to the pool. She was there waiting when Rob arrived.

After swimming a few laps, Jenny was ready to bake herself in the sun. She slathered sunscreen on every exposed inch of flesh, then stretched out on a chaise longue.

"This is great," she said when Rob claimed the

chair next to hers. "I'm glad you talked me into this. Once this heat wave passes, cooler weather will probably settle in for the rest of the year."

"Yeah," Rob said with a snicker. "And you can watch for loverboy easier from down here than from your apartment."

The woman called Maude glared through the sheers covering her patio door and watched the bitch down at the pool. The throbbing pain behind Maude's eyes was nearly blinding in its intensity. Panic threatened to overwhelm her.

"Where is he? Where is he?"

It was the bitch's fault. Why hadn't Jenny Franklin driven her own damn car, as she should have? As she always did? Why did she have to trade cars with Brett again *today*?

Where could Brett have driven Jenny's car? And why today, of all days?

Is it going to be like the last time? Is Seth going to die in Anna's place?

Maude hissed in a sharp breath. Where the hell had that thought come from? Seth and Anna? The last time?

A new level of pain sliced behind her eyes.

"I won't think about it. It's not important. Brett is the only thing that matters. He has to be all right. He *has* to be!"

But he'd driven the bitch's car!

The sun was hot, the air was heavy with humidity, and Jenny was on the verge of falling asleep, so good did the heat feel as it seeped into her bones. A sharp curse from Rob roused her.

She forced her eyes open and shaded them with her hand. "What is it?"

The look on Rob's face had her bolting upright. The last time she'd seen that look was two years ago when he'd told her about the strange thumps in his chest that told him something was wrong. She'd laughed at him when he'd suggested it had something to do with her family. She'd thought he was teasing her. Barely two hours later she'd learned her father had suffered a heart attack.

Now Rob wore that same look. "What's wrong?" she demanded.

"I don't know," Rob told her in frustration. "You know I never know the what of it."

"But you usually know the who. Who is it? Talk to me, Robert."

"Jenny, it's probably nothing. Just forget it, okay?"

"You're scaring me. Since when has one of your thumps turned out to be nothing?"

With his jaw tight, Rob merely shook his head and looked away.

"Rob, dammit, tell me." Then she felt a thumping in her own chest when she realized what his reticence meant. Her skin turned clammy. "Oh, God, it's Brett, isn't it?" She jumped up and grabbed her towel. "Something's happened to Brett."

"Slow down, Jenny, we don't know that anything's happened."

Jenny froze at the gate of the pool area, hanging there for one long, suspended moment. Then, as if catapulted from a giant slingshot, she burst through the gate. "Yes we do," she cried as she raced toward the police car that pulled halfway into her parking spot but stopped a good ten feet short of nosing up to the curb. The man in the passenger seat, the one with the stark white bandage on his forehead, was Brett McCormick.

Small rocks bit into the bottoms of her bare feet and hot pavement burned them, but Jenny barely noticed as she ran across the parking lot toward Brett. She rounded the police car just as he climbed out. Shock drew her to a sharp halt.

She'd seen the bandage, but not the angry scratch that it didn't quite cover. Nor had she seen the sheer rage she read now in his eyes.

"Brett? Oh, Brett, what happened?"

She was nearly on him before she realized he was leaning on crutches.

Rob, seeing that Brett was at least on his feet, approached at a slower pace. "Hell, man, don't tell me you did the world a favor and totaled that damn eyesore of a Monte Carlo."

"As a matter of fact, I did."

Jenny cried out in protest.

With one crutch tuck up tightly beneath his armpit, Brett raised his other arm toward her. "Come here, Jen."

She rushed into his embrace, careful not to bump his crutch. "Oh, Brett, what happened? How badly are you hurt?"

"I'm all right," he assured her as he held her awkwardly with one arm. "I'm all right. But your car—"

"To hell with my car! You're obviously not all right. You're wearing a bandage and a pair of crutches," she cried.

"A scratch on the head and a wrenched knee, that's all, I promise."

It was silly—she knew he wasn't seriously injured; he was, after all, standing up and holding her—but Jenny wanted very badly just then to cry. She struggled against the impulse and blinked away the pressure behind her eyes.

"Come on, Jen," he said softly, "we're drawing a crowd. Let's go inside."

Jenny slowly pulled a few inches away and glanced around. No one was approaching, but the dozen or so people around the pool were staring. Jenny wouldn't have cared for herself, but she knew Brett wouldn't appreciate finding a photo of himself, bandage, crutches, and all, gracing the next issue of the *Times-Picayune*.

She was surprised when Brett invited Rob and the police officer inside with them. After she went to Brett's room and put on one of his shirts over her bikini, Brett made the necessary introductions. The policeman was Officer Mike Morgan. Jenny forced herself to pay attention to that much, but her mind kept straying to the renewed anger on Brett's face.

"What happened?" she finally asked.

Brett lowered himself to the sofa, wincing once as he inadvertently put weight on his injured knee. "I'm afraid," he said, propping the crutches against the arm of the couch, "that I wasn't kidding about your car, Jen. It's totaled."

"How did it happen?" she asked.

Brett and Officer Morgan shared a brief look before Brett finally sighed and met her gaze. "Your brakes went out."

"Oh, God." A queasy feeling rolled through her stomach. "You could have been killed! Brett, I— dammit, I just had them checked last month and the mechanic said they were fine."

A muscle along Brett's jaw bunched. "They probably were."

"Then wha—"

"Jenny, someone cut your brake lines."

"You're not serious." Her remark sounded stupid, but no more incredible than what Brett had just said.

The grim look on his face, coupled with that harsh anger in his eyes and the ticcing muscle along his jaw, told her otherwise. "Good God, you *are* serious."

"Yes, ma'am," Officer Morgan said. "I'm afraid he is. In light of some of the things Mr. McCormick has told me have been happening to you lately, I need to ask you a few questions."

Jenny's hands turned to ice. "What things? What questions? Surely you're wrong about the brakes. It's an old car and I know I haven't taken very good care of it. Surely—"

"Jen," Brett interrupted. "The lines were cut. There's a puddle of what I'm sure is brake fluid out there in your parking spot. Someone deliberately tampered with your car, dammit."

"Easy, McCormick," Morgan cautioned.

"Easy, hell! Someone tried to kill her, and it's obviously not the first time. What I want to know, Morgan, is what the police intend to do about it."

"Everything we can, which is why I'm here."

Brett squeezed his eyes shut to hold in the rage. Someone had tried to kill Jen. He couldn't get over it, didn't want to get over it, dammit. He wanted to find the person responsible and put his hands around the bastard's throat and squeeze. Hard.

He couldn't keep his eyes closed for long, however, because he kept picturing that embankment coming at him as the brake pedal slammed clear to the floor without a hint of slowing the car. He kept picturing what might have happened to Jen had she been driving the car. It had taken every ounce of his strength to keep from plowing head-on into the concrete wall at fifty miles an hour. He'd missed the wall and had taken out about fifty feet of city flowerbed before crashing through a wooden fence and totaling the car around a telephone pole.

God, Jenny could so easily have been killed.

He pulled his mind away from that frightening thought to hear Morgan ask Jen about the incident downtown last week.

"And the name of your client?"

Jenny looked startled. "Surely you don't think Terrance Reeves had anything to do with it?"

Morgan shrugged. "We just need to check out every possibility. After all, who else knew you would be downtown that night?"

Brett watched the sense of unease steal over her face. Good, he thought. Not that he wanted her to be afraid, but he wanted her cautious, by God. Too many things had been happening. "Damn," he muttered.

"What?" Morgan asked.

"I just remembered her tires."

"Tires?"

"Somebody slashed them, right out front here."

Morgan flipped to a new page in his small notebook. "When?"

After Brett and Jenny had given the details, Rob remembered the incident with her shower.

With growing horror, Brett began to realize the situation was even worse that he'd thought. It wasn't only a matter of someone trying to kill her. That would be terrible enough on its own. But what he was thinking was even worse. "She's being stalked."

Morgan pursed his lips and nodded slowly. "That would be my guess. I'll have a detective get in touch with you tomorrow, Miss Franklin. He'll want to go over everything again to make sure you haven't forgotten anything. In the meantime, I'd advise you to keep a sharp eye out. Don't go anywhere alone.''

"Don't worry," Brett said grimly, watching her face turn more ashen by the minute. "I won't let her out of my sight.''

Chapter Fourteen

Jenny closed the door after Rob and Officer Morgan left. Instead of turning back toward Brett, she stood there a long moment, her arms wrapped around herself in a futile attempt to stem the chill seeping into her bones. Visions of Brett's mangled body trapped in the twisted wreckage of her car tormented her. "You could have been killed," she whispered.

"So could you, if we hadn't traded cars," Brett answered grimly.

"But we did trade!" She whirled and caught him using both hands to lift his injured leg to the coffee table. "It wasn't me who was hurt, it was *you*. I can't stand it that you were hurt because of me."

Brett held his hand out. "Come here, Jen."

With a sharp cry, she flew to his side. "I'm scared, Brett."

"I know, babe, I know." He wrapped his arms around her and held her tight. "The police will catch this creep, then you'll be safe."

"It's not me." Jenny clung to his warmth, his strength, the signs that he was alive and safe. She pressed her head hard against his chest and closed her eyes in gratitude as his heartbeat thundered in her ear. And she trembled. She couldn't seem to stop. "It's not me I'm scared for, it's you. God, you could have been killed because of me."

"I'm all right, Jen. Look at me." He pulled her arms from around his neck and pushed her far enough away to see her face. "I'm okay, do you hear me? I'm not the target here. You are."

"But—"

"No buts," he said fiercely. "It's you this creep is after. You have to remember that. I don't want you worrying about me when you need to be concentrating on being careful for yourself."

Jenny gaped at him. "Not worry about you? Ask me not to breathe, why don't you? How can I not worry about you?" She ran her hands over his face, careful to avoid the bandage on his forehead. "Are you sure you're all right?"

Brett turned toward her touch and kissed her palm. "I'm sure. I promise." He didn't know how to ease her fear for him, since he himself was eaten alive with fear for her. It gnawed at his insides like a hungry rat. "I don't want you worrying about me when we should be worrying about you."

She cupped her hands against his cheeks. "I'll make you a deal," she said, her voice shaking, her gray eyes dark and stormy. "You worry about me and I'll worry about you."

Brett watched helplessly as tears flowed down her cheeks. He whispered a curse and pulled her close to sip the tears away. "Okay, okay," he whispered. "Don't cry, babe; God, don't cry."

Jenny twisted her head away. She didn't want his

lips on her cheeks. She wanted, *needed,* to taste him, to take his mouth with hers hard and fast and prove to herself that this was Brett, that he was here with her, alive and safe and whole. With parted lips, she kissed him, unable to stifle the whimper of fear and need that rose from her throat.

Brett met her sudden fierceness with a need of his own. Jenny felt it, tasted it, reveled in it. Heat surged to her loins, shocking her before she recognized the classic need to reaffirm life. She had always scoffed at such things, believing that in the midst of great fear or trauma, sex was the last thing that would occur to her.

She wasn't laughing now. She was practically ripping the buttons from Brett's shirt to get at his skin, to run her hands over him and feel the smoothness of his flesh, the firmness of his muscles. With his shirt open, she trailed kisses down his neck to his chest and was gratified by the sudden leap in his pulse.

"Jen?"

Jenny raised her head and looked at him.

Brett's breath lodged in his throat. A barrage of impressions assaulted him. Her lips were wet and puffy, stirring his blood as they parted and begged for his. Her eyes were heavy-lidded but fierce, like a tigress set on protecting her own, yet deep in those gray depths he saw need, sharp and strong, mixed with her fear for him.

His own fear for her answered, and he understood then what she wanted, why she wanted it. His body's response was quick and undeniable. "Yes," he whispered. "Yes." With his fingers threaded through her hair, he eased backward and took her with him until he lay the length of the cushions and she lay sprawled atop him.

She was careful of his knee. With gentle yet strong

hands, she eased his injured leg from the coffee table to the couch, then slid her thigh across his.

Her weight, slight but warm and pressing against him in all the right places, felt like heaven. She was alive and in his arms, right where she belonged.

He wished he could have taken more time to appreciate how sexy she looked wearing his shirt, but just then he was much more interested in getting her out of it. He reached for the buttons.

Jenny surprised him. With one foot braced on the floor beside the couch, and her other knee tucked between his hip and the back cushion, she raised above him and straddled his hips. Her fingers flew down the row of buttons. The shirt became a blur of white as she tossed it toward the chair across the room. Her green bikini top followed.

Brett swallowed. He wondered as she knelt above him with her breasts proudly bared if she had any idea how much power she had over him. Under less volatile, less erotic circumstances, he could be reduced to begging for her smile. But now, like this, watching her rise and slip off the bottom half of her suit, then straddle his hips again, he was in her complete control. He didn't think she had any idea of the power she had. Just then she was too intensely focused on what was happening between them. And when she eased down against his chest, her bare breasts pressing flush against him, and kissed him, she took his breath away.

He wrapped one arm around her shoulders to hold her closer while his tongue teased hers. He splayed his other hand at the small of her back, on that fascinating, silky spot where her back ended and her hips began, and pressed downward, forcing her against his hips. Her answering moan tightened his loins.

He surged upward against her, grinding his hardness between her legs.

Ah, God, Jenny thought as a hollow emptiness threatened to swallow her. Pressing against his hips helped, but not enough. Not nearly enough. She kissed him fiercely, her heart thundering, her breathing harsh. With one hand, she reached between them and released the button on his jeans. As she reached for the zipper, his hand joined hers and together they freed him, only shoving his jeans down far enough to get them out of the way.

She wanted to touch him, hold the length of him in her hand and tease him until he was wild with wanting her, but she was too wild with wanting him to take the time.

Brett couldn't wait. He lifted her by her hips, then brought her back down. With her hands braced against his chest, she reared up and took all of him, searing him with her heat. His breath hissed as he clenched his teeth against the pleasure of thrusting home.

He trailed his hands from her hips to the curve of her waist and up her ribs and cupped her breasts. With his thumbs, he teased her nipples into hard points.

She gasped for breath and twisted her breasts against his hands, her loins against his loins. With their eyes locked and their bodies joined, they took each other higher, faster, until the fear of the afternoon was burned to cinders by the sheer heat of their passion.

Jenny felt the quickening in Brett's thrusts and let herself go. The end came hard and fast for both of them, then held them tight and refused to let them go for long moments of pure ecstasy.

* * *

Some time later, by silent, mutual agreement, they left the couch for the comfort of Brett's bed. They spent the rest of the day and night there, making love over and over again with a tender desperation neither of them could deny. Finally, with their arms around each other because they couldn't stand to let go, they slept. And Jenny dreamed.

The dream came upon her as it always did, soft, and quiet and filled with the wonder of love. Then, as was its habit, it turned into the nightmare that had haunted her for twenty years. She woke abruptly, gasping for air, clutching at the pain in her ribs, and searching, frantic and terrified that she would see Maudie and her gleaming bloody knife in every corner of the room.

Something about the dream was different now. The horror was there, and the fear, but this time, Anna's memories had been stronger. Not her memories of Seth or the night of the fire or even the murders, but her memories of all the little accidents that had befallen her before that fateful night when the warehouse burned.

The loose wheel on the carriage and the broken cinch strap, either of which could have resulted in her breaking her neck. The cottonmouth in her bureau.

Those specific memories of Anna's were part of the nightmare and always had been, but never before had Jenny remembered them so vividly as she did tonight.

Even before she recovered her breath, the knowledge filled her. It was happening again. Her slashed tires, the attacker downtown, the brakes on her car tampered with. The past was replaying itself.

There was no logic behind it, no reason for her to

believe that evil had followed her and Brett into this life. But she knew. She knew with a certainty that chilled her. Anna and Seth were not the only ones being given a second chance.

Maudie.

The name snaked silently through the room as though it had been whispered aloud. It crawled through Jenny's mind like a many-legged phantom and turned into a block of ice in the pit of her stomach.

Maudie wanted Jenny away from Brett.

It was crazy, totally insupportable by anything even resembling logic. But it was true. Jenny knew it deep down in her bones. Maudie was back.

Beside her, Brett shifted in his sleep. Jenny was grateful that for once, her nightmare had not wakened him.

Brett! Dear God, he'd almost been killed today, in her place. It could happen again. The entire past could replay itself—Brett could die in her place, just as Seth had stepped in front of the bullet meant for Anna.

Jenny's heart thundered loud in her ears. Her breathing altered until all that came were sharp little gasps of panic. The inside of her mouth turned to cotton.

Cotton. Cotton bales. Warehouse.

No!

"Oh God, oh God," she whispered. "What am I going to do?"

She wanted desperately to throw herself against Brett, to wake him and feel his strong arms hold and protect her, yet she knew she wouldn't wake him.

He would never believe what was happening. As

upset as he'd been over their last discussion about reincarnation, he would call the men in white coats to take her away if she told him that even now, in the safety of his apartment, with his arm lying heavily across her waist, she could feel Maudie's malevolent presence in the room like a gathering storm.

No, she couldn't say anything to Brett. But she could protect him. She gazed longingly at the dark shadow of his form next to her and knew that the only way to keep him safe would be to stay away from him. It was the only way she knew to keep him from getting caught in whatever trap might be set for her next.

But God, it was going to be hard to leave him. She loved him so damn much that the mere thought of not being with him, not seeing him, not hearing his voice, was enough to make her heart crack. Yet the alternative, to stay with him and have him caught in the crossfire, as Seth had been, was unthinkable. There was nothing she wouldn't do to keep him safe, no matter the cost to herself.

She would spare herself the ordeal of trying to explain to him, however. She was too much of a coward to put either one of them through what would surely be a bitter argument, and for no good reason. Brett would never believe her, would never understand.

What hurt the most was that she'd never told him she loved him, and now he would never know.

Brett didn't like waking up alone.

The thought startled him. Until Jen, he'd wakened alone every day of his life. When had she become such a habit?

And where the hell was she? After yesterday, he didn't want her out of his sight.

"Jen?" He crawled out of bed and checked the bathroom, the kitchen, the living room.

She was gone.

Puzzled, he checked his watch. It wasn't quite eight. She didn't usually go to work this early. Besides, she didn't have a car, so he didn't see how she could call on her clients today.

He picked up the phone and dialed her number, but got only her answering machine. Thinking maybe she'd gone upstairs to get a change of clothes and decided to take a shower while she was there, he left a message saying breakfast would be ready and waiting for her when she came back down.

She didn't come back down. She didn't call. After an hour, Brett started worrying. He worried more when she didn't answer her door or the phone.

Dammit, he was supposed to be watching out for her. Some frigging maniac was apparently stalking her, and what does she do? She takes off on her own.

How, he wanted to know, and why?

Jenny paid the exorbitant cab fare, then the even more exorbitant fee to rent a car. She went by the police station and learned where they had towed what was left of her car, and she contacted her insurance agent.

At ten-thirty she kept her scheduled appointment to set up a new computer system for Madam LaRue, Fortune Teller and Voodoo Priestess.

Most people considered Madam a con artist out to scam the tourists who wandered into her tiny shop in the French Quarter, but the tourists and locals, even those who scoffed at Tarot cards and voodoo charms, spent enough money to keep Madam in diamonds and Jaguars. Some called her a charlatan, others, an actress of mediocre talent, still others, an out-and-out thief.

No matter what they called her or how much people claimed they did not believe in the woman's powers, the white-haired, seventy-year-old woman with skin the color of café au lait had an active database of clients from all over the world that took up two megs on her hard drive. Most doctors and lawyers could not make such a claim.

Under ordinary circumstances, Jenny would have enjoyed puttering around the dark shop with its curtains of beads, eerie, primitive music, and mysterious smells. The odd pieces of bones and rocks, bins of colored stones, shelves of colored bottles purportedly filled with, among other things, love potions, and small bags of strange leaves and whatever else Madam put in them were intriguing and fun to peruse.

Today, however, Jenny preferred to get right to business.

Madam had other ideas. "Your aura has changed," she said in her raspy, ruined voice. Some said her larynx had been crushed by a client whose love potion had not worked. Others said her own lover had tried to strangle her many years ago in a fit of jealous rage. Madam herself, when asked, merely smiled mysteriously.

"You are in danger, *n'est-ce pas?*"

Shaken, Jenny offered a shaky smile. "What makes you say that?"

"I see these things, *cher*. While you work, I make you a gris-gris for protection." Piercing black eyes sliced into Jenny as though the woman were seeing clear through to her soul. "Strong protection," Madam added, barely moving her lips.

Rather than argue that she didn't need a magic charm, Jenny turned away toward the computer in the back room and settled in to work. Voodoo or not, she figured she wasn't in any position to turn down whatever help came her way. A little magic couldn't hurt.

Installation of the new hardware and software went smoothly. In less than three hours the system was up and running, the software loaded, and all data transferred.

Through it all, Jenny managed to avoid thinking of Brett for, oh, perhaps two or three minutes at a time.

She shouldn't have just walked out in the middle of the night as she had. It was rude and cowardly. Unconscionable. What had Brett thought when he woke and found her gone? Had he been hurt? Angry?

Jenny leaned toward the bottom shelf next to the desk and slipped the last diskette back into Madam's storage box. If Brett had disappeared from her bed without a word, she would have been devastated.

"Cut."

Jenny had thought she was still alone in the back room. Madam's raspy voice from right behind her startled her. She jerked upright and turned to find Madam seated in the chair next to the desk. Her white hair was smoothed back into a neat chignon. The flowing black caftan she wore made her hair glow like moonlight. Long earrings of large chunks of crystal, red, and gold, stretched her lobes. The matching necklace hung in two ropes to her waist. What most people assumed was cut glass, Jenny knew to be diamonds and rubies. Across Madam's lap she held a tray, in the center of which rested a large deck of cards. Tarot cards.

Jenny smiled. "You know I'm a heretic. I don't believe in the cards."

Madam did not smile as she usually did when Jenny refused to partake of her services. Her black eyes stared deeply, almost hypnotically. "Ah, but de cards, *cher*, dey believe in you. Humor an old woman. We will keep it short. No Celtic Cross, merely a three-card spread. Dat should suffice. Cut de deck into three stacks."

Jenny meant only to humor one of her best-paying clients, but when she touched the deck of cards, a hard shiver raced down her spine. She jerked her hand back. With a nervous laugh, she reached again at Madam's urging and quickly cut the deck into three uneven stacks without meeting the woman's piercing gaze.

Madam turned over the top card on the first stack. *"La Roue de Fortune,"* she murmured. *"The Wheel of Fortune."*

Jenny's nervous laugh came again. "Does that mean I'm going to be a contestant on a TV game show?"

Madam was not amused. *"La Roue de Fortune* represents de continuing circles of life, from tears to laughter, birth to death, and back again. Nothing is new. Everything will happen in its proper order, again and again, for de wheel is de flowing circle of all things, with no beginning, with no end, like life itself. All things are interwoven, each dependent on d'other, each flowing from what came before into what is yet to come, yet has already been. *L'infinité.* "

Moisture beaded Jenny's clasped palms.

Madam turned over the top card of the center stack.

Jenny froze. Her heart seemed to stop while ice formed in the pit of her stomach. The card pictured a skeleton in a suit of armor. In the foreground, a rose bloomed. Across the top, uppercase letters spelled out a single word: *DEATH*.

"As I said," Madam intoned, "you are in danger. De card, *cher*, does not mean you will die. It can mean a transition, from old to new, from here to there. But take care, *cher*, take care."

Jenny tore her gaze from the macabre card. "I was kind of hoping you'd turn up the *Lovers* card."

One corner of Madam's thin lips quirked upward. "I don't need de cards to tell me dat, *cher*. That you have a lover is written in your eyes for all to see."

"Had," Jenny said with a sad smile. "Had a lover."

"Mmmm," was all Madam said as she turned over the last card. *"The Moon*. Secrets. Mayhap lies. But not," she said thoughtfully, "from the one you love."

No, Jenny thought, translating the cards to the thoughts in her mind. The secrets and lies were Maudie's.

"Thank you," she said to Madam for the reading. "Here, let me . . ." Jenny meant to stack the cards neatly into a single pile and return them to the tray, but one card flipped out and landed face down on the floor.

Madam looked down and frowned. She reached out with her long, bony fingers and turned the card over. From her position, it was upside down. She hissed. *"Devil*. Dat is not your card."

"Why do you say that?" Jenny asked before she could stop herself.

The old woman's eyes pierced her. "Who were you thinking of when dis card fell?"

"No one in particular," Jenny lied.

Madam arched one silver eyebrow. "Indeed. Well, de *Devil* represents obsessive love. But you, *cher,* your obsession and your love are honest, not hurtful. De card was not only upside down, but facedown. You be careful, *cher.* Dis obsession of someone else's can hurt you. Hurt you bad. *Prênez garde!*"

Chapter Fifteen

Tarot cards, for heaven's sake, Jenny thought on her way home. And a gris-gris. Some mysterious collection of unknown items wrapped tightly in a small square of red calico and tied with twine. Jenny couldn't remember the last time she'd seen genuine twine. She couldn't believe there was twine in her purse right now, holding tight the secrets of a voodoo charm. Only in New Orleans. Next, she'd be into tea leaves and palm reading.

Yet Madam's cards had reflected things happening in Jenny's life that no one else could know. Even though Jenny did not believe in them, they had reaffirmed her belief that life and death were coming full circle. They reminded her of the reasons she had left Brett in the middle of the night.

No matter her reasons, slinking away like a coward was unforgivable, and she had to do something about it. But what?

It was three o'clock when she pulled into her parking spot. Her stomach was in knots. Her hands were cold and shaking despite another sweltering day—and she couldn't rightly blame their coldness on the car's air conditioning. What was she going to say to Brett? Or was she going to chicken out and creep directly up to her apartment, praying every step of the way that he didn't see her?

Dammit, Jenny, how do you get yourself into these messes?

There was no answer, except that she'd had help getting into this particular mess. Help from her friendly neighborhood stalker.

A sharp vision of a skeleton in armor sent a frisson of fear down her spine. The stalker was why she had to stay away from Brett. She had to keep Brett safe.

She glanced at his living room window. The blinds were at their usual angle, which meant that if he was there looking out, he could see her, but she wouldn't be able to see him.

Refusing to let herself think about the possibility of him watching her avoid him, she got out of the car and climbed the stairs to her apartment. The feel of invisible eyes crawled along the back of her neck every step of the way. Not Brett's eyes—someone else's. A stranger's eyes.

A hard shiver raced down her spine.

Brett stood behind the blinds of his living room window, disdaining the damn crutches but favoring his wrenched knee, and watched Jenny emerge from a strange car. Probably a rental, he thought. He saw her glance toward his window, then away. Saw her turn from the sidewalk that led to his door and take the stairs. He heard her climb them, heard her walk to her door, heard her door close as she went inside her apartment.

He told himself that she'd gone upstairs merely to

change clothes. Any minute she would come racing back down to him, all smiles and laughter, and give him some rational explanation for running out on him in the middle of the night.

"Listen to yourself, man," he muttered. Hell, he was acting as if he owned her, as if she weren't allowed to come and go as she pleased.

But dammit, this didn't feel like a simple coming and going. This felt like . . . abandonment.

Brett shook his head and turned his back to the window. Abandonment, hell, he thought as he picked up the crutches to ease the weight on his protesting knee. His feelings about Jen's actions reminded him of every other time he'd realized that a woman was through with him. She'd gotten whatever it was she'd wanted—or realized she wasn't ever going to get it, or found an easier way to get it—and it was *adios*, sucker, bye-bye Brett. That's what this felt like.

Except it didn't make sense. That wasn't a carefree I'm-through-with-this-bum look on Jen's face when she'd gotten out of the car a few minutes ago. She'd looked . . . torn. Lost. Unhappy.

What did I do, he wondered, *to push her away?* He'd held her, made love to her, sworn to protect her. And she'd been with him every step of the way.

Even now, knowing he'd obviously read more into their relationship than was there, he still wanted to hold her, make love with her. He wanted to see her smile, wanted to hear her laugh. He wanted to see the wheels turning in that sharp mind of hers. He wanted to protect her and keep her safe from the threat that loomed over her. He wanted . . . hell, he wanted everything. And she, apparently, wanted nothing more from him.

Except, dammit, that didn't sound right. Didn't feel right. Her actions didn't fit with the Jen he knew.

And maybe, he thought, grabbing a T-shirt and pulling it on, maybe it was time he found out just what the hell was going on.

He was halfway surprised when she answered his knock on her door. The look of fear that crossed her eyes before she glanced sharply away puzzled him. He didn't wait for her to step aside and invite him in. He maneuvered his way past her on his crutches and closed the door, sealing them inside her quiet, cool apartment together.

"What's going on, Jen?"

She licked her lips and backed away from him as if he were contagious. "I don't know what you mean," she said breathlessly.

"I guess that explains a lot, doesn't it?"

Her forehead wrinkled with a frown. "It does?"

"Yeah." He crutched his way to the breakfast bar and fingered the dead begonia. "It tells me I've apparently been taking things between us a little more seriously than I should have."

"Brett—"

"No, that's all right, Jen. It's not your problem if I wake up in the morning and wonder why I'm suddenly alone. It's not your problem that I've worried all day if you were all right. You weren't coming back, were you? You were just going to disappear, ignore me, and get yourself killed."

Good Lord, even to himself he sounded like a petulant child. He let out a sigh of disgust and started for the door. "I'm sorry." He stopped at the door and looked at her. "I've never been this involved, this close to a woman before. I guess when you left the way you did you just took me by surprise. Don't worry about it. I won't bother you again. But Jen, the police don't want you going anywhere alone, so take care, will you?''

Jenny watched him tuck one crutch beneath his arm so he could open the door. That was a goodbye speech if ever she'd heard one. Pain knotted in her chest and stomach. If this was the way he'd felt when he'd awakened alone and not heard from her all day, God, no wonder he looked like hell.

He'd taken the bandage from his forehead, leaving the angry scratch visible. He hadn't shaved since sometime yesterday, and his clothes were as rumpled as his finger-combed hair. She'd never seen a man more appealing in her life. And she'd hurt him, so now he was hurting her, and it was all so damned unfair.

He grasped the doorknob, and Jenny took an involuntary step toward him. A tiny whimper of pain escaped her tight throat.

He paused and looked back at her, but her vision blurred so badly that she couldn't read his expression. ''Brett, I . . .''

She heard a muffled curse, heard the soft thump of his crutches over the carpet, then heard the crutches hit the floor as he discarded them and wrapped his arms around her.

''What's wrong, baby? Tell me what it is.''

She felt the rumble of his voice where her face pressed against his chest. His arms were strong and warm and made her feel so safe. ''I'm scared, Brett,'' she whispered.

''Of course you are.'' He eased her toward the sofa, then down until she sat on his lap. ''Anybody would be scared to think someone was stalking them.''

Jenny sniffed and swiped the back of her hand beneath her eyes. ''It's not me I'm afraid for. I told you that. It's you.''

"Me? Why would you be afraid for me?"

She scooted off his lap and scrubbed her face with both hands, then looked at him solemnly.

"What?" he prompted.

Jenny looked away. "I had the dream again last night."

His hand came to rest on her shoulder. He squeezed gently. "What can I say, Jen? I'm sorry. Did it upset you so badly that you felt you had to leave?"

Jenny was shaking her head before he finished speaking. "It wasn't that, not exactly. Brett, you could have been killed yesterday because of me."

"You could have been killed, too."

"But I wasn't even driving the car."

"You would have been if your air conditioner hadn't quit, or if the weather had been cooler. Either one of us could have been killed, and we're both scared."

"But it's *me* somebody is after. I can't stand the thought of you getting hurt because of me," she cried.

"Jen, I—"

"Don't you see, Brett? It's happening again," she said urgently.

Brett stilled, a wary look coming over his face. "What are you talking about?"

Awareness came over her slowly. "You know," she said, her pulse pounding. "You know it's happening again, don't you?"

Brett looked away quickly. "I don't know what you're talking about."

"You do. You know as well as I do that it's all happening again. Maudie tried to kill Anna, but Seth got in the way. Someone is after me, and you nearly got killed."

Brett pushed himself from the sofa and limped to the middle of the room. "You're not off on that reincarnation crap again, are you?'' He ran his fingers through his hair. ''Jesus, you are. Hell, the next thing you're going to tell me is that not only are you Anna and I'm Seth, but Maudie must be—who, Kay? Grace? Give me a break.''

Jenny waved a hand in the air. ''Even I can see that they're both a little too convenient. Besides, I can't quite picture either one of them grubbing around under my car in the middle of the night, can you?''

Brett rubbed a hand over his face. ''I don't believe this. Dammit, Jen, the book is *fiction!* I made it up, for crying out loud.''

''Did you?'' Jenny met his fierce gaze without flinching. ''Did you make it up, or did some part of your mind remember it?''

''That's bullshit and you know it. Nobody comes back from the dead. It's a fairy tale, Jen, a goddamn fairy tale. When you're dead—''

''You're dead,'' she finished for him. ''I know.''

''Damn right. Nobody comes back.''

''Who didn't come back to you?''

Brett stiffened and looked away. ''People die all the time.''

''Who, Brett?'' she asked softly, even though she thought she knew the answer. He'd spoken more than once of his mother and brother, but there was one person he'd never mentioned. ''Your father?''

Brett turned his back on her and rammed his hands into the front pockets of his jeans. The action made his shoulders hunch. ''What about my father?'' he muttered, his tone bordering on belligerent.

Jenny slipped from the sofa and placed a hand on his arm. ''I was hoping you'd tell me.''

He shrugged her hand away. ''There's nothing to tell.''

But there was, Jenny knew. If not, he wouldn't have

hunched his shoulders even more, as if to protect himself from a painful blow. "I'm sorry," she offered. "I guess it's none of my business. If you'd rather not talk about it—"

"He's dead, all right?" Brett shouted. "He's dead and gone." Softly he added, "And he's not ever coming back. That's how it happens, Jen, for real. People die and they don't come back."

Jenny could hear the pain in Brett's voice and knew there was more he wasn't saying. She should let it go. He was entitled to his private pain. But something in her wouldn't let it lie. "How did he die?" she heard herself ask.

Brett tilted his head back and closed his eyes. After a deep sigh, he stared blankly at the bookcase on the far wall. "I killed him."

Jenny's shock lasted less than a heartbeat. "You did not!" she cried.

"Yes," he said coldly, "I did. I can't believe we're having this conversation. I'm outta here." Ignoring the crutches he'd left on the floor, he limped once more toward the door.

Jenny's faith in Brett McCormick was absolute. She knew in her bones that he could not have been responsible for his father's death. She wasn't about to let him walk out of her apartment on such a bold-faced lie. She bolted after him. "No!"

As he reached the door, she grabbed his arm with both hands and spun him around. Because of his injured knee, his balance was off and he stumbled back against the door.

"What the hell?" he muttered.

"You're not leaving here until you explain what you meant," she vowed, still holding on to his arm. "I know you better than that. I know you couldn't have killed your father."

His jaw flexed. "You don't know any such thing. Let go, Jen. You had the right idea when you sneaked out of bed in the middle of the night. I should have just let you go."

"Then why didn't you?"

Suddenly the tension seemed to drain right out of him, from his head out through the soles of his feet. He slumped there against the door, his eyes looking dull and filled with defeat. "Because," he said, sounding incredibly tired, "I'm a fool."

"No," she whispered, pressing herself against him. He looked so cold and lonely, she wanted only to warm him, to let him know he wasn't alone. "Come."

He made no objection when she led him to the couch.

"Wait here," she told him.

She glanced back three times on her way to the kitchen to make sure he stayed put. The instant she was out of sight, she raced across the kitchen and opened the bottom drawer at the end of the counter to use as a step so she could reach the cabinet above the refrigerator.

Last summer her oldest brother and his wife had planned to come down for a visit, and in preparation, Jenny had bought a bottle of Chivas Regal. The trip had been canceled at the last minute, and the bottle had been languishing over the fridge ever since. Now seemed like an appropriate time to get it down. If ever anyone looked like he could use a stiff drink, it was Brett.

Jenny's hands shook as she splashed Scotch over a couple of ice cubes. She carried the drink and the bottle back to the living room and handed the glass to Brett. Everything else that had happened lately was forgotten. The only thing on her mind just then was easing that look of devastation on Brett's face, banishing that haunted look from his eyes.

She waited for him to take a sip, but instead of sipping, he knocked the drink back like it was water. An instant later his eyes popped wide open and his breath came out in a wheezing gasp. "Good God, that's straight Scotch."

"Would you like some more?"

He eyed her warily for a moment, and she was grateful to see that his haunted look was gone. Then he surprised her by holding out the glass for her to refill. His hand was shaking nearly as badly as hers.

She waited once again, but this time he sipped. When the glass was half empty, she tucked her feet up beside her on the sofa and turned sideways to face him. The light in the room was growing dimmer as the sun settled toward the west. In her bedroom, she knew, it would be brighter, but here in the living room, evening was coming.

After a long silence that was considerably less than comfortable, Jenny said, "Talk to me, Brett."

He held up his half-empty glass and gave it a sickly smile. "Talk, she says. She wants me to talk about how I killed my father."

"Why do you keep saying that?" Jenny demanded.

Brett downed the rest of his drink. "Because it's true," he finally answered.

"What did you do, put a gun to his head and pull the trigger?"

Brett closed his eyes and let his head fall to rest against the back of the couch. He swallowed heavily. "It would have been better for him if I had. Easier. Cleaner. Quicker."

Jenny pressed her fingers against her lips to hold in her whimpering cry, but the sound escaped.

Brett rolled his head toward her and opened his eyes. "I don't believe I'm telling you this."

Anger seized her, and she nursed it, let it build. "You're not telling me anything so far. You're just tossing out cryptic comments to see how badly you can shock me. So far, I don't believe a word of it."

"Well believe *this,* babe." He leaned forward and refilled his glass, not caring that the ice was all but gone. "A bullet in the head is a hell of a lot more merciful than having a fifteen-year-old son who's so goddamn irresponsible that he can't even close a fucking gate when he's told to, so you're left to be trampled to death by a two-thousand-pound bull."

The guilt and anguish in his voice, plus the words themselves, sent Jenny's breath from her lungs with an audible hiss. "Oh, God, Brett."

"God? What God is that? The God that let my father linger in a coma for six months before he finally died? No," he said taking another swallow of Scotch. "I don't believe in God, Jenny-girl. No God, no afterlife. Heaven is a pipe dream, and hell is right here on earth."

Jenny had never before hurt so badly inside, not for herself, not for anyone, as she did for Brett. She could barely imagine what he must have felt all these years since his father's death. She tried to put herself in his place, believing herself responsible for her own father's death, and her stomach heaved in protest. Oh, God, how utterly *horrible.*

His father's death had been an accident, yet she understood that Brett might never see it that way. He might always bitterly blame himself. "Oh, Brett . . . I'm so sorry."

He gave a harsh laugh. "What for?"

"For bringing it up, for making you remember

such a tragic accident. I'm sorry you blame yourself. I'm sorry you still hurt so much.''

The bitter defiance in his face slowly faded until there was nothing but bleak sadness in his eyes just before he closed them and leaned his head back against the couch again. "No, I'm sorry. It's old history. It has nothing to do with you. I shouldn't have brought it up.''

"Shouldn't have—. Nothing to do with me? Of course it does! Anything that affects you this much affects me, don't you know that? I don't believe for a minute that your father's death was anything more than a terrible, tragic accident. I don't believe for a minute that you're to blame. And I don't understand why what happened to your father makes you believe so strongly that there's no such thing as an afterlife or rebirth. I'd think you'd want to believe your father was at peace in some better place.''

"That kind of belief can destroy a person.''

Shocked, Jenny stared openmouthed for a long moment before responding. "You don't mean that.''

"I do. I watched it destroy my mother,'' he said dully. "She was totally unprepared for Dad's death. The whole time he was in the coma—six months or more—she was convinced that any day he was going to open his eyes, get well, and come home, and everything would be the way it always had been. Nothing any of us said ever got through to her. So when he died, she lost it.''

The raw grief he tried to hide roughened his voice. Jenny couldn't keep herself from scooting closer to him in some futile notion that her nearness might help ease at least some of his pain.

"She spent the next fifteen years spending every dime she could get her hands on. She hired every two-bit shyster who promised to put her in contact with the dearly departed. Jesus, the seances we had in that house. She was so positive she could reach my father beyond the grave."

"And you were fifteen and feeling responsible for his death."

"And ripe for the plucking, just like she was. Oh, yeah, I fell for all that crap for a while. But it didn't take me more than a few weeks to realize it was all a scam, that all those creeps with their satin turbans and fake crystal balls were just after her money. And they got it, too. My brother had to quit college and come home to run the farm, but he and I both had to get part-time jobs to pay for all the con artists my mother dragged home."

Without thinking, Jenny threaded her fingers through Brett's hair. When she realized what she was doing, she started to pull away. She didn't want to distract him. He'd apparently been holding this in for a long time, and he needed to get it out, needed to talk about it and put it behind him. God, how she ached for him. But when she started to slide her hand away, he rolled his head and trapped her fingers between his cheek and the back of the sofa. The ache in her heart grew.

"The sad part was, sometimes the things they told her sounded so much like something Dad would have said that it was hard not to believe in what was happening. But it was Mom and her prompting that had the so-called mediums telling her things like, 'Tell Brat it wasn't his fault. Tell Brat to stop blaming himself.' They were telling us what she wanted me to hear."

"Brat?" Jenny asked quietly.

"That was Dad's nickname for me."

She smiled. "I'd like to hear the story behind that someday."

Brett almost smiled back, but stopped short. He

shook his head slightly. "Finally the mediums quit being able to *locate* him in the hereafter, or wherever," he said with a sneer. "Mom got frantic without her regular seances. Then somebody suggested reincarnation to her, that maybe she couldn't reach him anymore because he'd been reborn. Christ, she fell for it hook, line, and sinker."

"What happened?"

"She got ahold of somebody from the Association for Research and Enlightenment."

"The group that investigates and researches physic phenomena."

Brett opened his eyes and scowled. "It figures you would have heard of them."

She gave him a small smile and flexed her fingers gently against his scalp. "What happened?" she asked again.

Brett snorted and closed his eyes again. "Fortunately, not much. She wanted them to run around checking all the babies that had been born since she 'lost contact,' or whatever, and see if they could figure out which one was my father. By then she was convinced he was back among us. The guy she tried to hire refused her money. Apparently there had been just too many babies born in the area," Brett added sarcastically.

"He said he couldn't go knocking on doors all over Indiana—and anyway, there was no way to be sure . . . what was it he called it? The entity, I think. Meaning Dad. No way to be sure he'd been reborn into a family who lived anywhere near us. How's that for a crock of shit? Not once did he even hint at the possibility that my father was actually dead and in his grave."

Jenny bowed her head and mashed her lips together to keep from commenting. The bitterness was back in Brett's voice, telling her that he wouldn't listen to anything she might say.

"And he *was* dead, Jen. He still is. So is everybody who's ever died. That's how I see it."

Jenny might have commented then, but someone knocked on the door. She frowned and got up.

Brett jumped up after her and grabbed her just before she would have opened the door. "Are you nuts? Somebody's stalking you. You can't just open the door."

Chapter Sixteen

Shaken, Jenny realized Brett was right. She couldn't just open the door. She shouldn't have *just* gone out this morning. She didn't know who was after her—it could be anyone. She jerked away from the door, her eyes wide, her throat clogged.

"Who is it?" Brett called.

"Detective Julien, New Orleans Police."

Brett and Jenny shared a look. Jenny's was resigned, Brett's grim. He opened the door.

Detective Paul Julien was of medium height, middle aged, and nondescript. Jenny's imagination took flight. The man should be working undercover. No one would ever be able to describe him, because there was nothing of note to describe. His hair was medium brown, as were his eyes. His voice was tinged with an average Southern drawl.

His questions, however, reminded her he was a detective with a purpose.

"Tell me everything that's happened to you lately

that has been out of the ordinary. Everything, no matter how insignificant.''

During the next couple of hours, it seemed to Jenny that she told the detective everything about her life, her friends, her clients, every move she'd made for weeks. She told him again and again and again.

"Tell her she shouldn't be alone," Brett said to the detective.

"It's not smart," Julien said to her.

"She's got this theory," Brett began.

Jenny stiffened. Was he going to try to make her look like a fool to Julien?

"What kind of theory?"

"Brett—" Jenny began.

"She's got this crazy notion that the stalker is only after her because Jenny's involved with me."

Julien scribbled in his notebook. "Is that what you think, Miz Franklin?"

Jenny let out a slow breath. "Yes, that's what I think."

"Do you have any specific reason for your theory?"

"Only this." She went to the kitchen counter where she'd left her mail and pulled out a plain white envelope. Under Brett's outraged glare, she handed the envelope to the detective.

"Where the hell did that come from?" Brett demanded.

Jenny swallowed. "It was in my mailbox this afternoon when I came home."

"What's in it?" Brett asked, his voice tight with anger.

Julien held the contents of the envelope—a single sheet of paper—up by one corner so Brett could read the handwritten block letters: STAY AWAY FROM BRETT McCORMICK.

A muscle along Brett's jaw twitched as he glared

at Jenny. "You weren't going to tell me about this, were you?"

"I handed it to him in front of you, didn't I?"

"Where's it from?" Brett demanded of Julien.

"No postmark, no stamp. Someone obviously bypassed the mailman and put it in the box himself. Or herself."

Brett turned on Jenny again. "So this is where you came up with the rest of your theory."

"The rest?" Julien asked.

"Yeah," Brett replied. "Jen thinks if she stays away from me, the creep will back off and leave her alone."

"What I *think,*" Jenny said tersely, "is that if I stay away from you, you won't get hurt in my place again, like you did yesterday."

Julien looked up from his pad. "Could there be a woman out there who, uh, wants you for herself, so to speak?" he asked Brett.

Brett ran splayed fingers through his hair. "I've been asking myself that question since yesterday."

It was news to Jenny. He hadn't said a word to her.

"But there's no one that I know of."

"What about obvious ones, like women you've dated?"

Brett shook his head. "There's no one."

Julien arched a brow.

"Detective, aside from my publicist and my secretary, Jenny is the only woman I've even had dinner with in months."

While Julien looked skeptical, Jenny felt warm pleasure fill her at Brett's admission.

"What about you?" the detective asked her.

"Me, what?"

"If the stalker could be someone who doesn't want you involved with Brett, then we have to consider that it could be someone *you* know, who maybe doesn't want you involved with another man."

Jenny was shaking her head before he finished. "I haven't even been out with anyone in months."

"Y'all were just walkin' around alone until you found each other, is that it?"

Jenny stiffened at the man's tone.

Brett narrowed his eyes. "If you've got anything pertinent to ask . . ."

Julien shrugged. "Of course, it's just as likely that the person we're after doesn't know either one of you."

"You mean he's just some wacko who's decided to go after Jenny?"

"It happens. But it's got to be somebody who keeps pretty close tabs on you," he told Jenny. "Someone who knows where you park your car, which apartment is yours, when you're not home, and sometimes, even where you are when you're working, unless that incident downtown was unconnected, but we can't afford to assume that it was. I'll need a list from both of you of everyone you know in the complex, and from you, Miz Franklin, of everyone who knows where you live. Think about it, work on it tonight."

He pulled a couple of business cards from his wallet and handed one to each of them. Jenny took his card with a hand that shook. She didn't like this, not at all. He was making it real to her again, when she would much rather stick her head in the sand.

But she'd decided against that yesterday when Brett had been hurt. She had to do as the detective asked. She had to give him all the information she could so the stalker could be caught.

But a list of her friends? The idea appalled her.

"Give me a call tomorrow," Julien added. "I'll run

by and pick up your lists. Include everyone you can think of, from the mailman to your best friend."

"Thank you," Jenny told Brett after Detective Julien left.

Brett, chilled to the bone once more at all the talk about someone stalking Jenny, turned from locking her door after Julien's departure and faced her. "For what?"

She gave him a sad little half-smile that cut straight to his gut. "For not trying to make me sound like a fanatic about reincarnation."

Brett shrugged, not liking this topic any better than the other one. "Your beliefs are your business."

"But you don't happen to agree with them."

"No," he told her. "You know I don't, and you know why. I think what we have, have had from the beginning, is maybe the world's strongest chemistry, maybe something more."

"Maybe," she said quietly. "Or maybe what you call chemistry is simply two souls recognizing each other."

A deep shudder wracked Brett, and with it came the sudden need to hold Jenny close. "Does it matter?" he asked. He placed his hands on her shoulders, gently urging her to step into his embrace. "What does it matter if it's chemistry or love at first sight or reincarnation? We're here, and we're together."

Jenny could no more resist the tenderness in his voice than she could the gentle pressure of his hands urging her against him. She placed her head on his chest and wrapped her arms around his waist and returned his embrace, her fear too close to the surface, her heart too full and achy to allow for words just then. He was right. What did the how and why matter?

"Yes," she whispered. "We're together."

His warm hands caressed her back, her shoulders. "Does that mean you're not going to stay away from me for what you think is my own good?"

She raised her head and looked at him, knowing her heart was in her eyes. Her hand trembled as she smoothed a lock of his hair away from the deep scratch on his forehead. "I should."

"You shouldn't. You can watch out for me, and I'll watch out for you."

"But you won't watch out for yourself. That's what scares me."

"Of course I will."

Jenny shook her head. "You'll be looking for strangers. This isn't a stranger. This is someone we both know, someone we trust."

Brett closed his eyes and tilted his head back. "I thought we weren't going to talk about that anymore."

"I know you don't want to." She gripped his shoulders, afraid he might pull away from her. "I know you don't want to believe the way I do—"

"It's not a matter of wanting to," he argued, dropping his arms and stepping back. "I *can't* believe something I know isn't true. Hell, Jen, don't you think it's just a little too convenient to have two people who supposedly lived a hundred and fifty years ago just happen to run into each other in New Orleans in this life, when you're from Oklahoma and I'm from Indiana? And now you want to throw a third person in for an even bigger coincidence. The goddamn book is *fiction*. Seth and Anna *never lived*."

"They *did,*" she insisted. "It's not fiction, not coincidence. You've heard of past-life regression, where people are hypnotized and taken back to a former life. It happens all the time. People—doctors, scientists, researchers—have done studies.''

"Spare me," Brett muttered.

"No, dammit, I won't spare you," Jenny cried. "This is your life I'm talking about. According to studies, people who were close in a former life or who had unfinished business with each other tend to find their way back to a common location and find each other. It's not a coincidence.''

"So you and I both subconsciously found our way to the mall?''

Jenny narrowed her eyes at his sarcastic tone. "I found my way to the mall that day very deliberately, looking for the man who wrote my dream in his book. Explain that!''

Something inside Jenny snapped. Before Brett could answer, she cut loose. "Do you think I *like* believing what I believe? Do you think it's fun having the same nightmare over and over for *twenty years?*" she cried. "Do you think I want to become Anna in my dreams, and watch Seth die in my arms time after time? Do you think I relish the thought that it's all happening again? Only this time it isn't Anna and Seth and Maudie, it's Jenny and Brett and some third person whom we haven't yet identified, and it scares the living hell out of me!''

"You think I'm not scared?" Brett yelled back. "You think my stomach doesn't tie itself in knots when I think of what nearly happened to you downtown the other night? You think I don't break out in a cold sweat every time I think of how close it came to being *you* in that car yesterday? What the hell does it matter what either one of us believes, as long as we admit somebody is stalking you and we do everything possible to keep you safe? I don't *care* who it is. I only want you *safe!* I don't want anything to happen to you."

The depth of emotion, of caring in his voice, knocked the fight out of her. Jenny stood unable to move, unable to breathe, for the longest time. He was right. What did beliefs matter, as long as they were together and safe? A bubble of sound escaped her throat. It sounded and felt like a sob.

"Don't cry. God, Jen, please don't cry." He held her close and kissed the tears away from her cheeks, then settled his lips on hers. With a groan, he threaded his fingers through her hair and deepened the kiss, tasting her tears, feeling the rightness of being with her, holding her, wanting her.

He'd run the gamut that day, from waking up alone and worried, to being convinced she wanted nothing more to do with him, to being terrified something had happened to her, to arguing, to . . . this. Was it love? Was that what he was feeling? How did a man know? He'd come so close to losing her, in more ways than one. The fear of how easy it would be to lose this woman made him desperate to feel her flesh against his, to imprint her on his very soul, and himself on hers. Was that love?

"Take me to bed, Brett. Make love to me."

"Ah, God." Her plea rocked him. He squeezed her tight and felt his heart swell, his blood heat. "I thought you'd never ask."

Chapter Seventeen

Brett sat in the waiting room of the dentist's office while Jenny worked on the doctor's computer system. To occupy his time, he pulled from his briefcase the stack of mail Kay had brought him yesterday. Anything to take his mind off being in a dentist's office. The Muzak wasn't quite loud enough to drown out the whine of a drill in one of the exam booths. The sound made gooseflesh rise across his shoulders.

He flipped through the envelopes, trying to work up even the smallest bit of concentration. His mind kept wandering to Jenny.

The past few days since Detective Julien had paid them a visit had been both tense and immensely satisfying. Tense because Brett had refused to let Jen go anywhere alone and she was a fiercely independent woman. For all that, though, she gave in gracefully and allowed Brett to drive her to her meetings with clients and wait there to drive her home again.

Satisfying and admittedly scary because he'd never felt so close, so *connected*, to another person. How was a man supposed to know if he deserved this kind of happiness? He didn't deserve it. Surely he didn't.

He jerked the next letter from its envelope and forced himself to concentrate. For the life of him, he had no idea what the previous three letters he'd already looked at had said.

He glanced at this one and suddenly had no trouble concentrating. A name halfway down the first page snared his attention. Coupled with the word "diary," the name sent a cold tingling across the back of his neck. He started back at the beginning of the letter and read it again.

Dear Mr. McCormick,

My wife and I recently purchased a few hundred acres along the Bayou Sara in West Feliciana Parish. Imagine our surprise when we began clearing a remote section of land and found a house so long since neglected that the former owner of twenty-five years had not known of its existence.

I do not mean to bore you with details; suffice it to say we have undertaken a major restoration project, and no, I am not writing to you for a donation. I write because during the renovation and restoration process we ran across a collection of old diaries dating from before The War. One of the diaries, written by a young woman named Maudie Hampton, bears a remarkable, indeed, startling resemblance to your novel *This Raging Madness*.

Be assured I am in no way accusing you of copying this diary, even though ... well, you should see for yourself why I cannot find words appropriate to describe the diary's uncanny resemblance to your book, or vice versa. But there is no earthly way you could have copied it, for it has not been out of my possession since its discovery some months ago.

At any rate, I thought you might be interested in taking a look at it. My wife, our six-year-old son, Jeff, and I are just completing the finishing touches on this our new home, which will see its grand opening as the parish's newest bed-and-breakfast inn, Oak Hollow, the last weekend in October. Not to belabor the point, but my wife, Susan, and I have long been fans of yours. We would be honored to have you as our guest if you would care to come for a visit to look at the diary. Assuming you would prefer privacy over the publicity surrounding our grand opening, you are welcome to come in advance of the event, at your convenience.

Sincerely,
John Jacob Templeton
Oak Hollow Plantation

Brett's logical, pragmatic mind would not let him think of any word other than "coincidence" regarding the diary and the name of its author. Maudie wasn't all that uncommon a name for that time period, and nearly everyone kept diaries back then. No big deal.

But the letter did intrigue him, as, according to the map Templeton had enclosed, the plantation was located in an area Brett had once driven through and liked. He'd thought that some day he might want to buy property there himself. He certainly wouldn't mind visiting the area again, touring all the old plantation homes. Including Oak Hollow.

The idea of getting out of town for a day or two excited him. He could take Jenny away from the city and the particular danger she faced and give the police a chance to catch the creep who'd been stalking her.

She wouldn't want to go. He knew that, because he'd already tried to talk her into taking a trip somewhere, anywhere, to get her out of town. She'd been adamant that she could not leave her clients without losing more business than she could afford to lose. Even the suggestion of a visit to her parents' farm hadn't budged her.

The diary, though . . . she wouldn't be able to resist the diary.

He heard her voice coming down the hall and quickly stuffed the letter back into its envelope. The minute they got home . . .

"What's this?" Jenny kicked off her shoes and took the sheets of paper Brett handed her as she propped her feet on his coffee table.

"Just read it."

He was up to something. "What does that gleam in your eyes mean?" she asked with laughing suspicion. "You look like a fox about to snare a rabbit."

Brett laughed. "You're the fox, but I am about to get my wish. Just read the letter, then tell me again you can't leave town for a few days."

"You want me to lose my clients?"

"No, I want you to read that letter."

Jenny rolled her eyes and unfolded the paper. "All right, but I still won't leave town. I told you . . . Holy cow! Brett! Did you *read* this?"

They left for Oak Hollow at one in the afternoon two days later. It took Jenny that long to make sure her clients would be serviced by a friend whom she occasionally covered for when he went out of town. It was his turn now to pay her back.

The day was clear and sunny, and the heat wave had finally broken, leaving the temperature near eighty. Brett's silver Corvette hugged I-10 as if the highway were a railed track specifically built for the low-slung car to run on. Jazz played softly on the stereo as the miles between New Orleans and Baton Rouge disappeared in less than an hour and a half.

Jenny watched the countryside whip past and fall behind as the city of Baton Rouge took shape. Then the city, too, was behind them as they took Highway 61 into West Feliciana Parish and the small town of Saint Francisville, twenty-five miles northwest of Baton Rouge.

As Brett turned off the highway onto the secondary road that led to the plantation, Jenny felt her tension increase. She kept telling herself that going to Oak Hollow was the right thing to do. The diary might be able to answer many questions, might even convince Brett of the truth of their past, maybe giving them some hint of how to deal with the current threat against her. She had to see this through. At least here, away from New Orleans, the stalker could not find them and Brett would be safe.

It wouldn't be easy. The lack of enthusiasm she'd always had for old plantations was rapidly turning into fear as they neared Oak Hollow.

Just the thought of visiting a plantation gave her the shivers. She attributed the feeling to her old night-mare, of course. That alone, without the added con-viction that she had once been murdered on a plantation, seemed justification enough for her fear. There was nothing irrational about it. It was perfectly reasonable, she figured.

That didn't make it any easier to realize she was about to visit a plantation, probably even spend the night—unless she could convince Brett to look for a motel back in Saint Francisville. She hadn't been paying much attention when they'd driven through town, but with a population of around 2,000, surely there was at least one motel. She could live with the smell of the chemical plants in the area for one night.

"You're pretty quiet," Brett commented.

Deep into her own thoughts, Jenny jerked at the sound of his voice. "What?"

Brett reached across the console and placed his hand over her fists. "What's wrong? You're jumpy, and your hands are like ice."

She forced herself to relax her hands. "Sorry. Just distracted, I guess."

"Are you nervous about this? I thought you'd be thrilled to get a chance to wave this diary in my face and say, 'I told you so.'"

Jenny knew he was teasing. He didn't for a minute think the diary at Oak Hollow was going to prove anything. In his mind he'd already marked it down to coincidence, no matter how similar it was to his book. She, however, couldn't bring herself to treat the subject so lightly.

"What if the diary . . ." She paused and shook her head. "I don't know. It's one thing to believe the things I do, but another thing entirely to have it proved true." When he didn't respond, she said, "No comment?"

"You already know how I feel about all this. I think we're going to find some similarities between my book and the diary, or Templeton wouldn't have written. But that's all it can be—similarities. Here's the turn-off," he added.

Jenny looked out the windshield as Brett turned

off the road. The sight of the red brick driveway made her feel suddenly off balance, as if she'd just stepped off a merry-go-round and the world hadn't yet stopped spinning. A long line of moss-draped live oaks marched down each side of the drive, the branches meeting overhead to form a living tunnel over the worn herringbone pattern of the brick lane.

Her gaze darted from one side of the driveway to the other sharply, as she suddenly felt certain there was something she was supposed to see, something . . . *The house.*

It rose at the end of the drive, majestic and white and two stories tall. The architecture was Greek Revival, a popular style among the old plantations, with a wide gallery encircling both floors, the upper railed in shiny black wrought-iron. Eight round columns stood tall and graceful across the front. Forest-green shutters framed magnificent multipaned windows. Red clay pots of varying sizes, some on delicate-looking wrought-iron pedestals, some resting directly on the wooden floor of the porch, sat at intervals against the house, with more spaced between the columns along the front edge of the veranda. Lacy green ferns, brilliant red geraniums, and white, pink, and purple periwinkles spilled out of the pots in a profusion of riotous color.

Jenny's heart thundered in her ears. The house seemed to call to her, to reach out invisible arms, warm arms, welcoming arms. So, she thought, feeling her pulse slow to a thick, steady beat. This was what déjà-vu felt like. There was something eerily familiar about the house, yet Jenny knew she had never been here before.

That off-balance feeling faded and the world around her slowly righted itself.

Not so for Brett. He drove the nearly quarter-mile

brick driveway slowly—brick was damn rough on a car, after all. The house was a knockout, like something out of a movie. There was no reason on earth for this prickling sensation along his spine. He was letting Jenny's imagination affect him, that was all. The power of suggestion.

It was an elegant old house, though, with a certain feeling of welcome about it, and a man had to appreciate it for its beauty alone. The historian in him itched to explore. He bet if he sat on that long shaded veranda he would be able to hear through the deep quiet the sounds of long-ago picnics out on the spacious front lawn. Maybe the clattering of iron-shod hooves racing up the brick drive, the rattle of a carriage, the laughter of children.

He pulled up before the front steps and killed the engine. For a long moment, he and Jenny sat and stared at the house, each of them lost in thought.

The wide double front doors were topped with a single huge fanlight window. One side of the door opened and a pale-haired man stepped out onto the veranda. John Templeton was of average height and wore pleated slacks, suede loafers, and over his starched white dress shirt, a whimsical pair of suspenders featuring bright yellow renditions of Tweety Bird up and down their length. For a man with a six-year-old son, he was older than Brett had expected, somewhere in his mid- to late fifties.

"Welcome to Oak Hollow," Templeton offered with enthusiasm and genuine warmth. "Since we aren't officially open for business until next weekend, you're our first guests. Come in, come in."

The entrance was a large, open room with a sixteen-foot ceiling dominated by an exquisite crystal chandelier. The scents of fresh flowers and lemon oil teased the air. The polished parquet floor gleamed like a mirror. Double-wide doorways led to a parlor on the left and a massive dining room on the right. Across the back wall, a carved mahogany staircase curved elegantly upward, and beneath it sat a padded bench next to a hall leading to the back of the house.

"This is beautiful," Jenny murmured.

"Thank you." John Templeton's smile spoke of pride. "We're pleased with the way the restoration has gone."

He might have said more, but the *slap-slap-slap* of footsteps raced toward them from the hall. An instant later, a young boy of about six, presumably the Templetons' son Jeff, barreled into the entry. At the sight of strangers, he caught himself by the door frame and halted abruptly.

"We have guests, Jeff," his father said.

Big brown eyes blinked once. "Oh, wow," Jeff whispered, then a huge grin split his face and his eyes lit as though it was Christmas morning and he'd just found his presents. Ignoring his Father, he let go of the door frame and literally leaped toward Brett and Jenny, grabbing each by a leg and hugging them tight.

Jenny bit back a laugh at the look of stunned surprise on Brett's face. One glance told her he didn't know quite what to make of such an exuberant greeting from a child. Then Brett's expression changed to one of sheer pleasure, which inexplicably pleased Jenny. For herself, the exuberant greeting was endearing.

"Jeff?" the boy's father questioned. "What in the world?"

Six-year-old Jeff Templeton arched his neck back as far as it would go and looked up at first Brett, then Jenny, with nothing short of total adoration. "Hi! I knew you'd come! I've been waiting and waiting, 'cuz I knew you'd come here!"

John Templeton slowly withdrew his hands from his pockets. Jeff was not a shy boy, but he didn't usually greet strangers with such unabashed enthusiasm. Interesting, Templeton thought. Very interesting. The connection was as close as he'd suspected. "Son, Mr. McCormick and Ms. Franklin have had a long drive, and you're supposed to be asleep. You get on back up to your room and finish your nap, or—"

"I know," Jeff said with a dramatic sigh as he released Brett and Jenny. He stepped back and gave them an irrepressible grin that revealed a deep dimple on either side of his mouth. Susan's dimples, John thought, more pleased every time he saw them. "—or I don't get no tappy-oca pudding for desert," Jeff finished.

"Don't get *any* tapioca pudding," John corrected without thinking.

Jeff turned to him and grinned. "That's what I said."

"Young man . . ."

Jeff raced for the stairs, a giggle trailing in his wake. "I'm goin', I'm goin'," he cried.

"Sorry about that," John said to his guests. "Six-year-olds are always full of surprises."

His mind was buzzing with questions but it was too soon to ask. Instead, John ushered his guests into the parlor. "Please make yourselves at home while I go find Susan and tell her you're here."

When he left, Jenny turned to study the room, but that off-balance feeling that she'd experienced at the sight of the red brick driveway struck again and made the room spin. Her head felt light. The edges of her vision blurred.

"Jen?"

The sensation fled as quickly as it had hit. The room righted and her vision cleared.

"Jen?" Brett said again, taking her arm and guiding her toward the rose-colored settee. "What's wrong?"

Experimentally, she shook her head. Everything seemed all right. "Nothing," she told him with a smile.

"Are you sure?" His brow wrinkled and the corners of his mouth turned down. "Sit down. You look pale."

"I'm fine," she assured him as she let him seat her on the settee. "Maybe just a little tired."

Brett opened his mouth to say something, but the sound of approaching footsteps cut him off. Jenny and Brett rose and turned to greet their host and hostess.

If John Templeton looked a good deal older than the average father of a six-year-old, his wife did not.

"Here they are," Templeton told his wife.

Susan Templeton was attractively plump, with auburn hair, friendly brown eyes, and a smattering of freckles across her nose. Years younger than her husband, she appeared to be in her early to mid-thirties.

"Jenny Franklin, Brett McCormick, my wife, Susan.

"Hello," Susan Templeton offered. "Welcome to Oak Hollow. I hear you've already met our son Jeff."

"Yes." Brett smiled.

"He's adorable," Jenny offered.

"He's a mess," Susan claimed with a dimpled grin. "But we love him anyway. Come. I'll show you to your room."

As she led the way up the curving staircase, she explained, "When we open for business at the end of the month—heavens, I can't believe that's next weekend! I'll never be ready in time! Anyway, our guests will stay in the converted slave cabins and the quarters above the carriage house, but they're not ready yet."

"The cabins are still standing?" Jenny asked, her earlier trepidation gone.

"Yes. They were surprisingly well built. Of course, the roofs and plank floors rotted out years ago, so all we really had to work with was walls, but they're coming along nicely. If you're interested, we can show you later."

"Interested?" Jenny cried. "I hope you don't mind, but I'm dying to see everything."

Brett followed Jenny and Susan, but their conversation faded as he tested the strength of his injured knee on the stairs. He'd returned the rented crutches to the medical supply company yesterday, but today was the first time he'd gone without the stretch bandage. To his pleasure, the knee worked fine. No pain, no discomfort, no stiffness.

Brett smiled secretly. When he was a kid, his mother would have kissed his knee to make it better. Today, a child had hugged it. Maybe that was why it felt so good. He could still feel the pleasing warmth of a small young arm wrapped around his leg. He'd forgotten, if he'd ever known, how much a smile or hug from a child could brighten a day.

And he'd forgotten, he realized as his pleasure faded, how easily a single word could trigger memories better left untouched.

Tapioca.

He tried to shut out the memories conjured by that one word, but they would not let him be.

Chapter Eighteen

This was my room.

The words startled Jenny. They burst through her mind in her own voice as though she'd said them aloud.

John had carried Brett and Jenny's scant luggage upstairs from the car to this corner bedroom at the back of the house and offered them plenty of time to unpack and rest before joining him and Susan for refreshments and a tour of the house.

Jenny scanned the room eagerly, wondering. Had this been Anna's room? What were the chances that a person could actually stumble across her own past life by sheer coincidence?

Or was it coincidence? Her dream, Brett's book, now the diary. Coincidence? Or perhaps fate . . . karma. God's deliberate attempt to give Seth and Anna another chance?

Jenny shook her head. She had no answers that anyone else would understand, but she knew in her heart all she needed to know. She and Brett were meant to be together. It didn't matter if this was Anna's old room or not. It was a room any woman would enjoy, even without the sense of welcome that seemed to wrap around her.

The bed was enormous, and so high off the floor that a tapestry-covered step stool had been provided to aid in climbing up onto the mattress. Four elegantly carved corner posts held the frame for the canopy. "Is this a real Hepplewhite tester bed?"

"Sheraton," Brett muttered distractedly.

"What?"

"It's a Sheraton tester bed."

"How do you know?" Jenny asked, wondering if he felt the pull and welcome of Oak Hollow the way she did. If so, it didn't seem to please him, if the bleak look on his face was any indication.

"I had to study them to get them right in my book. This one's a Sheraton."

"What makes it a Sheraton?" *Come on, Brett, talk to me. Tell me why you suddenly look so sad.*

"Casters," he answered.

"Casters? What about them?"

"Hepplewhites are from around 1785 to 1800 and don't have casters. Sheratons came afterward, 1800 to 1820, and do have casters."

"I'm impressed."

"Yes, it's in excellent condition."

"I meant with your knowledge," Jenny said. "But I agree, the bed is beautiful." She glanced around the room, noting the attention to detail in the hand-crocheted lace dresser scarf, the oil lamp with a rose-painted globe on the dressing table. The bedspread and canopy were of white eyelet. At the foot of the bed sat a lyre-backed sofa with curved arms, upholstered in rose-and-white-striped silk. Near the fireplace sat a daybed covered in rose velvet. Jenny couldn't begin to date the pieces. What she knew about antiques wouldn't fill the head of a pin.

She did know that stepping into this room, indeed, into the house itself, was like stepping back in time. There was a sense of things past in the air. She imagined that if the walls could talk, they would tell of long-ago secrets and happenings, whispers and parties and the laughter and tears that made up everyday life in the years gone by.

She wanted to draw Brett out, get him talking, but he looked so sad that her throat closed and nothing came out. He stood with his back to her, but she could see his reflection in the mirror over the dresser. Just then he looked as young as Jeff Templeton, and more lost than any man should ever look.

"Brett . . . what's wrong?"

He turned away from the mirror and stared out the French doors into the upper branches of a huge old magnolia in the backyard. "It has little *things* in it."

"What?" Jenny followed his gaze to the tree to see what he was talking about.

"Tapioca." Brett said.

Tapioca? Worried, Jenny watched him carefully. "Brett?"

"He used to tease me by offering me his tapioca." Brett spoke slowly, as if in a trance, his gaze focused inward to a past only he could see. "My dad. He knew I hated tapioca. I always said I wouldn't eat it because it had those little beady-looking things in it. He used to laugh and say they were what made it so good."

Brett blinked and looked around as if surprised by his surroundings. "Now, there's a piece of work." He forced a laugh and pointed to what Jenny could only term an indoor outhouse. The original portapotty.

Standing in a corner, partially hidden by a dressing

screen, the item in question was a beautiful two-foot walnut cube with a hinged lid propped open to reveal an enameled chamberpot inside. Jenny barely spared it a glance. She was still too concerned about Brett to be so easily distracted. "Brett?"

He heard the hesitation in her voice and turned to see her brush a strand of hair from her cheek. So graceful, that hand. So clever and competent on a keyboard, so soft against his skin. Arousing. A mere touch from her hand, and he could go up in flames. It was easier and more pleasant to think of that than old memories of a lost childhood.

He shook his head. The memories were old ones and belonged in the past. He couldn't believe he'd spoken of them aloud. By the look in her eyes, he knew he was scaring Jenny.

"Hey, I'm sorry." He slipped his arms around her and pulled her close. God, she felt good. "It was just something I remembered, that's all. It's nothing, Jen. Just forget it. I'm all right."

And with the words, with the feel of her pressed against him, the guilt and pain that always came with memories of his father faded, and he *was* all right.

Electricity, central heating and air conditioning, modern plumbing. An up-to-date kitchen. None of those things detracted from the atmosphere of the house, from the feeling of walking through authentic history as the Templetons led Jenny and Brett on a tour before dinner.

The house itself was large, with five bedrooms and three full baths upstairs; two of the bedrooms had their own sitting rooms. Four of the bedrooms were painstakingly restored to their former life in the early 1800s. One was not.

Here was a little boy's room, a little boy of today. Three-inch-tall plastic men in space regalia, complete with laser weapons, stood in neat rows, faced off and ready to do battle with a two-foot-tall fuzzy purple dinosaur. One wall held a hockey poster, a Louisiana State University pennant, and a giant picture of Big Bird. Dirty sneakers and socks poked out of the open closet door, and beneath the bottom edge of the Space Invaders bedspread, a soccer ball was visible.

The rooms weren't small, but the high, molded ceilings gave an additional feeling of space without destroying the coziness.

Downstairs, in addition to the huge entry and the parlor in which Brett and Jenny had waited to meet Susan, there was a second parlor. The two rooms, each with its own fireplace, were separated by double sliding doors. The front room was the gentlemen's parlor, the back, the ladies'.

On the opposite side of the entry was a large dining room with a table big enough to seat twenty. The door at the far end led to a modern kitchen with a walk-in pantry as large as Jenny's living room. Past the kitchen was the morning room, tucked into a sunny corner with two adjoining walls of floor-to-ceiling windows, with a dining table for eight and a pair of French doors opening onto the veranda.

With every step Jenny took, the house, the period furnishings, the very air seemed to call to her with the echoes of past lives, of history rich and strong—happy history, sad history. In the hallways she heard the silence of long-ago laughter and tears, arguments and good cheer. Life and death and everything in between. But none of the rooms affected her, welcomed her with warmth, the way the upstairs corner bedroom did.

Across from the morning room there was a study,

then a library with walls lined with books. The library, too, had French doors leading onto the veranda. John pulled them open and ushered Jenny and Brett outside to the cushioned wicker furniture and refreshments awaiting them.

There they met Hester.

"Good afternoon." The black woman stood nearly six feet tall and appeared to be in her late forties. She gave a regal nod to Jenny and Brett. "Welcome to Oak Hollow."

Susan made the introductions. Hester Fielding was their cook and housekeeper. When Oak Hollow opened for business next week, she would be in charge of the maids they'd hired to care for the house and the guest cottages. She and her husband, Arnold, had lived in West Feliciana Parish all their lives.

"She's been down in New Orleans for a few weeks taking care of her aunt and has only been back a few days. Let me tell you, we certainly missed her. I'm not sure how we managed without her while she was gone."

"You managed just fine, and you know it," the woman said. Then she spoke to Brett. "Are you the one who wrote the book about this place?"

Brett stiffened. "What book is that?"

"You know, *This Raging Madness.*"

"That's my book, but I didn't know about this place when I wrote it. The book is fiction."

The woman's black eyes narrowed. "Fiction. Yes."

Brett turned away abruptly. Jenny wanted to call him back, but she didn't. She turned to Hester, but any words she might have uttered dried up on her tongue. Hester was watching Brett with a look that chilled Jenny to her soul. A look of . . . knowledge.

"Where's Jeff?" Susan asked Hester.

The woman's face changed instantly. Now it

beamed with pleasure. "The young rascal is out helping Arnold plant the last of the marigolds around the cabins."

"I'm sure your husband doesn't consider it *helping*," John muttered beneath his breath.

"Now you just hush," Hester scolded. "That's between Mister Jeff and Arnold. Those two have an understanding."

"Arnold is our groundskeeper," Susan explained.

"He's an excellent one," Jenny offered. "The grounds are beautiful. The formal garden in the back must be a full-time job in itself."

They spoke of the yard, of flowers, of the restoration of the house. The evening air was skin temperature and soft. Jenny delighted in sitting on the veranda and watching the day wane. She wondered how many families had sat just here, on this spot. How many times had they watched the sun set or rise? Had a terrified woman sent her men off to war down that brick drive? Had she stood here and watched Yankees trample her garden and cut her trees for firewood?

As the conversation swirled around her, Jenny smiled at herself. If Yankees had cut down Oak Hollow trees, someone had replanted immediately, because the live oaks and pines and magnolias were tall and stately as only age could make them.

Almost too soon for Jenny, Hester called them to the formal dining room for dinner.

The housekeeper might have lived in rural West Feliciana Parish all her life, but no one could have served a more elegant meal. Yet for all the elegance and formality of the occasion, the atmosphere was warm and casual. John and Susan treated Jenny and Brett as if they were old and dear friends.

After dinner John led them to the library and

opened the roll top desk. "Here's the diary I told you about. I think you'll find it . . . interesting."

Brett didn't want to take it. Templeton held the diary out and Brett felt a sense of hatred roll through him. Not his hatred; it came from the book, as crazy as that thought sounded. Waves of it. He had the sudden impression that if he opened the leatherbound volume, hatred and evil would come spewing out.

He shook himself. It must be this house, he thought, trying to explain away his unease. The house, and Hester's cryptic comment about his novel.

"We found it stored in a trunk in the attic," John said of the diary. "It's in remarkably good condition. The paper is still smooth and supple, the cover intact. Not even any mouse nibbles around the edges," he added with a smile.

Cursing his own stupidity, for hesitating, for coming to Oak Hollow, for a dozen things, Brett reached out and took the offered book. Nothing happened. No tentacles of hate reached out from beneath the cover to entwine themselves around his wrist. No evil seeped through to burn his skin like acid. It was just a book. An old, old diary that would give him new insight into a way of life long past. Research for future books. Just research.

"Thank you," Brett managed.

"After you read it, we'll talk."

Brett barely heard him. He stared at the book for a long time. When he looked up, he was alone in the room. Vaguely he remembered hearing Jenny offer to help Susan and Hester clean up after dinner. He sighed. Might as well get this over with.

He took the upholstered walnut easy chair because there was a table next to it bearing a lamp. Upon sitting down, he discovered the chair was what used to be termed an "invalid chair," the forerunner of today's recliner. He'd seen one like it in Andrew Jackson's library at the Hermitage when he'd toured it a few years back. If he was going to do research, he figured he might as well research the full benefits of an early nineteenth-century invalid chair. He pulled the lever that raised his feet and settled in.

If his hand trembled when he opened the cover of the diary, no one was there to see but him.

My Journal
New Year's Day, 1857
Maudie Hampton

As this is the First day of a New Year, I do hereby Resolve that I will once and for all be Eternally and Forever rid of my interfering Cousin. The Bitch has gone too far and has somehow managed to trick my Dear Beloved Seth into pursuing her! Some—the bitch's brother Randall, for one—are saying Seth intends Marriage. I Shall Not Allow it!

Dear Seth doesn't mean it, anyway. He merely intends to slake his Manly Lust on the slut. It is Me he intends to Marry. He shall have no other to Wife but Me.

I Hate her.

February 22, 1857

My poor little Cousin Anna was nearly bitten by a Cottonmouth today. What a shame it was— a shame that Anna's maid, Delilah, stepped into the room at just the wrong moment and distracted her. If not for that Interfering Negress, Anna would have reached her hand into that open drawer and been Bitten.

Does Delilah know? Did she see me put the

snake in there? She's too smart to say anything. She knows I could have her whipped, sold, or Killed if I wanted. But she's clever, so I shall be even more clever. And I Shall get even. Mayhaps not directly, but through her grandfather. Yes, that's the thing. I'll get back at Delilah through Old Saul. He is such a trusting Fool, it will be simple to get that old black Buck into trouble.

Now, however, I must think of something new for Anna. Seth is entirely too enamored of her. I should have seen this coming that day at the barbecue last fall. That's when he first noticed that the little Bitch has grown up. I should have done something then. But it is Not Too Late.

The handwriting was sometimes difficult to read, but the ink was dark, not faded by age. Brett read page after page, unaware of the passage of hours as he read what could not be explained. It was his story. This was *This Raging Madness*, but not as he'd written it. The events, he realized as he made his way through the journal, were the same; the viewpoint was not.

Brett had told his story occasionally from Maudie's point of view, once in a while from Randall's, or from Mr. or Mrs. Hampton's, Anna's parents. But mostly he'd told the story from Seth or Anna's viewpoint.

The diary in his hands was the same story, but strictly from Maudie's eyes.

And damned if Brett could explain the why or the how of it. He squeezed his eyes shut and told himself again it was a coincidence. Just a coincidence.

If only the voice inside his head wasn't starting to sound so damned uncertain.

* * *

It was after midnight when Brett finally joined Jenny in the bedroom. She had wanted to go to him in the library but had managed to talk herself out of it. She had pushed him so hard on the subject of reincarnation last week that he'd told her things about his past, about his beliefs and fears, about his father, things he hadn't wanted to tell her. Jenny was reluctant to push harder just yet.

Whether he admitted it or not, he was coming around to her way of thinking. After all, despite everything—the excuses, his letting her think this trip was her idea—he had come here to Oak Hollow because of the diary. Writers were an innately curious lot, and Brett was no exception. If the word "reincarnation" had never been spoken, he would still not have been able to resist taking a look at the diary.

Actually, now that she thought about it, leaving him alone in the library with the diary hadn't been all that difficult. She was admittedly nervous about reading it. It was one thing to think, to believe, to say she knew she had lived before as Anna. It was quite another to come face to face with what could turn out to be proof.

So she'd left Brett to read the diary alone. He'd spent hours at it, and now he was back with her, but he wasn't. He was withdrawn and distracted, and suddenly Jenny's nervousness threatened to turn into fear.

The bedside lamp cast a warm, golden glow across the bed where Jenny waited for Brett to join her. He gave her a distracted smile, tugged off his clothes, and crawled into bed with her without so much as a word.

Tension radiated from him in waves. She could feel it, and it hurt something down deep inside her. He was blocking her out, practically screaming at her to keep away from him, and she couldn't. Somewhere amid all the tension and withdrawal, despite the deliberate distance, she felt his pain, and it was intolerable to her that he should hurt.

"Brett?"

He stiffened. She was going to touch him, and he couldn't let her. The foulness, the hatred, the sheer evilness from that damn diary was all over him. He could feel it, layer after layer coating his skin like thick slime. It had spewed off the pages like venom from the cottonmouth described there—dangerous, deadly. Pure poison. Holding the diary, reading it, left him feeling . . . dirty. He couldn't bring himself to taint Jenny with such foulness, no matter how badly he wanted to hold her.

It had come on him the minute he'd opened the cover and read the name Maudie Hampton—a fierce urge to grab Jenny and hold her, wrap her tight in his arms, protect her from danger. He still felt the need, but he felt too dirty after holding those vicious words in his hands, seeing them with his eyes.

He threw off the covers. "I'm going to take a shower."

A moment later he stepped into the claw-foot tub in their private bath and pulled the shower curtain closed. The old tub wasn't exactly early-nineteenth-century, but it was old enough that it didn't really break the mood of the rest of the house.

Hot water pounded on his head and shoulders. For long moments he let it beat at him. With the guest soap left out for their use, Brett scrubbed from his scalp to his soles and back again until his skin felt raw, until the water turned cool. Until he realized it wasn't working. He couldn't wash Maudie Hampton's foulness away with soap and water.

With any luck, he thought as he dried off, Jen would be asleep by now and wouldn't notice anything was wrong.

His luck, however, wasn't holding. The instant he slid naked between the sheets, she was there, reaching for him.

"Brett?" The uncertainty in her whisper cut him. He'd done that to her with his silent withdrawal. He'd made her unsure of her welcome.

Then she did something to him, something he should have anticipated but hadn't. She touched him. Just her fingertips against his shoulder, that was all. A simple touch, warm and gentle, but it had the most incredible effect. The arousal was expected. Her touch always aroused him. The heat that spread from her fingertips to his chest, his groin, was no surprise. Neither was the love he felt through her touch.

The surprise was that her touch accomplished what all the hot water and soap at his disposal had not been able to. It cleansed him. With one simple touch, she wiped away the soiled feeling he'd brought upstairs with him against his will. One touch from her, and he was free of it.

He breathed her name and pulled her to his side.

Jenny felt the need in him through the way he grasped her arms. She breathed a sigh of relief. His withdrawal had scared her. She should probably ask him what had been wrong, but just then she couldn't bring herself to open any doors but this one. He needed her. Just then, that was enough. Tomorrow would be soon enough for questions.

She spread her hands across his chest, loving the feel of him, loving him. Her lips followed her hands, and she loved his taste, too, a little salty, a little soapy.

She loved the way his breath hitched, the way his hands tightened on her arms. The way his hair-roughened legs shifted restlessly next to her smooth ones.

Brett gathered his strength to turn, to gently roll her to her back so he could feast on her, but he found himself trapped. Delightfully, wonderfully trapped. She laced her fingers through his and with their palms pressed together, pulled his arms above his head and imprisoned his hands against the pillow. She smoothed her soft cheek over his rough one, making him wish he'd shaved, but she didn't seem to mind the day's growth of beard.

She kissed his forehead, his temples, his eyelids, and made his heart ache with her tenderness. For long moments they tasted each other, their lips and tongues stroking and dancing. Her taste was sweeter than honey, more potent than wine. She nibbled her way to his chin and along his jaw, then down his neck to the hollow where his pulse pounded.

He waited, his breath coming sharper by the moment, as her lips trailed down his chest. Finally, she was forced to release his hands or stop her downward journey. He prayed, and was rewarded when his hands were freed and her mouth traveled lower.

Now, he could touch her.

But no, she slipped from his grasp and kissed him all the way to his soles. It was torture, feeling her soft, hot mouth on him. It was heaven. She didn't miss a single spot. Not a one. But neither did she linger anywhere. She moved on, ever on, making him restless, needy. Driving him toward the edge.

He was nearly at the breaking point, ready to grab her and roll her beneath him and plunge into her when she straddled his hips and brought him home.

Ah, God, there had never been a time in his life when he felt so complete as when she took his hard, aching flesh into her softness. He ran his hands up her ribs and cupped her breasts, gratified to see the way she tossed her head back, please by her moan of pleasure when he flicked his thumbs over her nipples. She rode him slow and easy, so slow he thought he would lose his mind. With hands that shook, he pulled her toward him and took the hard, pointing tip of one breast into his mouth. He suckled; she moaned. He did it again, then again, and wanted to laugh with sheer triumph when her inner muscles contracted around him in time with his suckling.

She pulled away, almost freeing him from her depths completely. In protest, he grasped her hips and pulled her back down, thrusting his hips up at the same time. Ah, God, it was good. So damned . . . *good.* "Jen," he whispered fiercely.

"Yes. " She pulled away again, then took him harder, deeper. Then again. And again. The heat built. Need overwhelmed them both. And the world exploded into a thousand brilliant colors.

"You didn't ask me about the diary," Brett said the next morning as they were getting dressed.

Jenny paused in the act of tugging on a shoe. Without straightening, she slowly lifted her head to meet his gaze. "No. I didn't."

He sat in the wingback in the corner, his elbows spread to rest on the arms of the chair. With his fingertips pressed together, he tapped them against his lips. "Any particular reason?"

She finished putting on her shoe, then picked up its mate. The caution in his voice had her choosing her words carefully. "I figured you'd tell me soon enough."

"I thought you'd be more curious than that."

"I am." With a last wiggle of her toes, the second shoe was in place. Jenny stood. "But I don't really need the diary to convince me of anything."

"You think it's all in there, don't you?"

"Is it?" she asked solemnly.

Brett flopped his head back against the chair and closed his eyes. "Yes."

Jenny's heart lurched. "All of it?"

"And then some." He voice sounded of defeat.

"Does this mean . . . you believe—"

"Don't." His eyes were still closed, but his voice sharpened over the word. "Just . . . don't ask, all right? Read the damn diary yourself."

Hurt, Jenny turned away. What was happening? She'd thought that if he ever started to believe, to understand that they had known each other before, they would be drawn closer. Instead, he was pushing her away.

"I'm sorry."

Startled—his voice was at her ear, yet she hadn't heard him move—she started to turn. His arms came around her from behind and pulled her back against his chest.

"I'm sorry," he said again . "I didn't mean that the way it sounded. I guess I'm just not taking this very well. On second thought, I'd just as soon you didn't read Maudie Hampton's diary."

Jenny turned in his arms. "Why?"

Brett pressed her head to his shoulder, then laid his cheek against her hair. "In my book, Maudie was crazy. She was mean and vicious—psychopathic."

"And?"

"No 'and'. But. In her diary, Maudie Hampton is mean and vicious. But she wasn't crazy, not like I wrote her. The real Maudie was . . . evil. That's the only word I can think of. Reading her diary made me feel like I'd been crawling around through a pile of dead bodies.''

"Gross."

"Yeah." He chuckled. "Sorry. But that's what I felt like last night."

Jenny understood, then, why he'd been so stiff and withdrawn when he'd come to bed. Why he'd jumped up and run to the shower when she'd reached out to touch him. He'd been trying to rid himself of Maudie Hampton.

An icy shiver struck deep inside her. He still didn't believe, didn't understand. The nightmare had come again last night, stronger and more real than ever. Maudie wasn't trapped in the past, she wasn't dead and gone, confined to living through the pages of her diary. She was here, now. In New Orleans, waiting for her. Maudie, whoever she was in this life, was the stalker. Of that, Jenny had no doubt.

Chapter Nineteen

They could go home, Brett thought. He'd seen all he ever wanted to see of that damn diary. It didn't mean a thing, except that some powerful coincidences had occurred. Peoples' names. Certain events. Similarities. Coincidences.

Yet he didn't suggest they leave. The stalker was still back in New Orleans, and Brett was in no hurry to expose Jenny to that danger again.

Susan and John didn't suggest that Brett and Jenny leave, either. Over breakfast, they acted as though they expected them to stay for a few days. And really, Brett thought, what could it hurt? As sick to his stomach as the diary had made him, there was still something appealing about Oak Hollow.

"Aren't you having your grand opening next weekend?" Jenny asked.

"We were supposed to," Susan said darkly. Sunlight streamed through the east window of the morning room and cut a swath across the red checkered tablecloth. "But the paper in Baton Rouge left our ad out last Sunday by mistake. We were counting on it to bring in business.''

"It's only Monday. Can't you run another one?"

"We could," Susan said. "We are. But an ad every day this week still won't reach as many people as the Sunday paper would have."

"And we *weren't* counting on the governor holding a fundraiser in Baton Rouge this weekend for Bosnian orphans," John added. "He's making a big media splash, and the press isn't interested in our open house when something like this is happening."

Jenny saw the look of speculation in Brett's eyes. "What are you thinking?" she asked.

"I'm thinking," he said slowly, "we need to fight fire with fire."

"Meaning?"

Brett grinned at Susan and John. "This open house you're planning—were you thinking of doing something like an Old South costume ball? And when exactly is the governor doing his thing?"

"A ball?" Susan said weakly.

"Saturday afternoon," John said in answer to Brett's question about the governor. "Why?"

"I've got a publicist who loves a challenge. Why don't I give her a call?"

Within twenty minutes new plans for Oak Hollow's grand opening were in motion.

Jenny tucked her arm through Brett's as they stepped out onto the side veranda. "You're a nice man, Brett McCormick."

He smiled down at her and twined his fingers through hers. "Why, thank you. I like you, too."

Like. Not love. It shouldn't hurt her, but it did, quick and deep, before she could push it away. She turned her face into the slight breeze, hoping he wouldn't see her pain. "I mean for what you're doing for Susan and John. Getting Grace to organize a costume ball for Saturday night. Do you really think she can get the governor to come?"

"If she can't, no one can."

"It's nice of her to go to all this work."

"Trust me," he said with a chuckle. "Grace doesn't do anything to be nice. She'll use this as the prelaunch of my November tour. She'll promote the hell out of me and both the last book and the next one, and if she does a good enough job, if my sales jump enough, she'll probably land the job as publicist with my publisher. *That's* why she was so willing to take on this open house. Ten bucks says she fills every guest room here before tomorrow night and they have to turn people away."

"Only ten bucks?"

"I didn't want to rob you blind."

"Kind of you."

"I thought so."

"Oh, look," Jenny cried softly as they rounded the house and saw the formal gardens. They'd caught glimpses yesterday from inside, but up close was much better. Red brick walkways bordered by deep green knee-high boxwood hedges meandered lazily from the house to the cottages and back again. Between the green borders, vivid splashes of color bloomed— reds, pinks, yellows, whites—geraniums, pansies, impatiens, begonias, roses, and a dozen other flowers Jenny couldn't name.

In the center of it all, like a queen surrounded by her colorful cape, stood a white gazebo covered in lacy latticework.

"Oh, look," she whispered again. It was round, perhaps eight feet across, with a cushioned bench encircling the interior. English ivy trailed up and over the arched doorway. The gazebo, set as it was in the midst of flowers, looked like some good fairy's enchantment, created on this bright fall day just for lovers.

Jenny shook her head. She was the logical one, the one who preferred computers to most people. Brett was the storyteller. So why was *her* imagination suddenly running away with her?

She glanced at him and caught him staring at the gazebo with a look of utter sadness on his face. Then she, too, remembered. In her dream, and in his book, Seth and Anna had met frequently at the gazebo. Except on that last night. There'd been too many people around, so they'd met at her father's cotton warehouse on the bayou. If only they had gone to the gazebo instead . . .

As if he sensed that her mood was the same as his, Brett looked down at her and tried for a smile. "Do you want to go see it?"

"No." Her smile was as sad as his. She swallowed. "Not today. I don't think . . . Not today."

By unspoken agreement, they strolled hand in hand through the gardens, ignoring the gazebo, and wound up back at the house. Hester was seated in a rocker just outside the back door. With a bowl in her lap and a bucket on the floor beside her, she was snapping green beans.

Jenny smiled. "Lord, I used to hate it when it was my turn to do that."

Hester returned her smile. "I find it soothing, myself."

"I think I would too, now. But when you're eight years old, snapping beans is more something to resent than to be soothed by."

With Brett beside her, Jenny started to reach for

the door, but the shrubbery at the edge of her vision began to shake. She looked over her shoulder and realized that Brett had also noticed. Hester caught their attention and, with a slight shake of her head, cautioned them to silence. Her lips were pursed and her eyes crinkled at the corners in silent laughter.

The glossy green shrub shook again. "All right, nobody move!" Jeff Templeton staggered into view from behind the bush. With one forefinger aimed like a pistol, he clutched the front of his grubby T-shirt with his other hand and stumbled onto the porch. "Is y'all Yankees, or is ya Rebs?" he demanded fiercely in an exaggerated Southern drawl.

"Well now," Hester answered slowly. "Seein' as how I can always tell a fine Southern gentleman by the way he dresses, we'd be plumb foolish to admit to being Yankees, now, wouldn't we?"

"That's right." Jeff gave a serious nod.

"So, who are we today?" Hester asked, fighting a smile.

"I'm Johnny Reb, and a dirty Yankee done shot me." He staggered beautifully and collapsed with a pitiful moan.

"Let's watch that dirty Yankee talk, boy. Yankees freed my ancestors from slavery, you know."

"Oh." Forgetting all about his deadly wound, Jeff sat up and grinned. "What's a antsetter?"

"Ancestors. My family."

"Oh. I knew that." Assuming his former pose, he let out a credible groan. "Well, I don't got no family left, and now this clean Yankee done kilt me. I'm gut shot, and I'm gonna die."

"You're liable to come closer than you think when your mother sees what you've done to that T-shirt," his father said, stepping out the back door.

"It's blood," Jeff announced gleefully.

"Looks like dirt to me," John told him with a smirk.

"That's cuz you got no majination."

"I don't have *any* imagination."

"That's what I said." Jeff lowered his brows and stuck out his lower lip. "Grown-ups. Humph." With that, he gave a mighty Rebel yell and leaped from the porch to dart around the corner of the house.

Jenny laughed and was pleased to hear Brett chuckle. She didn't like to think he might still be troubled over the diary.

John's smile faded. When he turned to Brett, his eyes were sharp. "Can we talk about the diary?"

Brett pulled in a deep breath. He didn't want to have this conversation, but the man had opened his home to them, so Brett resigned himself and gave a reluctant nod. When they started inside, Jenny hesitated. Brett reached for her arm and took her with him.

The three of them settled in the study. Old furniture, fresh paint, cut flowers, and a swath of golden sunlight made the room feel comfortable. John took the wingback. Brett and Jenny sat on the settee next to it.

"You read the diary?" John asked.

"I did."

"And?"

"And what?"

Leaning back in the chair, John propped his elbows on the padded arms and templed his fingers together. "I suppose I should have had the diary authenticated before you came."

"You mean, to prove its age?" Jenny asked.

John nodded.

"Why didn't you?" Brett asked.

"I guess I thought that since you'd written essentially the same story in your book, you wouldn't need the proof.''

"Meaning?"

"How do you explain the similarities between the two?" John asked, instead of answering Brett's question.

Brett stiffened. "You admitted in your letter that there was no way I could have seen the diary, no way I could have copied it."

"I know I did, and I meant it. I still mean it. I'm certainly not accusing you of any such thing."

"Then what is it you want? The diary may be real— I have no reason to believe it's not," Brett said. "But the book I wrote is fiction."

"You made it up?"

"That's right."

"Have you considered that there might be another possibility?" John asked quietly.

Brett felt the skin on the back of his neck prickle. He glanced at Jenny and caught her intent look. God help him, he knew what was coming before he asked, "What possibility is that?"

"I suppose I should start by telling you that before I retired last year I was a practicing parapsychologist."

Brett shot Jenny a look. "Did you know about this?"

Wide-eyed, Jenny shook her head. "How could I?"

Brett started to rise. He braced his hands beside his thighs and gathered his muscles. He didn't need this, didn't want it. Dammit, this man was going to start talking about past lives and reincarnation, and Brett didn't want to hear it.

"I apologize for taking you by surprise this way," John said. "Perhaps I should have warned you in my letter."

"Warned me of what?" Brett demanded, knowing somewhere inside that he wasn't going to leave. Not yet. He was going to sit here and listen to Dr. John Templeton, because too many things had happened, too many coincidences he could no longer explain. He sank back against the settee. "What is it you want from me?"

"I don't want anything from you." Never had a man looked more sincere, more trustworthy. "I was just curious, and I thought you might be interested in the diary."

"Curious about what?"

"About how you came to write your novel."

"It's fiction, Templeton. I made it up."

"Made it up? Or perhaps remembered it?"

Too restless to sit, Brett pushed himself from the settee. "What is this, a publicity gag for your grand opening? Come to Oak Hollow and meet the former residents in their latest incarnation?"

"Residents? Plural?"

"He means me," Jenny said.

"I don't understand."

"Neither do I," she said with a twist of her mouth. "But I do believe it."

John leaned forward in his seat. "Believe what, Jenny?"

"Wait," Brett said before Jenny could speak. "I want an answer to my question. Are you after publicity?"

"No," John answered calmly. "It never entered my mind. Although, if someone were to ask Hester a direct question, I'm sure she wouldn't deny that some of her ancestors are buried in the slaves' cemetery out back."

John leaned back again and studied Brett. "We wouldn't need you and whatever connection you might have to Oak Hollow, Brett. If we were after sensational publicity, we already have Jeff."

Brett paced to the fireplace. It was cleaned and stacked with wood, just waiting for a match and a cool evening. He braced a hand on the mantle. "I assume you're going to tell us what that means?"

"I'd like to, because I think it might ease your mind on a couple of issues. When Jeff was about four, he started making up stories. We didn't think anything of it at first. Many children invent imaginary playmates, and Jeff is an only child and spends a lot of time entertaining himself. But the stories grew more and more elaborate, much too elaborate for him to simply be making them up. He kept talking about living on a plantation. Susan and I expended a great deal of energy trying to figure out how a four-year-old could have learned the things Jeff seemed to know about life in the antebellum South."

John shook his head and laughed at himself. "I don't mind telling you I felt like a fool when it finally occurred to me that perhaps he wasn't making it up after all. I mean, past lives are part of my profession. I dealt with similar experiences every day in my practice but failed to recognize the same thing in my own son."

"You're saying that Jeff remembers a former life?" Jenny asked cautiously.

"Not as much now as he used to," John said. "The memories are fading as he gets older. But every now and then . . ."

"That's . . . incredible," Jenny said.

"Not really. Small memories here and there of a past life are a great deal more common than most people believe. Some call it déjà vu. Have you ever heard of past-life regression?"

"Hypnosis?" Jenny asked.

"Yes. I hypnotized Jeff before he turned five and took him back. He's our connection with Oak Hollow,

Brett, the reason we have no need of you for publicity, if that's what we were after. Besides, I'm not quite unprincipled enough to resort to parlor games of that sort. Must be my strict Presbyterian upbringing."

Brett leaned against the mantel and felt resignation seep through him. Parlor games aside, he didn't believe in reincarnation. But others did. "You're saying your son once lived at Oak Hollow?"

"He did. He was Randall Hampton."

A cold chill rushed down Brett's spine. "The son of the house."

"That's right. Under hypnosis, he gave us details we have since been able to document. Details no four-year-old child could possibly have known or even imagined. During our research to find evidence that Randall Hampton had once lived in the area, we found this property, and everything fell into place. We were able to trace back far enough and prove many of the things Jeff told us."

"Did . . . did Jeff ever mention Randall's sister?" Jenny asked. "Or a friend?"

"You mean Anna and Seth."

Jenny nodded. As she told John about her nightmare and everything that had happened since she read *This Raging Madness,* Brett's stomach twisted itself into one huge knot. For the most part, John remained calm and professional, but excitement sparked in his eyes.

"Hell," Brett muttered, "if I believed in this crap, I'd bet the two of you were twins in a former life."

"You don't believe in reincarnation," John said.

Brett shook his head. "What difference does it make what I believe?"

"If what Jenny suspects is true, that whoever is after her is somehow connected to all this, then it might make a great deal of difference. Failing to learn from the past leaves you open to repeating it.''

"Learn what?" Brett demanded. "That Maudie Hampton murdered her cousin? Do you have any cousins around, Jen?"

"Brett—"

"It doesn't matter," he said curtly, cutting her off and turning to John. "Knowing everything there is to know won't make a damn bit of difference. Even if Jen's right, that still doesn't tell us who the stalker is, does it?"

John sighed. "No, it doesn't. But if Jenny is right, it tells you who the stalker isn't."

"I know, I know," Brett said tiredly. "We've been all over this. Jenny believes the stalker is someone we know and trust. But it doesn't fit with everything we know about Maudie. Anna may have trusted her, but Seth didn't. Randall didn't." He shook his head again. "None of your theories tells us who's after Jenny. I brought her here to give the police a chance to catch the bastard. Compared to that, the diary means nothing."

"You can say that after having read it? After seeing the proof with your own eyes that most of the things you wrote in your novel actually happened, right here at Oak Hollow? The people, the events? If you're that determined to deny that this story came out of your own subconscious memories, then I advise you to steer clear of the family cemetery behind the carriage house."

"Oh, God," Jenny whispered.

"I'm sorry." John reached over and put a hand on her arm. "I didn't mean to upset you."

Brett had heard enough. With angry strides he crossed behind the settee toward the door.

He felt the walls of the study closing in on him. Desperate to escape, he flung open the door.

With John's words ringing in his ears, Brett did the only thing he could—he headed outside, for fresh air and sunshine, for sanity.

He had no patience for the formal pathways through the garden, no desire to see or speak to anyone. What he needed, he thought as he headed past the stable into the woods that bordered the bayou, was about a rick of wood to chop. As a boy he'd hated the chore, but right now he wanted to smash something, to hack away at something that didn't want to be hacked.

Jenny rose to follow Brett.

"Do you mind some advice from a professional?" John asked her.

She paused and glanced at him over her shoulder.

"Give him a little time to himself. I hit him with quite a bit just now, I think. Why don't you give him a chance to mull it over?"

Jenny took in a slow, deep breath, then let it out. "You're right. My going after him won't help. He doesn't want to believe reincarnation is possible."

"Do you have any idea why?"

She did, but it wasn't her place to discuss Brett's past. "You'll have to ask him."

"Fair enough. You don't seem to have a problem accepting that you've lived before."

"How could I not accept it? I've been having that dream since I was ten years old."

"Do you still have it?"

"Yes." She rubbed her hands up her arms to ward off a sudden chill. "It gets . . . more real every time."

John leaned forward. "How do you mean?"

She shook her head and paced toward the fireplace, where Brett had stood. "I don't know. I guess I feel more threatened by it now."

"By the dream?"

"No, I know the dream can't hurt me. But the menace, the threat of danger seems so much more real, so close, when I wake up."

"Have you ever been regressed?"

"No. I've never felt the need to. I don't need to know any more than I already do. To be honest, I'm not at all curious. I just want the damn dream to leave me alone, and I want Brett to be safe."

"And you think he's not."

She shook her head again. "Not as long as someone is after me. He was nearly killed the day he drove my car." She shivered. "I'm just so frightened that history will repeat itself."

"That he will die in your place, as Seth died in Anna's."

"Yes."

"Did you read Maudie's diary?"

"No. Frankly, I'm not sure I want to."

"I don't blame you. It's pretty grim reading for me, and I'm an outsider to all this. But Jenny, if you're right and the person who's after you now is the same one who murdered you once before, don't you think it might behoove you to learn everything you can about her . . . or him?"

Brett ducked under a low-hanging branch and kept heading away from the house. He knew he was acting like a first-class jerk. There was no reason for him to have stormed out the way he had, no reason for the denial he kept nursing, but he couldn't seem to stop. He didn't want any of what had been discussed to be true; so, he figured with a wry twist of his mouth, if he denied it enough, it wouldn't be true.

A nice piece of stupidity if ever there was one. His reactions were way out of line and totally inappropriate. He had some serious thinking to do, and he knew he'd damn well better get to it before he returned to the house and had to face Jenny. And Dr. John Jacob Templeton, parapsychologist. A shrink, para or otherwise, would have a field day with him.

Not following any path, he walked deeper into the woods until all signs of civilization disappeared. The air was still and smelled heavily of pine. He found a bald cypress and sat down on one of its exposed knees to think. As screwed up as his head was right then, he doubted he could think and walk at the same time.

The answers to his problems were inside him. He knew they were there, had been there all along. He just didn't want to look. He didn't want to open the door on past pain, didn't want to subject himself to that. He'd come close when he'd told Jenny about his father. The door had cracked open that day, but thank God he'd been able to slam it shut again.

Like a child peeking through spread fingers at a scary movie, Brett stole a cautious, fearful look into his own heart. His palms turned clammy and his chest heaved with the effort to breathe. He tried to slam the door again, but it was no use. Behind eyes squeezed tightly shut, behind all the anger and denial, despite his will and the effort he expended to push it away, it was there. The root, the source of nearly every argument he'd ever had with Jenny, the reason for his refusal even to discuss the possibility of reincarnation, the answer to why he'd never forgiven his mother for her seances, why he so vehemently denied there was any such thing as life of any kind after death.

For if there was, if spirits could contact the living, if souls could be reborn into a new life and somehow gravitate toward those they'd known before—if souls had any choice at all in the matter—then that meant that the tiny seed of hope inside Brett that maybe he wasn't responsible for his father's death was in vain.

They'd been so damn close, he and his father. There hadn't been anything Brett couldn't tell or ask his dad, not anything. His dad had set a strong example of how a man ought to live his life, and never had Brett admired anyone more. God, the pain of his loss was still bone deep, even after all these years.

If there had been any way in heaven, hell, or anywhere in between, for Frank McCormick to reassure his son that he was not to blame for Frank's death, he would have done so. He would have bargained with God himself to keep Brett from suffering.

Unless it was true. Unless that one infinitesimal fragment of hope was wrong. Unless Brett really *was* to blame.

What that had to do precisely with reincarnation, he wasn't sure, but somehow, it all tied together in his mind.

Loose bark crumbled beneath his fingers as he gripped the cypress knee beneath him. He barely noticed the small stirring of air that caressed his face and told him his cheeks were wet. He felt raw, like his skin had been peeled away from his body and left every nerve ending exposed. He'd been careless, criminally so, and his father had died and left him to suffer the guilt alone forever with no chance to win forgiveness.

Inside his chest the pressure built and built until it erupted into a deep roar of anguish that set birds to flight and sent small mammals scurrying for cover.

* * *

Jenny was going to read Maudie Hampton's diary. She really was. But first she wanted to see Brett, talk to him, touch him, know that he was all right.

He obviously wasn't all right. He didn't come back for lunch. Arnold said he'd seen him take off into the woods to the west, but Jenny would not follow him. If he'd wanted her company, he wouldn't have gone off alone.

Besides, wandering the woods alone was unappealing at best. To think that she might come upon the very spot where Anna and Seth had died . . . No, she would sit out here on the back veranda and wait for Brett. The afternoon was warm, the sky clear, the garden and yard deserted.

She wondered where Brett was, what he was thinking, how he was feeling. The information from John was a lot to ask a man to accept when he didn't want to accept any of it.

From somewhere deep in the woods came a sound like none Jenny had ever heard. Chill bumps rose along her arms. It sounded as though some creature were in mortal pain. Jenny was no stranger to life and death in the woods—she'd grown up on a farm— but she'd never heard a sound so filled with anguish.

She rubbed her hands up and down her arms to chase away the chill.

"Brett," she whispered. "Where are you?"

He didn't know how long he'd been in the woods, nor how he'd come to be kneeling belly-down over a jutting cypress knee. The last thing he remembered was sitting down to think . . .

Ah, God. In a rush it all came back to him, the pain, the anguish. The guilt.

But there were things he understood now that he hadn't when he'd sat down. He understood that he'd spent all these years since his father's death waiting for someone to forgive him, to tell him it wasn't his fault.

It didn't matter anymore, he realized as he pushed himself from the cypress and began to walk aimlessly. It *was* his fault, and nobody was going to come along and pat him on the back and tell him all was forgiven. That was the reality, and he'd damn well better learn to deal with it. If he couldn't, he had no business pushing himself any further into Jenny's life. She deserved a man with his head on straight, a whole man with a whole heart, who could hand that heart to her intact, if only she would take it.

Jenny.

He couldn't face her yet. She wanted him to believe, to accept that he had lived and loved as Seth Taylor more than a hundred and thirty years ago, and died as Seth Taylor on this very plantation. John expected him to believe it as well. Brett felt like the only person in the nudist camp who wore clothes. He was right, and he was comfortable with it, but it didn't serve any purpose for him to be in constant disagreement with Jenny, never mind John.

Were their theories really so far out that he couldn't at least accept the possibility? If he was honest, he had to admit that their explanations made a hell of a lot more sense than his constant "coincidences." How many coincidences could a man pile one on top of the other before they toppled and buried him?

He smelled the water several yards before he broke from the trees into a large clearing on the banks of the Bayou Sara. Dank, heavy, the air was ripe with humidity and the smell of rotting vegetation.

Millions of people believed in reincarnation, he reminded himself. Who was he to say that he was right and they were wrong?

A small wooden pier hugged the bank at the water's edge. Three new boards in the middle testified that someone was keeping it up. He wondered if this was still Oak Hollow land or if he'd strayed onto a neighboring plantation.

He stood in the middle of the clearing and let the midday sun beat down on him. It felt good after the coolness of the dense woods. He breathed deeply and concentrated on relaxing. It was time he headed back to the house. Jenny would be wondering what had happened to him.

A gust of wind rippled the grass and stirred the bordering pines and scrub oaks. He thought he caught a whiff of smoke in the air. A moment later the ground seemed to shift.

Impossible. The ground didn't shift in Louisiana, did it?

Ghostlike, the gray outline of a building shimmered before him like a heat wave as the edges of his vision dimmed. Around him the clearing seemed to spin. There was a tremendous roar in his ears. And heat. Such heat blasting at him as though he were standing before a furnace. Or a burning building. Or the gates of hell.

A blinding pain struck his left temple. Brett squeezed his eyes shut against the agony and swore. What the hell . . .?

As fast as it came, it disappeared. All of it. The pain, the roaring in his ears. The phantom building.

He was cold. Deep-down-to-the-bone cold, yet he knew the day was warm.

It was this place. There was something here, something he didn't want to know about, didn't want to see, would not acknowledge.

Jenny. He wanted to see Jenny, *had* to. *Now.* He needed to touch her and hold her and know she was all right.

As he stepped back into the woods, he glanced over his shoulder at the clearing and thought of Seth and Anna, two people he'd met in a dream and who would not leave him alone. If they had ever lived, then this, he knew, was where they had died.

With another shiver, he turned his back on the clearing and headed home. He would not bring Jenny to this place.

Chapter Twenty

Jenny saw him come out of the woods beyond the stables. She'd thought she would sit here and wait for him, give him these last few moments to himself, but one look at his ravaged face told her something was drastically wrong. In a flash, she was up and running, rushing toward him.

The way he caught her to his chest when she reached him confirmed her suspicions. "What is it?" She held on tight and searched his face. "What's wrong?"

He kissed her as though he'd been away for a month, hard, desperate, hungry.

"You're scaring me," she whispered when they came up for air.

"I'm sorry." He met her gaze, and his eyes were fierce. "I didn't mean to. I just . . ." He raised his face to the sky and closed his eyes while his hands roamed up and down her back. "I shouldn't have run out on you the way I did."

"Not then," she told him. "Now. Just now, the look in your eyes. What's wrong, Brett?"

He let out a slow breath and rubbed his cheek against hers. "Nothing now. You always make everything feel right. I was in the woods telling myself what a jerk I was being, and I just wanted to get back to you. Come upstairs with me, Jen."

She shivered as his warm breath tickled her ear. "Now? In the middle of the afternoon?"

His teeth teased her lobe. "You have something against the middle of the afternoon?"

Jenny hesitated. Cupping his head in both hands, she pushed him away and searched his face again. This time his eyes were clear and bright, bluer than blue. And hot. "The only thing I have against the middle of the afternoon is that we're here, and the bed is a long way away."

His smile was quick and lethal. "Then what are we waiting for?"

They went into the house through the back door and took the back stairs to their room. On the landing they met Hester.

"I was just returning the quilt that belongs in the room you're using. I think I finally got all the musty smell out of it, but if I didn't, let me know."

"I'm sure it will be fine," Jenny said. She stepped into the room and saw the quilt instantly. Its many bright colors had faded with age, but the Grandmother's Flower Garden pattern was unmistakable. Hester had left the quilt draped over the foot of the bed.

One look, and Jenny felt her throat tighten inexplicably. Pressure built in her chest and behind her eyes. She stepped closer, brushed the old, old fabric with the tips of her fingers . . . and burst out crying.

For one awful instant, Brett stood frozen in the

doorway. Then he bolted to Jenny's side. "Jen? Jen, what's wrong?"

Hester stuck her head in the door. "What happened?"

Brett held Jenny from behind as she stared at the quilt and sobbed like a baby. "I don't know. She just ... Jen? Baby? Ah, hell, Jen, what's wrong?"

When she turned to him, her eyes were big and swamped with tears. "I don't—know," she managed between sobs. "I looked at the q-quilt, and—I don't know. I just ... f-felt so *sad.*"

"My, oh, my." Hester's eyes were wide and stunned. "My, oh, my."

"What's going on?" Susan joined Hester. "What's happened?"

Jenny sniffed. "Nothing. I'm fine. Lord, this is embarrassing."

"I think," Hester said slowly to Susan, "you'd better show her the other diary."

Startled, Susan said, "What for?"

Jenny and Brett shared a look. "What other diary?" they asked in unison.

June 6, 1857

Oh, Great Lord in Heaven, help me. We buried our Dear Sweet Anna today, and her own Beloved Seth. They perished when our cotton warehouse on the Bayou caught fire and burned. I can only assume they went there to be alone for a few moments before their Engagement was to be announced. But at Midnight during the ball, when Randolph rose to make the Toast, the Happy Couple was not to be found.

A shout drew us to the back Gallery, where we saw the flames leaping into the night above the treetops. Such a terrible, tragic accident to befall two people so young and so deeply in love.

That was three days ago, on Anna's nineteenth Birthday. It is too, too, cruel, Randolph says, for God to have taken our Daughter on her Birthday. This morning he said, "Mary, I cannot endure it that our Daughter is gone." I wanted to agree that I, too, could not bear it, but for my Husband's and Son's sake I put on a strong face and told them that of course we could endure it, because we have no Choice. God would not give us this Pain if he knew we could not withstand it.

Randall, the Poor Boy, is beside himself. But he is not a Boy, and that I must remember. At twenty-and-six he is a Man. Not only did he lose his Sister, but Seth was his Best Friend. I shall have to see about a Wife for our Son, to take his mind off this most tragic of Losses.

As I write tonight in this Journal I have one hand resting on the quilt Anna and I made together. The Grandmother's Flower Garden quilt we made from the dresses of my Dear Departed Mother. It did so help Anna to get over her grief last year at losing her Favorite Grandmother. Perhaps if I keep it near me now I will remember the tears, both happy and sad, that my Dear Daughter and I shed as we pieced the top and quilted the layers together. As I keep this quilt at my side, so shall I Forever keep our Daughter in my Heart.

Dear Lord, take my Beautiful Angel to your breast and hold her dear. While this Earth has grown dark and dismal with her passing, Heaven will be the sweeter for her Presence.

With Susan and Hester on either side of her on the parlor sofa, John in the adjacent chair, and Brett standing behind the sofa with his hands on Jenny's shoulders, Jenny slipped the satin bookmark in place and closed Mary Hampton's journal.

She understood now about the quilt, why it had moved her to tears. She nearly started crying again, reading how Mary Hampton had kept the quilt at hand to feel closer to her daughter.

But Mary Hampton had thought Anna and Seth's deaths were *accidents*. Not a word was mentioned about Maudie.

"I don't believe it." Terror and anguish and red-hot fury boiled in Jenny's chest. "I don't *believe* she got *away* with it! She got away with murder!"

Hester slowly raised her black eyes to Jenny. "Who *are* you?" she whispered.

Jenny glanced up at Hester, then away. She couldn't speak past the lump of emotions in her throat.

"You're her, aren't you?" Hester asked quietly. "You're Miss Mary's Anna."

Next to Jenny, Susan gasped.

"Did you tell him the story?" Hester nodded toward Brett. "Is that how he knew to write it?"

Jenny craned her neck to look at Brett. An ironic smile curved her lips. "I didn't have to tell him anything. He knew."

"My, oh, my." Hester stood slowly. "Oh my, oh my. You'd be him, then. You'd be Miss Anna's Seth."

Brett's hands tightened on Jenny's shoulders. "My name," he said fiercely, "is Brett McCormick. Who the hell are you?"

"Me?" Hester let out a low chuckle. "Why, I'm nobody important."

"Not much," John said with a laugh of his own.

"Just the living proof that what took place in Brett's book really happened."

"Now, Dr. John, don't go making a specimen out of me." She rose from the sofa and stood before Brett and Jenny, her head held at a regal angle, queen to subjects.

"Susan told you that I've lived in this parish all my life, and that's true. So did my mother before me, my grandmother, my great grandmother, clear on back to my great-great—oh, my, there must be about four greats in there before we get back to Granddaddy Saul. He was a grown man when they brought him here from Virginia to help build Hampton House. That was the name of this place back before The War. Hampton House. It was built by Randolph Hampton for his wife Mary and their young son. By my calculations, that would have been around 1835. Near as we can figure, that was the year Delilah was born— Granddaddy Saul's youngest granddaughter—and she was the first child born here, white or black. Miss Anna came along about three years later."

"Hester is the one who helped us find this property," Susan told them. "Our investigation of the things Jeff said under hypnosis led us to this area. Hester is a recognized authority on local history, as well as a storyteller at the library in Saint Francisville."

"When we told her about some of the things Jeff had mentioned, she knew exactly who and what we were talking about," John added.

"That's right." Hester smoothed a hand down her skirt. "Some of the things they told me were the same stories that had been handed down in my family for generations."

"In fact," John said, "she knew a great deal more about this place than Jeff did. She's the one who showed us the house that wasn't on the survey. And she told us about Maudie and Anna and Seth,'' he added quietly. ''She told us six months before Susan found the diaries in the attic. At least a year before your book was published, Brett.''

Brett released his grip on Jenny's shoulders and rubbed his hands over his face. What they were telling him—all of them, Jenny, John, Jeff, Hester, the diaries—was that the things he'd thought had come strictly from his imagination had actually happened.

He dropped his hands and stared at Hester. ''Tell me this. If your ancestors were slaves on the original plantation, why would you come back here? Why would you want anything to do with this place?''

Hester's smile was full of dignity when she answered. ''You mean, why wouldn't I want to burn the reminder of our slavery to the ground?''

''Something like that.''

''I have a great respect for history, Mr. McCormick, even unpleasant history. Yes, my ancestors were slaves, but I find that nothing to be ashamed of.''

''I didn't mean you should.''

''No, I suppose you didn't. While I greatly resent what happened back then, I'm proud of my family. White people can crow all they like about the glory of these fine old mansions, but the truth is, it was *my* family who actually built this one. A hundred and sixty years ago my ancestors built this house with the sweat of their brows and the blood of their backs, and look at it. Left neglected since before I was born, but it's still standing. I take great pride in that. Besides,'' she added with a laugh, ''my ancestors may have been slaves, but I'm not. The Templetons pay me a small fortune to take care of this place.''

''You can say that again,'' John grumbled good-naturedly.

Hester arched a regal brow. "You're welcome to hire someone cheaper."

"Never mind." John raised his hands in defense. "Forget I said anything. But you might put Jenny's mind somewhat to rest and tell her that Maudie didn't entirely get away with murder."

Hester paused. There were many things she could tell Jenny, things even John didn't know. But she could not bring herself to tell Jenny that Maudie *had* gotten away with murder, many times.

"Later in Miss Mary's diary she finally starts to suspect that Maudie had something to do with Anna and Seth's deaths. She wasn't ever able to prove it, but she did confront Maudie."

"What happened?" Jenny asked.

Hester shook her head. "Mary's diary ends there, and Maudie's ends at about the same time." But not the story, Hester thought, and not the murders. There was another diary, in which Maudie tells how she silenced Mary Hampton for good by arranging a fatal accident.

This time, however, Maudie was not as careful as she had been in the past. This time there'd been a witness—Delilah. The year was 1863, and The War, as most folks today still called it—"The Wo-wah"—raged all around them. Slaves were running away in droves, set free by the Union soldiers.

No Union troops had come to Hampton House, but Delilah had heard the talk of freedom. Knowing how Maudie liked to write down in her journal everything she did, Delilah had waited two weeks after Mary's death, then sneaked into Maudie's room and stolen the book. She couldn't read, but she knew what was in there.

When Miss Maudie discovered the book was missing, she knew Delilah had taken it. Delilah threatened to give the book to the authorities if Maudie didn't write out papers giving her and her family their freedom. Maudie refused and the women fought. In her mind no longer a slave, Delilah fought for her life, for her freedom. Maudie hit her head on the sharp corner of the fireplace in this very room and died. Old Saul had helped Delilah throw the body into the bayou that night.

Just standing in this room now filled Hester with such anguish over what her family had suffered, yet such pride that they had stood up for themselves and wrested their freedom from the hands of evil.

But that was a family secret, never to be told to outsiders. Jenny Franklin didn't need to know all that. She didn't need the added heartache of knowing Maudie had killed again.

"Word has it," Hester told Jenny, "that Maudie fell in the bayou, hit her head, and drowned. Right there at the dock where the old warehouse used to be."

The dock, Brett thought. Where the warehouse used to be. Where Anna and Seth were murdered. *The clearing.* He'd stood on that very spot less than an hour ago and smelled smoke, felt the ground shift beneath his feet. He'd felt the presence of death. Now he learned it wasn't only Anna's and Seth's deaths, but Maudie's, too. "Poetic justice," he murmured.

"Yes," Jenny whispered. "Poetic justice."

Then Brett laughed. "I'm afraid I didn't let ol' Maudie off so easily in the sequel."

John straightened in his chair. "You've written a sequel?"

"What did you do with her?" Hester's eyes twinkled.

"When Randall figures out what she's done, Maudie takes off across the country, leaving a trail of dead bodies. What happens when he catches her is *not* pretty." Brett grinned for the first time in hours.

"Randall," Jenny muttered. "What did happen to Randall?"

"He was killed in The War," Susan offered softly.

Brett eyed John, then Hester. "See? I told you I made it up."

"Not the first one."

"I made that one up, too." The reply came automatically, but he wasn't sure how much of it he believed any longer.

"Did you?" Hester asked softly. "Or did some part of your subconscious mind remember it? Even a cat has nine lives, you know. Don't bother," she said to cut off his objection. "There's denial on your lips, but in your heart you know the truth. Yes, sir, Mr. Brett McCormick. Your heart remembers."

In the tide of emotions over Mary's diary and Hester's revelations, Jenny had nearly forgotten about the quilt, until she and Brett returned to their room later that afternoon.

Hexagons within hexagons, color within color in ever-widening bands until they met and joined another hexagon on each side. A veritable garden of flowers. Grandmother's Flower Garden. Each tiny piece hand-stitched to the next, then the next. Made with devoted hands from the worn clothing of a lost loved one, as both a heartfelt reminder and a practical necessity for warmth in the winter months.

Such painstaking work. Jenny could almost feel the prick of a needle against her fingertip, the press of a thimble. She could feel the heartache and love that went into each stitch. The tears shed and laughter shared around the quilting frame when the layers, with their warm cushion of batting between them, were quilted together.

"Are you all right with that? Do you want me to take it out of here?"

Jenny's heart constricted at the concern in Brett's voice. "No." She turned to him. "No, I'm fine now. It's a beautiful quilt. We might be glad of it if that storm in the Rockies makes it this far while we're still here."

She strolled to the French doors and opened them. "For now, the weather is wonderful, though, isn't it?"

"Is that what you want to talk about?" he asked. "The weather?"

With her hands braced behind her, Jenny leaned back against the door frame and rolled her head to look at him. "You knew she'd gotten away with it, didn't you?"

"Who?" He strolled to stand beside her in the doorway.

"Maudie, with murder. You read her diary, so you knew."

"Yeah," he said, looking out at a sky such a brilliant blue that it hurt the eyes. "Yeah, I knew."

And it was going to happen again, Jenny thought, if they couldn't figure out who was stalking her back in New Orleans. She was glad to have Brett away from there, away from the danger, glad to be here . . . Oh, good God. Why hadn't she thought of it sooner? If she returned to New Orleans alone, she could draw the stalker out, get him to make a try at her, and Brett wouldn't be anywhere around to get caught in the middle!

"What's that look mean?"

Jenny cursed to feel a blush stain her cheeks. "What look?" she asked stupidly.

Brett eyed her with blatant suspicion. "Well, it *was* a look that said you were up to something and I damn sure wasn't going to like it when I found out. Now it looks more like guilt. Spill it, Jen."

Jenny did her best to school her features in a semblance of calm innocence, but feared she failed miserably. She couldn't control her pulse, but she gave her breathing a shot. "Actually," she said to him, "you probably won't like what I was thinking."

"Why am I not surprised?"

"It's nothing drastic, I promise." She wandered to the edge of the veranda to the spot that had become her favorite place to lean out and view the gardens and guest cottages. "I just realized that when we came here, we planned to stay only a day or two. Now we're involved in all these plans for next weekend." She turned to face him, bracing herself against the wrought-iron railing. "Brett, I can't leave my clients for that long, and Harley only agreed to cover for me for a few days. I really need to get back to New Orleans."

Brett opened his mouth, no doubt to protest, but she cut him off.

"That doesn't mean you can't stay, though. You have to, really, now that you're going to be the draw, so to speak, for the ball Saturday. I mean, Grace will be here, and she's inviting the governor. You really do have to stay, and I understand that. It's not like it will be forever. I mean—"

"No."

"—It'll only be a few days. You'll be busy, and—. What do you mean, no?"

"You're not going home without me."

"I don't recall asking your permission," she said coolly.

"That won't work, either."

"What?"

"Picking a fight with me. We don't have anything to fight about. If you go home, I'm going with you. That's all there is to it."

"You can't," she claimed. "You have to be here for the ball Saturday night."

"So we'll drive back Saturday for the ball. You're not going back without me. In fact," he added with a slight grin, "you can't. Unless you're planning on stealing my car."

"I don't see what the big deal is," she grumbled.

"The big deal is, I know you better than you give me credit for. You think you can go home and leave me stuck here out of your way while you make a target out of yourself for that damn stalker."

Another blush betrayed her.

"Jen, look. Maybe I was wrong about some things. Hell, even I have to admit that all these things around us, things we're learning, things we've felt, can't all be coincidences."

Jenny's heart leaped. "Do you mean that?"

"I don't know. But I'm willing to admit . . ." He braced his hands low on his lips and threw his head back. His eyes slid closed. "I'm willing to admit there might be possibilities that I hadn't considered."

"Brett . . ."

He opened his eyes and met her gaze. "But I don't buy that this creep in New Orleans has anything to do with any of it. I don't care if you once lived as Anna Hampton or Lizzie Borden. All I know or care about is that someone has been trying to hurt you, and I'm not about to let you out of my sight. If you go home, I go with you."

With her heart pounding, Jenny moved to stand before him. She placed her hands on his chest. "Do you mean that?"

"Damn straight I mean it. You're not going any-where alone."

"No, I mean about the other. Are you saying you're willing to admit that what we have here might be something more than simply the world's longest string of coincidences?"

She saw the ambivalence in his eyes, but his hands were warm and gentle when they covered hers.

"The truth? I honestly don't know anymore, Jen. But I'm feeling things . . . Hell, maybe it's this house, with its history and its atmosphere. I don't know. I may never know. Does it matter? Does it have anything to do with how you and I feel about each other here and now?"

"Of course it doesn't, not like you mean." It was time, she thought, to think of other things for a while. She didn't want to push him anymore, didn't want their different beliefs to come between them, and they would if she kept hounding him.

Other things, she thought, deliberately relaxing against him with a smile. "Just how do we feel about each other?"

His answering smile spoke of relief, and . . . other things. "Why don't you come with me," he said, wrapping his arms around her and pulling her into the bedroom, "and we'll . . . talk about it."

She wound her arms around his neck and held on as he lowered them both to the bed. "And if I don't want to talk?"

"Even better. I seem to remember that we had specific plans for how to pass the afternoon when we came up here earlier."

"I . . . ah . . ." And then she couldn't talk, because he was kissing her senseless.

* * *

"I don't know what that publicist of yours is doing," John told Brett that evening over dinner, "but we're already getting reservations for guests and RSVPs for the ball."

"What're aressveepees?" Jeff wanted to know. He ran the separate letters together and made a single word out of them.

"Répondez, s'il vous plaît," Susan answered.

"Oh." Jeff frowned. "I knew that."

John pierced him with a look. "Eat your green beans, Johnny Reb. That nice lady on the back porch today who patched up your gunshot wound and saved your life cooked them especially for you."

Susan rolled her eyes. "And you claim Hester encourages him."

"Of course Hester encourages him," Hester said, as she brought in a second batch of dinner rolls and placed them next to Brett. It hadn't taken her long to realize he had a weakness for them. "It can't hurt a man to remember his past mistakes and shortcomings so he can do a better job of things this time around."

Jenny watched, fascinated, as Brett and Hester did battle with their eyes. Hester was pushing him in ways Jenny never had. And if Jenny wasn't mistaken, Hester was making headway.

"Is that how it works?" Brett asked the woman.

"That's how it ought to work," Hester answered. "Those who don't learn from the past are likely doomed to repeat it."

That thought stayed in Brett's mind throughout dinner. The idea wasn't new to him. He understood the principles of reincarnation. A soul kept returning to life on earth to learn, to grow, until it reached a state of ... perfection? That wasn't the right word. Grace. Until it reached a state of grace.

He agreed that the theory made some sense. He agreed that *something* strange was happening to him, around him. There were, as he'd admitted to Jenny, entirely too many coincidences, even for the most devout of doubters like him.

Still, he wasn't ready to embrace the idea of reincarnation. He wasn't ready to admit that he had lived a hundred and fifty years ago. That his name had been Seth. That he had loved a woman named Anna. He preferred the here and now, and here and now he was Brett McCormick and he loved a woman named Jenny Franklin.

The thought perhaps should have startled him, that he loved her, but it didn't. That was what this constant insatiable need was for her smile, her touch, the sound of her voice. The peace he felt with her that he'd felt at no other time in his life.

He'd never admitted it before, not even to himself, but yes, he was in love with Jenny Franklin. And suddenly the idea shook him.

He couldn't, *wouldn't,* let anything happen to her.

Chapter Twenty-One

Preparations for the weekend began in earnest on Tuesday. The house became as busy and crowded as an anthill with the invasion of additional household staff and constant phone calls from the media, the governor's office, Brett's publisher. There were conferences with caterers and musicians and florists.

For the ball, the sliding doors between the front and back parlors would be pushed open, leaving one long room that ran the length of the house. Under Susan and Hester's critical eyes, furniture would be moved against the walls, and carpets rolled up and stored. The oak floor would be waxed and polished to a mirror shine.

A buffet would be set up in the formal dining room, and the caterers agreed to wear period costumes.

"Costumes!" Susan shrieked. It was Wednesday morning before she realized everyone needed costumes. Within minutes of her cry, the family, Jenny, and Brett were piled into John's passenger van and headed for Baton Rouge to find costumes. Hester remained behind to oversee the preparations.

Whispering and laughing, Susan and Jenny hid in the dressing room of the costumer and refused to let John and Brett see their dresses.

"Can I see, Mom?" Jeff demanded from outside the closed dressing room door.

"No," Susan called back. "You'll squeal."

"I will not."

"Yes you will."

"No I won't. Dad!" he called. "Mom won't let me in! I think she's on to us!"

Susan gave a deep chuckle and helped Jenny out of her gown. "What'd I tell you? They sent a spy."

The five of them stopped for lunch before heading back for Oak Hollow. Once there, everyone but Brett scattered to various jobs, leaving him at loose ends. Even Jenny was busy loading new accounting software onto John's hard drive.

Brett figured he'd be busy enough tonight and tomorrow. Kay had called and was on her way with a list of changes his editor was asking for on his current book. Hell, the book had been bought and scheduled for publication on the basis of Brett's synopsis. That had been months ago. Now, without seeing the finished manuscript, some yo-yo had decided there needed to be changes.

Brett promised himself he wasn't going to call his editor and tell him exactly what he thought of him until he'd seen the changes being requested. He should have insisted that Kay fax them, but she'd been planning to come anyway. Grace had recruited her to help handle on-site details for her over the weekend. Grace herself would arrive tomorrow.

Leaning now against the doorway to the front parlor, Brett smiled at the excited gleam in Susan's eyes.

"What do you think? Enough room for people to waltz?"

"Plenty of room," John answered. To prove his claim, he seized her dramatically in his arms and with sweeping steps and a booming count of "*One*-two-three, *one*-two-three," waltzed her down the length of the room and back again.

Susan tossed back her head and laughed.

The edges of Brett's vision turned gray. Beneath his feet, the floor seemed to tilt. He gripped the door frame to steady himself. He tried to call out a warning—of what? Earthquake? In Louisiana?

This felt like the same thing that had happened to him in the clearing beside the bayou. Maybe he was coming down with a bug. That would explain the dizziness, and the way his strength seemed to drain out through the bottoms of his feet.

Feelings, impressions drifted around him in ever-nearing circles. Whirling. He felt himself whirling, and there was music, grand and full bodied. Laughter floated to him again, but it was both closer, yet farther away. Not in distance . . . in time. His laughter, and *hers*.

The rustle of silk, the murmur of voices beneath the music. Excitement. Love. A young woman with glorious blond hair looking up at him with total devotion as he waltzed her around this very room.

"What are you doing?"

The sound of young Jeff's voice jolted Brett back to the present.

The present. As though he'd been . . . in the past.

Absurd. But his fingers ached from gripping the door frame and the strains of a waltz still hummed through his mind.

He'd been here before, had waltzed in this very

room with the woman he loved. Right before he'd lost everything.

"Your mother and I are dancing," John told his son.

Imagination, Brett thought. His had always been vivid. He used it to make his living. He'd seen a similar scene in dozens of old movies. His mind had just chosen that particular moment to conjure one up, that was all.

He swallowed. That was all it was. Some old scene from some old movie.

If it had felt more personal than that, it was just his imagination. Just as it was his imagination that called up a growing sense of foreboding.

He had a sudden, desperate need to see Jenny, to hold her. Acting on it, he pushed away from the door and strode toward the back of the house, faster, faster, vague yet potent warnings shouting in his head, panic rising to his throat. By the time he shoved the swinging door out of his way and burst into the kitchen he was nearly running.

Jenny stood with her back to the door and held a crystal glass up to the light of the window to check for spots. She really shouldn't be handling Susan's good crystal, she thought, as the tension in her shoulders wound another notch tighter. She was jumpy and on edge, and it was a miracle she hadn't broken a glass yet.

There was no reason as far as she could see for her nerves to stretch as they'd been doing all afternoon. No logical reason. There was just this . . . feeling, as though something terrible was about to happen. She didn't like it, not one damn bit.

Maybe it was the house, or reading Mary Hampton's

diary a couple of days ago. Jenny had yet to read
Maudie's, and wondered now if she even would.
Whenever she thought about it, dread knotted in her
stomach.

Maybe it was the ball, just a few days away. Would
it remind her of her dream? She hadn't dreamed of
music or waltzing, but in her dream she had just left
the party. Was that what had her grinding her teeth?

Something was going to happen.

When the kitchen door whacked against the wall,
she shrieked and whirled. The glass slipped from her
fingers and shattered in the sink.

"What's wrong?" Brett demanded.

"What is it?" Jenny cried at the same time, her
heart knocking against her ribs.

Brett rushed to her side, his gaze sweeping the
room.

"What?" Jenny cried again. "There's no one
here."

He gripped her upper arms and searched her face.
"You screamed."

"Because you scared the crap out of me, crashing
through the door like that. What happened?"

He let out a rush of breath and pulled her to his
chest. "Nothing. I just . . . I just wanted to see you,
that's all."

Jenny felt the tension in him. It matched hers.
"Let's get out of here and take a walk."

They cleaned up the broken glass, then left by the
back door. Hand in hand, they entered the maze of
short hedges and colorful flowerbeds. The sunshine
felt good on her head, her shoulders. By the time
they reached the gazebo, Jenny could feel herself
start to relax. Brett's hand, too, eased its bruising grip
on hers. Yet neither suggested they enter the gazebo.

As they'd done every time before, they walked past it in silence.

Beyond the cottages, past the carriage house, where the sound of a hammer rang out on some last minute repair, past the barn and stables, Jenny and Brett entered the shelter of the woods. There was variety here, pines, cypress, and live oaks vying for space and precious light. Their branches intermingled and spread cool shade beneath. The air smelled sweet and damp, of fertile soil and growing things.

They didn't talk, but only shared the peace, the silence. At the edge of a small rill that led to the Bayou Sara, duty reminded them both that they should be helping John and Susan, and in any case, Brett would not take Jenny any closer to the clearing he'd found along the bayou. They angled back toward the house and came across a clearing they hadn't seen before on the far side of the carriage house. The old family graveyard.

Jenny stopped short, not sure she wanted to inspect the aged headstones resting there.

Brett, too, hesitated, but something stronger than common sense pushed him forward. He'd written a novel. He'd made up a story from the depths of his imagination and put it on paper. Now, every turn he took led to more proof that what he'd written had actually happened. The feel of the house. Maudie's dairy. Mary's diary. Hester's family history. Jenny's nightmare.

No one had to authenticate the diaries for Brett to believe they were indeed as old as they stated they were. Would the headstones in the family plot confirm what he could no longer deny?

"Brett?"

"I have to, Jen."

A filigreed wrought-iron fence enclosed the twenty

or so graves laid out in haphazard rows. The grass was neatly trimmed, and flowers had been planted in places. Brett wondered idly who decided which graves got flowers. There were tall, ornate headstones of angels and cherubs, and more sedate rectangles and squares of granite and marble. Moss grew in cracks. Wind and sun and time had smoothed sharp edges. People had been buried here as late as 1910, he noted as he walked the short rows.

The skin along the back of his neck prickled. Without knowing why, he turned and looked behind him, to the last row, the one he'd yet to walk.

"Jesus." There they were. The Hamptons, Randolph and Mary, side by side beneath a double granite marker. Randall Hampton had been laid to rest beside his father, both men apparently killed during the Civil War. A deep sadness settled in Brett's chest as he stared at Randall's grave. This man had been Seth Taylor's closest friend. They'd shared their first drink, their first smoke, their first woman. They'd been as close as brothers. They would have become brothers with Seth's marriage to Anna.

Brett studied the elder Hamptons' headstone. Mary had outlived her husband by one year, her son by two. How had it felt to bury them both after losing her daughter? And where—

There. Oh, sweet Jesus. *Anna.* Her name seemed to whisper through his soul. She was buried next to her mother, and the sight of her grave sent grief, sharp and hot, crashing into him. *Anna.* And next to her, Seth. A chill raced down his spine. The dates of their deaths matched. June 3, 1857. Anna's nineteenth birthday.

From outside the fence Jenny saw Brett swallow heavily and knew what he'd found. She didn't want to go and look, didn't need to, but she couldn't seem to stop herself. Quietly, reverently, she walked through the gate and stood just behind Brett's shoulder, at the foot of Anna's grave.

Deep, profound sadness flooded her. This was no stranger's grave. This was the final resting place of the last earthly remains of a part of Jenny Franklin. That life, the one that had been Anna's, had been cut short, far too short.

Anna and Seth should have had their time together. They should have been allowed to love each other and raise a family and grow old together.

Jenny expected to feel anger for the way that other, older part of herself had been cheated, but all she felt was this crushing sadness. She squeezed her eyes shut against the pain.

She must have made a sound, for the next thing she knew, Brett's strong arms were holding her with infinite gentleness.

Brett hadn't heard her approach. By the time he realized she was there, tears were streaming down her cheeks. He slipped his arms around her and eased her head onto his shoulder.

They held each other a long time, until he felt Jenny's tears subsided. Until some of the sadness slipped away.

"Anna and Seth, whoever they were, have been dead a long, long time," he said quietly. "Jenny and Brett are very much alive."

"Yes." Jenny wiped the last of the moisture from her eyes and looked up at him. The gray depths were sparkling clear. "And I think we should celebrate that fact."

Brett smiled slowly. "Oh, yeah? What did you have in mind?"

"Weeellll . . ." She lowered her lashes and pursed

her lips. "I'm sure if we went to our room we could think of something."

Whatever dark feelings he'd had fell away. "I'll race you."

Laughing, they dashed from the graveyard to the house, from the damp shadows into the sunlight.

They never made it upstairs. Kay and Grace had arrived.

"Brett, there you are." Kay rushed toward him and held out a hand, which Brett took.

Kay looked . . . different, Jenny thought. She'd lost weight and had had her hair cut and styled. She was a very attractive woman. And when she turned her dark-eyed gaze on Jenny, she fairly radiated animosity.

So, Jenny thought. That's the way the wind blows. She'd been right all along about Kay's feelings for Brett. The secretary was in love with him.

From Grace there was merely a measure of reserved coolness. She was brisk and polite and all business. She and John and Susan went to John's office to discuss details of the ball.

Brett and Kay took over the library.

Brett, too, noticed the changes in Kay, and he remembered both Jenny's comment and Grace's warning about Kay's feelings for him. That was why he made sure to leave the door open and his laptop between them. He watched every word he said, every move he made, to make sure he kept things friendly and professional.

He felt uncomfortable as hell the whole time.

They broke for dinner, and Brett was relieved to be with Jen for a while. He made a deliberate point of touching her, kissing her in front of the others. He wanted to be certain Kay understood. It occurred to him to wonder how Grace was taking his rather public attentions to Jenny, but Grace responded with the same amused tolerance as did Hester. Brett was relieved.

After dinner he and Kay went back to work, but things only seemed worse. Now, instead of quick glances and shy smiles, she looked . . . hurt.

Dammit, he didn't want to hurt her. But better a small hurt now than to let her think he would ever look at her as anything other than a friend and business associate.

God, he couldn't wait to call it a night and get upstairs to Jen. Only with her did he feel he was on solid ground.

The one called Maudie lay in the dark that night and stared at the ceiling over the bed. The throbbing behind her eyes was no less painful for all its familiarity.

It was time to end it. This ridiculous liaison between Seth and that little bitch—. No, not Seth. The ache in her head grew worse. Brett. Brett McCormick. The bitch was Jenny Franklin. And the bitch had to die.

I've tried before, but this time I won't fail. She will not leave this place alive.

It was the only way. The only way of getting Brett to notice *her*. The bitch had to die. And soon. *Soon.*

Chapter Twenty-Two

The next morning, as Brett watched Jen slip out the bedroom door, he felt the edges of his temper start to fray. He wanted to spend more time alone with her, and he needed to come to terms in his own mind as to just what the house, the diary, the headstones in the cemetery meant. There seemed to be little time for either.

He desperately wanted to keep Jenny safe. That was why he'd brought her to Oak Hollow, why he'd insisted that she stay when she'd wanted to go home the other day. Now, he felt the skin on the back of his neck grow tighter each hour and couldn't say why. He had a need to take her away from this place, these memories, his obligations be damned. Jenny was more important than any obligation.

But how would he get her to cooperate when she was so damned determined to keep *him* safe and somehow trap the stalker on her own? Did she think he didn't know that was why she'd wanted to go home alone?

He threw off the covers and swung his legs over the side of the bed. If he didn't get a move on, he'd still be in the shower when she came back with their morning coffee. He'd offered to go get it himself this morning, but she had refused. She said she was enjoying the routine.

Since they'd been here, she had gone downstairs every morning and brought back a tray. They'd sat together on the veranda, sipping coffee and watching the day come to life. Jen liked to lean out from the railing and touch the morning sunlight with her fingers.

God, he loved her.

He'd just stepped out of the shower and into his jeans a few minutes later when he heard her scream.

As Jenny entered the kitchen, the aroma of croissants wafted from the oven and made her stomach growl.

Hester laughed with approval. "They'll be done in a minute. Take some with you. You could stand to put on a few pounds."

"You sound like my mother," Jenny grumbled good-naturedly. Then she smiled. "But I can't resist fresh-baked bread of any kind and neither can Brett, so I'll wait."

By the time Jenny had the tray ready, with two mugs and an insulated carafe of fresh, hot coffee, the croissants were done. Hester lined a small basket with a linen napkin and placed four steaming rolls inside. A couple of saucers and knives, a small bowl of honey butter and another filled with Hester's homemade blackberry jam, and Jenny was set.

She carried the tray out through the dining room and up the stairs. At the second step from the top, the carpet shifted beneath her foot and tossed her hard against the banister. She felt it give beneath the impact, heard it crack. In sheer desperation she threw her weight in the opposite direction. She lost her balance, and her hold on the tray. The tray went over the banister and crashed to the floor below. Jenny screamed as she felt herself tumble head first down the stairs.

Carpet scraped her arms and burned. She tried to stop her descent but managed only to knock her wrist hard against the banister. Her head and back, knees and shins and rear took a beating. On and on she fell until finally she thought to cover her head with her arms.

At the foot of the stairs she lay dazed, trying to take stock of her injuries. By the time she realized the worst she'd suffered were a few bruises and carpet burns and one severe dent in her dignity, Brett was at her side. She felt like a clumsy fool.

"Are you hurt?" His voice and hands were frantic as they rushed over her. "What happened? Don't move, you might have broken something."

"I did."

"What? Where?"

"The dishes," she said with a groan. "I'm fine, but I dropped—"

"Jenny!" Susan cried from the landing.

"What happened?" John demanded as they started down the stairs.

"Watch out for the loose carpet," Jenny called out.

"Are you all right?" Susan cried.

"I'm all right." By the time she sat up with Brett's help, John and Susan had joined them. "I'm not hurt. Just my pride, I think. And maybe my rear," she added ruefully as she rubbed at an ache. "Oh, Susan," she moaned. "Look at the mess."

The china had shattered, as had the bowls of honey butter and blackberry jam. The mess was horrendous.

Jenny groaned again. "I'm so sorry. I slipped at the top of the stairs, and the tray—"

"Forget the tray." Susan squatted beside her as Hester arrived. "Are you sure you're all right? You could have broken your neck."

"I'm fine, I'm fine."

And she was, until later in the day, when the carpet layer came to repair the loose strip on the stairs and informed Susan that the carpet appeared to have been cut with a knife.

Jenny's insides turned to ice.

"But that's impossible," Susan cried.

The carpet man allowed as how he could be wrong, but the look in his eyes said otherwise.

That's when Jenny knew. It was starting again. The stalker was here, at Oak Hollow.

The house had been filled with strangers for the last two days—caterers, carpenters, the new maids. It was entirely possible that any one of them could have cut the carpet. Then there were Kay and Grace, neither of whom would blink if Jenny Franklin fell off the face of the earth.

One of them, then. It almost had to be, no matter that it seemed entirely too obvious, too pat.

Then Jenny remembered how Brett had wanted to go down for coffee that morning. If he had, and if he'd hit the rail where she had . . . She shivered. The banister would never have held Brett's weight. She'd felt it give beneath hers. With Brett it would have given way entirely and he'd have fallen straight to the first floor. He could easily have been killed.

"Oh, God." It was happening again!

But how would Grace or Kay have known Jenny would most likely be the first person to use the stairs that morning? There was no way either of them could have known a thing like that. Even John probably didn't know. Only Brett and Hester . . .

The echo of Susan's voice from last week when she'd introduced them to Hester rang in Jenny's ears. *She's been down in New Orleans for a few weeks taking care of her aunt and has only been back a few days.*

Oh, God! Hester . . . *Hester?*

Jenny wrapped her arms around herself to combat a sudden chill. Maybe the sun would help, she thought distractedly. She stepped from the veranda and crossed the sidewalk into the yard. *Think! Think!* she told herself.

As Jenny strolled across the yard, then around the house and through the gardens, waiting for Brett to finish the last of the revisions his editor had requested, she realized just how farfetched was the scenario she'd built in her mind. Counting Kay and Grace, there were six adults and one child who slept upstairs. Any one of them could have hit that loose patch of carpet. If someone was after Jenny, they would surely have aimed a little more directly.

With a shake of her head, she was fiercely glad she'd kept her paranoid suspicions to herself. Brett would have had her paying an official visit to John for therapy if he'd known what she'd been thinking.

Yet Brett's thoughts weren't so far from hers as he stepped through the back door to join her in the gardens. His heart had yet to slow to normal since hearing her scream that morning. His knees weren't quite steady yet, either, nor had the tremor in his hands gone away. The staircase was steep. Surely it was only by the grace of God that Jenny hadn't broken her neck. At the least, an arm. For the first time since he didn't remember when, Brett actually prayed that day. He gave thanks for Jenny's safety, her life.

And just now he added another prayer of thanks, for her smile.

"All through?" she asked as he neared.

His answering smile came easily. "All through."

They joined hands and, as if on signal, turned and strolled through the gardens. Their steps slowed as they passed the gazebo, but as usual, neither mentioned going inside, so they walked on by. Near the stable, they met Jeff, down on his hands and knees, grubbing in the dirt.

"Hey, squirt," Brett said.

Jeff turned and grinned. Dirt was streaked across his cheek and chin. "Hi, Mr. McCormick, Miss Franklin."

"And who are you today?" Jenny asked.

He held out his filthy hands. His grin broadened and his dimples flashed. "Today I'm just Jeff."

"No Johnny Reb today?"

He scrunched up his face as if in fierce thought. "Naw. Not today. I was him yesterday. I'm just me today."

"There you are." Susan came hustling around the corner of the stable. "Oh, hi," she said to Jenny and Brett. "Come on, Jeff, time to wash up for dinner."

"I guess that means us, too," Jenny said.

Brett held her back. "We'll be along in a minute." He waited for Susan and Jeff to leave, then pulled Jenny behind the building.

"What are you doing?"

"Stealing a kiss." And he did. A long, slow kiss that heated her blood and made her forget about grubby little boys, Johnny Rebs, and loose carpet. Made her forget everything but Brett.

"What was that for?" she asked breathlessly when the kiss ended. "Not that I'm complaining."

"You'd better not be." He kissed her again. "I just wanted to kiss you. I missed you today."

"I missed you, too." She leaned against him and savored his warmth, the solid feel of his body supporting hers.

"Are you sure you're all right, Jen?"

She leaned back to look at him. "Wha—oh, you mean because of this morning. I'm fine, I promise. Just a bruise or two is all."

With his arms around her, he held her gently. "You scared the bejesus out of me."

She smiled. "Me, too, actually. But I'm fine. Really."

The second accident came the next day in mid-morning. One of the new housekeeping staff had just finished cleaning Jenny and Brett's room and stepped out through the French doors onto the upstairs veranda to retrieve the mug Brett had left on the small table out there. She heard a child's laughter from below and innocently leaned against the railing to look down into the garden, where Jeff was following Arnold around.

The railing shifted beneath the maid's weight, throwing her off balance. She cried out and stepped back just before the section of railing broke loose and fell nearly twenty feet to the ground.

This time there seemed to be no question in anyone's mind that the railing had been tampered with. John called the parish sheriff.

Jenny turned cold as ice. The implications were obvious to her. That section of railing was the very spot where she leaned every morning. Brett grew furious, because he, too, was beginning to suspect someone at Oak Hollow was out to hurt Jenny. Dammit, was no place safe for her?

The one called Maude watched all the anxious activity and silently fumed at having failed once again. There would be no more subtleties. No more failures. The next and final effort would be direct, it would be successful. Maybe then the crippling pain in her head would let her be.

By Friday the tension in the air at Oak Hollow was as thick as the humidity. Even young Jeff seemed to pick up on it, for he was quieter than usual and played in his room all morning.

Both recent "accidents" were uppermost in everyone's mind, but so, too, was the costume ball and grand opening, now only one day away. Add to that Oak Hollow Bed and Breakfast's first paying guests—three cottages were filled, with more guests due to arrive that afternoon—repairs on the upstairs veranda railing, a clogged sink in the carriage house, a mixup on the flowers, half of the caterer's shrimp order ending up at the Angola State Penitentiary a few miles away by mistake, and things were getting interesting.

When Jenny came at Brett with a spare apron and suggested he help in the kitchen, he fled for the door.

"Where are you going?" Grace's voice rang out sharp and clear through the entryway.

"Out of everyone's way," Brett answered.

"You can't go outside."

Irritated, he turned on her. "Why the hell not?"

"Because Tanya Baker just checked into cottage number four, that's why."

Brett groaned.

"You remember Tanya, don't you?" Grace

propped a hand on her hip and smirked. "The Tanya with the camera, microphone, and notepad who freelances for *People* magazine?"

"Yes, Grace." He felt defeated. "I remember Baker." He would not be going outside this afternoon, after all.

"I've already told her no one would be seeing you until tomorrow night at the ball. Don't make a liar out of me."

"Yes, Mother," he grumbled.

But for all his grumbling, he was grateful Grace had warned him. Tanya Baker had always given him a fair shake in her articles, but he wasn't in the mood to be interviewed today.

For the rest of the day he did a decent job of staying out of everyone's way, and even managed to help now and then. But by the time dinner was over and everyone was heading off to bed for the night, he felt like a caged cat.

He caught Jenny at the foot of the stairs. "How tired are you?" he asked.

Jenny didn't have to glance at her watch to know it was after ten. She'd been on her feet all day and was ready to drop. Just looking into his blue eyes revived her. "What did you have in mind?"

His smile was quick and fleeting. "Nothing drastic. Maybe just a walk to the end of the drive and back."

"In the dark?"

"Yeah."

"So the reporter won't see us?"

"Don't make me sound so romantic."

Jenny laughed and took his hand in hers. "Come on. Let's go outside. In the dark. I'll try to take your mind off the reporter."

Brett's smile was genuine this time as he led her

to the front door. "Oh, yeah? This could get interesting."

The night was cool and calm, but far from dark. Electric replicas of old fashioned street lamps lined the brick driveway, casting long, eerie shadows across the lawn. Overhead the sky was velvet black with a glitter of stars sprinkled throughout.

The quiet was broken by a chorus of frogs and night insects, but the natural sounds soothed rather than grated. As Jenny and Brett strolled across the yard at the edge of the light, she felt him begin to unwind.

"You stayed pretty busy today," he commented.

Jenny shrugged. "I guess I did." She started to say that the work had kept her mind off the stalker, but she swallowed the words. The stalker was here, somewhere close. Jenny could feel him. Or her. But Brett was still too tense. Tomorrow night he would have to smile and shake hands, sign autographs, pose for photographs, and be interviewed. He needed to be rested and relaxed.

He pulled her to a stop beneath a spreading magnolia. "What are you thinking?"

He was scarcely more than a shadow in the darkness, but she knew she'd be able to feel his presence even if they weren't holding hands. "I'm thinking it's time I took your mind off that reporter in cottage number four."

With his arms around her, Brett threaded his fingers together at the base of her spine and touched his lips to her forehead. "Oh yeah?"

Jenny tilted her head back and pressed her mouth to his. "Oh . . . yeah."

The kiss was gentle, reviving, like a cool drink after a desert trek. Brett moaned and took them deeper, feeling his hunger for her pulse in his veins. Lord, what she could do to him. One kiss and he was breath-less and hard.

He had a sudden flash in his mind of how empty and colorless his life would be without her, how mean-ingless. *This* was what life should be, this hot wildness racing through his veins, making him feel alive, her answering wildness as she pulled his shirttail free and clutched at the bare skin of his back.

Other pictures flashed through his mind. Old head-stones side by side. A mangled Monte Carlo. Jenny, alone and frightened on a dark New Orleans street. A loose strip of carpet. Wrought-iron railing falling from the upstairs veranda.

Fear seized Brett's soul. He could lose her. No matter what he did, he could lose her to the stalker. In desperation, he backed her deeper into the shadows against the thick trunk of the magnolia and ground his hips into hers, wanting, needing her, trying to get closer, closer.

Brett's urgency set Jenny on fire. Heat and moisture gathered low in answer to his hardness thrusting against her. Her breasts seemed to swell in need and anticipation. Unable to wait, Jenny took Brett's hand and placed it over one breast. She wasn't wearing a bra and the heat of his palm seared her, made her arch more fully into his touch.

Brett growled in satisfaction when her nipple hard-ened. But it wasn't enough. He wanted to feel her flesh, taste it, sink himself into her. With hands that shook, he pushed her blouse up above her breasts and took a nipple into his mouth.

Jenny cried out and arched away from the tree, urging him to take more, suck harder. She was pant-ing now, in excitement, in need. The throbbing heat between her legs grew unbearable. "Brett, oh, God, Brett, please."

"Yes," he breathed.

No further words were needed. Brett unfastened her jeans and shoved them down along with her panties. Jenny managed to kick one leg free before he slid a hand between her legs and cupped her. Her knees buckled.

With his heart threatening to pound free of his chest, Brett lowered her to the cool, damp grass. She brought her legs up around his waist. God, he could feel her heat clear through his jeans. Need clawed at him from inside. In seconds he was free of his jeans and sinking himself into her slick depths.

Jenny moaned in sheer relief at having the aching emptiness filled with the only thing on earth that mattered—Brett. But the relief was short-lived. He moved inside her, against her, driving her urgency to startling new heights. Grass prickled beneath her. Overhead the thick branches of the magnolia blocked out the night sky. None of it mattered. Only Brett. Only Brett, thrusting harder, faster, again and again, desperately, frantically, until fire and need and hunger came together and exploded inside her.

Brett drank her cry with his lips, and smothered his own at the same time. With one final, mighty thrust, he emptied himself into her, pouring all he had, all that he was, giving her his very soul, as if by so doing, he could somehow make time stand still and banish the threat to her safety.

And then he wasn't thinking at all, because his climax wouldn't stop. It kept coming, kept coming, until it wrung him dry and he collapsed into Jenny's waiting arms.

It was several long minutes before either had breath enough to speak, but words would have seemed an intrusion. Slowly Jenny became aware of the world outside Brett's embrace. Crickets sang, cicadas trilled their loud buzz. Nearby, a mockingbird ran through its repertoire, and somewhere beyond the house, perhaps near the barn or in the woods, an owl hooted.

"I can't believe we did this," Jenny said, a smile spreading across her face.

Brett raised up on his elbows and peered down at her through the darkness. "Did what?" The gleam of his teeth told her he, too, was smiling.

Jenny laughed. "Rolled around on the grass like a couple of overheated teenagers. Or rather, rolled around in the chiggers." She squirmed againt the grass. "I think something bit me."

Brett laughed in sympathy and nipped at her collarbone. "Come on, confess. Don't you feel a little bit like an overheated teenager?"

"Believe me," she said, running the fingers of both hands through his hair and bringing his lips to hers, "as a teenager, I had no idea it could be like this."

They shared a long, slow kiss. As the fire began to rekindle, Brett pulled back. "I think we're pushing our luck."

Jenny sighed. "You're right. I'd die of embarrassment if someone happened to come along about now. And if we don't get out of this grass, we'll probably both be sorry."

Amid groans and laughter, they helped each other up and back into their clothes. Brett's earlier anxiety had been burned away by their lovemaking. The night was dark and unseasonably warm, and Jenny Franklin was at his side. He slipped his arm around her shoulders and guided her through the trees toward the house. Nothing, surely nothing could mar the perfection of what he and Jenny shared. It was too good, too right.

So good and right that halfway up the lawn he pulled her to a stop and kissed her again.

Behind his closed eyes, the brilliant flash of a strobe invaded. A shutter clicked.

He tore his mouth free and glared at the intruder. "Goddammit, Baker."

"Sorry, McCormick." With the beam of her flashlight, a young woman sauntered out of the darkness. "I couldn't help myself. I've never seen you with a woman before."

"Get lost, Baker," he grumbled, breathing a sigh of relief that she was coming from the direction of the house, which meant she couldn't have seen them earlier.

Ignoring him, Tanya Baker juggled her camera and flashlight until she had a free hand to extend to Jenny. "Hi. I'm Tanya Baker. And you are . . .?"

"Don't tell her unless you want to read it in *People* next week."

"Why should I care about that?" Jenny grinned at him. "Think of all the new business I could get."

Brett's chest tightened. His mind screamed a denial. She couldn't mean it. She couldn't.

Faces swam before his eyes. Girls who wanted to be seen with the high school football star. Coeds who wanted a good grade from their history professor. Women who wanted a fling with a famous author. Users. Graspers. Hangers-on.

Jenny wasn't like that. She couldn't be.

He saw her wince and only then realized he was gripping her arms hard enough to leave bruises. He dropped his hands to his sides.

Jenny would have given anything to understand what was going through Brett's mind just then. The parade of emotions across his face—outrage, pain, denial—what had she said to cause them? Now his eyes questioned, pleaded, but for what, she didn't know, and would not ask in front of the reporter.

The reporter. Oh, God, what must she think of this silent byplay? Thank God she hadn't found them earlier. Jenny forced a smile and told her, "I'm nobody important."

The hurt was back in Brett's eyes. "The hell you're not." He gripped her arms again, but gently this time. "You're the most important person in my life."

Jenny's throat swelled with emotion and her eyes burned. With trembling lips, she moved into his embrace and returned it with all her strength as she breathed his name.

A tidal wave of relief poured through Brett. Relief that his irrational fear had been groundless, shame that he'd doubted her for even a moment.

"Damn. Where the hell's my tape recorder?"

"If you find it," Brett muttered, "I know what I'm going to tell you to do with it, and it won't be pretty. Beat it, Baker."

"Jesus, the bachelor stud of the book world gets smitten and I don't have my goddamn recorder."

While the reporter fumbled through her canvas bag, Brett kissed Jenny. "Come on," he whispered. "Let's get out of here."

Jenny smiled. "What about her?"

Brett followed her gaze. He saw Baker with a flashlight in one hand trying to hold a notepad against her knee and write on it at the same time with the other as she muttered to herself, "Most . . . important . . . person . . ."

"She's got the story straight. She's on her own."

Since they'd already been discovered, secrecy seemed useless. They took the lighted driveway back to the house and locked the front door behind them before going upstairs. In their bedroom, Brett leaned back against the closed door and pulled Jenny into his arms. The lamp on the dresser gilded her hair in gold.

"Baker was right, you know." He buried his fingers in Jenny's hair and cupped her head in his palm.

"What?" Jenny grinned as she nestled into his touch. "That you're the bachelor stud of the book world?"

He grinned back. "That, too. But I am smitten. With you."

"Did you say bitten, as in chiggers?"

He squeezed her backside. "I said smitten, as in, with you."

"I think I like the sound of that," she whispered against his lips.

A sound, a feeling, something made the hairs on the back of Brett's neck stand on end. He jerked his head up.

"Wha—"

He pressed his hand over Jenny's mouth and pointed across the room to the wardrobe. He felt Jenny stiffen as she spotted her clothes trailing out one gaping door.

Brett pushed her behind him and, motioning for her to stay put, moved silently across the room. Without giving himself time to think, he yanked open the second door. An empty clothes hanger fell out at his feet, nearly scaring the crap out of him.

He bent to pick it up, but reached for Jenny's red sweater instead. Or what was left of it. It had been shredded. So had her black slacks, her jeans, and everything else of hers that had been in the wardrobe.

"Did we leave the bathroom door closed?" Jenny asked quietly.

Muttering a curse, Brett lifted a severed sleeve of her sweater. "No . . ." She had crossed the room and was reaching for the bathroom door. The closed bathroom door that he knew they'd left open. Her jaw was set. The fire of anger lit her eyes.

"Jen, no!"

His warning came too late. As she touched the glass doorknob, the door flew open, knocking her sideways against the dresser. Brett had a single glimpse of a tall figure in black clothes and ski mask leaping at Jenny, a pair of scissors held high in the attacker's gloved hand, when the lamp on the dresser teetered, fell, and broke, plunging the room in darkness.

Jenny screamed.

Brett nearly choked on the terror in his throat. In that instant he realized that no matter what had happened in his past, a future without Jenny would be darker than this room.

He'd mouthed words of love, but only to himself. He'd thought he'd meant them, but until this moment he'd failed to fully realize that without her, he had no life. And he'd never told her. "Jenny!" *He'd never told her he loved her.*

A crash. A grunt. A curse. In the scant illumination filtering through the French doors, all he could see were shadows, lunging, jerking. And light glancing off chrome scissors.

Brett raced for the bedroom door, where he hit the wall switch, flooding the room with light. He lunged across the room toward Jenny, but he was too far away. Too damn far!

Jenny shoved and knocked the assailant off balance, then turned to run.

Brett was inches away—*inches!*—when the blades of the scissors arced, then sliced down her back. She screamed again.

The attacker whirled and fled toward the French doors and escape. With a roar of rage and terror, Brett leaped and tackled, bringing the attacker crashing to the floor. They rolled until Brett ended up on top. He slammed the hand with the scissors against the floor and put his free hand around the culprit's throat.

Out in the hall, doors slammed open. Jenny cried out for help. And Brett suddenly realized the thrashing figure beneath him was a woman.

With a curse, he slammed her hand against the floor again and sent the scissors sliding across the hardwood floor.

"I'm sorry," she whimpered.

His vision clouded with rage, Brett ripped away the ski mask. "Good God."

Jenny gasped. "Kay!"

John and Susan and Grace burst into the room. "What the hell?" John cried.

"Jenny's hurt. Somebody take care of her. Call an ambulance. And the police," Brett bit out.

Chapter Twenty-Three

It was dawn before Brett was finally able to put Jenny to bed and hold her gently against his side. He didn't want to be gentle; he wanted to wrap both arms around her and hold on with all his might. Dear God, he could have lost her last night. He wasn't sure his heart rate would ever settle down to normal again.

Kay. Jesus, he would never have thought quiet, shy Kay capable of attempted murder. She was in custody, thank God. It was over. Jenny was finally safe. Maybe now her dreams would be more pleasant than that damn nightmare that had haunted her for so long.

The paramedics had arrived thirty seconds behind the police. While Kay was being handcuffed and read her rights, Jenny was being treated. The EMTs wouldn't allow him to ride in the ambulance, so he'd followed. Or rather, John had driven him. Brett had been in no shape to drive, and he'd known it. He was scared out of his wits for Jenny, and ... hell, anger didn't begin to cover what he'd felt toward Kay. Rage. Fury. Those words came close.

Self-blame had been there, too; it was still boiling around inside him. Jenny had pegged Kay's feelings for him the first time she'd met her. Even Grace had warned him that Kay was getting too fond of him.

Had he listened? Hell, no. Not know-it-all Brett McCormick. He hadn't paid enough attention. Jenny could have paid with her life for his carelessness.

Hell, McCormick, it wouldn't be the first time your carelessness killed somebody, would it?

"Brett, don't."

He'd thought she was asleep, what with all the drugs they'd pumped into her at the hospital when they'd cleaned her wound and determined it didn't need suturing.

"Don't what?"

"You're blaming yourself for what Kay did."

"Reading my mind, are you?"

"Maybe. Or maybe I just know you well enough to guess. You're blaming yourself and it wasn't your fault. You're not responsible for her actions. It's over and done with. She's in jail, and history did not repeat itself. I'm too glad to be alive and have this all behind us to let you lie here and blame yourself."

"Hell, Jen, I can't help but feel responsible. If it wasn't for me, this never would have happened."

Jenny tried to rise.

"Don't you dare. The doctor said to take it easy and get plenty of rest. You're supposed to be asleep."

"I'll go to sleep as soon as you look me in the eye and take back that idiotic statement you just made."

"Jesus, after all you've been through in the last eight hours, where do you find the energy to be pissed?"

"What can I say? You just bring out the best in me. Now, repeat after me, I am not responsible for Kay's actions."

"Jen," he said.

She pinched his side.

"Ow!"

"Say it, or I'll pinch something else." Her hand slid across his abdomen and headed south.

"I am not responsible for Kay's actions," he said in a rush.

"Very good. Now, say it like you believe it."

"Would you go to sleep?"

She arched her neck until she could look him in the face. "On second thought, I guess maybe you are responsible."

Brett's gut clenched. "What?"

"I mean, there's just something about you that makes women fall in love with you. I might react the same way she did if I saw you giving all your attention to another woman."

Relief swept through him, leaving him weak. She didn't blame him. "What other woman?" he asked.

"I was speaking hypothetically."

"Jen, there is no other woman."

Her smile was soft and spoke of exhaustion. Dark circles hung below her eyes, and her face was still ashen. "I know that, Brett. I just want to know when you're going to learn that every bad thing that happens to someone close to you is not your fault."

Hell, maybe she *had* been reading his mind. "I don't know." He eyed her carefully, a smile suddenly teasing his lips. "So, women fall in love with me, do they?"

She shrugged and looked away feigning disinterest. "So I'm told."

Brett lost all urge to tease. "I did learn one thing last night, Jen. When I looked across the room and saw those scissors swinging down on you, I learned that life without you just wouldn't be worth living. I sure as hell hope you're one of those women you mentioned, because I love you. I think I fell in love with you when I saw you at the mall that first time.''

Jenny looked into his deep blue eyes and knew that for her, love had come long before then, more than a hundred years before. But she wouldn't tell him that, because for once there were no shadows in those blue eyes. "So did I," she whispered. "So did I."

She slept then, with a smile on her face, and Brett slept, too. When he woke, it was just past noon and for the first time in weeks, maybe years, his mind was clear of all doubt. He would no longer blame himself for everything bad that happened.

He'd accepted the blame for his father's death. If there was any way to go back and change things, he would. But there was no way. He accepted that, too.

He wasn't fool enough to believe he wouldn't still be haunted by his father's death, wouldn't still feel responsible, but he had a chance for true happiness with Jen, if she would have him, and if he could present himself to her with a whole heart, one not tormented by the past.

His heart pounding with equal parts of excitement and sheer nerves, he eased from the bed without waking her.

Tendrils of soft fragrance drifted into Jenny's sleep and woke her gently, pleasantly. Roses. She smelled roses.

She blinked her eyes open and found herself staring at a bright red rose lying beside her head on the white pillow.

Brett. She smiled and touched the velvet-soft petals with the tips of her fingers. His gesture touched her deep inside and made her feel like she was glowing from head to toe. How she loved him.

She was stiff and sore and her back ached and throbbed beneath the bandage, but she was alive, and Brett was alive, and the world was a beautiful place.

She made it to the bathroom and back with little trouble, but the effort was unbelievably tiring. After piling pillows against the headboard, she eased back against them and brought Brett's offering to her nose and inhaled the sweet, sweet fragrance. Her eyes closed in sheer pleasure.

That's how Brett found her when he carried in her breakfast tray. Her eyes smiled at him over the top of the rose.

"Good morning." He carried the tray to the bed.

She glanced ruefully at the clock on the bedside table. "I think you mean good afternoon."

He braced the tray's short legs on either side of her thighs and brushed his lips across hers. "For you, it's morning. Hence— *Volià.* "With a flourish, he whipped the cover off the tray.

"Breakfast in bed?"

Brett pulled a chair next to the bed and sat.

With a hungry look in her eyes, Jenny shook out her napkin. "Bacon, eggs . . . fresh croissants. And what—Sugar Crisp!" She laughed, delighted, and beamed at him. "Now I know you love me if you went into town for Sugar Crisp. I happen to know there wasn't one single sugar-coated piece of puffed wheat in this house."

Brett's pulse started a slow, heavy pounding. "You're right on both counts."

"Both?"

"There wasn't any, and I do love you." Sweat

popped out on his palms and down his spine. "Jen . . . I, that is, we never—I mean, would you—"

"Hi, Miss Franklin."

Brett's breath left him with a soundless whoosh. He didn't know whether to welcome Jeff's interruption or strangle the kid. He should have closed the damn door.

"Hi, Jeff," Jenny answered. "What have you got there?"

"Flowers," he claimed proudly, holding out a sweet, ragged handful of blooms.

"Ah, so I see," Jenny said. "They're very pretty."

"Yes, ma'am. I picked 'em myself. Mom said I could. She said they might make you feel better."

"Of course they will. How thoughtful of you to go to all that trouble." She smiled and held out her hand.

Jeff hesitated, then rounded the bed and gave the flowers to Brett. "You give 'em to her," he said solemnly. "I'm not supposed to touch the bed or anything."

Brett bit back a combination curse and laugh. Some of the flowers had evidently been pulled up by their roots. His hand was full of dirt. "Uh, thanks."

Jeff skipped back toward the door. "I'm not allowed to stay. Mom said so. 'Bye, Miss Franklin."

" 'Bye, Jeff. Thank you for the flowers."

"You're welcome." He grinned, exposing twin dimples, then stopped halfway out the door.

"Hester's gonna let me lick the bowl when she makes chocolate pie if I'm not late." Without a backward glance, the boy cheerfully darted out the door and bounded down the stairs.

Voices rose from the backyard and floated through the closed French doors. Somewhere downstairs a phone rang. In Brett and Jenny's room upstairs, there was only the sound of breathing.

Brett stared at the empty doorway with a strange look on his face, half hope, half fear. Wincing against the pull on the skin across her back, Jenny set her breakfast tray aside and scooted to the edge of the bed. "Brett?"

After a long moment, he turned his head to face her and she couldn't begin to read the emotions in his eyes. "Would you be interested . . ." He glanced down at the flowers in his hand. "That is, have you ever thought about having a kid or two? I mean, I don't think for a minute that I'm good enough for you, and I probably have no right to have kids, but—"

"Not good enough?" Jenny cried. "No right to have kids? What the hell do you mean by that?" she demanded, outraged.

His jaw bunched, and his grip on the flowers tightened until two stems snapped. And suddenly Jenny knew, without being told, that Brett was speaking of his father's death. Anger and pain mixed inside her, but she managed to smother the anger, for she knew it would do her no good. The pain, she couldn't seem to control. "You're talking about your father," she told him. "Let it go, Brett. Let go of your guilt and self-blame. You don't deserve it. His death was an accident. A devastating, tragic *accident*. It doesn't matter who did what—"

"It matters to me," he nearly shouted. Then he shook his head. "I'm sorry, I didn't mean to yell. I thought I had all this worked out in my head. I thought I'd found a way to live with it. But when I think of one day having to explain to a kid of my own that I'm the reason he doesn't have a grandfather—"

"You're not," Jenny snapped, losing her battle with

anger. "You're not guilty of a damn thing, but I could tell you that every day for the next ten years and you wouldn't believe it, would you?" She waved an arm in the air—the wrong arm, and winced.

"Why should I waste my breath trying to convince you of anything? Your mind is made up and you're not about to change it. You're never going to let go of all that guilt, are you, because it's too damn comfortable. You've held onto it all these years like a security blanket so you can use it as an excuse to keep from getting close to anyone."

His eyes narrowed. His jaw flexed. "I'm pretty damn close to you. Or I thought I was."

Jenny waved his words away. "Go ahead and blame yourself all you want. I don't care. Stay all wrapped up in your guilt and let it eat away at your insides."

"What do you want me to say?" he yelled.

"I want you to say, 'My God, you're right, I didn't cause my father's death!'"

"You're right! I didn't cause my father's death! I—" The words dried up on Brett's tongue as that afternoon so long ago on the farm slammed back at him with vivid clarity. The cool wind, the dry, brittle stubble of the field beneath his boots. The smell of alfalfa. The bellow of that damn bull in the pasture.

"My God," he whispered. "You *are* right! I remember! I . . . good God, I remember—I *did* close the gate. Closed it, threaded the chain through, and latched it!" He blinked and swallowed and looked at Jenny. "I *did* close the gate."

"Say it again," Jenny ground out.

"What?" He cocked his head.

"I said say it again, damn you."

His eyes slid shut as an ancient weight lifted from his chest. "I didn't kill my father."

"You're damn right you didn't."

Brett opened his eyes and realized she was still angry. He felt like the king of the world, and she was ready to spit nails at him. He threw his head back and laughed. "We're not supposed to fight until after the wedding."

Jenny looked at him as though he'd lost his mind. "What wedding?"

"Ours."

"I beg your pardon?"

"What did you think I meant about having kids? Jeff interrupted my bumbling proposal. When he walked in I was about to ask you to marry me."

Jenny's heart slammed against her ribs. Her locked breath crowded her lungs. Yearnings and dreams crowded her heart. "You were?" she managed.

"I only plan to do this once, so I guess I'd better do it right." He slid off the chair onto one knee before her and cupped her hips in his hands. "I don't know if I've loved you for weeks, or decades, but I know I love you, I know I've never loved anyone but you. I want . . . I want a life with you. I want to sleep with you every night and wake with you every morning. I want to give you children, if you want them. I want to make love with you from now until we're both so old we can't, and then I want to hold your hand for the next hundred years or so after that. I want to be your husband. I want you to be my wife. Jennifer Franklin, will you marry me?"

Tears streamed down her cheeks and her lips trembled. She slid from the edge of the bed straight into his arms. "Yes. Dear God, yes."

Jenny scarcely noticed, but throughout the day the sky darkened as clouds built overhead and the wind picked up. The storm from the Rockies threatened to do its best to put a damper on Oak Hollow's Grand Opening and Costume Ball. No one in the house seemed to care. They were too busy with last-minute arrangements.

Over Brett's objections, Jenny insisted on getting dressed and going downstairs. He had reheated her breakfast, and afterward she had taken a short nap and sworn she felt much better. Her back hardly hurt at all.

It wasn't until the costumes were delivered that Brett realized Jenny was still planning on attending the ball.

"You're not," he told her bluntly.

She stood in the middle of the entry and gave him an arched look. "Excuse me?"

"Jenny, be reasonable."

"When have you ever known me to be reasonable?"

"There's a first time for everything," he muttered. "The doctor said you were supposed to rest for a few days. I don't think he had dancing and partying in mind."

"I don't plan to overdo it, but I'm not missing this ball."

"I thought we weren't going to fight until *after* we got married," he said in exasperation.

Susan halted on her way to the kitchen. "Who's getting married?"

Brett grinned. "We are."

Jenny gave a toss of her head. "Maybe."

"Jen," he complained.

"Really?" Susan's eyes widened. "No kidding?"

"She said yes. I distinctly heard her say yes," Brett said firmly.

"Oh!" A wide smile spread across Susan's face. "John! Hester! Jenny and Brett are getting married!"

Hester heard the shout and rushed in from the back hall. "Married? Somebody's getting married?"

Jenny was still giving Brett a mock glare. She opened her mouth, but he covered it with his hand and said, "We are."

"My, oh, my." Hester finished drying her hands on the dish towel she carried. "How about that."

John came in from his study. "Just think," he said. "The last time around, the announcement never got made. But this time there's no one to interfere. You can make the announcement at the ball tonight. It's perfect. Fitting, don't you think?"

Grace ambled down the stairs just then. "Make what announcement?"

"Grace," Brett said before anyone could answer. "I need to talk to you, if you have a minute." He turned to Jenny and said, for her ears only, "I need to tell her myself, Jen. She's going to gripe about my image, and you don't need to hear that crap. It'll only take a minute, I promise."

Jenny didn't intend to fall asleep while Brett broke the news of their upcoming marriage to Grace. She'd only thought to go upstairs and lie down so she could prove she was rested enough to go to the ball. She kicked off her shoes and eased herself onto the bed, then pulled the old quilt across her because it felt so comforting. She was asleep almost instantly.

Once asleep, she didn't intend to dream, either. But she woke an hour later in a cold, terrified sweat, calling Seth's name and searching the room frantically for Maudie.

"Oh, damn," she groaned. "Not again."

She willed her pulse to slow, her heart to stop pounding. Willed the horror and panic to recede.

Why, dammit? Why was she still plagued by dreams of blood, betrayal, and death?

The euphoria she'd felt earlier over Kay's arrest and Brett's proposal waned. Damn the dream! It was robbing her of happiness that was rightfully hers, and she wouldn't stand for it! It was over. The fear, the threat—gone.

Yet now that she thought about it, she realized that Kay's arrest had not given her the slightest feeling of vindication, of closure, and it should have, shouldn't it? Thinking about last night, the events seemed . . . anticlimactic.

Shouldn't there have been something more drastic than merely a softly weeping woman being taken away in handcuffs? Where was the smoke, the fire, the lightning of retribution? The bone-deep feeling that an old score had finally been settled, an old enemy vanquished?

They weren't there. Jenny searched her mind, her heart, and found none of those things. All she felt was sore and tired.

And lucky, she admitted. Incredibly lucky. Brett was safe, she was safe and relatively unharmed, and the ordeal was over.

So why didn't she feel better? Why had the nightmare returned to plague her? Why was her mood suddenly as troubled as the sky?

The sense of foreboding snaking through her had nothing to do with the building clouds.

Chapter Twenty-Four

The stirring strains of a Strauss waltz drifted up the stairs and through the closed bedroom door where Jenny had promised Brett she would stay.

She'd lied. She had never agreed to marry a man before. She'd be damned if she was going to spend the first night of her engagement alone in her room while he waltzed the night away.

She had managed to recover from her nightmare before Brett had returned to the room after talking with Grace that afternoon.

"How did she take it?" Jenny had asked. She knew Grace didn't want to see Brett tied down to one woman.

"She took it pretty well, considering she'd rather see me gelded than married."

"She *said* that?" Jenny demanded, outraged.

Brett laughed. "No, but that's what I expected her to say. Actually, when she realized I was serious, she immediately started figuring out how to use our upcoming marriage for more publicity. I suspect she'd like to handle our wedding herself, but unless we want it turned into a major media event, I suggest we make other arrangements.''

Jenny had grimaced. "How does elopement sound?''

Brett had sidled up to her and nudged his hips against hers while placing his hands boldly on her backside to pull her closer. "Tonight?''

"She really would geld you. *People* magazine is here, the governor is coming, and John and Susan are counting on you to dazzle their guests. I think we should put in at least a token appearance at the ball, don't you?''

That's when he'd started in on her. "We? You shouldn't even be out of bed, much less thinking about a costume ball.''

"The doctor didn't say anything about staying in bed.''

"He said plenty of rest, and no vigorous activity.''

She'd rolled her eyes. "I don't call standing around visiting with people 'vigorous.' ''

"Jen, babe, be reasonable.''

She hated it when he called her "babe." It made her go all soft inside and made her want to do everything possible to please him.

"You're still pale and weak. Come on, humor me.''

She hated to admit she did feel weak. "What am I supposed to do with myself all night while you have fun?''

"Fun? I have to put on my public face and smile at everyone and be interviewed and photographed, when I'd rather be here with you. Tell you what. You go back to bed, and stay there," he added, "and I'll come up later and check on you. If you're still feeling up to it, you can come down for dinner. How's that?''

"Rotten. You're treating me like a two-year-old.''

"But you'll do it?"

She must have been even weaker than she'd realized, because she'd knuckled under like a spineless wuss. The second nap, however, had refreshed her. No nightmares had disturbed her this time. She figured that during her earlier nap maybe her brain just hadn't gotten the message yet that she was safe, that the danger was over. She felt fine now—better than fine.

Her movements were slow, so as not to pull at her wound, but her progress was steady. She was going to dance with the man she loved—whether he liked it or not, she thought with a devilish grin.

She turned slowly before the mirror. Yards and yards of yellow silk over even more yards of petticoat swished and swirled around her, catching the light and throwing it back, dazzling the eye. *Did they really wear them cut this low in front?*

She gave another tug on what was euphemistically called a neckline. The back, fortunately, was high enough to cover her bandage. The doctor had said the bandage could come off tonight, but she didn't want to chance ruining the dress.

She left her hair down and liked the effect the curling iron gave it. Upon close inspection, she looked rested and alert.

A fan. Every Southern belle worth her salt should have a fan. Ah, well, she supposed she'd do all right without one. If one look at this neckline didn't knock Brett McCormick's socks off, no fan was going to catch his attention.

Her neck was too bare, though. She ran a hand over the expanse of naked skin and wished for a locket . . .

"You have to marry me to get the matching locket."

"Seems like a lot of trouble for just an ol' locket."

"Come on. It's heart-shaped,"

Jenny smiled poignantly at her reflection. Poor Anna and Seth. He never got to give her the locket. They never got to announce their engagement that night at the ball . . . never got to dance with each other as an official engaged couple.

Tonight, she vowed, Brett and Jenny would.

Full circle. The *Wheel of Fortune,* she thought, remembering Madam's Tarot card. Jenny stood now on the threshold of what had once turned into her worst nightmare. But the nightmare was over. More than a hundred years too late, but finally they would announce their love to the world and dance the night away.

With a final turn before the mirror, she gave a satisfied nod and walked out into the music. It wasn't until she was halfway down the staircase that she realized the dress she wore looked like an exact duplicate of Anna Hampton's ballgown.

It was fitting, she decided.

The music swelled, filling the house, filling Jenny with the kinds of emotions generated only by a Strauss waltz. People were everywhere, laughing, talking, most in historical costume, some not. They spilled out of the dining room where the buffet dinner was set up, into the polished entry hall, and filled the two connecting parlors. In the center of each parlor and even in the entry, couples swayed and swirled in time with the music.

Jenny spotted Brett at once. The mere sight of him, tall and lean and looking oh-so-handsome in his formal black cutaway, was enough to steal her breath away.

He stood surrounded by people. Jenny thought she recognized the reporter from *People* among those around him. The governor was there. Brett, with his back to her, had his head tilted down to hear what the governor was saying.

Oak Hollow's ball was a huge success. Jenny was more than pleased for John and Susan.

The music changed, and amid a great deal of good-natured laughter, a few brave couples—John and Susan among them—attempted the Virginia Reel. Trouble was, no one really knew how to do it. But there was no lack of enthusiasm on the part of the dancers or those watching from the sidelines. Jenny had a great time clapping and tapping her toe in time to the music along with everyone else. She was sorry Brett wasn't at her side, but he and several others were still deep in conversation with the governor.

After the reel, Jenny accompanied John and Susan to the punchbowl. "That," John said breathlessly, "was *work*."

"That," Susan said with a laugh, "was *fun*."

"The evening looks like a huge success," Jenny told them. "I'm so pleased for both of you."

"Thanks," Susan said, squeezing Jenny's hand. "I'm so glad you made it. After all your hard work helping us pull this off, I would have hated to see you have to miss it." She leaned forward with a conspiratorial grin and whispered, "Does Brett know you're down here?"

Jenny fought a smile and took a sip of punch. "Not yet. I think I'll just wait and let him notice on his own."

"Excuse me." One of the costumed servers hired by the caterer stepped to Jenny's side. "Miss Franklin?"

"Yes?"

"I was asked to deliver a message to you."

"Yes?"

A twinkle lit the waiter's eye. "Mr. McCormick would like you to meet him in the gazebo."

Jenny smiled slowly as a warmth spread through her. How perfect. They had purposely avoided the gazebo since their arrival. Now, with the past behind them, the trouble put to rest, it was time. The gazebo would be the perfect place to meet. "Well, I guess he knows I'm here," she told Susan.

Jenny set her cup of punch on a small table in the entry hall set up for discarded dishes and threaded her way through the crowd.

With eager steps, she pushed open the back door and stepped outside into the night.

"All right." Brett folded his arms and pursed his lips. "Where did she go?"

"She who?" Susan asked.

"You know who—Jenny. I saw you and John talking to her a few minutes ago. She was supposed to be resting, dammit. Where's she hiding?"

Susan frowned. "I don't know what you mean. She went out the back way as soon as she got your message."

Brett slowly lowered his arms to his sides. "What message?"

"That you wanted to meet her in the gazebo." Susan grinned. "You romantic devil, you. John never had a waiter deliver a message like that to me. The closest he ever came was the time he had a fry cook tell me he was going to be a while in the men's room because Jeff had thrown up on John's shoes."

Brett was scarcely listening. A chill skittered down his spine. A message sent by him—that he hadn't sent. Foreboding, full-bodied and consuming, washed over him. With a curse, he spun on his heel toward the door.

"Where are you going?"

"To find her." Frowning, he threaded his way through the partygoers toward the back hall, urgency building in him with every step.

Directly over Oak Hollow the warm air from the gulf met the colder air pushing east from the Rockies. Trees swayed, limbs danced, leaves rustled. The sky boiled with clouds, low and black in the night. Thunder rumbled. Lightning flashed in the distance.

Small, ankle-high landscape lights lit the brick pathways in the formal gardens between the house and the cottages. When Jenny stepped from the porch, the wind lifted her skirt and billowed it out. It seemed such a teasing, playful thing that she laughed, delighted.

The gardens appeared to be deserted. She supposed everyone was inside enjoying the food and dancing. Anchoring her skirt as best she could with both hands, she took her time following the brick path between the short boxwood hedges to the gazebo. The air was humid and cooling, but the power of the approaching storm was there as well. It was invigorating, and it gave her a heady rush after she'd been in bed and idle most of the day. The impending storm made her feel alive and vital. Excited, as anticipation filled the night.

Thankfully, the gazebo was deserted. She would have hated to have interrupted a couple who might have sought a moment of privacy, as she and Brett were seeking. She was glad, so glad, they were putting this final piece of the past to rest.

She thought to wait for him on the steps so they could enter the gazebo together, hand in hand, but she didn't trust the sky. Then, too, if someone other than Brett came outside, she didn't want to get dragged into a conversation. She wanted Brett all to herself.

Muttering over the impracticality of such full skirts, she grabbed handfuls of yellow silk, hiked the skirt up as far as she could, and took the two narrow steps up into the gazebo.

Here the wind did not reach, nor even much of the light. Through the vine-covered lattice she could see the back of the house on one side, the cottages on the other, but no one would be able to see inside without coming close, for the door faced the garden and the woods beyond.

The back door of the house opened and a man and woman stepped out, laughing. Jenny recognized them as the couple in cottage two. They'd checked in a few days ago on their honeymoon. They'd gone all out and rented costumes for tonight. Now, arm in arm, staring at each other with total adoration, they strolled slowly along the brick pathway to their cottage.

Newlyweds. Jenny smiled, eagerness expanding in her chest. She and Brett would soon be newlyweds. They hadn't discussed a date yet, but for now, it was enough to know that he loved her enough to want to spend the rest of his life with her. She loved him so much that at times she ached with it.

Thunder boomed overhead, making Jenny jump. The wind picked up, bringing with it the sweetness of autumn roses and the sharper tang of marigolds from the flowerbeds around her. Lightning flashed across the sky. The storm would break soon. She hoped Brett hurried.

The door to cottage two closed with a soft *click*.

Wrapped up in her own thoughts, listening to the thunder and wind, Jenny didn't hear anyone until the scrape of a shoe on brick alerted her. *Brett.* Eagerly she rose from the cushion and rushed to the gazebo steps. "There you are. I was beginning to think— Grace! I'm sorry, I thought . . ."

Jenny's throat dried up and cut off her own words. Something was wrong. The fine hairs on the back of her neck stood on end. Something was drastically, dangerously wrong.

"I know what you thought."

The voice. Grace's voice, it was . . . different. Gone were the smooth, cultured tones, the easy manner. In their place was harshness, grim determination. Rage.

"Grace?"

The wind tore at Grace's hair, at her billowing skirt. She threw her head back and laughed.

No, not laughed, Jenny thought . . . cackled, like a witch stirring her boiling cauldron.

There was something . . .

Jenny sucked in a sharp breath. *Maudie.* The thought came unbidden, but strong. It wasn't the dress so much, although it was that same royal blue that Maudie wore in Jenny's nightmares. No, it was more subtle than that. The voice. *The eyes.* One lid drooped, twitching. And there was nothing in those cold-hot depths even remotely resembling sanity.

Thunder crash. Jenny flinched.

Grace cackled again. "Did you think I'd let you have him?" she shouted above the wind. "I'm through trying for an accident! He's *mine!* Do you hear me? He's *mine!*"

Ice formed in Jenny's veins. "Accident?"

"I would have been rid of you weeks ago if you'd driven your own car that day."

"That was *you?* No." Jenny shook her head in denial. "That was Kay. We caught her last night. You know that, Grace."

"Kay!" Grace spat with disgust. "That little fool wouldn't have the nerve. Oh, she slipped the note in your mailbox—I saw her myself. But she couldn't work up the guts to do anything that might actually hurt somebody. Last night was a fluke. She was so head over heals for Brett that I think she actually went a little crazy. The tires, your brakes, the carpet on the stairs, the loose railing—that was *me*, damn you. All Kay managed was to get in my way. Sure, she loves Brett, but so what? She's only loved him for a year or so. *I've* loved him a lifetime—longer than that—more than a century! He belongs to *me!*" she screamed, advancing slowly.

Jenny gasped as a gun appeared in Grace's hand. "Grace—"

"No mistakes this time. No more accidents. This time you're going to die for trying to take him from me, and he's not here to get in the way like he was last time. That was your fault, bitch."

Jenny stared down the bore of the pistol and shuddered. Sheer terror gripped her insides. "You don't know what you're doing, Grace."

"I know exactly what I'm doing." She pulled the hammer back on the pistol and took aim.

"No!" The shout came from Brett as he raced toward them from the back of the house.

"Stay away!" Grace leaped forward and pressed the barrel of the gun to Jenny's temple.

Brett skidded to a halt on the brick pathway, his heart in his throat. "Let her go, Grace."

"Never! You know you don't love her. I don't know what she's done to make you think you do, but it's *me* you love, it's always been me. She came between us the last time, and now here she is again. She has to die, surely you see that. You're mine! Mine!"

Terror turned Brett's insides to ice. One glance at

Jenny's pale face ripped a hole through his sanity. He took a step forward.

"No!" This time the scream was Jenny's. "Stay back, Brett, please!"

He knew, God, he knew what she was thinking. Stay back so he wouldn't be killed in her place, like that last time. "To hell with that," he snarled.

A huge bolt of lightning crashed so near that the ground shook. For a split second that seemed to hang on for an eternity, the garden was brighter than daylight, so bright there was no color. Everything was bleached white. Jenny looked like a ghost.

And in that one brief half-second, when Brett and Jenny's eyes met, the barrier of time slipped away and it was all there, all the memories from before, the love, the laughter, the pain. Every word Anna and Seth had ever shared, every touch, every kiss.

And Maudie. Who she'd been, what she'd done. Who she was now. The memories, the knowledge were there.

Brett had time to think, *Good God, it's true, all of it.* He *had* lived as Seth Taylor, Jenny as Anna. And Grace . . .

The smell of ozone was strong—or was it brimstone straight from the pits of hell? In the sudden absence of lightning, vision was impaired.

Grace choked and coughed on a lungful of lightning-singed air.

Brett lunged. Jenny screamed. She threw herself between him and Grace and shoved him off balance. Brett grabbed her and took her to the ground with him when he fell.

Grace followed them with the barrel of the gun.

Over Jenny's shoulder, Brett saw Grace's finger tighten on the trigger. He literally threw Jenny over the hedge into the marigolds. The bullet hit him in the shoulder.

Jenny screamed again. "Brett! Oh my God, no!" Plowing back through the boxwood, she scrambled for him, tearing her dress, not noticing, not caring about anything but reaching his side. "Brett!"

Grace—no, she was Maudie now—filled the night with vile curses.

Jenny ignored her and placed a violently trembling hand against Brett's chest. She was shaking too hard to tell if he was breathing. A sob wracked her as she called his name over and over.

Then, suddenly, he moaned.

"Thank God!" she breathed.

He tried to say something, but she hushed him. "You'll be all right. It's okay."

Incredibly, he reached up and shoved her away. "Get out of here," he demanded harshly.

Unbelievably hurt by his curt rejection, Jenny crawled back to his side. "No! I won't leave you." Some sixth sense made her glance up.

In a chilling replay from more than a hundred years ago, Grace—Maudie—tossed the gun to the ground. "I don't need that," came the strident screech of her voice. "We'll do it right, just like last time. Only *this* time, *you're* the only one who'll die. Seth will be mine! Forever!"

From some secret fold in her skirt she pulled a huge, menacing butcher knife and lunged at Jenny.

Jenny barely managed to scramble out of the way of the deadly blade. Fear hampered her; the wound on her back from the night before hampered her. The damn skirt and petticoats nearly rendered her immobile, but she lurched sideways at the last moment, at the same time grabbing at Grace's billowing skirt.

The two women went down in a tangle of arms, legs, and yards of silk. Grace raised the knife again. Jenny grabbed her wrist and hung on with all her strength to keep the gleaming blade from plunging into her chest. The mark on her ribs throbbed in remembered pain.

Not again, Jenny vowed. *Not again, by God.*

She doubled her free hand into a fist and connected with Grace's chin, knocking her back and breaking the hold she had had on Grace's wrist.

Brett didn't have the breath to cheer the move. He knew Jenny's reprieve was only momentary. Visions of that eight-inch blade plunging into her soft flesh nearly paralyzed him, but he forced himself up from the ground.

The gun. He had to reach the gun.

But Jenny couldn't wait for him. The blade flashed before her eyes. She ducked sideways, and Grace grabbed a handful of her hair and yanked.

Jenny cried out, caught, unable to free herself. She scratched, she kicked. She would have cursed, but didn't have the breath.

No matter what happened, she told herself, Brett was alive.

But she didn't want to die! She would not give Grace—Maudie—the satisfaction!

She reached for Maudie's knife hand again. The two struggled for control. Maudie was strong, filled with the overwhelming strength of madness. Jenny's strength came from fear, from sheer determination. From righteous rage.

They rolled through the marigolds, crashed through a new planting of boxwood and into the rosebed. Thorns, sharp and vicious, raked Jenny's already damaged back. She couldn't hold back the cry of pain.

"You're *dead,*" Maudie hissed.

"No!" Jenny gathered herself and gave a mighty shove.

Grace tumbled backward, but took Jenny with her. Jenny felt the handle of the knife dig into her shoulder. Then it gave.

A look of stunned surprise crossed Maudie's face.

No, Jenny thought in shock. Not Maudie. The woman lying beneath her in bewildered pain now was Grace. "Wha—?"

Jenny knew then. Without looking, she knew. She pulled back slowly and gasped for breath.

Grace lay there panting, both hands wrapped around the handle of the knife that pierced her chest. "Jenny?" she asked tentatively.

With the gun in his hand, Brett dropped to his knees beside them.

Grace looked at him, and as she did, her eyes changed again. Maudie was back. "Mine," she hissed. She glared at Jenny. "I'm going to kill—" She lunged upward, then fell back with a gasp and stared sightlessly at the turbulent sky.

"Is she dead?" Jenny asked, her chest still heaving for breath.

Brett pressed two fingers to the artery in Grace's throat. "Yes." He threw the gun down and dragged Jenny to his heaving chest. Alive! Thank God, thank God, Jenny was alive. Brett couldn't hold her close enough or tight enough. "Are you all right?" he managed breathlessly.

Jenny swallowed. "I don't think so." She clung to him shaking violently, and smelled blood . . . his blood. She shuddered. "You're hurt."

"But I'm alive, and so are you." He squeezed her hard despite the pain in his shoulder. "We beat her this time, Jen."

Jenny slowly raised her head to look at him. The wind tore at her hair and she had to hold the strands back from her face. "This time?"

He stared at her in solemn wonder. "It was all there. When the lightning struck, all the memories were there. Everything that happened between Seth and Anna—you and me. I remembered it, Jen, just like I remember what I ate for breakfast yesterday."

Jenny met his look squarely. "I know."

"You, too?"

"Yes."

"And now? Do you remember it now?"

Jenny searched her mind, then shook her head. "No. It's gone. But it was there, like you said. All of it. I remember remembering it, but now it's gone."

"Me too. But there's one thing I haven't forgotten from that life, or this one."

"What's that?"

"How much I love you. How much I have always loved you, will always love you. And how much you love me."

Jenny smiled through her tears as the first drops of rain pelted the earth. "You mean your heart finally remembered mine?"

"Yes," he said fiercely. His good arm tightened around her waist. "I remembered your heart, your soul, your love. And I swear to you I'll never forget them through this life or the next or the one after that." He kissed her with all the reverence that such a vow deserved, with all the love his heart and soul had to offer.

Epilogue

Jenny shrieked with laughter. "Put me down, you idiot. You'll hurt your shoulder."

Brett stepped into their Garden District house and kicked the door shut behind him. "My shoulder is fine, has been fine for a month, as I believe I've proved numerous times during the past two weeks."

"Somehow, I don't think lazing in the Caribbean sun on our honeymoon put that much of a strain on your damaged muscles."

"I was talking about what went on under the Caribbean moon, thank you very much."

"Oh." She looped her hands around his neck. "In that case, you'd better put me down for sure. You may have overworked that shoulder during the past two weeks."

"You complaining?"

"Absolutely not. But I think—"

"I think you talk too much." He shut her up with a kiss. It was long and slow and made his heart pound. With his lips still on hers, he slipped his arm from beneath her legs and let her stand before him. With his arms now free, he pulled her flush to his chest and deepened the kiss until they were both breathless.

"Mmm, yes," she murmured, resting her head on his good shoulder. "I think I'm going to like living in this house."

Renovations had been completed in late January, a scant week before they were married. The press had had a field day with their wedding, but the star of the coverage hadn't been the author who'd finally taken a wife. Reporters had gleefully latched on to the fact that Brett's best man had been a six-year-old boy named Jeff.

Young Jeff's memories of his life as Randall Hampton were gone now, but the connection, that special bond his soul had had with Brett's and Jenny's was still there. Brett felt the special kinship and vowed to treat it as the treasured friendship it was. If people thought it odd that a grown man's best friend— indeed, his best man at his wedding—was six years old, that was their problem.

"Oh, look!" Jenny pulled from his arms and stepped into the parlor just off the entry. "Someone sent flowers."

Brett smiled as she read the congratulatory card from the contractor who'd done the work on the house. "He did a good job, didn't he?"

"It's wonderful, Brett. It looks like it was just built, yet it has that feeling of history to it, like Oak Hollow. But I don't feel anything bad here. This house feels . . . good."

"Yes," he murmured. "The first time I saw this place, neglected, deserted, tumbling down, I knew I had to have it. Funny, but with everything I've learned about myself lately, I would have thought I would find some personal connection with this house."

"You could have one, you know."

"What do you mean?"

"Remember in your book? Seth built a house in New Orleans for Anna. They were going to live there once they got married."

Brett smiled at her. "Wouldn't that be a hoot? Maybe we should check the old deeds and see if we can trace it." Then he grimaced. "I don't know, though. I'd hate to think I paid for the same house twice. Three times, if you count the renovations."

Jenny clucked her tongue at him. "A rich, successful author like you? You can afford it. Besides," she said, looking around the room. "Whatever you paid, it was worth it."

"What's this?" He picked up an envelope left prominently on the round occasional table beneath the front window and read the note scribbled across the front.

McCormick:
    I found the contents of this envelope beneath a loose brick in the master bedroom fireplace. Happy house, happy marriage.

It was signed by the contractor.

Curious, Brett tore open the envelope as Jenny leaned over his shoulder to see what it contained. Her gasp of surprise echoed his silent one. The heart-shaped gold locket looked brand new, as though someone had tucked it away no more than a week ago.

"I wonder who it belonged to," Jenny murmured. "I wonder how old it is. Does it open?"

Brett pressed the tiny latch on the side, and the heart popped open.

His chest tightened.

Jenny made a whimpering sound in her throat. Her

hand shook violently as she reached out to touch the locket.

With a tremor in his voice that he couldn't conceal, Brett read the inscription.

> To my darling Anna on our wedding day, may you always, throughout time, remember my heart, as I will remember yours. All my love for eternity, your devoted Seth.

FOR THE VERY BEST IN ROMANCE—
DENISE LITTLE PRESENTS!

HISTORICAL ROMANCE FROM PINNACLE BOOKS

LOVE'S RAGING TIDE   (381, $4.50)
by Patricia Matthews

Melissa stood on the veranda and looked over the sweeping acres of Great Oaks that had been her family's home for two generations, and her eyes burned with anger and humiliation. Today her home would go beneath the auctioneer's hammer and be lost to her forever. Two men eagerly awaited the auction: Simon Crouse and Luke Devereaux. Both would try to have her, but they would have to contend with the anger and pride of girl turned woman . . .

CASTLE OF DREAMS   (334, $4.50)
by Flora M. Speer

Meredith would never forget the moment she first saw the baron of Afoncaer, with his armor glistening and blue eyes shining honest and true. Though she knew she should hate this Norman intruder, she could only admire the lean strength of his body, the golden hue of his face. And the innocent Welsh maiden realized that she had lost her heart to one she could only call enemy.

LOVE'S DARING DREAM   (372, $4.50)
by Patricia Matthews

Maggie's escape from the poverty of her family's bleak existence gives fire to her dream of happiness in the arms of a true, loving man. But the men she encounters on her tempestuous journey are men of wealth, greed, and lust. To survive in their world she must control her newly awakened desires, as her beautiful body threatens to betray her at every turn.